The Dark Of The
STARS

A Novel

William Hamilton

Original cover and interior art created by Dr. Mary Bliss

Cover design by Lewis Agrell

Authority Publishing
11230 Gold Express Drive, #310-413
Gold River, CA 95670

The publisher is not responsible for websites (or their content) that are not owned by the publisher.

THE DARK OF THE STARS
by William Hamilton
YAF011000 2. YAF011000 3. YAF000000
ISBN: 978-1-949642-93-3 (paperback)
ISBN: 979-8-88636-000-4 (hardcover)
ISBN: 978-1-949642-94-0 (ebook)

Printed in the United States of America

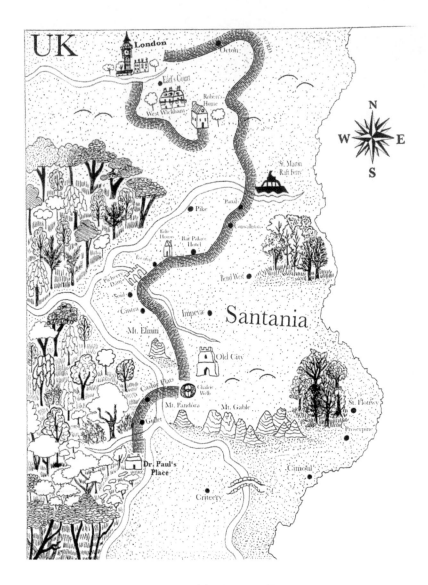

Map created by Lauren Payne

PART 1

London

THE MILKMAN'S
VAN

1

CotterPins

Few people visited this house in London, and with good reason. There was nothing remarkable about it. Hidden by weeds at the end of a short, cracked-asphalt drive, it was dull white, lacking all the warm touches of home, tucked forgettably away in a cul-de-sac. In fact, the mailman often skipped the place entirely. Robert himself never would have been here if it weren't for a social worker, who'd insisted upon it. He doubted his foster parents would've minded much if he simply disappeared.

Eager to get on with it, he knelt at the end of the drive, by the kerb, hammering at the bolt in the pedal of his bicycle, the privet hedge where it leaned shaking with every blow. So intent was he in this pursuit that he barely heard the rattle of a milk crate, the garden gate click, feet passing him, and a bottle put down on the doorstep.

Returning, the footsteps paused, and a shadow fell over him.

"That's no way to hit it out," said a voice.

Robert did not look up but noted the pointed shoes of worn grey leather with pinkish dust in the cracks. He disliked that style of shoe, and almost felt the same about the slightly foreign accent of the speaker, but not quite as much.

To make the man leave, he muttered sourly, "We didn't order milk for today. Won't want any for a month. Sam and Linda left for Spain this morning, and I'm leaving as soon as I've fixed these blasted pedals."

A pause. A tsk. "Well, flattening the bolt like a rivet won't help. Give me the hammer and I'll show you what to do."

Robert tipped his head back and regarded the milkman, who was now squatting at his side. His hair was too long and billowed around his head like a vapour, and his chin suggested he'd never yet needed to shave. He seemed about three years older, a slight young man in frayed jeans and a shirt with a psychedelic pattern of rainbow colours. He was not like any milkman Robert had ever seen.

I suppose I have nothing to lose, Robert thought, handing him the tool.

"Sam and Linda, eh?" the milkman said, surveying the situation.

"Yes. The place is theirs."

"They went off to Spain and left you."

It wasn't a question, so Robert didn't answer. It wasn't the first time he'd been left out of things by his foster parents. They made it no secret that while they found the checks Child Services sent them quite favourable, Robert himself was merely tolerable.

Placing the biggest hammerhead under the pedal, the milkman picked up the nut Robert had placed on the ground, screwed it a little way back on, and struck it with the light hammer. Removing the nut, he struck again, this time on the threaded end of the pin, which flew out and rolled upon the drive.

"That was neat," said Robert, examining the pin. "You haven't even damaged the thread. Thanks!"

He hoped his voice did not indicate his dislike of milkmen who dressed like this one and were smaller than him by at least a few stone. After all, he'd done him a favour. He added, "I'm in a bit of a hurry. I'll replace this and leave the other pedal. It's loose, but ought to hold."

"It won't. Fetch me a hacksaw and punch and I'll fix it for you."

"We've a saw, but I don't think there's a punch."

"Then I'll use the cotter pin I knocked out instead. Get the saw."

"The what pin?"

"Cotter pin. That's what pins that hold pedals are called."

"You've worked in a bike shop?"

"No, but they're called that."

"Were you a builder's mate recently?"

"Why do you think that?"

"Brick dust on your shoes. And you're new to this milk round."

The milkman laughed. "It's not brick dust. I'll maybe explain in a moment, but first, fetch the saw."

Robert started toward the garage at the rear of the drive, but upon hearing the telephone ring inside, dashed into the house.

It was John, his friend. At first, he was glad to hear from him, but shortly into the conversation, the black mood he'd had while kneeling on the sunny drive, hammering the pedal, returned. After listening to a myriad of poorly-constructed excuses for a short while, he said, "So you're not waiting for me."

"We've waited for two hours already! Don't sound so pissed off."

"Might I find you tomorrow at Spalding youth hostel?"

"Yes. Hey!" said John. "I'd wait if it was only me but there's four of us. And Vic has set his heart on getting to his girlfriend's house this afternoon. He's very keen on her, and her parents expect us."

"I know. I understand. See you, I suppose."

He did *not* suppose, truthfully, and did not go immediately back to the bicycle. There wasn't much point, now. He'd be stuck in no man's land, likely for the whole rotting summer. The milkman would've left by now, anyway. Why had his friends stayed at Victor's house and not come to see what had delayed him? In that band of friends, he had always feared being one of too many. Now, he was sure of it.

He slowly climbed the stairs, at each step becoming more deeply certain that he would not be at the youth hostel the next day. In his room, Linda's sewing room, which was barely more than a closet, two bicycle panniers and a rucksack lay beside the bed, with a partly rolled sleeping bag on top. His legs felt heavy as he reached for a family photograph—the only one he had—and stared at the kind faces of his parents. They weren't beautiful, but they'd been *his*, and the way they'd wrapped their arms protectively around his chubby five-year-old frame *had* been rather a beautiful feeling. One he seemed to forget more and more, with every passing day.

He sat on the bed and at last bowed his face onto the bag—his father's—inhaling the smell of feathers and his old sweat. Through his mind tumbled the words he'd heard from John, along with words he should have said back. Jealousy, divergence, lost comradeship, moments of lost happiness…

Behind his closed eyelids, he saw his parents, that day on the jetty. He'd seen a rock among gentle waves, a cracked mass that looked like a solid slab, though it tilted sharply toward the sea, slick and black with seawater. He'd stepped on it and turned back to cry to his parents how close he'd climbed to the waves, how *brave*. But with frost and the buffeting waves of winter, the rock mass cracked beneath him.

The broken rock fell, and he fell...

Karl persuading
Robert to come on
his expedition

2

Karl's Offer

A hammer was clinking outside when Robert woke. He jumped up from his bed and hurried downstairs. Surprisingly, in the drive, the slight but now less feeble-seeming young man was bolting the second pedal in place.

He stood up as Robert approached, pushed the bike toward him, and said, "I've fixed it without the saw. But maybe you don't need it now?"

"Why not?"

"I heard some of what you said to the black widow in there."

"Black widow?"

"A large black spider with a poisonous bite. All telephones were black until recently, and all of them can bite."

"How can they?"

"Like when a lady rings to say she doesn't want to see you again."

"That isn't poisonous. It's just sad."

"Anyways, I gather your trip has flatted," said the milkman, juggling the hammers, and Robert finally understood. The phone call seemed ages ago. How long had he been asleep?

"No, just delayed. It wasn't a girl I was speaking to; it was my mate. I'm leaving tomorrow with them, so I still need this." He mounted the bike and

7

tested the pedals saying, "Thanks very much. I'm always bending my pedals. What's your name?"

"Karl."

"I'm Robert. I hope I haven't delayed your round too much."

"No problem," the milkman said, but hesitated and glanced across the neat hedge separating them from the next-door garden.

Robert asked, "Sure?"

"Well, a kind of problem emerged with a green dress and a red face. She complained that I hadn't left the milk on her front step. Her old delivery man did it just so. She went indoors saying she would phone the depot."

"I'm sorry. That was Mrs Lampson. She likely has already phoned, seeing as how she lives to find fault. But I don't think they'd sack you for one complaint, would they?"

"Ah. I suppose that doesn't matter because this is my last milk round. Tomorrow I'm going south. Perhaps you're coming with me," said Karl, sending the hammers higher and higher.

Robert laughed. "Why should I?"

"Because you answered my advert."

Robert looked hard at Karl who, watching the hammers with darting eyes, had an odd, knowing smile on his narrow face. It suggested pride and self-reliance but also a wish to please. He was juggling both hammers with such astonishing ease that Robert had to wonder if he'd been a circus performer prior. "Advert?" he asked, as memory flooded him.

A few weeks earlier, Sam, at breakfast, had read out an advertisement from his morning paper:

Daring? Crazy? Safari South 1963 still has places for a few travellers. To Bend West and Pike overland by new Cimoul road. Apply Box 286.

His foster father had said it sounded like an offer of apprenticeship in drug smuggling, white slavery, or both.

But Robert had been intrigued. After Sam had discarded the paper—he never let Robert read it until all the sections had been ripped apart and thoroughly perused—Robert had fetched the classifieds from the trash and torn the advert out, showing it the next day at school to John and Victor. They had looked up Bend West, Pike, and Cimoul in an atlas index, could not find them anywhere, and decided the advert was a joke. Purely out of curiosity, they'd written a mainly facetious reply, but in case the advert had something serious behind it, had given their names and addresses. Afterward, there'd been no response.

"Did you put that advert in *The Times?*"

Karl nodded.

"Are you leading a Safari South expedition?"

"Yes."

"How come you're doing a milk round where I live?"

"Snob! Why shouldn't a milkman lead an expedition?"

"Well, it seems a bit dodgy."

"I was working Shelford's Dairy when I placed the advert. Just a temp job while I got things in order here in London—one has to pay one's bills, you know. Yesterday I swapped around with Tom Drayton, your usual delivery man and the one Mrs Lampson clearly prefers, so we could meet today. Mrs Lampson will be most relieved to know I'm only temporary."

"You did that for me?" Hardly anyone ever had put much thought into Robert. In fact, though the ordeal with his friends leaving him behind had been a disappointment, it hadn't really surprised him. "I could have been gone when you came."

"Ah. But you weren't."

"As it turns out. But have you seen John Stookey, Victor Parsons, Colin Fielding, and the others who answered?" Those were his friends.

"Yes. Briefly. No good. You're the only one I'm offering a place to."

The young man's pale eyes were fixed keenly on Robert's face, glinting with an air of mystery. Under his flippancy, Robert sensed something hard, probing for hardness in himself, almost like a hand on the bicep of his arm. He felt a sudden chill.

"Why me?"

Slowly Karl's looked changed to a smile as he seemed to think a while, then he said, "Remember my ad? Some of the others were probably daring enough, but only you are crazy enough to accompany me out through the moors."

"Why do you think I'm crazy?"

"Instead of getting a touring bike with ten gears, you have a heavy workman's bike with three. You've loaded it with pannier frames, a basket, and a saddlebag with a ton of tools you don't know how to use. You obviously ride up hills standing on the pedals and yanking the handlebars till you wreck the cotter pins. I tell you mate; gouging both cotter pins at once on the pedal axle is quite a feat. It only proves one thing."

"I'm crazy."

He nodded. "All right. Two things. You're strong, too."

Robert was silent. His friends had often laughed at the oddity of his bike and way of riding it. But the whole of it was, Sam and Linda wouldn't let him have a new bike—they had the money but didn't see the need. For a moment, he thought of his pals, freewheeling from Swanscombe toward the Dartford Tunnel, glad to be off, joking to the wind—yet perhaps some were thinking of him and a little sorry. He said defensively, "I do know how to use most of these tools. If I'd been in less of a hurry, I could have worked out how to mend the pedals myself, like you did. What else does my bike show?"

"You're one of God's chosen fools."

"Fool yourself! Why should that help your expedition? *If* it even exists."

"It means that in tight places you'll react in unexpected ways, which is sometimes useful."

"So on this trip of yours, I'll be the odd man out, as usual? Thanks Karl, if that's your name, but if I'm crazy, you are…unbelievable. As an expedition leader, anyway. If you're serious, I need a plain explanation. You must be crossing the channel. Are you going to Africa via Gibraltar? Where are these moors? Where are Pike and the other places you mentioned in your advert?"

For a moment Karl frowned impatiently, but then his evasive half-smile returned. "I haven't time to show you the route just now, Robert. We will not cross the channel. The moors are due south. You'll learn about the other places in time."

"Unless you go to France or Spain, the nearest thing to a moor south of London is Leith Hill or Ashdown Forest."

"There are moors south of London. With the right weather conditions, you could see them from here, if you were high enough. I am leading an expedition to the country of Santania, past the General Moors, Souls, Pike…to the glorious city of Cimoul on the Vascoma River, and I want you to come."

"I've never heard of such places."

"Cimoul exists. Indeed. It is not easy to get to, but to get there we must. People need both of us—for their lives." Robert noticed that Karl's face was deeply flushed as he went on, "Come on. You've already half-decided. Like me, you're an outsider to your friends. Forget them. Tomorrow, I'll call here and we'll go. All you need for the trip is long trousers instead of those shorts. No money. I'll pay for everything."

The skin tightened on Robert's scalp. "You will? How? How old are you, anyway?"

"Eighteen. Just. And I've no parents either, so I, too, won't be missed around here."

The boy frowned. "How do you know *that?*"

Karl stared at him with a queer sort of smirk. "I know much about you, Robert."

He didn't like that look. "Get three things straight. First, don't *Robert* me so much and I won't *Karl* you. Second, don't criticize my friends. Thirdly, you know all about me, but I know next to nothing about you. I'm not coming unless I have more. If your trip means smoking pot on Beachy Head you can keep it, and keep it even more if you're running drugs. You look dotty enough or dangerous enough or–or—for me to suspect that."

Lame finish, he thought, having almost said "or beautiful enough" but had decided not to, as the idea had just occurred to him. But his words had clearly startled Karl, who hesitated, then said quietly, "Yes, drug running is involved. You might call it a white drug racket. We're taking life-saving pharmaceuticals to the people who need it."

"Then why call it a racket? Can't you take it openly?"

"Impossible. I'm undercutting someone else's racket, which is really bad. The difference is, our drugs work, and his…"

"Don't? Then why on Earth would people take them?"

He checked his wristwatch. "I've not the time to talk of this all. I'm simply going to carry two cartons of pills in the back of the jeep and hope to God I don't get caught."

Following Karl's glance to the front gate, Robert noticed for the first time a strange vehicle. Under the yellow flowers of a laburnum tree by the front gate was what seemed a child's drawing of a car. The bonnet, mudguards, and grill were like an American army jeep, but the wheelbase was much longer and supported a homemade-looking metal box with circular windows like portholes. The vehicle's lower half was pale blue, the upper half white, and the tyres and wheel hubs were stained with red dust. It was certainly not owned by the dairy. Since a wild query about drugs had produced unexpected information, Robert decided to try again. "Any other wonders and dangers? King Solomon's Mines? Princesses? Film stars?"

Karl said quietly, "Well, when the medicine is delivered, we might look for diamonds. There is supposed to be a cache of diamonds, the biggest anyone ever owned, though the owner is dead now. Finding those would be dangerous. As for princesses, you might find a Russian one in Cimoul, which is where the most useless émigrés go. There are no real princesses in Santania—the place is a republic. But there are quite a few attractive girls."

"Voluptuous? Dazzlingly dark? Ready to overwhelm me with their gratitude for saving them from disease?"

Robert expected a sharp rejoinder and was surprised to see Karl's eyes glistening as he said, "The ones who know you are helping me will be grateful, of course."

"That won't make them fall into my arms."

"You're no film star, but you're tough, and they like that."

"If you were truthful, you would say I'm damned ugly."

"But there you would be a rarity—all that English schooling. That European *haute couture* which they lack. You wouldn't be ignored."

Karl's smile now suggested a kind of leer. *He wants to tempt me*, Robert thought, and said flatly, "That sounds like a dream."

"It is," said Karl earnestly. "You are dreaming it. Why else would you be talking to a milkman for this long when you could be pedalling off on your bike, alone? So, you will come?"

"I might come if I believed for a moment where you are going. You seem sincere, and the expedition certainly seems interesting, but I need more."

Karl turned his hatchet-like face away and said distinctly, "We'll go south on the new Santania road to the General Moors, where we can go to where the roadworks end on the far slope of Mount Pandora. Following the Vascoma River, we deliver one box of the drug in each village—Bend West, Souls, the farthest point of our journey being Cimoul. We do not cross the English Channel."

Mount Pandora? Vascoma? Robert's favourite subject in school was geography, yet he'd never heard of these places. Likely, they were more points he'd never find in an atlas. How was it possible to get to these places without crossing the Channel? The man was dotty, making up stories, and wasting his time.

Robert sighed and said, "Then I'm not coming. Thanks very much for mending the pedals."

He went into the house.

Indoors, he heard Karl yelling angrily from the gate, "So you're scared! You should be—you *would* be if you knew everything! I haven't told you half! About the diseases and people vanishing! And the diamonds! The doctor's the stuff of nightmares. Why did I think you might do? You! You couldn't face a blackfly on the creeks!"

He's mad, Robert thought.

A moment later he heard the rattle of milk bottles as the car began to leave, then heard Karl calling over that, "I'll ask you once more tomorrow."

Good, Robert thought, because one look about the desolate house reminded him of his desperate need to put all of this wretched life behind him.

3

Mirage

In his upstairs bedroom, Robert finished packing to leave the next day, still unsure whether to join his friends or go youth hostelling alone with just the sleeping bag to Devon or Cornwall.

Either. Doesn't matter. Just get out of here. Never come back.

That was his father's voice, speaking. His father had been a biologist at the university and, never satisfied with being in one place for too long, had taken Robert on many an adventure. Barely a weekend went by that they weren't exploring some locale for interesting life. In fact, that was what they'd been doing that day, on the jetty, when Robert was seven, looking through pools in the crevasses between the rocks for whatever sea creatures the tumultuous tide had brought in.

Adventure is in your blood, after all.

Afterward, he sat a long while on the chair beside the bed doing nothing, not even thinking. This was sometimes a useful exercise. On rousing himself from what was not exactly sleep, he often felt, not just rested, but as if life had somehow improved from the dreary nothingness that had overwhelmed him since the death of his parents. Day was ending, though the sun was still in the sky. A pink square of light moved across the wall opposite the window, growing narrower and redder.

He stood up, stretched, and said aloud, "So! Mr. Mysterious Milkman!"

He smiled, snapped his fingers, and stepped to the window. It overlooked gardens and the backs of houses in a lower street, for his home was on a ridge which sloped down to the distant fields of Kent. Through gaps between the lower house backs, he saw more suburban houses, small lawns and trees, mainly apple and laburnums. Between shadows of buildings, the setting sun added colour to the scene. The laburnums were like yellow flames, the walls and lawns were red and copper-green.

To the south, over the houses, was a wide, dark bank of cloud-like high moorland, very far away, the edges rough with what seemed to be cliffs. As he gazed, the cliffs seemed clearer, their pinnacles and clefts drifting toward him through the evening air, but when he blinked in the fading sunlight, they again seemed far away. The slopes of the moor beyond were obscured by a mist. To the south, above the mist, a cloud-like cone seemed to radiate downward, then beyond it, his eye just made out a ghostly cone of the same kind, much fainter. He realized both were volcanoes, mantled in snow. Mist and sunset-pinked clouds veiled the whole landscape.

At that moment, he heard his father's voice. "Come on, Robbie, let's go check it out!" His father was always eager to take him off on one adventure or another. Intensely curious, he'd be the first person to investigate such a vista. And Robert would've been by his side. He could almost feel his father, nudging him toward it. If only he'd had his father's mettle, he'd set off, without question...

But it's only a mirage and nothing more, Robert thought. *That is how desperate and insane I've become.*

Later, he lay in bed, trying to sleep, but the mirage of moorland and volcanoes returned as clearly as when he'd seen them from the window. He wondered, idly, whether such a mirage came from Africa, the Himalayas, or the Andes. What layers of air could have refracted it? How had cyclones of Biscay or the Atlantic, storms over Amazonia, and the curvature of the Earth let the image through? Or...was there indeed more to the South than he'd read about in his schoolbooks?

What did it matter? He wasn't going anywhere.

Perhaps for the rest of his life. Unless...

4

West Wickham

The next morning, after sleeping badly, Robert rose late, lunched before twelve, and left home for Devon on his bicycle, yawning and wobbling over the handlebars. Wearing light khaki trousers in place of yesterday's shorts, he pedalled furiously, never looking back upon the dull house he'd lived in for the past year. It had never been his home, anyway.

Standing on the pedals to push himself uphill on a narrow road to West Wickham, he broke into a sweat. Panting, he moved aside for a vehicle coming from behind him. It slowed as it passed him, and he recognized it long before he'd turned his head to look—the odd blue and white jeep.

With a friendly smile, the milkman leaned from the window and asked, "How are the pedals?"

"Fine."

"They'll last till next year. Coming with me?"

"Right. I've decided. I'll come."

Karl pulled ahead and stopped at the roadside. Robert jumped off the bike and broke into a run to catch up. The jeep had no one else inside.

He asked where the rest of the expedition was and was not surprised when Karl said, "This is all."

"Just you and me? You expect a lot of trust."

Karl got out at the road's concrete kerb and said, "I would have told you that yesterday but was afraid to put you off. Well, now I am going to tell you the very worst. *I* am the main danger of this trip. I have occasional needs when I turn into a treacherous mean shit. It's a kind of disease."

He stood looking down at his shoes. Robert said, "What am I supposed to do then?"

"Put up with me till I recover, after a few hours or days. If you have to use force, do it. I'll be grateful afterward. It really is a disease."

"Incurable?"

"Some doctors are working on it. I wasn't always this way." He paused, wistful and serious, then asked, "Have I made you change your mind?"

"No. I have bad moods too. Anyone does."

"Not like mine."

"I still don't follow all this but I'm glad you warned me—I mean, I don't believe anyone ever changes completely. How do I know when one of these… seizures…happens?"

"I start acting like a mean shit, like I said, asking you to do something silly or even evil. Look out when you notice that. Later, you might help to cure me." Then more eagerly, he added, "Believe me, you're going to see that I need help as much as the disease victims. Some recover by themselves. I never will. Not with the medicines available today, at least."

He stopped and watched Robert closely as if for some sign, then said, "Okay?"

At Robert's nod, he suddenly opened the back door of the jeep, lifted the bike, with its tied-on rucksack, panniers, and the rest, and laid it as one piece on top of a travel-stained heap of camping equipment, suitcases, and cloth bags. Watching him, Robert realized Karl was not only dexterous but strong. He was one of those deceptively weedy types who in reality are like iron.

"Good, now that that's settled, let us go to collect the drugs, shall we?" Karl asked when they were situated in the jeep.

"Where's that?"

"Swanson's. You've heard of it, then?"

Robert shook his head.

Driving into London city proper, they hardly spoke. Robert, letting tiredness take over, lapsed into a somnolent daze. Threading through the dense traffic past Crystal Palace, Streatham, and Battersea, his companion had a good excuse for silence, but right now, Robert didn't mind it. The destination didn't matter, nor the purpose. He was pleased to finally be on his way, *somewhere*, whatever adventure it might bring.

5

The Naturalist's Shop

The entrance to a Victorian building near Earl's Court had an arrow-shaped sign pointing upward before the stair. Painted upon it were the words, *Swanson—Naturalist's Museum Suppliers, 3rd Floor.*

As they went up, a man came behind them taking two steps at a time, and pushed past them, rather rudely, Robert thought. The man wore a dark suit and a black hat like an upside-down flowerpot. From his shoulders swung a photographer's satchel and a long tubular black case. He entered a glass-panelled door at the top of the stairs and didn't hold it for Karl, who dove forward to catch it.

In the bright light overhead, a large turtle near the ceiling seemed to be swimming down toward the door between a high cabinet of drawers on one side and a crammed bookcase on the other. Part of the incredibly large, outstretched wing of an albatross hovered beyond.

Robert passed the bookcase, eyeing the rest of the albatross, soaring over a big table spread with papers, where a neat, grey-haired lady sat. Around the table were drawer-lined alcoves and smaller rooms so crowded with display cases, stuffed animals, aquaria, glass jars with huge corks that made movement between them difficult. The photographer had gone straight to a glass dome containing a glittering flock of hummingbirds. He crouched behind it, staring so hard at one of the bright-winged things that Robert thought he looked like a hungry cat.

The woman at the table glanced at the newcomers, then told a plump, pale man opposite her, "Certainly note the numbers of any that interest you, but please excuse me just now."

This man reminded Robert of a rabbit—funny that now, the shop was making him see everyone like animals.

The lady greeted Karl as a friend, with a hearty wave and smile. He called her Mrs Foster, put his full rucksack on the table, then sat and unpacked from it boxes and cloth bags. The first box he opened contained a beetle so huge that at first, Robert thought it a wax model, with its toad-like warts and wire-cutter mandibles. After his first astonished glance, Robert felt tiredness creep over him again, together with a wish that such a beetle did not exist. He wished God had not created it. Not wanting to see what was in the other bags and boxes, he looked for a chair beside a cabinet and noticed the rabbit-man pulling out drawers and making notes on a white index card.

megalior
megalissimus

After meandering carefully through the narrow aisles, Robert found a chair in an alcove behind him and slumped into it, taking in the unfamiliar assortment of oddities. Not to seem idle, he too, opened a drawer. It contained close-packed rows of moths with wings patterned like tiny Persian rugs so lovely that he fell into a contemplative daze, wondering whether his father had ever been here, amongst these curiosities. It was certainly up a biologist's alley.

He was roused by a voice saying, "You are an enthusiast, I see."

It was the rabbit-man, smiling at him benignly. Robert said awkwardly, "Well, they're beautiful."

"Indeed!" said the man. "And to whom do I have the honour of speaking? Ah! Robert *Jones*. I am Van Huffel!"

"How did you...?"

He raised his eyebrows, blinked rapidly, and said, "Delighted! We met years ago at Hannah Nysson's garden party which you won't remember, being a child at the time. I knew your father well—a significant worker. He revised Ulops and made many other contributions to the rhynchophora. Oh, that immense group—the weevils as they are commonly known. What a loss he was to science and, of course, to me personally..."

His flow of words was so rapid that it overcame Robert's efforts to change the subject. At the first pause in the monologue, Robert said, "Can you tell me anything about the black widow spider?"

The man stopped, obviously disoriented by the interruption in his train of thought. "Yes. Black widow, *Latrodectus mactans*, the Americas south. Poisonous bite, often fatal to children." He paused. "Your mother died too, in that accident...when? Five years ago?"

"Seven. Is it in Africa too?"

"Surely your father knew. The stage is set for it, with so many cargo ships between these continents, but I am not aware that mactans are yet in Africa." He shook his head. "Terrible shame, what happened to them. It was a storm, yes?"

For a moment, Robert was bobbing under the black waves, gasping on saltwater, reaching for shore as the tide pulled him out. He blinked such thoughts away. "How does it bite people?"

"Curious, just like your father, eh? The question is...*Where* does it bite them! Remarkable. It is said to bite men four times more often than women. A real puzzle! And where does this excess of bites fall?" He blinked rapidly and almost whispered, "Predominantly on the penis." He smiled, and the course of interrogation on his parents was forgotten.

"Good Lord, why?"

Keeping his voice low, Van Huffel said, "Not to—ah—disturb others, for a shop like this should be as sacred as a library, I would call your attention to the outdoor privy, still common in warm regions where the spider abounds. Had you noticed when watering plants in your father's conservatory—how well I remember it! What orchids!—that drops of water falling on spiders' webs make the spiders run out, believing them to be flies? Remember that the dear, dark old privy, the home of reflection, is a natural habitat for spiders. In a novel by Dostoevsky, one of his nastiest characters suggests Hell will be like such a lavatory..."

Robert yanked himself back before he could think too much on his father's conservatory, where he lazed in the sun like a cat while his father, always busy, toiled on his projects. Behind the high cases of drawers, Robert heard Karl say, "How much is this little sketch?"

Mrs Foster replied, "That damaged sheet? I don't know why I have it. The tattooing on the upper lip is unusual—such a simple, stark pattern, I suppose belonging to a tribe he wished to record. And while it is not in his best style, it is genuine Dewey, from the same sketchbook as this little landscape."

"His last sketchbook," said a deep voice which likely belonged to the cat-man. "How did you come by it?"

Mrs Foster said, "Yes, late in his career, I should think. I came by it like I came by everything here—someone, I don't remember, sold it to me. But part of the design is torn. You can have it for ten pounds. Any sketch by Dewey, that one, for instance, Mr. McNeeve."

Van Huffel straightened. He muttered, "Excuse me," coughed, and hurriedly left the alcove, blowing his nose.

Robert followed.

Mrs Foster stood by an open art folder on the table, which was now scattered with small watercolour sketches of birds, insects, and tropical scenery. Opposite her, Karl held a sheet of paper, lightly rolled. He seemed at pains to look calm but was clearly not, for his forehead shone with moisture. Also at the table was a newcomer, a lady wearing sand-coloured slacks, a satiny pink shirt, and a broad-brimmed man's outdoor hat. Though not young, she had a look of beauty or at least attractiveness that had been faded long ago by age. She must have just entered and was glancing restlessly from one face to another.

"Dewey?" she said quietly, her eyes misting slightly as she studied the paper in Karl's hands. "You're to buy that sketch, then? Karl…"

Karl nodded, about to say something, but was interrupted.

"McNeeve?" exclaimed Van Huffel, blustering his way close to Robert's companion. "Karl McNeeve? May I have the pleasure?"

The lady, who had brown spots upon her skin from the sun, smiled at Robert. She had tiny gold stars inlaid on each of her two upper front teeth. He smiled back but his surprise at the stars must have shown because she pressed her lips together and switched her attention to the cat-man, who was standing by a case with an open book in his hand. The lady smiled at him too. He snorted and backed out of sight.

"Karl McNeeve," said Van Huffel breathlessly. "Sir, your fame spreads wide! You are the last, best hope of Santania. I plead for your alliance."

6

Octon

Karl clearly did not like Van Huffel's fawning, or the woman with the stars in her teeth. He deposited several banknotes on the table uncounted, collected the sketches and boxes of drugs in a rush, and headed out the door without a word, Robert on his tail.

"Why was that man so eager to make your acquaintance?" Robert asked him, flummoxed. "Are you famous?"

Karl ignored the question. "I'm in a rush."

"And the woman? Don't you like her?"

"What do you mean? I don't know her well enough to have formed any opinion of her. She would've asked for a lift from me."

"And that's bad?"

"Not bad. But I told you, it's you and me, that's all."

"You stiffened when she came near."

"Rubbish, boy. I have heard of that lady and would have liked to have talked to her. Given another place and time. But we are in a rush, are we not?"

"Heard of her? Did she leave a name?"

"No. But it's obvious who she was."

To you, perhaps. Not me, Robert thought.

Karl must've read his mind, because he said, "His wife, in a manner of speaking."

"Whose wife? Van Huffel's?"

"Don't be daft. Dewey, of course."

"Dewey? You mean the naturalist who drew all those pictures you were gazing at?"

"The same. Also, the man who formerly owned that large diamond cache I told you about."

"Oh. I think she wanted that picture you bought."

"She sold it to Mrs Foster. And now she wants it back? Too late, I'd say. It's mine." He patted it.

"But why wouldn't you have given her a lift?"

"I would have, but we are short on space, and I'm trying to get on the road incognito. This jeep isn't the one I came up in. I mustn't attract attention leaving London just now."

Again, that begged the question of his fame. But Robert had more sense than to ask a second time. "All the same, I think you're mean after the way you behaved when she cried over that picture. She must have loved him."

"She didn't. Cry, I mean."

"Yes, she did. I saw it."

Karl was silent for a moment, and then said sadly, "Yes, I was mean. I told you I could be. Later, on the road, you'll probably see me doing meaner things. But I'm worried about her if she keeps breaking down like that. And she should be warned not to speak so openly about Dewey, even if she was a kind of wife to him, though she was very young when he died."

"Her gold stars don't seem to fit a pioneer life. She seems more like a lounge singer, if you ask me."

He laughed. "Oh, the stars fit well enough. Not all pioneers are pilgrim fathers. She must have met Dewey in the first diamond rush. For him, there was never a second one."

"Karl, you must tell me this story properly."

"Soon. At the first camp."

They were now out of London among a jumble of broken chalk hills. Karl seemed to be looking for a turning. They passed a cement works, then came back and repassed it. Karl finally swung abruptly down a stony lane past a terrace of dingy, dust-whitened houses where someone had spray-painted on the gable in big clumsy letters TO THE SOUTH, with an arrow pointing the way they were going. The arrow could as easily have been pointing to a piece of obscene graffiti spray-painted on the cement factory's side wall farther on.

Fifty yards beyond where the wall ended, Karl stopped the jeep and said, "This is the real start and your last easy chance to turn back. Still want to come?"

"Yes."

"Even though, as I said, part of the danger…is in me?"

"Yes, but you should be more explicit about the dangers. It's too easy to seem brave when I don't know them."

"I'll tell you all I can when we're really on the road."

"When there's no chance of going back?"

"Oh, you could still turn back if you wanted. It would just be more difficult."

"So, now, do we cut our thumbs and become blood brothers?"

Karl laughed and said, "No need. Also, if our blood groups are compatible, never accept a transfusion from me."

"Because of disease? Is it that of the blood?"

"Yes, because of the disease and something worse."

The jeep lurched forward past a long chain-link perimeter fence of the cement work, under an arch of ruinous railway viaduct, then across an unfenced field of stubble towards the back of a disused church, deep in nettles. Outside it was a notice that read, *Please do not break in. There is nothing of value to steal.* Beyond the church, a small, tarmacked road began again.

This led to others, but signs were few and soon Karl seemed lost again. He stopped by a small public house, asked Robert to go in and enquire the way to Octon, saying meanwhile he would check on fuel for the jeep—at Octon they would pass the first petrol station for a long way, and he'd have to fill up, "or we'll be sunk," Karl had added cheerfully.

Robert did not like the pub or the silence that fell in the crowded public bar as he entered. Nor did he like the drunk who asked why he was going to Octon. Robert tried to ignore him. The drunk asked for a lift. Robert said his car was completely full. The drunk asked where he was going after Octon. Robert ignored him.

The drunk said, "South, of course. Camping or motel-ing?"

Ignoring him again, Robert asked the barman for two boxes of matches. The drunk asked Robert if he had hammocks for camping, and that was the first moment that Robert realized that in all his adventures with his father, he'd never been out camping before. Speaking as if his thoughts were elsewhere, Robert politely and humorously said he had no intention of camping and wouldn't know how to sleep in a hammock if he had one. He paid for the matches and edged toward the door. All the eyes in the dark room followed him.

The drunk came with him to the door, looked out at the road, and said, "So, no car. Best of bloody walks to you, liar boy."

What Robert liked least was that the more insolent the man became, the less certain Robert felt that he was as drunk as he pretended. He found the jeep parked round the first bend ahead, with Karl inside, ready to go.

It was dark when they reached Octon, which was odd. The day seemed to have been very short. Karl filled both the petrol tank and two five-gallon cans they were carrying. He shopped in the store beside the garage, going in twice to carry out loads of provisions. Beyond Octon, they came to roadworks and Karl turned down what seemed the half-made spur of a motor way.

In the beam of a headlight, a sign came out of the darkness. They passed it slowly and Robert made out faintly behind a layer of rust, the words, *M17-S17 SOUTH CIMOUL.*

So it *did* exist. At least his companion hadn't lied about that.

A few hundred yards past the sign, Karl bumped the jeep off the road and up a track to the left. He switched off the lights, parked the jeep behind a hedgerow, and said, "This is our first camp. Try not to use much light."

"Have you a tent?" asked Robert.

"No. This is the dry season. We'll hardly need one."

"Do you have hammocks?"

"Yes, two. Huh! How did you guess?"

Robert frowned.

For a moment, Karl seemed confused, but then said, "But there are no snakes yet. We'll be safe in our bags on the grass."

PART 2

Road

1

Road Sickness

R obert was too tired when they reached the first camp, and so Karl told him nothing about the adventure they'd set off on. The next day, as they travelled south on a little-used four-lane road, Robert had no attention for the tale. Their motoring had hardly begun, and Robert was already ill, his stomach swarming like a kettle of bees. As they went on, Karl had been giving him increasingly worried looks. *I bet he wishes he chose a different travelling companion,* Robert thought miserably.

At the first filling station, Karl kindly made him a nest of sleeping bags and rucksacks on the back seat of the jeep. The sun, warm on his face, felt nice on his clammy skin, though the dust kicked up from the tyres choked him. Through eyes that did not want to look, Robert saw the top of a palm tree fluttering wind-shredded leaflets with dry brown hills behind.

Karl brought him milk. Robert sipped it and said with a gaiety he found hard to force, "You are the milkman still."

That day, or perhaps the next—they all bled together—they came to the end of the tarmac and hit the first corrugations of the road at speed. The jeep waltzed half sideways across the road. After Karl braced to the wheel and felt out the best speed, a dull and endless vibration began. For a time, Robert sat up. He could hardly believe their vehicle could withstand such shuddering for more than a few miles; he thought it must crack every weld, shake every bolt.

Karl was weaving to miss potholes but could never miss them all. Tyre-thrown stones whanged under the floor.

"How far is the road like this?" Robert said.

They were in a cutting of red clay banks, then the banks dipped from sight and they were on an embankment with a fence beside and a marsh beyond. Behind the marsh was a wood matted with vines.

"It's like this the whole way," Karl said. "Worse as we get near the highlands. Better in some places if a grader has been over it. Tarmac doesn't start again until Proserpine, about 700 kilometres north of Cimoul and we're not going nearly so far. It will take twelve days to reach Bend West, if the jeep holds out."

After thirty miles, they had their first puncture, and Karl said they would be lucky not to have another before reaching the next service station. He got out, efficiently took off a wheel, and removed nails and splinters that had been hammered into the tyres by the bumps of the road. Robert asked what would happen if the service station didn't mend punctures. Karl said they all did. The next puncture came two miles later. Karl set off, rolling one of the wheels, but before he was out of sight Robert saw him picked up by a lorry. He was back two hours later when it was nightfall, and they slept in the grass on the verge of the road.

So began for Robert a sick whirl of days. Karl predicted one or two days of "road sickness," but Robert's illness lasted eight. There were days of heat and dust and sun and endless shivering in the jeep. There was a roar of unsilenced lorries passing and after each, a wave of dust penetrated the jeep and made him cough. Dust drifted like tiny sand dunes into his empty shoes on the floor, lay as a grey film on all their baggage, caked the sweat on Robert's arms, and made the spittle on his teeth gritty. Roadside stops were even hotter. Robert sat on the shady side of the jeep, or half under it, while Karl did things to the engine or went away with a punctured wheel. Even lying in full sun was preferable to the oven of the jeep when it wasn't moving. He glimpsed strange scenes that seemed to make no sense. A sign in Japanese pointed down a track to neat gardens with tiled rooftops, half-hidden among orchard trees. In a village, a little barefoot boy floated a peapod in a gutter of brown water, while a beautiful woman with a headscarf was sweeping from a doorway into the street. For a moment, when she looked up to watch them pass, he could've sworn she had his mother's face. Yoghurt was all Robert could bring himself to eat. They mainly passed nights in their sleeping bags on roadside sand. One night was cold and the rest were far too hot.

Yet nights were the best time, and he remembered some peaceful, beautiful scenes amid the strange, senseless chaos of the rest. There was a lagoon in dense, soft darkness where they tried to wash. They stood on a sliding, newly bulldozed slope of mud beside water with a floating carpet of pale flowers like hyacinths, and further out the lights of a village cast yellow paths across the black water. In the dark sky above them, the stars were sharp and strange. Even so, after a few minutes, Robert's delight sank back into the nausea of his sickness. He hated that water, the mud, the tangled roots of hyacinths between his toes, and the lump on the skin of Karl's shoulder, gleaming in the faint light from the jeep's headlamps back on the road.

Perhaps after the third day, the road had been cut or bogged so badly by floods that it was better to take to the fields beside it than negotiate the deep wheel ruts left by big lorries. They lurched slowly for miles along winding tracks through scrub, or over corduroy rafts laid down through marshy woodland, the jeep raked by hanging vines above and stripped saplings below. Once they reached a rickety wooden bridge where decking timbers had to be picked from the riverbed and replaced on the bridge before they could cross. From hating the swaying when they moved, Robert came to detest even more the heat and stillness in the back seat when the jeep was motionless, and he silently cursed Karl's attempts at friendly conversation. But now, each day very few vehicles were passing them.

Not for the first time, Robert wondered if this was a mistake, a folly going after his dreams of being his adventurous father's son, and if life with Sam and Linda, barely any life at all, would have been better.

The black man

2

By the Ford

On the eighth morning, Robert woke to find himself in his sleeping bag on the dry sand of a riverbed. A little way off, the river lay in shallow pools, water sparkling in the light of a newly risen sun. Beyond the pools were more yellow sands, low rocks, and over these low-hanging branches held up a tapestry of vines, and over trees and vines arched a sky of pure blue, the colour of beauty and truth. Down through the chasm of trees on each bank, a black and white duck flew, and the duck seemed like Robert's illness, flying away. In the sunlight, every green leaf of the woodland wall was like a star on the day of creation. The mud tastes in his mouth, and the dullness in his mind, were gone, along with his wish not to see or be seen.

Karl was filling their fire-blackened tea kettle at one of the pools. Robert again pulled the sleeping bag up to his ears and wriggled a little to make the sand settle to his shape. Through shaggy tree roots of the nearby bank, he saw a swarm of creatures, like small black grasshoppers which, as he turned, went hopping away. In the branches of a tree above perched a green parrot with a red crest. It peered curiously at him through gaps in the leaves, then pecked at something on the branch below its talons. Then one of the black things (a cricket, Karl told him later) came back across the sand, hopped onto his sleeping bag, and looked at him over a fold. Its face was like the front of a bus, with two black fishing rods waving at him from the front windows. Robert ignored it. With a leap, it vanished, and soon he was asleep again.

When he woke a second time, Karl was squatting near a small fire on the sand and talking to a nearby man on horseback. The man's face was black as coal and his body splendidly strong. He wore a broad-brimmed hat, and on either hip, Robert saw the silver-gilt shine of the butts of a pair of pistols. Karl was gesturing to him and the kettle and billy on the fire, obviously inviting him to tea and breakfast. Robert saw the man shake his head but unhooked a flask that hung from his saddle and poured milk from it into a pannikin Karl held out. From another bag, he took a yellow fruit like a melon but longish, wider at one end. Robert heard Karl say, "Until our next meeting."

"Until then, go with God," said the man, and he rode away into the trees.

While Robert washed, he saw Karl go into the jeep, come back with a small sheet of paper, and after, holding it up to the sun looking for something in the paper's translucent image. When he had finished or given up, he stood in thought, suddenly shrugged, and returned to the jeep and removed something from the toolbox under the front seat. Robert came to the fire after washing and dressing and saw Karl rubbing one end of a full roll of new toilet paper on a slab of rock.

"What are you doing?" Robert asked.

Karl grinned and said, "In the art fraud business they call this giving the work a patina of age."

He eyed the now brown and roughened end of the roll like an artist examining a tiny, complex sculpture.

"Modern art doesn't need a patina of age."

"This one does. It must look like it's been bumping around, forgotten and mouldy, in a toolbox for a year or more."

"What are you *really* doing?"

"I'll tell you sometime."

"Who was that man?"

Karl, poking the fire, did not answer at once, so Robert asked mischievously, "Will he come into our story again?" because when Karl did not postpone answering a question, the answer was often informative.

"We might see him again," said Karl. "He is a part-time police officer in Saint Flortwy, south of the moors, and we're going through there. He's descended from slaves who broke free and made their own communes outside the frontier over a century ago. He's on leave to look after his farm and has given us milk for our tea and a cocoa fruit to go with our rice. I've made more rice today because you look a lot better. Are you?"

"Yes, I am completely better, thanks to your kindness and good care, though not to this damned road you brought me on. I never knew a road could be so bad."

"Then you've seen little yet."

"But now," said Robert, "I think it's time you told me where we are going and what we are going to do, as you promised."

"Then I will. It's time for a day's rest. We can take it easy on the sand in the shade of the trees."

They had breakfast. Robert put his milk in his rice and added sugar; Karl drank his separately and then ate rice along with the remnant of stew from the previous evening. (The stew and the rice, as usual, had spent the night on the roof of the jeep—it was quickly cool there in the evening and well out of the way of roaming animals.) After the rice, Karl cut the cocoa fruit in two and they sucked the sweet white pulp from the big seeds.

"To start off with, one thing that's puzzling me—and this is more...metaphysical, I guess, than the rest," Robert said. "When I go back to England, if I go, am I going to be...completely out of this again?"

"Out of what?"

"Cocoa fruits,"—he waved the yellow beaker-like half shell in his hand—"and mangoes, for instance, these are things I had once vaguely heard of, they kind of happen in the tropics. Same with termite mounds, and eucalyptus, and other things you've shown me. When I'm back, am I going to have forgotten ever having eaten and seen and touched them? And, if I ever go to a tropical country, will I have to re-learn what it's like?"

Karl frowned and said, "I guess I'm puzzled by that too, although the problem for me has lost force with time passing, because I don't think I ever shall be 'completely out,' as you put it. I was born out here, you know."

Robert was startled. "You were?"

"You knew that already, though. The reason I know is the same as the reason my answers are always half what you expect—like you're asking whether we would meet that man again. This is a dream, and you are imagining me."

He eyed his companion doubtfully. "Rubbish. I don't dream so vividly. What about all those people we met in London—at the Swanson shop for instance? Are they in it or out of it? What about an ordinary place, like the grocery at Octon, where you bought provisions?"

"That last is easy. Did you ever see a grocery store anywhere else in England with a stack of dried fish on the floor?"

"Oh, but I didn't go in."

"So, I remember, although you have eaten some of the fish—under protest, I'll admit. As for the people at Swanson's, I'm not sure about Mrs Foster, perhaps she is like me, a door-keeper—I don't know. These are hard questions. And your first one, about what you will remember, is the hardest of all. Somehow, I feel that, after you return, you may keep some faint idea of where you went. That might be an explanation for that old thing, the so-called déjà vu." He paused with a questioning look. Robert nodded. "But on the whole, I don't care for that. More probably I think you will just forget completely, as if you had never been here."

"Then what is the point of all?"

"Maybe there isn't a point. If there is one, my favourite guess is that in a dream like this, your Maker might be testing the mettle of a creature that he has made—that is, of you—to see what tasks, encounters, and so on it would be right to put in your way in real life. Thus, this is a part of his game."

"Of God's game, you mean?"

"Yes. There's plenty of room for special types to be meeting special tests, without its being very visible in failures of the laws of nature."

"Er, so…on this theory, I—and you—are in some way special types, then?"

"Once before you asked roughly the same thing." He imitated Robert's voice with nervousness exaggerated: "'Are you offering the place in the expedition just to me? Why me?' My answer's the same as I gave then."

"That was—that I am one of God's chosen fools?"

Karl laughed. "Fool, indeed. But you're still just a boy, with much to learn. Age makes no difference. You've been held back, though, for years, with those idiots Sam and Linda. You'll get there, though, which is more than I can say for most."

Robert was silent a moment and then he blushed.

"Don't feel flattered yet," Karl said, laughing again. "Chekhov wrote a story called 'The Black Monk.' In it, a man has a vision that calls him one of God's chosen, and so makes him become a misery to those he loves. In the end, his own misery, born out of his conceit, kills him too."

"You are very unmilkman-like today, Karl," Robert said. "Where did you read all this highfalutin literature? And where did you learn all those plant names, and science and philosophy that you keep telling me? Have you been to university?"

"I started last fall but crashed out. Oh, I was bored, I suppose. Too many dull instructors, too, thinking their narrow patch is everything. The only course I liked, for some reason, was entomology. Insects are splendid; weirdness with no end in sight. That's why I got the net. I collect them."

"What did you do when you dropped out?"

"Learned to juggle. Joined a circus."

"Ah, so you did! I've felt like doing something like that. What I'd like first of all, is to experience life and to think about it; not just learn without ever having done—without having the grit of something in my toes. That's why I didn't take a summer job right now. I wanted to travel this summer, see things. Somehow, I just hang around keeping in touch with friends who don't care much for the same. Most of them are still at school doing what's expected, scholarships and extra subjects and the lot."

"So, I knew you did right to come! I knew I did right to choose you!" Suddenly, Karl shouted like a man selling china in a street market, "So, instead, leave all behind, come safari-ing south with Karl McNeeve, your customized guide, and tutor!" Karl waved an arm and snapped his fingers. "I bet you'll get more grit, Rob, than you bargained for on this trip! Yet, despite the real danger, I do believe you will, at last, get back to London—if you want to."

"I should think so!" Robert had truthfully never expected otherwise. "You don't expect to?"

"I don't know."

"But if you say you were like me at the start, why don't you think you will 'get back'?"

Still with excited eyes but a little sadly, Karl said, "Just wait. You too may be tempted to stay. There'll be plenty to do here, I can tell you right now, more than in stuffy old England. Perhaps my feeling is because I've seen more of it.

I am three years ahead. And I am taking big risks in what I am doing now." Karl stood up.

"Well, what is there plenty of to do? Are you going to tell me?"

"All right. Fine. I will tell you a story." He sat down closer, making himself comfortable. "Many years ago, a man named William Brunel Chamard, US citizen, visionary, early inventor, later aircraft-manufacturing millionaire, took part in the planning, financing, and equipping of the projected London-Cimoul road, and bought from government agents a large tract in the back country. At this time, the basin of the Vascoma was so little known that even the geographical limits of the mountain range were hardly mapped and considered rather impassable, so the land was deemed worthless.

"During the completion of the road, Chamard died, leaving the land and the project to his only son, a medical doctor, Edwin Paul. A few years later, the new road first touched the massif and the volcanoes. I suppose it was then that it was discovered that the area contained diamonds. There was a rumour among the woodsmen cutting the first pioneer track for road, of a naturalist-prospector who kept boxes of diamonds under the nest of sticks where he slept in a remote hut. Most thought it was rubbish, until a road worker brought back a diamond the size of a pigeon's egg that he himself had found on the stream bed, which was from that day called Diamond Creek.

"However, at the same time, an astonished and angry nation was learning that the site of an extraordinary find of diamonds, plus the country's highest mountain, plus another volcano, belonged, with all mineral rights included, to one young man, Edwin Paul Chamard, who was not even a native of Santania.

"That led to lawlessness and total cessation of work on the road. With the season's first downpours came the first illegal diamond hunters. Down with the rain came blackflies, mosquitoes, river blindness, malaria, dysentery, and strife. Then, as the season changed, and the hot mists began to clear, out of the river came diamonds. There were many, but never enough for the seekers. All potholes were ransacked over again. The first murder on the creek was that of a discoverer, the odd-ball naturalist; this was followed by others among the new hunters, a number they will never know.

"Eventually, the area was declared a National Resource, and more diamond collecting took place, legally…until most of the diamonds were pulled from the land. They are becoming increasingly harder to find. To quell the natives,

Dr Paul arranged that a large part of the proceeds of the sale of the diamonds was allocated to a public health drive against the diseases of the area, of which there were many: malaria, river blindness, leprosy, and trachoma, plus syphilis and leishmaniasis which had been encouraged by the opening of the road. The drive was called the Campaign Against Malaria and Indigenous Diseases, or CAMID. He was declared a national hero for his efforts to foster health in the native population. Despite that, the area surrounding the creek is considered one of the most dangerous, with new diseases popping up all the time, and has some of the highest disease death rates in all the world. It has been deemed, by the WHO, very unsafe to travel there."

Robert frowned. "Well, I'm sincerely glad that *we're* going there, then!"

Karl lifted a finger. "Or so he says. But it is also believed by some that such a claim is a way to keep the illegal diamond hunters at bay. For a long time, there has been a very believable rumour that a huge hoard of the most select and perfect diamonds ever found by man lay somewhere buried near the Vascoma, concealed by the naturalist shortly before he died. This cache is supposedly larger than all of the diamonds brought out of the area thus far and remains hidden to this day."

"You're saying that this has been Dr Paul's way of keeping the treasure to himself?"

He nodded. "That's what I think. Moreover, a terrible disease has been sweeping through the country, and I think that the officially distributed pills that CAMID supplies don't contain any effective drug. They have bitterness and may be something like caffeine that gives the person a feeling that the pill has done something. But they are worse than useless. Anyone infected with a disease who takes the drug, hoping to get better, will become hopelessly addicted…or worse."

"So you expect to go to these places and provide the real cure?"

He nodded. "Yes, we're just taking samples to certain men I trust and that I've already told my suspicions to. There are three: The road engineer at the road head on Gable, a Dr Clemson at the hospital at Souls on the Moors, and one doctor that I trust in the CAMID team in Pike. Certainly not everyone in CAMID is corrupt, and this one I know isn't. There's lots who will be delighted to see pills that work. Anyway, don't worry. I don't believe our lives will be in danger just through this one job. The real dangers of this trip, as I see it, will begin after we have been to Pike…" He stopped and shook his head. "Our first stop."

"This whole thing is absolutely fantastic. How did you come to be involved in this?"

Karl was silent, shifting his shoulders uneasily and staring at the sand. Then he said, "I worked for Dr Paul. At CAMID."

"You did? He will not be happy if he finds out what you've been up to. He took a very foolish risk in letting you go on this trip. You might have gone straight to Scotland Yard, or, say, to the offices of the *Daily Telegraph* with your story. You might never have collected any drugs."

"Firstly, he didn't exactly let me go. I raised the idea of a trip to London to do various things, buy instruments we need, photocopy papers from journals, et cetera, and he agreed and sent me. But that was a long time ago. When I didn't return, he had to have realized his mistake."

"Then his risk was simply letting you out."

"I'm sure he'll find that that was a bad risk," said Karl rather gloomily. "For a time, I thought I might never return. I stayed in London, trying to decide what to do. After a while, I decided I simply couldn't let him continue on as he has been. I'm sure he already knows I'm back. He's got many friends. Eyes everywhere."

"What does he look like?" Robert asked.

"Little taller than you. Kind of fattish, but still very strong. Fair hair, balding a little… But look, I don't want to talk about this. I'll tell you some other time." He flicked spurts of dry sand with the end of a stick. He was sitting with his back against an old driftwood log and Robert was outstretched on the sand near to him. They were in the deep shade of branches near where they had slept. It was where Robert had seen the crickets at dawn, although there were none there now. Outside their well of shade, a harsh light radiated from the white sand of the riverbed. The sand quivered; now and then a wind rolled the hot air in under the trees, striking their bodies like buffets from a soft balloon.

Karl closed his eyes and screwed his face, as with a bad taste. "I'm hoping we shan't see him, but if we do, you may be sure I'll point him out. Of course, if he sees me, I may have to introduce you. He's amazingly active around the moors—certainly no sort of recluse of a king. And, believe it or not, he possibly was—and certainly thought himself to be—a very benign potentate to his people in the early days. Many families in the moors have reason to be grateful for the lives that he saved. He brought improved cattle to the area and persuaded people to dump a lot of the sillier folk remedies for livestock and human diseases."

"I thought you said the folk medicine was very good."

"Some of it is quite remarkable, but that part comes from the indigenous tribes. These people of the moors are quite different from the indigenous; they are of very mixed origin. The clash of different traditions has kept some of what was good, but also destroyed much, and has thrown in a lot of utter nonsense. Voodoo beliefs. Anyway, as I was saying, early on, the people respected Dr Paul so much that even feuds would be submitted to him for arbitration. It was when he began to see that real progress—the coming of real engineers, real doctors—was incompatible with continuing his kind of power, that he turned sour completely. And how sour, how utterly rotten and terrible, I haven't told you yet—about the rumours that spread against the road people—abduction, murder... It's like the story of Ivan the Terrible. But...some other time."

"But how can he be like this and still be a wandering friar, as you say? What does he get out of it all for himself if he lives in hardship? Ivan the Terrible had a palace, didn't he?"

"The fact is, no one knows where he does spend half his time: he appears and disappears. To a lot of the people, this gives him a god-like aura, an appearance of supernatural power. And whatever he does during his absences— he might well have a palace in Cimoul for all I know, his income from his father's investments would very easily cover it—whatever he does, the god-like charisma and veneration, might be reward enough—even without that savage and psychopathic power he wields. I hope you see now what an important mission I have brought you on and how powerful a madman we have to beat. It's generous to call him mad, instead of a mass murderer. For that's what he is also, even the swapping of the pills alone amounts to that."

"But we're not going to beat him, are we?"

Karl shook his head. "No. I suppose I'll be happy to save a few lives, is all." He levelled his gaze at the boy. "Now, you sound frightened."

"I'm not," he said, though it was a lie. He'd begun to feel tendrils of fear, creeping up his back. "Even if only half is true—I'd like to help. I only hope I won't be just an added danger to you. I think I'm not very brave. I'll fight any—but that's because I've grown. I'm as tough as they are; but I'm not sure how much courage I'd have facing a gang of hard men in the real world—or this real-unreal world of yours down here."

"I'm not any surer of myself than that," said Karl gloomily. "I have some reasons to be less sure. See how even thinking about it is making me sweat. Let's move to something else, Robert. I can tell you more about it some other time."

Karl was indeed sweating heavily, and his face looked grey under his usual brown. Robert agreed, though he still had a thousand more questions, because he wondered if this wasn't the beginning of one of his "moods" that Karl had warned him about. He said, lightly, "I feel as though we are in another world. I wonder if in another few days, I might forget what civilization is like altogether. And then you're right—never will I be able to return to London."

When he next spoke, Karl was more jovial. His eyes darted across the blackness beyond their circle of light. "We are not *that* far away from other human life. In fact, I think we are being followed."

"Followed! What?" Robert scanned the dark, now, too. "Are we being hunted?"

Karl laughed. "Don't worry. Let's sleep now. We shan't be attacked in the night."

3

Butterfly

Indeed, as they trekked deeper into the forest, the road had grown narrower and less rutted from vehicles that had gone this way before, until it seemed as if it'd never been travelled at all. No one had passed them in days, and yet Robert carefully considered Karl's words and wondered if they were indeed being tracked.

To add to his suspicions about being watched, Karl did not want to bathe in the nearest pool but in one beyond a band of rocks and palms that half-crossed the riverbed a little upstream. It was better anyway. The pool, dammed by the rocks, was just deep enough to swim in. After splashing, soaping themselves, and splashing again, they began to wash their clothes, keeping close to the outlet stream so as not to dirty the pool with the washing water. Robert continued to wear his shirt, soaked as it was, because of Karl's warning about sunburn.

A brilliant orange butterfly floated to Karl's washed shirt, where it lay on the sand. It uncurled its long black tongue and began drinking from the wet material.

"Hey! Karl! See this! You should have brought the net!" Robert whispered. "It's another of those...."

"Another what?"

"The same butterfly. Those you said were so rare, you remember?—the day we stopped by the lagoon—where the ibises were?"

"Man! You've sharp eyes," Karl said soberly.

"So you were wrong about it being found only in that area."

"Sure. I make mistakes."

"Why, it's exactly the same, Karl."

"Sure, it's exactly the same. Anyone can see. Same colour and size."

"But you aren't even watching. It's the same in everything. It has the same silver spots. Shall I fetch the net?"

Karl did not answer but reached slowly towards the butterfly, which continued sipping his shirt. In a moment Karl held the wings and picked up the butterfly and looked at it. It closed its long feathery legs against its body and did not struggle.

"Sure. Silver spots. So it does have them, now that I look. And it has that purple too, which you can see on helistes."

He held it gently from underneath and let it open its wings.

"So you admit that it's the same now? Is that what you said was following us?"

"Ha. A bit smaller. If it weren't for a few things that still worry me—"

"You'll collect it, now you've got it. won't you?"

"I'm damned if I will."

"Why?"

"Because, as anyone but a wall-eyed townie would know, this is totally different—not even the same family as helistes pennalia. Actually, I'm just trying to spot what you've spotted that might make it not be phaedrasantanensis, the old Cloth of Gold."

"Was that one rare at all?"

"Rare! That's the commonest butterfly for the past five hundred miles. There are lots here by the stream on the sand." He gave Robert a superior nod.

For someone who's never been to uni, he certainly knows a lot about these things. "Then here's another damn Cloth of Gold."

Robert threw the wet brown sock he was holding at Karl. Karl ignored it and gently opened his fingers. He let the butterfly drop onto his palm where it did not fly away but lay flat on its side. Presently, it stood up and walked around his palm extending its tongue and licking the skin.

"They all like sweat, mine especially," Karl said, watching it raptly. "They love me, even though I collect them."

He tossed the butterfly into the air and with strong curling glides it flew away. He grabbed one of his socks that was floating at his knees and threw that at Robert. It crossed with a second sock thrown by Robert in mid-air. Karl jumped up on the rock behind him. From tooth-tightened lower lip, he emitted a piercing whistle, and then just as Robert hurled Karl's sock back, he took off in a racing dive across the pool. Robert followed him, swimming underwater, pawing the sand with his hand to hold himself down until he could see the white columns of Karl's legs. He seized the ankles and tried to stand up, but Karl sat heavily on his back. They rolled together spluttering in the water, each trying to be on top.

At a moment when both heads happened to be above water at the same time, Karl said, "What did you do with the sock that I threw at you? Did it sink?"

"Chucked it into the palm. It stuck up there."

"Hell!" Karl looked up at the palm which was one of those with a fearsomely spiny trunk. He looked up through a storm of yellow butterflies mixed with some of the orange. They were flying all above the pool, having been disturbed from where they were sipping water from the sand at the side by Karl's dive. "I'm going to get yours—but first I'll—"

Robert dove for the deep water again. This time his underwater swim brought him to the face of the big rock. He came up alongside it, grabbed a ledge, and partly hauled himself out of the water. He could see the pale form of Karl's body under the green water, moving a little off target towards the rock. He turned to the rock face again and made ready to heave himself up further by a ledge to be ready to drop on Karl. Then he saw, on the mottled surface of the rock a few inches from his eyes, an odd shape. Embossed ridges radiated from a sort of divided lump on the surface of the stone. It was as if someone had carved something there—like a letter of an ancient alphabet. Suddenly, he realized that it was an enormous spider flattened against the surface of the rock. As he pushed back through the water in alarm, the embossed shape suddenly loosed itself, slipped into the water, and shot off across it, past Robert's shoulder. Some twenty feet away, it flipped up and vanished against the dark wall of a rock that was in shadow. When Karl came to the surface and grabbed his waist, Robert patted him urgently and said, "Karl! There was a giant spider. It runs on the water. Is it dangerous?"

Karl released Robert's waist and supported himself likewise from the ledge. "I know the kind. They're harmless. But I don't like spiders. Where is it?"

"Across on that black rock."

"It's shallow there. Let's go see it."

The water was waist-deep. They approached cautiously and at last made out the spider whose body in the shadow was even more invisible than where Robert had seen it first.

After they had peered at it from an arm's length distance, Robert suddenly grasped Karl by the shoulders and thrust him forward, almost on top of the spider, at the same time he leapt and dived sideways across the pool.

When he surfaced, he was surprised to see Karl neither following him nor smiling but clutching his shoulder with an expression of pain and anger.

"Don't ever do that again!" he shouted.

"What's the matter? Did the spider bite you?"

"No. He's gone off. But you mustn't hit me there."

"Why? Oh, because of that lump. What is that lump, Karl?"

"It's called a cyst—but it's painful and you mustn't touch it."

"Okay, I'll take care. There's your sock, by the way." He pointed to it floating on the surface of the pond. Seeing Karl was still holding his shoulder awkwardly and stroking it, he said, "I'm sorry I pushed you; it was a joke."

Karl was silent awhile, still carefully feeling his shoulder.

"It doesn't matter," he said at last. His anger had gone but his face was red. "It's quite true that spiders and centipedes give me the creeps—something that I never feel with insects…. But it's what comes later if I get that shoulder hit—I mean, there'll be swelling and pain." He shrugged. "Let's go back down and spread our things."

As they were laying out their clothes in the sunlight by the jeep, draping them over bushes and grass tussocks, Robert said, "I noticed your lump a while back. It has a little scar alongside it. Did you once try to cut it or lance it or something?"

Karl said nothing for a moment and then said, "Yep, I tried to lance it myself once with a mirror and a knife I'd sterilised in fire. It wasn't a success, as you can see."

"I suppose you had to do it left-handed."

"I am left-handed. No, the problem was the mirror. It was stupid—a bloody mess—and I've never touched it since then. It does no harm if I don't let it get rubbed or hit."

Robert had unpleasant intuitions about what the lump might be. He had heard of something called a sebaceous cyst but thought they were supposed to be like outsize blackheads, which everyone had...and painless. He sensed that Karl wasn't telling the whole truth about it. Was it possible that the scar was left when there had been an attempt to remove a tumour, and the tumour had regrown?

Karl seemed healthy enough in general, but at that moment, he did not look entirely well. He was perspiring heavily, and his movements seemed clumsy. He seemed tired out but had an odd smile. The shirt he was hanging from the twigs of a bush fell to the red earth, but he did not pick it up. Instead, he sighed and said, "Do you know, I have four-quart bottles of beer in the bottom of the big food box? I'm going to get one out and put a wet cloth over it and stand it in the shade. Even though it's British beer, it doesn't like to be drunk boiling, like in this weather. Today's our holiday and we can have it with dinner. But just for now, I'm going to sit in the shade."

"Are you okay?"

"I'm okay."

"You should be wearing a hat, Karl. Like you say I ought."

The sun was indeed brilliant, a pitiless rain. Karl's thing might be sunburn or sunstroke.

Karl lay in the shade on the sand for the rest of the afternoon. He seemed comfortable enough and showed no sign of fever but had a rather vacant expression. Well, he had mentioned that he could be a mean shit. Maybe this was one of those episodes. If so, it wasn't that bad. Robert had hurt him; Karl had had reason to be cross with him.

Robert sat among the reeds at the edge of the river, feeling a little uneasy. The outburst of today's hedonism would have seemed unsurprising in any other companion he had ever travelled with, but up until now, Karl had seemed so unswerving in his wish to be south as soon as possible.

It is as if he's escaping something, Robert thought.

It was while he was deep in thought, there on the riverbank, that he could've sworn he glimpsed the reeds parting, and a single eye gazing at him. But when he lifted his gaze to look closer, the reeds snapped back again, and the eye disappeared.

4

Stranded

The next day, once again on the road, they quarrelled. Karl had been moody all morning. About lunchtime, he asked Robert if he needed to eat—he said that for himself he had a tummy bug and was in no hurry. They were on a bad stretch of road and Robert was still weak from his sickness, so he wasn't hungry either. They passed a village without stopping, which surprised Robert. Since villages were becoming more scarce, normally a stop, if not for a meal, at least for fuel and provisions, was automatic. Afterwards, for many hours, no other village followed. Sometime after that, by some deep woodland along a river, they came to four sticks holding up a roof of palm leaves and under it a brown woman sitting by a pile of red palm hearts and some other small edibles spread out on the grass. She jumped up and stretched out two of the palm hearts towards them, beckoning them to stop and sample. Karl did not slow down.

"She looks like you, just about to juggle the hammers," said Robert with a forced smile, thinking of the food they were now passing. Karl gazed ahead and the jeep thundered on.

After one more hour, they passed a shack calling itself a restaurant. Karl muttered that it was small and had no petrol. At last, in mid-afternoon, where the road cut straight to the horizon through a dry and dust-coloured forest,

Robert asked coldly if they shouldn't at least stop to picnic. Karl slowed just a little.

"Why, are you hungry?"

By then, even his queasy stomach was in want of something. "Of course. It must be nearly four o'clock, and we haven't eaten all day."

"Why didn't you say you were hungry earlier?"

"It's your jeep, your expedition. You pay for what we eat. I was being polite."

"Polite! Ha, you've got manners like the bloody Queen. It just so happens there hasn't been a decent place to stop. We could have stopped at any one of those shacks if you'd said. I didn't feel like eating and thought you didn't. Now we're low on petrol and every stop wastes a little. Why don't you climb into the back and get some biscuits?"

Robert leaned over behind, but the vibration was such that he couldn't open the catch on the food box.

"Can't you slow down?" he shouted, his words jostling along with his body.

Karl slowed a little more and the vibration grew worse. Robert guessed he was driving at just the speed that would make it as bad as possible. He struggled with the jolting boxes a little longer and then, in the calmest voice he could manage, he called, "A can has fallen and I think is leaking—maybe into your pills. I think we should stop while we sort this mess out?"

Karl stopped the jeep in the middle of the road and continued to sit at the wheel, not looking around. There was a strong smell of petrol everywhere.

The sun bore down upon Robert. Sweat slipped down his arms. "Er…do you think you could move in the shade?"

Karl leaned across the front and looked back at the forest on their right. Then, turned again to the front, with narrowed, dreamy eyes, threw the gear stick in reverse and lurched the jeep backward off the road, curving it into the thicket of bamboos, which here made up the undergrowth of the forest. The canes splintered all around them and, with the jeep embedded among the arching rods rather like a tennis ball that had landed in long grass, Karl stopped the engine. He still did not glance at Robert.

Robert climbed back into the cab, forced the door open, took a machete from under his seat, and began to hack his way to the back of the jeep. Outside there was still the stench of petrol, and choking dust rose in stiff waves. After he had made a yard of clearance at the back and had opened the door, he called to Karl, "I'm putting this last can of petrol into the tank. Okay?"

No reply.

After he had poured in the petrol and flung the empty can up on the pile, he began eating handfuls of biscuits from the food box. They tasted of dust and petrol. Then he held up the big water can and tilted it to his lips and let the tepid, plastic-tasting water swill biscuit paste and crumbs into his throat. The water also seemed to have got the petrol smell into it.

He heard Karl crunching in the bamboos on the other side and expected he would come to the back to join him, but then Karl climbed back into the driving seat. Now Robert poured last night's bacon stew from the billy onto his pannikin and ate that, using his fingers to pick up the solid bits and drinking the rest. At last, he said, "Karl, you ought to eat something. Shall I bring you some stew?"

"Plenty of time."

"Shouldn't we be moving on?"

"Can't."

"Can't? Why?"

"We're out of juice."

"How can we be? I told you, I've put in our spare can."

"That's gone. I just looked underneath and saw the last bit of it running out."

"Running out? What the hell do you mean?"

"A stone holed our tank."

"Hell! Why didn't you look sooner?"

"You said something about a can on its side at the back. I thought the smell must be from that." Karl spoke wearily.

"Why, it's your cuckoo driving that's made the stone fly up and hole the tank. Now you blame me. It's ten to one we wouldn't have reached anywhere either, even if we hadn't stopped here. And if you hadn't bored into this stupid canebrake, I'd have seen the petrol dripping and we might have plugged it, and certainly not have wasted the spare can."

"Like how would you have stopped the leak?"

"With a twig, chewing gum, anything… Anything to hold it till we got to the next place."

They were side by side on the front seat again. Karl laid his head back, his face blank and grey. "I have a plug. That's not the problem. Right now, we've got no petrol."

"Aren't you the least bit worried? We haven't seen another human soul in *ages!*"

No answer. His expression of total indifference so angered Robert he could hardly look at him. He longed to seize him roughly by the arm, shake him awake, force him to turn full face to him, to shake him more until he could see anger, like his own, reflected there, in his stupidly staring mug.

And yet shortly Karl seemed to be asleep.

Robert ground his teeth noisily. Later, he slapped Karl's knee.

"Wake up, quick, I hear a lorry. It's going our way," he said. "We'd better be out on the roadside, hadn't we?—and wave it down."

Karl sat up and listened. Then he grabbed the gear lever, forced it into first gear, and turned the key to connect the self-starter motor. Running on the battery, the jeep groaned slowly out onto the road. A big truck bore down upon them.

ANNETTA

5

Chance Encounter

Robert saw a blurred shadow coming toward them on the path. He wiped the dust from his eyes and gazed at a familiar face.

It was the lady he had seen in Swanson's shop, the friend of Dewey the prospector, the lady who had cried over his sketches and who had wanted a lift south. She was neat still, wearing the same clothes that he had remembered. She was holding her hat on with one hand and under her hat, her sand-coloured hair whipped left and right. She smiled at Robert and her smile showed those gold stars on her white teeth. Behind her now, the dust kicked up from her lorry was retreating slowly over the clattering corn stalks and high into the air. He had no time to watch or think about this wonder, for the lady, framed by the red dust behind, was asking him about possibilities of combining their resources for an expedition south, seeming not to remember the boys at all.

"Fare paying if need be," she continued, though he had missed most of her words since she chattered incessantly.

Robert blinked. She had come like a genie out of a bottle, yet, in her chirpy voice, it seemed she was offering them twenty dollars or so for a passage to the south, happily paid.

Karl was silent, and indeed Robert wasn't even sure if he was listening. A crazy and rather muddled stream of speech poured like birdsong from her smiling and ageing lips. Her teeth flashed their stars from one to the other;

her words too seemed to scamper about between them, slightly elusive, like eager puppies.

When he could pop a word in, Robert said, because there was no possible way of refusing her—it wasn't gentlemanly, and even if they were inclined to be ungentlemanly, they needed her supplies—"Why, sure. We seem to be out of petrol. You came at just the right time."

She clapped her hands together, rather like a child. "Oh. Splendid. Let me get my things. And you're in luck—I have two full cans of petrol on me!"

She looked at Karl for confirmation, but he simply stared straight ahead, gnawing on a blade of grass he'd picked from the side of the road. "I suppose it was just a matter of time. You were following us long enough."

Robert's eyes popped. He looked at the woman, who appeared for the first time, embarrassed. Though she said nothing, he knew that Karl had spoken the truth. When she went back to collect her things, he hesitated. "If we'd never broken down here, would she have followed us the whole way, alone?"

He shrugged. "She wasn't alone. I was keeping tabs on her. Now, go help the lady with her bags."

They drove south long and hard that day. Annetta, for that was her name, sat between them on the bench seat. Karl had replied to her mention of a fare with an odd, dry courtesy to the effect that he would accept nothing, and she was welcome to come with them as far as she wished but must not mind a bit of a crush. It was indeed pretty close in the front. Her body pressed on Robert's from shoulder to thigh and when Karl reached for the gears, her calf too had to move over and press. Robert thought how trim and muscular she seemed, how hardened by some hard life, almost like Karl. This paralysed his usual lounging and he held his neck stiff, head facing forward. If he wished to look at her, or even look past her, at Karl, he had to fix on some passing landmark on their left—a tree all bright with flowers, perhaps, or the flashing green wings of a parrot—and let it draw his head round. But he found himself captivated by the crow's feet spreading from the corners of Annetta's eyes, so like the marks on his mother's and a thing that no one could call beautiful.

In contrast, Karl seemed quite at ease, though he never spoke. Annetta did all the talking and seemed to have no problem with it. When, in talking to Karl, Annetta referred to Robert as "your friend here," and then she would touch his knee with her hand and turn a dry smile upon him, lighting golden stars; and Robert would smile back at her quickly, and then look straight ahead, or out of the window.

"Oh, your friend here, he's young and he's big and strong and his hair waves up so neat, and yet he's so bashful—and won't look at me. There, he did—and see how sorry he is already!"

"Leave him alone."

"He likes to look at birds and things out there, he has time for that," she said.

"Sure," Karl answered for him.

"But the sins and the glories of people and all their needs, those pass him by."

There was silence. Robert was lost, much as he'd been growing up, when his parents would have their dinner parties and engage in "adult" conversations that he wasn't sure he wanted to understand.

Karl asked her questions about the road, and they compared knowledge. Robert wasn't sure whether Karl was asking seriously or just testing her. It seemed as if she knew the names of places on the road but little else, and often she confused even the order of the towns, as Karl pointed out to her.

"You're right. I take it back then. Pattal must be before Conwalliston. But such tiny places, how can I tell them apart? I never stopped at either except when we had to fill up, and once when a friend's carburettor broke. Or that's what he said, although I've heard that story more often than I've believed it, and many others. In Pattal, there was a place that said it was an inn, but they wouldn't let us stay. The man there was fat and very religious; he had a lot he wanted to shoot off about when he saw us. And he had one of those what-chamacallits—a goitre—on his neck."

"It's common on the moors," said Karl.

"I wouldn't contradict you, love, because I've only been up to the moors towns once and that I don't remember well. They say it's in the water, the goitre? That's why I always ask for bottled water. So…. Pattal, Conwalliston, I hardly knew them, but you're right, Pattal comes first."

A few minutes later she said, "But about the goitre, love, it's all Furnace water on the moors, and that's different. Even Diamond Creek, though next to Furnace, is different. It's those creeks, straight off the rocks or that clayey stuff, that makes the goitre. People on the moors that have it must have moved up from Pike and Bend West and Calla Holla and those places."

Robert had had a kindly old aunt with goitre. His father had said it was from mineral deficiency and had used it as a reason to ensure he always ate his vegetables as a child. "What makes you think the goitre's due to creek water?"

"Oh!" Annette gave a sideways glance to Karl. "I used to have a friend who lived by one of those creeks and he got it."

"Came while he was there?"

"His neck always was, you know, not fat, but a bit bullish. But when he started getting the colic and fevers—which weren't malaria, love, I know that—he said it was the creek water making him sick. Something about chemicals—iodine and mercury. Terrible dysentery. I used to fetch him water to drink the oxbows at Gullet, and he said it was much better—although I could hardly bear to watch him drink it, it was so green and full of the wrigglers I couldn't get out. So, if that stuff did him good, it must have been the creek water that had made him ill, mustn't it? And that creek water itself isn't crystal, even in the dry season. It's mucky—with that clay. You could soon tell the creek wasn't called Diamond because of the water! Even lake water didn't help in the end. He died."

"Of what?"

"His goitre, I guess, and all."

"Can you die from one? Maybe dehydration? A person with dysentery needs a lot of water, right?"

A pinched wrinkle appeared over the bridge of her nose. "What would the water matter, love, for that? It was just water, after all. I used to think I should make him drink less of it, so his tubes could dry out a bit." She tried out a smile and a shrug but looked rather upset.

"People with dysentery must have lots and lots of water to replace what they're losing."

"But people can go a long time without water if they try. I'd manage a day on the road sometimes, waiting for a lift, or when I was put down in some out-of-way spot. And I never thought much of that. Your tongue gets sticky, is about all."

"No. I've read that a day without water could kill a man with bad dysentery."

A bushy savannah was gliding past. Robert had hardly noticed until now, but suddenly, in tense silence, he saw it, those strange trees and sunlight, and wondered if he could survive for a day in the endless, dry shrubbery without water. Had hers been savannah like this?

Suddenly she burst out, "Oh, I killed him!"

The wide flat savannah swung past for what seemed a long time. Through the shoulder which pressed on his own, Robert felt her chest heave with a long indrawn breath.

At last, Robert could take the wondering no longer. "It's Dewey you're speaking of, isn't it? The naturalist—the diamond man. I know it is. You were his…er, friend."

Annetta gasped. "You know of him?"

"Only what Karl has told me."

"And what is that?" She leaned forward and clutched Karl's wrist holding the wheel so that the jeep swerved and sprayed up sand from the loose ridge at the side of the road. "Are you a diamonder too?"

"No, but Karl here is an insect collector, kind of. That was Dewey's other line, wasn't it?"

She beamed at Karl. "A collector, yes, he called himself that…" she mused. "He drew marvellous pictures of them."

"I've seen them. You've forgotten that I met you once before—in London. Do you remember a shop—a naturalist's shop—in London, where some sketches of his were being sold, just a few weeks ago?"

She was silent. She looked first at Karl and then at Robert. At last, she said, "I do remember something now."

"You were his wife, right?"

She smiled sadly. "I wouldn't go that far."

"But did you travel with him, before he died?" Robert asked.

"Maybe…"

"But a few moments ago, you were saying you were bringing him water when he died."

She didn't answer the question. Instead, she said, "Those drawings were the last he ever made. I'd sold them to Mrs Foster—I needed the money, you see—and then I regretted it. I was there to buy them back. But I was too late. They were already sold." She looked hopefully at Karl.

Robert looked at Karl, too, waiting for him to volunteer that he'd bought them, and perhaps out of kindness would return them to her. But he did not, and Robert began to wonder if he *had* indeed purchased them. He hadn't seen them since they'd set out from London.

Speech ended for a while. Tyres and springs thudded on the corrugations and the boxes bounced in the back. Hot wind fluttered in Robert's burning face. His sideways glances showed that Annetta was becoming increasingly dismayed and uneasy, even now that they had stopped talking. Presently, in a fainter voice, she said, "Boys, friends—I believe you are friends, who wouldn't take an advantage of a stranger—friends, you won't repeat down here how I might have known Dewey? Some might begin to think…and then, believe me; Annetta Fairby's as good as gone, give a day or a week. She's a ghost with the others—if you tell that."

"Gone!" Robert's eyes went wide.

"Yes! Many think I know the location of the diamonds. *Many* diamonds—surely you've heard the rumour. If they knew I was travelling with Dewey during his last days, they'd get ideas."

Robert stared at her. "*Do* you know?"

Karl spoke at last, his voice teasing. "Yes, Annetta. You must. Do tell us where the diamonds are."

"Karl!" said Robert. He leaned forward to look angrily across at Karl, who returned a brief glance, shrugging, and tightening his lips.

Annetta had gone chalk-white. There was silence again. The passing land, the immense, rough carpet of savannah that their wheels pushed back, was here drier and hillier. There was loose sand on the road, and sometimes they ploughed it so deeply that the jeep, checked as if in a huge puddle, would almost stop. The forest was scrubby and there were patches of open grass. The few big trees were of a kind they had not met before, with trunks like bulging bottles of grey stone.

Her eyes, her teeth, her stars, flashed from one boy to the other, and finally, she said, "Everyone who knows who I am asks about the diamonds. Where did the diamonds go? How big? How many? Who saw them? So it goes."

She writhed in her seat, swung her head side to side, put her hands palm outwards between her eyes and the bright sky.

Karl said coldly, "Did you sell any of the diamonds yourself, Miss Fairby?"

"I haven't sold them. I've said it a thousand times: I never had any, and I don't know where they are... Stop, please, this is as far as I want to go. I want to get down."

"I didn't ask if you sold them—Robert, help keep her off the brake, will you?—I asked if you sold *any*."

"If I'd sold one, even the smallest of those he kept, it's not likely I'd be travelling here, asking lifts, with my one bag. He left nothing and I sold nothing. I never asked him for nothing except love, and I'd never have asked for that except he loved me, like I never knew anyone could. Put me down. I don't want to go any further. You're not the friends I thought if you don't put me down."

"You know where they are. You're travelling back to claim the diamonds. Admit it. Why else would you be coming back?"

"Karl!" Robert repeated, at his wit's end. If she did jump down from their jeep, he wouldn't blame her. "She already told you. Leave it alone."

They were going fast again now, on a long straight stretch through grassy savannah, Karl was almost shouting, angrily and derisively, over the thunder from the pounded and shimmering noonday road. Annetta sat hunched between the boys with her face buried in her hands.

Then she said, "I am travelling back here—to the place I swore I'd never return—for Dewey. Not for diamonds. I have a mission of another sort, and I fear I'll never sleep soundly again until I complete it. Now, do not ask me another question about it, and we will all get along just fine."

The bottle
shaped tree

6

The Raft

They drove through the night. Morning rose, bringing bright sunshine with it. The trees grew taller and greener, the soil yet more brilliant red. At last, they came to a bit of a traffic jam, a raft ferry over the White River.

An enormous, wounded lizard, a red slash on its side, was lying and dying in the river. It was not a lizard, really, but the long hill of the far bank covered with forest trees like scales that went up to the blue sky in a serrated line like the frill of a green tree lizard's back. The wound was their road to the south, winding upon that far side. The red soil slanted up among huge trees, starting from a floating pier. They could just see the pier through the trees, and the raft that was to carry them. It carried two lorries that looked much too big and was crowded with cars and pickups as well. It trailed a yellow streak in the water.

They themselves were in a line of vehicles waiting for the raft on a steep downhill. The road was cut through high banks of crimson sand. Forest towered over the banks and the trees were hung with creepers, and a huge trunk had fallen right across the narrow cutting like a bridge and creepers hung from that too in festoons and curtains. Creepers flowered on the banks, tumbled down through brakes of tall grasses, and poured out among the dark green weeds of the roadside. They flowed onto the road and were crushed and cut by tyres. Everywhere the creepers held up their bubbly sprays of yellow flowers;

behind the flowers were green heart-shaped leaves and behind the massed leaves the crimson soil of the banks.

The road curved as it went down and, from where they waited, the landing on their side of the river was out of sight. The raft seemed to be coming faster now that it was nearer. It went behind the red bank to the right.

Karl muttered under his breath at his own stupidity, to have arrived this day of the week and at this hour. He said that with this queue in front they would not even get to the next crossing. All the while they must sit in the hot jeep and hide from notice.

Robert marvelled at the sheer number of people. After being off on their own for so long, this was surprising. He needn't have worried about forgetting what civilization was like. Lined in front of them were an open jeep and a Volkswagen Beetle. Some way ahead of that was a green, oldish lorry with sides and tyre guards gaily painted with frame lines and scrolls. It had unsawn lumber. A large Mercedes, purple and fawn with road dust, went quietly past; at the bend ahead it paused, then reversed and came to a standstill alongside them. The driver was busy with some papers which he rested on his wheel. Now and then he stopped and stared across at the boys.

Then a lorry, the first from the raft, came up the road and the blue car had to reverse ahead of it to get out of its way. Engines in the waiting line all sprang to life as the lorry came by. But nothing followed this premature action, as there was a long wait, and one by one the engines died to silence again. From far ahead, they could hear shouts and the furious whine of a big motor. The man from the jeep in front of them climbed out and went down the road. Then, there was a girl there too on the far side of the road, shading her eyes to look down the hill. She crossed to the green lorry and talked to someone in the cab. Robert thought she should shade her eyes from her white blouse; it was so bright that it dimmed the sunlight. But really, it was something else, something he couldn't quite put his finger on, that dazzled him. Her slender form, her outstretched pointing arm, the sparkle of sunlight on her hair…it all stung his own eyes. Robert sighed.

Karl said that risk or no, he was going down to see what was happening. Robert wanted to leave the jeep, too, but mostly because he wanted to see if that girl was really as beautiful, up close. He found himself suddenly wishing that his clothes were not so dirty. How did those people keep theirs so clean, the man in the blue shirt, that girl, with all this pink dust in the air? It was one thing to drive past people or to huddle in the jeep, most of your stains hidden. It was another to walk out there, past all the cars...

But a moment later, he could stand the wait no longer. He stepped out and hurried after Karl.

As the boys drew near, the girl watched them coming for a moment and then went around the front of the timber lorry as if to avoid them. But enough of her showed as he passed that Robert's breath checked in his throat. She was as she had seemed in the distance; shapely, perfect, lovely beyond measure. He thought that he saw the corner of a turned away smile.

It turned out that the second lorry was stuck on the raft's ramp. Its weight had tilted the whole raft and had made a vee between deck and ramp. The lorry with the racing engine rocked but could not climb the steep ramp. Some men were laying out a cable down across the dock from a jeep that was facing uphill on the open side of the road.

The man they had seen leave the other jeep was hurrying up the road towards them. He had on a clean straw hat and wore a red vest that hung low about his heavy brown arms and hairy chest. Sunglasses were clipped in a leather holder on his belt and his stomach bulged over them.

"Towing her," he puffed to Karl as he passed.

"Are you getting your jeep to help?"

"Yep."

"I'll bring mine, too."

"Shouldn't bother, comrade. Two will pull it. Come later, if she still won't shift with mine."

"The jeep's helping will get on the raft first, I suppose?" said Karl. "Say you wouldn't let me go down, would you? I'm in a hell of a hurry to cross."

"Sorry, I can't, mate. Like to help, but I'm in a hurry too, see. They're reaping my cane across there." He strode on.

Karl muttered a curse under his breath. "Let's hope they need another jeep for the pull. If so, we can get on before this line of cars," he told Robert.

Robert walked back up the road. The other jeep passed him going down and he could see men getting ropes ready to link it to the first.

He heard a girl's voice behind him. "Sir!" She was leaning from the cab of the green timber lorry, but it was not the girl in the white blouse. This one had a face thin and brown, and sharp aquiline nose, and black hair.

"Sir! Aren't you from the blue and white jeep up there?"

"Yes," said Robert.

"A man was trying to get into it just now. We wondered if you knew about him."

Robert looked at their jeep but could see no one, but worried for Annetta, who was sleeping in the front seat. He said, "Where did you see him? Where did he go?" He remembered that they had not even bothered to shut the windows.

"He was on the other side by the bank," said the girl. "He was reaching in through the window. We thought he might be taking something and might be…" Here her speech seemed to run out and she just stared at Robert. "I just told you, in case you wanted to know," she added.

"He's there still, Edie," said another girl's voice, rather strained, from inside the cab. "I can see him in the mirror this side."

Robert went to the roadside, passing the old-fashioned out-held headlights of the lorry. He glanced up the line of vehicles and then he turned and ran down the hill to Karl. He told him about the man.

A cracked, empty gourd lay in the road. Karl kicked it as he walked up straight towards their jeep. He had chosen a line where it would be hardest for a man at the far side or at the back to see him coming.

Robert went to where Karl had told him to wait, by the timber lorry. He stood near the cab and jerked his low voice towards the open window, to the girls, "Thanks for letting us know." He tried not to sound nervous.

The thin brown head nodded, with a swift, amused smile. He wished it had been the other girl. When it vanished, the far more beautiful face appeared behind her, this time, focusing on him, pushing back a falling wave of light brown hair with two fingers.

She flashed a merry smile and said, "Are you his cousin?"

"Whose?"

"Why, his—Karl McNeeve's?"

Robert was confused. How could she know Karl's name? Who was she? At last, he said, "No," rather abruptly.

"Okay. I just wondered," said the girl. Before he could ask anything more, she, too, vanished into the car with a tinkling of suppressed laughter.

Just then, Karl went out of his sight round behind the back of the jeep. Robert crossed past the old headlights again and walked swiftly up the bankside of the line of cars.

Backed against the tall weeds at the roadside was the driver of the blue Mercedes. Karl was facing him one pace away, blocking his way past the back. They could hear the second lorry from the raft coming up the hill.

"You had no business to touch it," said Karl.

"I touched nothing of yours," said the man. He looked lithe and cool in his clean blue shirt.

"You tried to open the back door. These are your handprints in the dust."

"Those are likely your own. The door hasn't been opened."

"I know it hasn't. It happens to be locked. That's why."

Karl's next words were drowned for Robert in the roar of the passing lorry. The jet of its exhaust from the pipe behind the cab swung up the curtain of vines under the bridging trunk. Yellow flowers tossed in the black smoke. The lorry went out of sight and the noise died and Robert heard the blue shirt man saying, "Well, I admit to that, my friend, I was curious how you'd fixed that old thing."

"Quite the enthusiast for repairs, for old cars. Of course. I guessed that from your own choice of model."

"Yes. It interests me professionally… How is it my business, you ask? Well, call me a lawyer if you like. It interests me when the handyman changes everything outside, does all this work, and still does not…?" He paused.

"Well?"

The Volks ahead of them was moving on down. "Hadn't we better go, Karl?" he said, wondering if Karl wasn't headed toward one of his mean moods. "I bet he didn't find anything worth taking, even if he tried."

"Well?" Karl persisted, louder now, ignoring Robert completely.

Karl leaned forward and hit him lightly, little more than a tap, on the shoulder.

The man backed up and said, "That's not a way to behave. You try that…"

"Nor a way to talk," Karl said, clenching his fist. He punched him again lightly on the mouth, and the man staggered back again, almost into Robert's arms.

The man spat and felt his mouth. "You'd better not try that anymore," the man said, holding up two fingers of each hand, placing them across each other like the bars of a cell. "It's this for you now. For assault too, shortly, as well as for a stolen jeep."

Robert followed Karl's angry glance to the side of the jeep and there saw that the dust had been carefully rubbed from the lower part. Embossed, shown up by the rubbing, he could see letters that have been covered over under paint and which he had never noticed before. CAMID.

The lorry behind their jeep was hooting for them to move, but Robert only stared. Karl worked for CAMID, hadn't he? He hadn't stolen the jeep. But if so…why had he covered the name?

"I know all I need to. I haven't taken names of witnesses who saw you hit me, but I may yet, so don't try it again."

The man's nose and lips were reddening, and he grew angrier as Karl motioned to Robert to get back into the jeep.

"Don't you run away from me!"

As the two of them slipped into the bench, Annetta woke and looked around. "What's all that—oh! We're at the crossing to St. Martin already? Excellent time!"

Karl pulled the jeep up at the end of the road, drove down onto the deck, and parked. Another car came on and that was the last. They began casting off ropes and Robert, trying not to seem in a hurry, walked to the floating dock himself, carrying his satchel and his sampling net over his shoulder. They had just begun winching the ramp as he stepped onto it.

The raft surged forward and began to turn towards the cluster of palms and the orange wedge of sand that marked the far landing place. Back at the landing they had left, the speck of a pale blue shirt moved back and was lost in the sparkling reflections of the waiting windshields. Karl watched him warily.

Robert said, "Do you think he'll get us in trouble?"

"Nah. And possibly Dr Paul already knows we're coming. But I didn't think the doctor would be so stupid as to believe he'd seen the last of me." He frowned and wiped dust from the windshield. "We didn't get on the same raft with the girl. Sad."

So he had seen her. One of Robert's first thoughts, when he had looked at the packed deck of cars down at the dock, had been how easy it would be to wander around among them and be near those girls—if they were there. And they didn't seem shy.

He said, "There were two, actually. I think they're too young for you."

"Yeah?" Karl gave him an amused, sideways glance. "Who're they just right for, then?"

He shrugged. "Didn't you think the fair one was pretty stunning too? You did, I can tell. And Karl, now I've just remembered something. You must know her. She knows your name."

"My name! Are you joking?" Karl looked at him in astonishment.

"*Do* you know her?"

Karl simply smiled a mysterious smile. Robert was just beginning to understand that it was always that way with him, as if there were millions of things just under the surface of his skin, things that would never make sense, no matter how hard he ventured to understand them.

7

St. Martin

At this side, as on the other bank, there were only one or two houses by the dock, along with a small shop for provisions. While Karl went inside to restock their supplies, Robert filled the tanks, then got out of the heat of the blistering sun. A thin spire of red dust sprang up in the gully and whirled up behind one of the houses. As the pink haze blotted the view of the river, the eddy spread and skipped out into the street. A fierce hot wind sent up sand and straws into Robert's face. He shut his eyes and held his breath. Then, as it lightened, he looked out under half-closed lashes to see if the dust had gone.

Annetta sat in the shade, fanning her face tiredly. Sweat beaded at her temples. "Are you all right?" he asked.

"I was just thinking of the last time I saw Michael. He was so weak and wasted he couldn't do a thing. But I think he might have been going to tell me something the night I didn't come back. Just before I went, he said, 'When you come back, I want to talk to you about you and the baby. Then he said—"

Robert's mouth opened. "A baby?"

She nodded. "He said, 'Come back quickly.' But of course, the baby wasn't a baby anymore. He'd grown. The poor dear was in such a state, he was hallucinating..." This was followed by an explosion of crying.

"Annetta, Annetta, please don't cry... It was not your fault. I'm sorry I ever told you about the water. I'm stupid. I didn't know it would upset you so much."

She patted his hand in a motherly way. And that made sense, for now, he realized, she *was* a mother. "You're sweet."

He thought of asking what became of the child, but at that moment, Karl appeared, his arms full of a crate of supplies. "You're to drive, Robert."

"What?" said Robert, startled. "Did you forget, I'm only—"

"Out here, the rules of London don't apply. Besides, my arm is getting stiff."

Robert now noticed that Karl was still sitting hunched up and was holding his arm. "Karl, what did you do? Let me see it."

He gingerly removed his hand for the inspection. Annetta, too, flitted round to the driving-side door to have a better look. After Annetta had wiped the mess from his arm with a leaf they saw a small puncture. "I rammed it up against the handle of the door," he explained.

Annetta said that the wound needed to be dressed with a special leaf which was very good for stopping bleeding and cleaning cuts; she called it by some pleasant and soft name—tessarra. All local people knew of it. The plant was quite likely to be growing where they were, but she had "a bad head for leaves and things." They would need to find someone to show it to them—such a person might also be able to show them a twig that Karl could chew to take away the pain.

"Did Dewey know about this leaf?" he asked.

"Him? He knew everything! He wrote about it in his notebook and pressed some leaves that he sent back to the museum. He believed it was marvellous, too."

"Might be something in it, then. But the cut's nothing; ache for a day or two and then mend. Dust helps. Gritty scabs stop the wasps biting them."

But Annetta insisted they look for a local person. They drove on with Karl holding Annetta's handkerchief to the wound. For many miles, there was no sign of humanity. Then came a low ridge, which turned out to be a treeless, sandy bluff on the far side of a river. As it drew slowly nearer, they made out a small farmhouse standing alone at the top of the bluff. Over it was a white flowering tree.

"You look as if you're in pain," said Robert, who was driving.

Karl didn't reply.

Robert was irritable. Perhaps in the confusion of that day he hadn't eaten enough, and it was now getting late and he was hungry, but that was not the only reason. Karl had treated Annetta horribly, almost as an afterthought, and he felt sorry for her, especially since she kept trying to curry favour with him, only to be rebuffed, again and again.

By sunset, Karl's wound had stopped bleeding, and they'd abandoned hopes of finding a local person altogether. Ahead, other dark ridges lay, one behind another like crests of advancing waves. The last ridges should have formed the horizon but they didn't, because above them was a purple mist, and above that something else. It seemed like a low bank of clouds but wasn't clouds; it was a high table land edged by a faintly-seen rim of cliffs. Just now they were touched by the last ray of reddish sunlight. The great rocks stood out clearly. They glowed and sharpened. Robert's hair prickled on his neck and he looked around. Instead of the houses of his vision in London, here there were crumbling, lateritic stones like ruins; instead of lawns, there was high, wiry grass, and instead of laburnums, maraati palms and all the fantastic, fruited and wax-flowered shrubs of the savannah. Now the sunlight was fading and the cliffs gone; only the dark, cloud-like mass of the table remained.

"Those are the General Moors, "said Karl. "But we don't go up onto them yet. Tomorrow we turn west onto the HPD. Barring punctures or something, tomorrow, we'll reach Pike."

Later, as the sun was nearly gone, they set up camp. Two hammocks hung from the low trees. A small fire burned up brightly. It lit other trunks around them and the trampled thin grass and the jeep standing by. Cups and plates and billies of the supper that Karl and Robert were preparing were arrayed on its bonnet. Annetta had gone off to the stream to freshen up.

Robert was still angry, and now that Annetta was not here, he said, "You're beastly to her."

Karl looked surprised. "I am not."

"You haven't said as much as two words to her," he protested. "And now I'm starting to think you're not out here as a humanitarian effort to deliver those drugs at all. I think you want the diamonds, and that's all."

Karl chuckled. But he did not deny it, as Robert had hoped.

"You could've told me that."

Karl was silent.

"That's what you're using her for, right? Hoping she'll lead you to the diamonds? She told us she knows nothing about them."

Again, he did not answer.

"Why is it so important for you to hunt for these diamonds?"

"Greed," said Karl, simply.

"Of course. That's certainly what it looks like. Any better reason as well?"

"Do I need one?"

Robert frowned. "Then it'll serve you right if she gets to hate you the way you hate Dr Paul. But, A, I'm not sure that you do hate him, and B, I don't suppose you'd mind, since you care about her so little."

"What makes you think I don't care about her?" said Karl quickly.

"Do you?"

He hitched a shoulder and winced. "I don't care for very much at all, these days."

Annetta came into the circle of firelight. She put her hat and something else down by a grass tussock and came up to them. In the firelight, she seemed transformed. Her satiny shirt shimmered yellow and pink, like the flames. From the faded traveller, twenty years had fallen away.

"My! What a boring party! What long faces! I couldn't help hearing some of what you said, love," she said to Karl. "No one need be sorry for anything. I'm not china and I won't break. Not till I choose to. I've been saying that since you were babies, loves, and haven't broken yet."

Her words were cheery, defiant, but far off was still that flaw, which Robert felt as if it was an ache in his own chest. The boys said nothing in response.

"Boys, if food's ready," she said, "I'll be glad to join you. I'm hungry."

No one spoke much as they ate. Karl was particularly silent. Annetta several times tried to reopen the conversation about places they both knew on the road. How long ago it seemed since they had first started on that subject! Yet Karl answered only briefly or ignored her. Annetta smiled at him, winningly at first, and then with resigned bitterness. Sometimes she seemed to be watching him with what seemed like fear, and once Robert caught her looking at him in the same way.

80

Underneath, she doesn't trust us, Robert thought. *Or there is something she is not telling us.*

As the night wore on and he grew more and more tired, Robert still hadn't decided which it was.

8

When he woke the next morning, Robert found Annetta asleep in Karl's hammock and Karl lying on the ground nearby. The blanket which Robert had spread on the bench seat of the jeep for Annetta had not been used.

Karl was very cheerful at breakfast and unusually attentive to Annetta. Contrary to his habit with Robert, he insisted on making coffee for her, recalling her complaint, in their conversation last night, about a certain wretched hotel they both knew of that did not even provide coffee. He dug deep in their food box and produced a jar of instant. Annetta accepted and smiled warmly at Karl; but after breakfast, while they were striking the camp, she seemed to avoid him, and seemed purposely to distance herself from the boys a little.

Later that morning, they came to a farm set against a wooded hill topped with a cliff-sided mesa, an outlier of the coming plateau. Even from the road, the place looked ill-kept and from the deep rain gullies of the track, it was clear no cart could have visited or left it for some months. But Bend West was ahead and Karl was eager for milk and eggs. While they hesitated, a cock crowed, and they turned in.

Soon the ruts were so bad that they left the jeep.

"I wonder what shock this one has in store for us," Robert said, as they climbed the red gullies.

Karl gave him a queer look and a grimace to say, "shut up" and did not reply. No one answered to the sounds of their arrival. The first thing Robert noticed, as they passed through the tall grass to the clearing, was a big white O painted on the door in front of them. At the back were half-ruined outhouses and a broken wooden aqueduct that poured its water into a thicket of big weeds in the middle of the yard. Everything seemed broken and deserted. But something human was there or had been, not long ago. A hen came out from a ruined coop, and a machete propped in the doorway bore a mere faint dusting of rust.

"Someone has lived on this farm since last wet season," Karl said. "I believe they are still here." He clapped his hands loudly. Still, no one answered or came. In the shack, they found a hen's nest with six eggs, built in a pile of old clothes.

The back door of the big house also had a white O on it but was hanging open. They went in. The rooms were dim and bare. Each had a white number on the wall: 2, 3, 1, 4. There was white dust everywhere, and the room smelled acrid and vaguely chemical. In one room, a nest of wasps on the ceiling had poured its whole population dead onto the floor. Then Robert found a room that had no number and only one piece of furniture, a bed, upon which a very thin person was sprawled, perhaps asleep, or perhaps ill.

He tiptoed from the room, but gathering his courage, came back to look. The figure lay very still. Creeping nearer, he realized it was a skeleton and its covering, the rags of clothes.

He called out to the others, his voice too soft to have any effect. It was as if he still feared to awaken a sleeper. No one answered.

The dead man's bed was upon a wooden pallet raised off the floor in the corner. Robert thought he saw something small move on the boards nearby. He bent closer, straining his eyes in the dim light. Tiny pebbles or seeds dotted the rags and the loose bones. It seemed it couldn't be one of these that had moved; then, out of the corner of his eye, one did. When he looked at it, it stopped. He looked more carefully at the pebbles and at white marks that marbled every one. They were tiny skulls. They lay scattered among the tufts of hair that had fallen from the dead man's head. Now he could see a death's head on every one of these pebbles and the mouths all full, almost bulging, and stained with blood. They were like babies of the big skull but fat where it was thin, and now, satiated, they all looked (like the mother) blindly up into the air:

they were like seeds it had sown. The loose hair moved. Easily, he might think the skulls had grazed there, feeding like sheep on the dry pasture of the fallen air…. Everything else, the blood and flesh that stained their teeth, had gone…

One of the little pebbles rolled, or crawled, from under a flap of skin twisted on the skull's side—or perhaps not skin, but it might be, what was left of an ear's cartilage, hung loose. Robert thought with horror how many of these must have been spawned out of the red flesh since the man had died; how they had grazed clean that yellow skull, and now lay resting. But was it so—had they finished? Soon, in the night, would they be busy again?

They were busy already. Several squirmed in the hair too… They had only been scared by his shadow or his footstep and had frozen for a beat.

"Karl!" he called, and then again. He was seized with a terror of the tiny horde that was now all moving and bustling among the hairs. "Karl!"

On Karl's palm, a minute later, two of the little skull-pebbles lay as they had done when Robert had first seen them on the boards. Then, one suddenly sprouted legs and walked off quickly towards Karl's wrist. Clearly, now Karl was here, they were only beetles.

Karl seemed pleased and slipped those he had into a glass tube which he corked. "Atrox necrophori," he said. "It's very big for a dermestid, and pretty rare. By the place, this one might be new—not necrophori." He gathered more for his glass tube. Then he took the real skeleton's head and turned it sharply aside. When he released it, the head curled slowly but not right back, and the pits of its eyes gazed at Robert. It was submitting. *Everything's very dry there; its springy sinews joining the bones that are making it do that*, Robert thought; but his thought was drowned by other thoughts. He'd seen dead creatures before, but the bodies of his parents, as they were pulled from the sea, were quite the opposite—bloated and waterlogged and heavy.

Nausea bubbled in the back of his throat as Karl darted his hand among the rustling throng of wildlife that had been revealed under the head.

"Huh! Scorpion!" He flicked at something. "These little hedgehogs are the grubs of the atrox you saw," he said, showing them to Robert. "Those, like silverfish, are silphids: their adults are totally different. If you see one flattish, like a terrapin…"

Robert shook his head to rid himself of the thought. "How can you?"

"What? Hurt this dead guy by collecting the bugs that ate him? Or do you mean just, fossick around here with my bare hands?"

"Both."

"You get used to it. Everything's grist, if you collect. Actually, I think I am doing the fellow a service—to me, it's like saying a prayer, saving him a year in purgatory—I mean, if I get a bit of him to end as a new species in a museum drawer in Cimoul … If you don't like to watch, Rob, go and find Annetta. Collect the chicken eggs… He's not going to mind if we take his eggs, any more than he minds me taking these… I think he's pleased. See, doesn't he look pleased?"

Karl turned the head right over towards Robert again. It grinned at him with a very dead grin. The front of the face hadn't yet lost quite all of its skin.

The nausea came back.

Annetta and Robert waited outside the back door. The shade of the mango trees was deep around them, but between them were patches of sunlight, and they stood in one of the patches. Robert felt a need for the sunlight. Behind them, the falling water seemed to gargle and chuckle and keep changing its tune—a lonely, insane sound.

"Do you understand what has happened here?" Robert asked Annetta. "Karl keeps fooling and won't tell me."

"A bit, dear. They write the white numbers when they spray the rooms for bugs—to show which ones they've done. It's CAMID that does these old farms."

"Did they spray the house owner in his bed and kill him too?" asked Robert with a hollow laugh.

"Of course not."

"What did you say?" Karl said to Robert. He had been washing his hands in the splatter of water under the aqueduct and had just come up.

"I just asked if, when they spray for insects, they spray the house holder in his bed and kill him as well." Robert looked straight at Karl.

"Good, then I'll tell you," said Karl. "No, they don't spray him; they give him pills which are supposed to cure the diseases caused by the insects they're spraying—the mosquitoes and kissing bugs and ticks. Or rather, they sell the pills, though they're meant to be supplied free. I told you about them, didn't I? The pills don't work, but coming from the respected man, are a bit believed in. He's so desperate to do something that he hardly notices that they don't work… Hope makes him believe in them. Or else he thinks he can't be using them properly. Anyway, he buys them; he even sells the last of the old furniture of his farm to buy them. And why not? Who is there left to use it? The children, his wife—they've all died, one by one. He has a relapsing fever himself, can't mind his farm, can't raise food. But who needs food either? With this disease, you don't want food. No one was hungry, even before… They need water but it's fine about that. He hasn't been able to mend the aqueduct his grandfather built so water doesn't come to the kitchen sink any more, but anyone can still collect it with that tea kettle from the break out in the yard. They can drink. But of course, they do really need food—and water and nursing … So, not having them, they die. Then there is only him. By habit, he goes on. The hens lay eggs; a few maize plants have seeded and he can cook cobs. Then one day, he doesn't get the expected remission in his fever. Now it's like subtertian malaria. He's too weak even for the water, the next day it's coma. Next day—that's it, he's there where you saw him. Come, let's go."

Karl spat this speech into the air of the yard, against the clatter of falling water. He said it like a man who'd seen such a thing, many times before. Though he spoke in a morose, serious way, when he finished, it seemed to cheer him a little. But his face was still taut with anger as they walked back across the field.

"A hundred years ago," Karl was saying, "when people relied on picheery bark as the cure for malaria and the like—the old remedy of the indigenous— instead of on pills, the whole plateau was covered with well-built farms like that one. Those aqueducts ran water wheels which ground corn and rice, and crushed cane and spun saws. Now almost all the big farms are in ruins. You'll see others if we ever go onto the plateau…he feeds on a dying people. He needs them to be sick and dying, so that he can rebuild the superstition, keep them weak. They have faith only in him. He wants to have Death stalking here, over whom only he has power, with his science and his miracles. He wants to be seen as a saviour…"

"Who is he, love?" asked Annetta.

Karl merely looked at her.

"Oh, this is that doctor's work?" Robert said, and followed his eyes to Annetta, who clutched at her heart. "Annetta, why are you staring so? Does the name Karl said mean something to you?"

"Someone I know has that as a second name, I think. Mine's called 'Dr Paul' by most people."

Robert looked at Karl, who didn't appear to be paying attention. "Yes. It's the same. Annetta, what is it about Dr Paul that frightens you?"

She shuddered. "Everyone that's been here knows him, of course. But I never could like him for all his goody goodness. And... I'm scared of him."

"Why, especially?"

"I don't like his stare."

"Why? Does he stare at you?"

"He sometimes seems to, but I don't know if it's only at me."

"But that's not all, is it, Annetta? It's more than his stare."

"Yes... Yes, it is."

Annetta said she would tell them in the jeep. She looked around at the blazing sun-soaked savannah and shivered. She didn't know why, she said, but it would be better in the jeep. As they climbed inside, Robert looked over at Karl. Despite their shared dislike for the doctor, Karl was too busy playing with the controls in the dash. It was almost as if he wished they'd talk of anything else.

Robert leaned in to her and whispered, "What is it? What is it that makes you afraid of him?"

At last, she spoke, her words barely a whisper. "He killed my son."

9

Bar Palace

When Karl went to make the first delivery of pills, he dropped Robert and Annetta off at an outpost five miles outside the Pike town limits—a combined filling station and shabby hotel called the Bar Palace. He explained that there was bound to be at least a watchman at the CAMID station, and by leaving Robert here, he would avoid the possibility of having to explain him as well as the jeep should he be questioned. He was also reluctant to take Annetta there, in case of danger. All three of them were now acutely aware of the risk of every unnecessary minute that the jeep spent on the road.

"Three hours at most. That's all I'll be," Karl said surely.

Annetta smiled at him and slowly shook her head. "It mayn't be, love, it mayn't be."

"Why?"

She put the fingers of both hands to her face and pulled the skin lightly in a way that at once made her look much older. She smiled. "Plans have a way of never working out as you hope them. Especially around here."

Karl waved that notion off before climbing into the jeep again. "Rob, don't let her go before I get back. Steal her hat and hide it, if need be."

Robert stared at him. "I didn't know you—"

"Cared? I can be a mean shit, but I'm not heartless. Watch after her." He waved and drove off before Robert could say more.

The post, the one building in a sea of forest, was a wrecked, sunken ship on a seabed, a derelict half-made and half-dead thing, a locker of Davy Jones with green waves far above it. The back was of cast concrete, but the slabs were cracked already, and the casting had ended when the ground floor was half-made, in some places in the middle of a wall. They'd run out of money. The whole front of the building was not concrete at all, but the usual pole-and-mud walls, the floors mud, and the thatch of palm leaves. Close behind the cracking concrete at the back came the writhing cascades of roots. Out of these, and out of slanting slabs of wood and bark as grey as the slabs of the hotel but far more graceful, rose the trunks of the trees—graceful as if to shame the crude angles of civilisation, lofty columns that split and split again, and held up nets and necklaces of vines and branches, and held up above that the rough green of a sun-shattered cloud, a frozen and bursting silent tornado of forest leaves. Just to the left of the building, between the grey columns, two defined wheel tracks entered a tiny jeep path, which disappeared downhill into the darkness of the forest.

The main entry was a doorless passage with a row of small rooms on each side. They appeared to be bedrooms. In more than one, Robert noticed a bed with a grey-stained mattress; one had a hammock slung across it and another was completely bare except for a hammock hook in a far wall post beside the window. The windows had shutters, most of which were closed, but even then, the rooms were not dark. There were long bright cracks between the sticks of the walls, where the mud had fallen away, and shafts of sunlight, striking through holes in the thatch, made brilliant sparks on the mud floors. At the end of the passage was a dim room with several tables and chairs. A step and a wide opening, curtained with a screen of dangling beaded cords to obstruct the flies, led up into a larger room, most of which was out of sight. Just ahead, through the curtain, more tables and chairs could be seen. It was brighter in there and the floor had ceramic tiles of grey and cobalt blue—evidently here began the more pretentious and unfinished concrete part of the hotel.

Robert and Annetta were about to go through the bead curtain when a man appeared behind the bar through an opening from the room beyond.

He began to ask what he could do for them, but had hardly opened his mouth when he suddenly leaned forward and cocked his head at Annetta, as if to see better under the brim of her hat, and exclaimed, "Annetta Fairby!

Annetta Fairby! Oh, happy day! Welcome to my humble palace! You have come! You have honoured me again! You've come to sing, I hope?"

"Indeed, if you'll have me, Taxim."

He held out both his hands and a sugary, toothy expression of delight appeared on his face. "Of course, of course!"

He went on about the rumours of the area. There had been a false start to the rains in the east—the floods had gone up but now were coming down again. The big fishing boats out on the Vascoma were coming back, and the newly returned crews would probably hire a van and come here from Pike for the evening. Palm-hearts and pineapples would start today for the cannery, and the cutters would stop off; then there were men clearing for a big new farm on the slopes near Celestia who would probably come, and a CAMID van also came Wednesdays too.

Annetta's enthusiasm for all this information seemed forced. Often, she didn't appear to be listening, as though her mind was elsewhere, and twice she asked the same question over again. At last, she indicated she would like to rest, saying that she had a touch of travel sickness.

"Of course, of course; and who should not be resting at this hour… Such heat! But no rain for two days and that keeps the mosquitoes asleep." The last was encouraging, if true, because none of the rooms had any netting, or doors or shutters that closed properly.

Robert was in a daze because of the heat, and, without thinking what he was doing, trailed after Annetta and their host into the passage. Taxim paused by one room and began by a gesture to offer it to Annetta but then pulled back his upturned palm and peered at Robert. "Perhaps a double for you and your…son?"

"Oh no, this is better," said Annetta quickly. "It's just for me."

Robert flushed and stammered something about his hammock. As he turned away, he noticed Annetta's bag in the bright square of light framed by the entry. It was like some lonely sea island, away out in the yard where it had been put down from the back of the jeep. He hurried out to fetch it. Sweating, he came back to the original room, which seemed slightly better than the others. It had, besides the bed, a little table with a ewer and bowl and a mirror with a cast-metal frame in an ugly design of silver leaves and scrolls. The links of a rusty chain showed between the metal leaves tethering the mirror to one of the logs in the wall.

Annetta took her case from Robert and asked him to call her when Karl came back. Meanwhile, she had "such a head—a migraine."

When Annetta had gone, Taxim's ready smiles flowed less freely. Back in the dark clay-floored room, he burst a can behind the bar, found a glass, peered into it, wiped it with a grey cloth, and then brought the beer Robert had ordered to a table and poured.

"I think I'll take it through into the other room," said Robert. "It's brighter."

"Oh no; if you please, drink here. The floor in the other is being washed."

"I don't see it being washed yet," said Robert.

"It will be washed. The maid will be putting up the chairs."

Robert heard voices and guessed there was company there that Taxim did not want to have disturbed. He sat down at the table. Taxim went behind the bar and tidied bottles and glasses; then, seemingly satisfied that his customer had struck roots where he wanted him, went out through the door at the back.

At least one of the voices from the next room was the sad, plaintive accent of a woman; but mostly it was the deeper voice of a man who spoke on and on. It sounded rather like his father would when he wanted to teach him a valuable life lesson. Robert could make out only a word here and there. It seemed vaguely medical.

Robert's beer was soon gone and Taxim had not returned. Robert located a filter behind the bar and refilled his glass with water. After perhaps half an hour had passed, during which he heard the clink of glasses but nothing that resembled chairs being put up, he rose, took his glass, and went through the bead curtain.

There were five people in the big room. The speaker with the deep voice was a large man, sitting at a table by himself. A teacup and a glass were in front of him, and he had a shallow bowl in his lap. His fingers were fiddling with something in the bowl. Two women, not young, were at the next table, on the edges of their chairs, leaning forward, listening to the man.

Behind them, several tables away and near the window, there was a dark shape which appeared to Robert to be an exceptionally large greyhound, and yet, odd for something that was so like a greyhound, it was seated and leaning back in a chair. Really, of course, it was human; or humanoid; somehow, from the very first glance, Robert did not like this person as a man any more than he liked greyhounds as dogs. Lastly, in a dark corner, an old man was drooping in a chair, apparently asleep.

Robert sat down a few tables away from the big man and the ladies, facing them.

"The milk-laurel tea was sheer foolishness," the man said. "Do you understand me? Why did you not listen before? It is bad, useless. For some conditions, it could even be dangerous. Because cow's milk is sometimes beneficial, why should you believe every plant milk must have medicinal effects? This is a foolish superstition. Rubber is made from a plant milk, but who, for his health, would consume rubber? Is that for any illness? Would you want to block your children's veins with elastic? Do not interrupt. I know that laurel milk does not form rubber—yet, in the wrong blood, laurel milk may yield principles still more dangerous... Far better to have seen me when she first fell ill."

"She...I could not...you see, Doctor, no one knew where you were."

"She is right, Doctor," put in the other woman eagerly. "It was the same with me. You are often away. We do not know where to find you."

"I have many who need my help."

Now that his eyes were accustomed to the dim light, Robert could see that the man's face was flushed and that he smiled without stopping. His words came slurred and deep.

"The use of milk-laurel was foolish superstition. Now, first I have to provide the remedy to undo the damage done by your tea and your neglect. For now, you may give him these. Next week, when you come again, according to your report, I may add the isser-fish liver to complete the remedy. I, and only I, know the value of each fish liver. I am the only person who is able to tell you what is required in this case, and even now, without my special preparation, the decoction would be useless. Each liver is good for some illness, but it must always be remembered that before it can neutralize, it must first collect the poisons in the body. Therefore, it must never be misapplied. Even the liver of a weak-fleshed fish, which, as everyone knows, the isser-fish is not, can be dangerous; the pure vitamin B12 that can be extracted from such a liver may be deadly if applied to the wrong complaint, or if given in too large quantities. Do you understand what I am saying?" He lifted a hand from the bowl and took a sip from his glass.

"Yes, Doctor. I try. I am sorry I made the mistake. My little girl was very sick and crying. It is hard to do nothing then... But we live in such ignorance here..."

The man interrupted her by turning to the other lady.

"When I have finished these pills," he said, still kneading with his fingers in the bowl, "I will attend to you. I regret that it takes time, but everything must be done properly. Now I must roll these out, and this is unclean!" He swept the pad of his finger over the tabletop in front of him and frowned at it. "Purity is essential; a trace, even a molecule, may bind the active site of a hepatic enzyme..."

As he looked around for another table that might be cleaner, he noticed Robert for the first time. He beamed warmly at Robert. He said nothing while he looked him over but reached for his glass and drank from it again. The large, tanned, powerful face was flushed and lightly beaded with sweat.

The man must be just a little drunk, Robert thought, as he'd heard it in his speech. He had blue-grey eyes, and behind his domed forehead, his wispy, straight fair hair was brushed back and out. It might have or might not have been greying, but it was hard to tell in the minimal light.

The man got up, holding his bowl in one hand and collecting his glass and teacup in the other, and came over to Robert's table. Standing, he was a great bull of a man, a saintly bull, with a halo of pale hair flaring behind him and he came swinging over between the tables towards Robert. In his deeply slurred voice, clearly expecting no refusal, he asked if he might join Robert at his table.

"There's plenty of space, sir," said Robert, moving his beer glass a little towards himself. The man had already been pulling out a chair and sat down. The ladies behind watched him and bent together, whispering.

"So, by your voice, you are from up north?" The man said. He again placed his bowl on his knees. He put the cup on the table alongside his glass. Then he went on kneading whatever was in the bowl, rolling brown pellets between his fingers.

"Yes," said Robert.

"From England?" He closely observed Robert, radiating a benevolent, smiling stare.

"Er...yes, I am."

"A fine country. I am often there." He drank from his glass and then tested the cleanliness of the table in front of him with his finger.

"Oh? Whereabouts?"

"It is a fine country. I like it. I like to stay at the Ascot Hotel. I visit the museums in London. Also, the Zoological Society. I am a foreign member. I bring them fish."

"I heard you saying something about fish pills. Is that what you are making?"

"Yes, young man. I know all about fish. The habitat, the food, and the chemical specificities of every kind…each fish has a chemical code…"

"Really? Do you know every kind of fish in the whole of Santania?"

The man lightly dusted the tabletop with flour, which he took in pinches from the cup.

"Oh, yes," he replied. "Even the government agencies in Cimoul seek my advice."

He tipped a number of ochre-yellow pellets onto the table and began to roll them between his palm and the tabletop.

"You travel a lot then, collecting fish?"

"Oh, I travel, of course. I have been up the Vascoma and all its tributaries, and down to the sea. The delta has fish of special interest to me. There the chemical specificity of the river fish has been shown to adapt daily to saline tides. The balance of ions…you know about ions?"

"Yes, a bit. But I don't see how you can have been up all the tributaries. Surely there are millions in any river that are too small for anyone to go up."

"I have been up them all. The White, the Juama, the Wicherrima, the Weiry—all. I have explored even as far as the creeks of England—the Thames—the Severn."

"But these are not tributaries of the Vascoma!"

"Oh yes, they are, young man."

"But those rivers rise in England."

"Of course. And they flow down to the Vascoma."

"No, they don't! You must have gone overland—or over sea—to get to the Thames and the Severn." Robert tried to hide a shaking in his voice, but he was quite certain of this, since geography had been his best subject in school.

"Oh, no. Up the river, up, far up the Vascoma. I have been the whole way." He drank from his glass.

"It's just not possible. The Thames flows into the English Channel—or is it the North Sea?—anyway, it amounts to the same—you must be thinking of another river called the Thames, not the London one."

"Oh, no, young man, I have been the whole way up the Vascoma to London in my yacht. My yacht is fitted for collecting." He beamed knowingly at Robert. He began to put the pills that his broad hands had rolled on the tabletop, back into the bowl one by one.

"Nonsense. It's just not possible," said Robert. *It's more than nonsense, it's utter rubbish. The man is fooling with me;* he thought to himself and made an effort to keep his face indifferent and calm. A dark shadow passed between them and the sunlit window; it was the man who looked like a greyhound on his way to the bar. His narrow, browless face bent coolly towards Robert as he passed by their table. Taxim was at the bar watching; the greyhound man leaned on it and spoke to him in a low voice and they both glanced in the direction where Robert and his companion sat.

"How is it not possible, young man?"

"Like I said. The Vascoma doesn't come from anywhere near England."

"Where does the Vascoma come from then?"

Robert frowned and while he tried to think of something to say, the greyhound man came back, bringing his beer to a table closer to where they were sitting. The large man motioned to him. "Scoreman, come here."

The man did and leaned in, and the two whispered together. Scoreman smiled with amusement, in such a way that Robert could only think the topic of conversation was, *Can you believe what this idiot thinks?*

Robert was baffled and angry. "I don't know the geography of this area well. But it flows west to east mainly, and then south of a range…So I am told."

"So you are told!" The man laughed heartily.

Then, as Robert's eyes swerved away in anger and fear from the red face that seemed to fill the room with its laughter and its claims of insane geography, he glimpsed a different, small and pale face parting the bead curtain. It was Annetta. Her look was blank, but a faint flash of her eyebrows seemed to call to him, to signal some warning.

Perhaps Karl has come, Robert thought. *I must find an excuse to leave this joker.*

He looked at the big man who, at this moment, wasn't looking at him but smiling at the balls that he was rolling with his palm.

Robert looked at Annetta, whose eyes were wide. "It is him, love," she mouthed. "Be careful…"

Now, his thoughts raced.

He glanced back again through the curtain, where she once stood. Her face had gone, so quickly he thought for a second he'd only imagined her. No one was near except Taxim, who was coming from the bar carrying a glass and a jug of light wine.

Robert's skin prickled. *So this quack doctor, this drunkard…is Edwin Paul Chamard.*

10

The Doctor

D espite the heat, Robert's blood ran cold.

This is the evil man Karl speaks of? The man who killed Annetta's son?

Taxim fluttered around the table, effusing hospitality. "Most honoured guests, another drink? Doctor, I have brought the same for you. Yes, I assure you, the same. Oh? I am sorry indeed; the limes were perhaps not ripe. I will put more sugar in at once."

As he went back to the bar, Robert muttered, in a voice so light it could barely be heard, "Er, excuse me. I thought I heard a car. It may be the ride I need."

Actually, he had heard nothing, but the need to escape had gotten so powerful that he couldn't breathe.

He stood up. To his horror, the big man stood up also, swaying a little. "I will come with you. We may continue our discussion of geography, eh? Perhaps there may yet be time for agreement. The Vascoma will not dry up, or change its course, merely as a result of our differences. Not all the imagination of youth can make a river do that."

Robert thought of poor Annetta's fear of the doctor. Was she still in the other bar? Had she had time to escape? As they neared the bead curtain, he pretended to trip in the half-dark and knocked over a chair.

"Watch it, boy," the doctor said with an amused laugh.

Robert picked it up, apologizing and stumbling through the bead curtain, setting all the glass beads and bamboo pieces to clatter.

Thankfully, she was nowhere in sight, in the bar or the passage to the front of the building. Still, it was near impossible to control the shaking of his legs. He did not look to see if the man was still following. And now, to his horror, he heard an engine ticking over just outside. He knew that sound all too well.

It was Karl's jeep.

It was out in the blazing court, broadside to his view. Karl was in the cab leaning across to talk to Annetta who stood, hatless, at the near side.

Robert froze before the exit. The jeep jerked forward, and only Annetta stayed. The jeep purred towards the rise where the HPD continued to the southwest. It climbed the slope of the soft and sandy road, rounded the corner, and disappeared.

Annetta, left islanded far out in the searing sunlight like her suitcase had been earlier, turned and walked toward them, in her tiny pool of shade. By Robert's side in the entrance, watching her, stood the doctor, thick arms crossed in front of him. Just behind him, at his shoulder, was the greyhound man.

Annetta started, paused an instant, and then came almost at a run to Dr Paul, with a delighted smile, holding out her palms to him.

Robert thought, *She's very frightened. I can see it.*

"So you are here, sir! You are here!" she said. "I did not know!"

"I am here. And so are you." One eyebrow was arched significantly higher than the other in suspicion. "Who was your friend in the jeep?"

"Oh, someone who gave me a lift back on the road. He saw me and stopped for a word. Just friendly."

"You are a passenger, perhaps, that he would not forget."

Annetta smiled her gold stars. "I doubt that! But I'm always glad if people remember."

"I seem to have seen his hard top before, on the moors," the man said coldly. "What is your friend's name?"

"He didn't tell me his name. What does a name mean to the hiker carried anyway, Dr Paul? Why, you're too rich, you've probably never been one, so you don't know!" She continued to babble as she laughed and made parting movements with her hands.

The men at the door stood aside to let her in. Dr Paul nodded to the man at his shoulder and they both walked a little way out into the yard. They stood together out in the sun, talking and looking now up the southwest-bound road where Karl had gone.

Just when Robert thought he could slink away, Dr Paul turned and came back.

"So it wasn't your lift after all?" He beamed at Robert again, but this time, Robert felt there was something sinister behind his eyes. The minute out in the sun had brought out big beads of sweat on his forehead, and one dripped across his temple and ran down his cheek.

"No," said Robert, trying his best to keep his voice even.

"Had you seen that hard-top before?"

"—Like that? No. It looked homemade."

"Homemade? That's what you thought? And you had not seen it before— Where has our nightingale gone? Ho, Taxim!"

Annetta was not in the dark bar room when they went in. The big room beyond the bar was empty, too. Even the old man had gone.

"Surely she will soon reappear," said Taxim apologetically. "She is tired, she has to rest. She had promised earlier that she will perform for the enjoyment of my special guests tonight."

"Splendid. I will wait and speak to her later then," said Dr Paul. He smiled. "Have you heard her sing?"

Robert shook his head. So his initial impression was right; she was a singer. This brought him no joy, though. Not now that he knew what Annetta must be feeling. This man had killed her son! Robert watched his smile with pure hatred. Taxim scurried for another glass for him. Soon the big man was sitting by the door, drunk and merry once more. He motioned to a straight-backed chair across from him, in the few inches of shade under the eaves.

Robert slumped into the chair, answered Dr Paul's questions vaguely, and said silly things that made Dr Paul laugh. But still, the doctor looked hard at Robert and sometimes seemed far from drunk.

The doctor kicked the chair back. "Now, if you'll excuse me for a moment, nature calls."

Robert nodded, hardly believing his luck. Here, he'd thought he was a captive, but now, freedom was close at hand.

The doctor loped through the doors. No sooner had the doctor disappeared than Robert was up and away, running on the road, spinning, as if a wasp was after him.

Robert went up the hill and as he was out of sight, turned right into the forest. He parted the tall weeds and grass and climbed over the heaped bull-dozed trunks at the roadside. Once under the trees, it was much cooler, and yet his heart drummed in his chest.

It was far easier than he'd imagined getting away, but he did not understand a forest of this kind and was soon swallowed up. To avoid being heard from the road, he'd had to go deep enough inside that it was now out of sight. He took a direction that would cut across the probable line of the jeep path but, because of the trees and strange roots that spread like upright boards from the bases of the trunks, and because of hanging tangles of creeper, and spiny palm stem, and stilt roots of other palms, it was impossible to walk straight. When, after a long time, he had not found the path, he turned and followed his tracks in the leaf mould back, to renew the attempt at a different angle. Soon, he found that the gym shoe prints he had been following had somehow changed into the deep-dented marks of a hoofed animal. A twisted, high tree above him looked like one he had seen from where he started, so he continued away from it, following the tracks toward another tree. Just at the point where he thought he should be right by its trunk, the tree he had thought to go to had somehow vanished.

Because it was dusk and he was looking up at all the trees, and the mighty cords lying against them, clad with ferns, he didn't notice at first the herd of forest pigs that had come feeding on fallen plum-like fruits that littered the ground under the tree. It was dusk and the pigs stood very still when they heard him coming; thus, he was right among them when suddenly they thundered on the ground with their hooves and bounded off into the undergrowth.

Robert was lost. After the confusion of the pigs, he could not even remember from what direction he had entered the space under the tree. He thought of the coming night. Karl was surely expecting him on the path or at the jeep and would be first impatient and then puzzled and then worried. He might then take risks in approaching the hotel to find him. He didn't want to risk going deeper into the bleak forest, getting even more hopelessly lost, and so, he stood there, motionless.

He wondered if the pigs would come back and whether they were dangerous and what else the darkening forest had that might harm him. Perhaps snakes. Leopards. A shrill and unvaried choir gathered about him and strengthened. It was mosquitoes. He moved his hands restlessly over his arms and neck and chest, driving them off. He didn't slap them because he was afraid of making a noise; he wanted to listen to the sound of the forest and to hear what was happening before he was heard by others.

This waiting and listening were stupid. He needed to move on before it was utterly dark, must try again to find the tracks that he had made when he came in. But how could he? Now there would be tracks of the pigs everywhere. Over the mosquito whine, the forest rustled; night creatures were coming out, or perhaps the pigs were returning, curious because he had fired no shot. Something moved in the branches overhead.

When he, at last, moved away from the shadow of the tree, the small, intensely green leaves of the forest undergrowth moved in around him again. The leaves and the dark between them were like a speckled net held close to his face, obstructing his vision. He had to push the leaves and the saplings aside as he walked. Then, off one of these saplings, a huge ant sprang onto his hand. As he flicked at its clinging and stinging body, it stung the pads of his fingers, clinging to them like burning tar.

Robert yelped. When at last he had flung it to the ground and crushed it underfoot, he fell to the ground, writhing and nearly fainting with the pain of the stings, screwing fists under his armpits and bending his head to his knees. When he stood up, the pain had made him forget yet again the direction he had been going in. He began to move almost at random as the forest became darker and darker. Spines jabbed his hands and broke off in his skin; showers of gritty rubbish and other small ants from some nest overhead fell on him. The ants fell into his hair and into the open neck of his shirt where they stung like nettles. After that, he tried to feel and shake everything in front of him with a short stick before he moved, groping forward like a blind man, but still brought down pale wasps from some unseen nest in a shower, stinging fiercely and smelling of honey.

Pale as they were, he could barely see them. The swift tropic night was down.

At last, he stumbled onto a path. He fled on it, soaked in sweat, dizzy with the pain of stings and bites and thorns, certain still that some unutterably strange thing was coming or had already happened. This was a ghost path; his crazed pain told him it was neither path nor forest either, but the tangled engine room of a ship or factory, with the great beams and shafts and wheels silent and yet steaming warm, waiting for the captain's bell and the new bursting of their violent life.

Light. One single light. He thought it might be the light of the real world, even of the hotel; but when he turned aside to look at it again it went silently curling its way up into the trees above, writing out its laughter at him into the dark air, mocking him. A firefly, only.

Right under the firefly, though, he found the jeep. But the jeep had grown old and had rusted. Its lifeless and twisted tyres were sunk in the leaf mould, its windscreen broken, creepers broke out, and in through the rust holes in the metal box of the back. Their cool leaves brushed his hands as, in horror and wonder, he ran a hand over the familiar shape. Yes, it was indeed Karl's jeep; here was the flat bonnet, the shelf mudguards, all as he knew them…and yet somehow, different.

He stepped silently close to the jeep: the window was wide open, its glass smashed and gone. He took a slow breath, listening, and then leaned suddenly in through the window and clawed into the darkness.

His arm gathered only some brittle and dead vine stems and webs and a shower of rust.

At the moment he drew back, he was seized from behind.

A weight fell on his back and an arm like a vice closed round his throat and threw him backward onto the ground.

The two lay struggling there, with the man leeched onto Robert's back still holding his throat and stopping him crying out, bending to all his movements.

But then the grip relaxed and, bending close above Robert's head, said, "So it is you, Robert. I'm sorry. You came here out of the forest—how'd you get there beyond me, for Christ's sake? And you acted strange. I had to be sure."

Heaving a sigh of relief, he rolled over and looked up at Karl, rubbing the bits of forest from his shirt. "We have to get out of here. But first, we have to save Annetta. She's with Dr Paul!"

"Bah," was all Karl said.

They got into the jeep, Karl heading back towards Bend West. "What happened to the jeep?"

Karl ignored him.

Robert had a mind to reach over and jam on the brakes. "We can't just leave her. After what he did to her son!"

"Bah," Karl said again.

"Karl! You are the most heartless person I ever—"

"She's in on it, with him." His voice was low.

Robert caught his breath. "What?"

"You heard me. She's a liar. After Dewey passed, she took up with him." He snapped. "Like that. That's the type of woman she is. And her son isn't dead. If he were, I'd think she'd call that a blessing. She cares for nothing but herself. Trust that."

"What? How do you—"

"I do. Drop it, all right?"

Robert stared. For a long time, he did not speak. She'd seemed so earnest. So truthful. Could it really have been a lie? But at that moment, he felt gullible, but he did not want to argue and feel more so.

They took the pioneer trail that had been made in scouting the route, to keep from the main road was difficult. It was rutted, stony, and overgrown. Driving was at best slow, and where the mist was heavy, because of the danger of deep ruts, they went at a crawl. Climbing over a high mound of a yellow-flowering creeper, plunging through a wall of small saplings, he jostled in his seat, thinking to himself.

He realized, at that moment, that he did not know who on this journey to trust. Not even the man sitting next to him.

PART 3

Plateau

THE
GENERAL MOORS

1

The Traitor

They camped on a short side road ten miles after the Bar Palace. All night, Robert thought of Annetta.

She'd reminded him of his own mother. And yet Annetta was a traitor. A snake. He wondered if he would ever see her again. He wondered if he would always be that bad a judge of character. If so, perhaps Dr Paul was deserving of being called a hero, and Karl was the one leading him astray? He simply didn't know.

In the morning, they refilled at the next village, including the spare cans, which Karl said could make it a long way towards Souls. Once they had joined the straight road coming up the slope, they entered a loose wilderness of sand that the thin wiry grass could hardly bind, and the wheels slipped and sunk constantly beneath them. They were already quite high. The HPD had become a tiny line of houses and mangoes and palms, and behind them, a huge view opened over all the blue ridges to the north. There again was that craggy outlier where the beetles had swarmed under the dead man in his ruined farm; there beyond the unending carpet of the wildland, the buff savannah grass and the blue woods, ridge behind ridge, confusing at last in a brown and purple haze at the horizon. Around and ahead, in contrast, was threadbare open grassland such as they had not seen, and tiny bushes in it hardly more than grass, and hills like the pit heap of old mines, and among these, the straight road going on and on. Higher still, their road started to twist and at last vanished among bare conical hillocks where sand and grass and sky met in a blaze of pale colours that hurt the eye—grey and buff, ruddy tints of iron in the slabs, and over it all the blue-white dazzling clouds and flare of the sun.

The wheels sank axle-deep in the sand and churned slowly. Karl was in the lowest gear and straining the engine to keep moving at all. They went at the clogged pace of a nightmare and almost every half-mile had to stop to let the engine cool and to replenish the boiling radiator from their can of water. At every stop, looking back, the carpet of the lowland behind them was more purpled, distant, and framed more narrowly between the brown hillocks they had passed which now, by illusion, seemed rising along with them. They passed no signs of human life at all.

At long last, the slope became easier and ground harder. The grassy hillocks around were of a gentler, more sinuous outline. Robert thought of them like bodies of naked women, lying asleep. The jeep came over the top following a dry valley. A hut came into view. As they drew nearer, a man was standing outside, shielding his eyes with his hands, looking towards them.

"What a place to live!" said Robert.

Karl said nothing. He seemed to turn inward to his own thoughts and looked very gloomy. At last, he said, almost as if to himself, "Where a man can live, he does."

"What?"

Karl did not answer. A while later he said, again as if to himself, "Heart of a heart of a…" and his voice faded.

"What? Heart of a what?" When Karl said nothing again, Robert sighed. It was often that Karl would go off muttering nonsensically to himself. Where Robert used to ignore it, now, his temper was short. He snapped, "I still do not think it was right to leave Annetta. How do you know she was in league with the doctor?"

At that, Karl looked over at him, a strange look on his face, as if he was not accustomed to being doubted. He revved and drove on at top speed, his face tight and hard.

"Why was she travelling with us if she was helping him?" Robert asked at last.

Their long track through the grassland had been slowly descending, and now the tussocks were less threadbare over the sand. In places, there were flat marshy meadows dotted with palms. With the meadow, a change came over Karl. Tears of the earth—stream water—trickling among leopard lilies and sleeping fireflies and stems of the white-topped sedges, salved him. His face had relaxed.

He replied, "Dewey did something in his sketchbook when he gave it to her on that last day, before he died. It wasn't a sketch, but he did add something to one. It was only a tiny thing, but he did it carefully, and it cost effort because he was very sick. So it was probably important."

"What was it?"

"It's hard to explain just here, but I will soon. I need to show you on a piece of paper—it will be better when we've stopped and I can get at the actual sketch, the one I bought at Swanson's. That's what she wanted. What she tried to get from me."

"She did? Rubbish! She said she *sold* them to Swanson's."

"She sold them before she realized what they contained. And she was there, at the urging of Dr Paul, to retrieve them. Only we got there first."

"And what does it contain?" Karl didn't answer, right away, so Robert pressed on. "I never saw her behaving in any way queer, or suspicious like that!"

"And because you never saw it, it never happened, eh?" His laugh was bitter. "I saw her snooping through my things. She never found it because I've hidden it as deep as I can…somewhere. I might tell you later. I'll also tell you how I think we might try to organise the search."

"Search?"

"For the diamonds, of course." Before Robert could answer, he added, "I'm afraid it's not very encouraging. We might have to start work in Cimoul or London, not here."

"Perhaps I could do the London end while you do Cimoul, when we finish our deliveries?" said Robert. "Then we could meet in the middle."

Karl glanced at him several times, and then said cheerfully, "Good. We'll see. The first clue I want, Rob, is three palm trees, strong ones, close together. That's the key to all that follows."

"How?" He leaned forward, interested.

"To hang two hammocks. Rob, I just want to quit fighting this wheel, and sleep. Steering is bloody terrible."

THE GIRLS AT THE SPRING

2

The Sisters

E arly next morning, they made a sharp descent into the country that Karl called the Vales. Still part of the General Moors, it was a land of meadows and woods and deep-cut ravines, farmed for cattle. It was dry at this season, and because of the dryness, Karl said, the farms here would all be drawing their water from deep wells. Farther down, in broader valleys with rivers that did not dry up, they would find rice fields.

At first, as they came down, they saw nothing, because it was all hidden beneath a lake of mist. Soft as the lake of a Chinese landscape, whose expanse one might expect to see marked by a distant fishing boat under a square sail, the mist stretched away to the blue reefs and promontories, and even knowing it to be mist, it was hard to realise the dryness of which Karl spoke. So too with the brilliant roadsides lit by the new sun. The grasses and leaves were all bright with the dew of the night. When they had plunged into the mist itself, the crystal sky was hidden and only a pale opalescent ball showed the sun was there.

The jeep had no wipers and from time to time, Karl had to stop, and Robert jumped out to clear the droplets on the glass. Once, climbing back into his seat, Robert thought of the mornings he'd gone with his parents to North Downs in Kent; sometimes the mist lay there over the fields, like an apparition. The thought made him melancholy.

They crossed a creaking wooden bridge and there, for the first time, was water and a small fall below in the ravine. Shortly, they passed two barefoot girls walking on the road. One carried a big bundle on her head, doubtlessly clothes that they had been washing in the stream. The other girl had a shotgun slanting on her shoulder. The boys glimpsed them only as the jeep came round a bend, out of the mist. They were at the roadside, stepping onto the green verge to be out of the way, and did not look up.

"They clearly love us," Robert joked after they had passed.

Karl did not laugh, as he seemed to be miles away. "It's a shame. There was a time, not long ago, when they would never have thought of a gun here. The diamonders coming up from the big road have changed things. You often see women carrying guns now."

"The one with the gun certainly needs protection," Robert said, still thinking of the girls.

"Was she the prettiest? I didn't see."

"By her figure at least."

A few miles beyond, they came to a banana orchard that leaned out its huge wet leaves over the road. The leaves were shining and silvery with dew and sparkling in the sunlight that was just breaking. Shreds of mist were steaming off over the grove into the blue sky. At the top of a path that led downhill, a small girl was standing with her mouth open, watching the jeep as it came by. Karl stopped and then backed up to her.

"Is there a farm down there?" he said.

"Yes," the girl said.

"Could we buy some bananas? It's your dad's farm, isn't it?"

"I'll go and ask," the girl said. She rushed off around the grove. The boys climbed down.

When the girl came up the patch again, she was carrying a bunch of bananas in one hand and a basket in the other. She was trying hard to walk fast and at the same time to hold out the basket from her side so it did not bump her knees. She was panting. She put the things down quickly on the grass in front of Karl and the boys saw that the basket contained eggs.

"Jiminy, you were quick! And eggs! Just the things for us." Karl smiled at her. "How much did your father say we were to pay?"

"Mother. It's my mother's farm," the girl said, still breathless. "She said you could have them, but not the basket."

"Hey, now—bananas may cost nothing, if this grove is hers. But she can't do that with eggs. Are you sure you remember what she said?"

"She said to tell you to have these, they'll only waste." The girl spoke in a great rush.

"I see I need to talk to your mummy," Karl said, smiling. "And I want to see your farm, too. Can you show us the way?"

They followed the girl around the grove and down an avenue of trees. The trees blotted the world in yellow flowers, in a tunnel of sulphur. The sky above, even the ground they walked on, was yellow. Only the trunks were black and the thick twigs arching up to be lost in the yellow drape above. Black bees, too, were visiting the trumpets. The trees had no leaves. The big fallen blooms, like yellow foxgloves, carpeted the path and also the yard of the house that they were coming to. The house was poor and small, of mud and wood, with a tiled roof of cheerful curly tiles, and the outside walls had once, at least, been plastered and then painted with a pale bluish or purple wash. Beyond the house, down the hill, there was another flowering dome of a much larger tree which tossed up armfuls of pink stars amid its leaves of brilliant green—and everywhere else, outside the house too, was this same lushness of flowering and greenery, almost as if a dry season, in its place, had never come. Over the door, a creeper held sprays of pale pink, crossing their own green hearts, and both the leaves and flowers stood out vividly on the brown mud of the wall and over the purple flakes of the wash still clinging there. All of the trees and the garden flowers, and the vines, seemed to be telling Robert that hope and kindness and gaiety and love of nature would be found in that home.

The little girl, running ahead, went into the dark doorway.

A tall woman came out and watched them as they came down. She looked narrowly at Karl as he drew near. "Why, it's Karl! Karl!"

Karl for his part stopped sharply on the last edge of the spray of the fallen flowers. "Mrs Oliveira!"

They beamed at one another until Karl spoke. "I came to pay money to a lady farmer—and to tell her that the day is past when she should give eggs for nothing to strangers—but now I know that I needn't waste my words. She knows what I am going to say already, and she will never change."

"Nor will you change, Karl, I hope. So we can talk about other things. Where are you staying? Come in and tell me all your news and be welcome again."

Karl pulled something from his bulging pocket. "Yes, I'll come," he said, "but, first, wait—I want you to have this, in case I get talking and forget. When I thought that the lady farmer mightn't take money for the eggs, I hoped that she might accept this instead." He held out a packet towards her. "These are pills for disease—real, McNeeve certified."

The lady smiled and took them. She held the packet stiffly from her and her smile began to fade oddly, not exactly in anger, but something like it. She looked at the ground and seemed to be struggling with words.

Karl had been watching her also, his face filling with regret. "I had forgotten," he said suddenly. "I didn't think. I'm sorry. I knew, of course, but had forgotten."

"It was sudden. But hard for all of us. You can imagine."

Karl nodded. "I heard and I wrote from Pike … But it means that you should have these all the more. For you and the others."

Mrs Oliveira turned away, still looking at the ground. "Oh, Karl, if you only had brought these four years ago…and just at this season, when the rains broke. Then it might so have changed things. He would have lived. Ah, but you were just a boy yourself, then. Let us not think."

Suddenly she looked around at them again, with an effort, smiled, and for the time she fixed her keen grey eyes on Robert. They were very bright, perhaps from tears, but still stern and piercing. "And who is your friend, Karl? You should introduce me."

Karl told her Robert's name and that he was a friend who had come here from London to help him with his work. She bowed to Robert and they went inside. It was dark. They sat at a big wooden table on hard stools topped with cowhide, and Karl and Mrs Oliveira fell to talking and Robert to dreaming, half-listening to them and again half-watching the spark of an ember in the raised fireplace where a black kettle stood on bars.

Karl had known her husband well. As a carrier, he had taken his trade all over the plateau. Because his work caused him to travel and he liked to travel, he had become something of an explorer in the wilder parts of the plateau. At times he had carried parcels for Karl's father and later, at his suggestion, Karl had lodged for quite a long time at the family's house in Souls whilst he had been collecting in the region. But since Karl and Mrs Oliveira had last met, the husband had become sick with a disease, had taken Dr Paul's remedies, and had died.

Then, Mrs Oliveira had been nearly destitute, but with the money she had obtained from selling his share of the lorry—she told that due to duplicity of the family of the other owner this had been far less than it should have been—she bought the land and ruined cottage here at the roadside and planted bananas and rice, and also some shrubs that had become profitable for a time because they yielded a drug. For a while, traders for a company in Cimoul had come to buy seeds, but recently she had been told they were using "chemicals" instead and she had not seen the buyers for a long time. Still, after living in a palm hut—now lost in the banana grove—for two years at this place, she had managed to rebuild the farmhouse where they now sat and had added the tiled roof. She had also bought two more fields on better land in the valley below.

"And the baby I remembered those years ago in Souls is now the little girl I met on the road—"

"That is our Annie," said Mrs Oliveira.

"—I should have known her when I saw her on the road because she's much like her father! Perhaps that is what made me stop. And what of Edie and Valery?"

"They are well. They are on an errand now. Last week, they went on a long trip with her uncle and now they must work hard to make up for it. They are washing."

"Where did they go on the trip?"

"To the St. Martin ferry on the White River. They went to take our iron-wood to the new sawmill to float on the White River, and to bring pine timber back—it is from England," she added, looking at Robert.

They heard footsteps outside on the stone flags by the door.

"Edie was at St. Martin?" Karl began but did not finish.

There was a bang of metal on wood in the entry room and the sound of a girl laughing. Then they heard whispers and suddenly a girl's head appeared in the door. Dark as it was, Robert immediately recognized the funny thin face and aquiline nose of the girl who addressed him from the lorry while they were waiting for the ferry at St. Martin.

"Mother—" she said while her eyes quickly roved around the room, resting a moment on Karl and then on Robert.

"Yes?"

"It's Karl, and his friend, Edie. You remember Karl, who used to stay at our house when he was passing through?"

"Yes, just. And I saw him at St. Martin. Mother, can I whisper something?"

She came in, thin and angular, and bent over the lady's chair from behind. What she whispered seemed far from short and the mother, at last, stopped her and said, "Well, I'm sure it was he who'd done something wrong and not Karl, whatever the fuss was."

"I know, Mother. That's what I said." She looked Robert over. "Where is your friend from, Karl?"

"Robert is from the north. England. He comes as my guest."

Her mouth made the shape of an O, and so did her mother's.

"Where's Valery?"

"The gun hit the doorway when she came in and she says it's hurt her neck." She giggled. "She was hurrying—and now she's tidying."

Then the other girl, Valery, was there. Again, as on the road at St. Martin, she struck Robert as a girl of breathtaking beauty, flawless in every curve of hair and cheek and limb. Her beauty hurt his eyes and would hardly let him look at her. He could only glance at her and then turn away. She in return glanced at him rather often, which made everything even more difficult. When she spoke to her mother, her dark eyes seemed to smile, and Robert was immediately lost in them.

ROBERT
TALKING TO
MRS OLIVEIRA
IN THE WINDOW

3

The Plan

"There was a real row at the ferry after they went. Uncle said it was almost a fight. We stayed in the line, but lots of others didn't."

"Let's not talk about it anymore, Valery."

"But it was quite exciting! Edie said the man Mr McNeeve hit was a coward because he didn't hit back. I said he wasn't because Karl's friend was nearby, and the man knew he hadn't a chance."

At this, Robert stood prouder and taller. So she *had* noticed him.

"Let's not talk about it," said Mrs Oliveira, louder. She clapped her hands. "Edie! Fetch okra from the yard and then sort rice for our lunch—there must be enough for Karl and Robert too."

Edie went out.

"He hits people if they just touch his car. And he's not very nice to ladies on the road either," Valery said in a teasing tone, side-eyeing Karl. She seemed determined to go on with her stories, whatever Mrs Oliveira said. Her voice was rather deep, and Robert thought it beautiful, like her person. Most of what she said was gossipy bordering upon rude, but the way she said it, it seemed like sweet music. "They didn't offer us a lift on the road when they saw us with all that heavy washing."

"Why do you carry a gun, if you want people to stop?" Karl growled, but even then, he seemed to be teasing.

"But if you see that it's us?" Valery flashed back. "You didn't even say hello to us on the road, back then."

"Of course, I didn't see it was you. Either time. I might have recognized Edie, but I didn't. She is so tall now. And I was preoccupied."

"Perhaps if your friend had been driving, he'd have stopped," said Valery, looking at Robert. "Well, I'll go and help Edie."

Without a great deal of protest—but certainly, none from Robert—the boys stayed to lunch. Robert was in a dream. The half-hour before lunch he wandered down the hill and stood under the pink-domed tree. Huge, unbelievable flowers thrust yellow tongues of pollen at him out of the pink stars of petals; but he saw them and didn't. Whispering the name Valery over and over in his head, he thought of the coincidence that was just too extraordinary. It was indeed as Karl had said, as if it had been in some way fated to happen.

Below him in the bottom of the valley, a line of cows was moving slowly along a dried stream bed. Edie was there at a well, rapidly pulling up the rope of a bucket, leaning out over the low wall, and her long brown arms going like pistons in the sun. For a moment, he watched her, wishing it was Valery. He'd have liked to see her, carrying on with the day's business, but she was nowhere to be found.

She was there at lunch, though, and sat beside him at the table, though she never looked his way. It was Mrs Oliveira who did all the talking, mostly asking Robert about life in England. Everyone was attentive and the girls often interjected a gasp or an "is that so?" when he talked about his ordinary life and schooling and mates back at home, making him feel like it was much more exciting than he'd originally thought it was. When he finished speaking of how he wasn't much good in his subjects at school and how Sam and Linda had wanted him to go for the summer, Edie sighed wistfully. "That sounds nice."

He looked at her. "Why, don't you have school here?"

They all shook their heads. "I learned to read from magazines," Valery said proudly. "And I taught Edie some. What happened to your parents?"

Mrs Oliveira shushed her, which it seemed, she was used to doing. "Valery, that isn't nice."

Robert smiled at her. She could've asked him anything at all, and he would've answered in a heartbeat. "It's all right. They're dead. They died when I was seven."

Edie poked at the okra on her plate. "I was eight when our father died."

After that, there was silence. When lunch was over, Edie got up and went to her mother. She stood up very straight at a little distance from her and said, "Mother, can Valery and I go to Souls with Karl and Robert today?"

"What's this?" said the woman, startled.

"You said I could come to Souls sometime soon."

"But now—why, you have only just come back—"

"We could stay at Uncle Peter's house and then come back with him. Valery says he'll be coming back here on Friday."

"Oh, child! You're only just back—what am to do with the farm? Who is going to do the watering? Who is to weed the field?"

"I did some yesterday."

"What has Karl said about this? Karl, this is not your doing, is it? Nor your friend? Who started this? They cannot go because—"

"*I* thought of it, Mother. I and Valery. We both thought. And Karl says we can go if you'll let us."

"All I said was that we could make space to take you," said Karl quickly. "But there is one big snag. We must go on today. And as we can't hope to get there tonight now, we'll have to camp on the way."

"Exactly," said Mrs Oliveira. "It cannot be."

"I thought we could stop for the night at Escobal, like I did once. We could sleep with the families. And Karl and Robert could camp."

"Child, don't argue so. Go and wash the plates. Then you must raise water for the cattle—"

"*Please?*" Edie begged.

"Not another word…you'd better both go and weed more of the manioc. It is terrible. And feed your birds—must I always feed them? Go. I need to talk to Karl."

Edie went to the door. Outside, she turned and mouthed something at Valery and beckoned. Valery stood up, smoothing down her dress. It was a much newer one than the limp, beaten-looking thing that Edie wore. She went out after Edie.

"Towards the end of your stay with us before," said Mrs Oliveira to Karl, once the girls had gone, "you said that your work was leading towards something that might become dangerous. Is that still so? What is this journey you are on? Is the reason for danger the same that you told me about before?"

"Yes."

"If they went, would the girls have to do things for you—like take the medicines to the doors of houses, or anything like that?"

Karl shook his head. "That is my business. Mine and Robert's."

"Good. They should not do that. They're young girls, and innocent of the way the world works. Above all, they should not be made enemies of your enemy."

"There is less danger in these Vales than anywhere," said Karl. "All the doctor can do here is supply those pills that don't work and send his company to cut down picheery trees, so that people cannot cure their diseases for themselves and must ask for his help. I told you about all that before. The chance of the girls getting sick, of course, is the same here as elsewhere in the Vales; and should it happen, we carry the medicine. So, they would be safe—"

"I was not thinking of that. Would you sleep, then, at Escobal?"

"If you wished, we could camp there. I don't know this homestead, but the girls could show us…."

"It is a farm. Edie could show you. They are good people, if very dark. They have much knowledge of their own kind. But they are not good farmers; consequently, they are poor like us, who are just beginning. Karl," she said, looking straight at him. "You know I would not allow this with anyone else but you. I would allow it with no one. Do you understand? No one. Even now, I am not sure…" She glanced at Robert with a look of disdain.

"I would answer completely for my friend," said Karl.

"Of course, of course, else he would not be your friend. But how does he answer for himself?"

Robert felt the very cold blaze of her eyes on him again and looked up to meet it but could find nothing to say.

"Of course," she said, at last, "if the girls have their work done in time, they may go." She got up and went to the window and looked out, her back to them both.

Karl said, "We will be ready to leave quite soon. But I need to dig into the big carton again. I'll go and do that now; Rob, you might like to go and help the girls. They're weeding, I think."

Robert went to the back door of the house and looked in the direction that Mrs Oliveira was looking from the window. Along the hillside he could see two heads bobbing busily among what seemed tall green weeds. He took a deep breath and stepped out into the sunlight, across the yard.

The woman's voice from the window called him back.

"Young man!—Robert! One moment!"

Framed in the window and facing the open sky, now he could see the long face better—freckled and lined, with the hair pulled back and gathered in a ball behind. It was less angular than that of her daughter Edie, and without that dark element that must have entered from her father.

"Robert, do you have a sister?"

"No, Mrs Oliveira."

"You have brothers?"

"No."

"You are the only one?"

"Yes."

"A pity. Then your mother is unlucky, as unlucky as I am who have no son at all, but two daughters whom I love more than anything. Since you have no sister, I cannot say what I was going to…"

She smiled at him for the first time.

"What were you going to say, ma'am?" asked Robert.

"That if they go with you, I would wish you to think of Edie and Valery as if they were your sisters and to protect them like sisters."

"I can try. But I'm not sure how people do think of sisters." As he said this, he at once felt stupid and blushed and added, "I wish I did have one; then I'd know."

At that, Mrs Oliveira smiled at Robert more warmly.

THE VOLCANOS

4

Toward Souls

Edie sat in the back seat of the jeep in a crevice that Karl had opened among high-piled suitcases, rolled sleeping bags, and hammocks. Her narrow shape and dark hair blended with jumbled gear, and even her limp grey cotton dress looked rather like a third hammock tossed onto the pile. She and the luggage behind seemed to accept each other in excellent spirit and she was very much at ease. Most of the time she leaned forward a little and watched the unfurling road with a keen, half-smiling interest. She watched Karl especially; Robert thought he caught her looking at himself less often, and more coldly.

Edie could look at them more easily than they could look at her, and this was not just because she was behind and they in front. For Robert at least, it had to be a very determined look that could pass the long and ever-breaking wave of hair that belonged to Valery, who was sitting between the two boys on the bench seat.

So, he saw Valery again and again momentarily, as if passing her in a crowd. But nothing could stop the two of them from touching all the time, or insulate against the electricity that was flowing fiercely into him. She was softer than Annetta and so flawlessly beautiful that he felt if he did have a chance to look right at her, he might never look away.

The valley was spreading out. Such softer meadows had hardly appeared when the broadening alley swung off to the left and the road began a long slanting course up a palm-girt hillside. They began to pass rocks, and then entered a little craggy ravine that led them up higher still until at last they came out on a dark green moor, which sloped gently up to rounded summits on the left and right. Tiny gullies zig-zagged up to the slopes like wrinkles on an ancient face. It was open, treeless land, dark green, and lush-looking from mists or rain. The curves of the skyline were much longer than those of the dry hills they had come through before, and the feel of the land was also different. It was no longer even dry grassland, but a moor.

"This is the high country I told you about," Karl said to Robert. "Or at least, it's the first wee bit of it. We'll not see much more of it until we are past Souls."

Where the road reached the saddle itself, it passed through a gap between banks. From there the gravel and moor grass jumped off into a purple hazy sky where floated huge fleeced white clouds of a strange shape. Clouds—a wind combed circus? No. Robert gasped. They were the distant awful peaks and snowfields of the two volcanoes, now much nearer. They linked hands through the haze in a long icy arc.

"Pandora, slightly," said Karl.

"They don't seem very high." Almost instantly, he thought that this was stupid to have said.

"High! You bet they are high. Think what snow means inside the tropics."

"Anyway, they don't look hard to climb."

"Oh yes, for you, maybe. Do you see the way they steepen near to the summit? You probably don't guess what those slopes are like. None of that's snow; it's ice."

"Has anyone climbed them?"

"I've never heard that anyone has even crossed between, leave alone climbed...Edie, has anyone ever crossed between the volcanoes?"

"No. Why should anyone? It is snow. There are not even mosses, no birds, nothing."

"Well, someone could have seen what is there, and just to say he's been, if nothing else," said Robert. "Personally, I'd love to try to climb them. Especially to the crater of that tallest one, Pandora."

"Oh, people have been there," exclaimed Valery. "Some scientists came. They went from Souls in a helicopter."

"Well, that's not the same as climbing them," Robert said, though he felt disappointed that the craters had been visited.

"Climbing would be stupid if there is another way. I think that a person who climbed them just in order to say that he had, would be a foolish boaster."

Robert felt warm and challenged to convince the girls that the climb would be worthwhile for its own sake. He wished he could seem strong and heroic to them, indeed, the sort of person who would climb difficult mountains not caring whether he was called a foolish boaster at the end or not, or indeed even whether anyone knew what he had done. But first, he needed to tell them why it was good to such a thing for its own sake and the right words didn't seem easy to find.

"Well, it's not boasting, at least, if you just do it for yourself. You can be proud because you've done something most would be afraid of."

After a moment's pause, Valery said, "Well, then I might like him a bit, for that." She smiled at Robert.

Robert felt pleased he found a right chord at last. His face tingled under the radiance of her smile.

They reached Escobal in the mid-afternoon, when it was still very hot. Karl seemed disappointed to find that the farm was merely in the next valley. He had hoped to go farther before they had to stop. But when he had pulled up the jeep in the shade of an enormous mango tree, he merely muttered about how they must make an early start for Souls the next day.

Valery smiled. "Oh. But these are our kin. We will be well-cared-for and fed. You'll see. You'll be grateful to have stopped, grouch."

A space of fierce sunlight separated the tree they had stopped under from the grove around the farm. They were all mango trees and all equally huge. Between the trunks, on the far side, there was a low house with a roof of curly brown tiles. In the middle of the grove, in the dense shade cast by the cloud of leaves, a bright spot of flame licked the air. It was the open front of a fire heating an oven in a clay mound. People were moving near the flame; pigs too, rooting among the dry leaves.

Outside the grove, in the sunlight, there were other trees with spikes of flowers like orange flames ascending out of their green crowns. Robert had never seen trees like these before, and he thought there was something miraculous and devilish about them, as well as beautiful. Beyond the flame trees were palms, and beyond the palms, meadows that sloped gently away, and then, far beyond those, the other side of the valley, which ran up to a line of crags and an edging of dark browns and green against the sky.

Robert drew his sleeve across his forehead so that the sweat that soaked his eyebrows would not run into his eyes. Out in the gap, blinding, burning sunlight poured down over everything, and, although it was hardly cooler, they were grateful for the shade of the mango trees as they went in. They walked towards the eye of the flame, which was the glowing open hearth of the stove.

On top of the stove was a huge iron dish with roots lying in a bubbling black lake. On the ground nearby, two women were pounding more roots with sticks, until they broke up into a white mash. In the open door of the oven in the clay mound, Robert could see a pile of the same white stuff. The ground around them was all beaten hard soil scattered with empty corn husks and twigs and with things that looked like very dirty false beards thrown out from a children's party. These, in fact, were the old stones of mango fruits; and the white stuff they were making in the dishes was flour of manioc. There were children there, all very dark, like the women. If they had been playing before, they stopped now, to stare at the newcomers. Now and then, a pig would come, grunting and snuffling among the litter, looking for bits of the manioc roots, and a child would dash at it and chase it away. A man, also very black, came up with a bundle of sticks on his shoulders which he threw down in front of the stove.

Everyone seemed to know everyone else, and Robert hung back from the greetings and watched as Valery and Edie embraced their kin.

Not far from where the man had thrown the sticks, there was a dried stretched cowhide on the ground. Karl and one of the women went over to the cowhide on the ground, or rather two hides, one on top of the other. Robert came closer still and at last could see what it was; a boy's head. Yes, a boy was lying on one hide and covered up to the chin by the other. He was perhaps a dozen years. He was asleep and was breathing heavily. Beads of sweat studded his black, frowning forehead under his curly hair. His hair was wet too, and there was a wet patch on the hide around his head.

Karl knelt beside the boy's head. He lifted the top hide, slid it back, and felt the boy's naked shoulder. Robert saw that it was running with sweat like the rest. The boy's breath came almost as if he was snoring. "What is this top hide here for?" Karl asked sharply.

"To keep flies off and not be too warm," said the woman. "It is cooler here than in the house."

"It should not be—how long has he been like this?"

"Yesterday, at lunch time, he took a little milk and some water. Since then, he has been asleep."

Karl jumped up and said, "Bring some water now. I won't wait for him to wake up—we must try to wake him and make him drink. I will start the new medicine at once."

He set off towards the jeep. Once out of the shade of the trees, Robert heard the pounding of the ground as he broke into a run.

Robert watched curiously and whispered, "Is it contagious?"

People looked at him, warnings in their eyes. Edie put a finger to her lips but answered, softly, "No."

A grey pig came snuffling near to the hides. A child dashed at it, shouting and waving a stick, and the pig dodged and rushed across a corner past the boy's head; it squealed, and its hooves drummed on the hard leather. The frown on the dark face clenched deeper for a moment and the drops ran together into a swarm of trickles; he stopped breathing and moved slightly as if he would turn. Then the loud breathing started again. It was the only sound in the grove. Now everyone was standing near the cowhides looking at the boy. No one spoke.

Suddenly, a rush of wind cooled their ankles, and there came a new sound: first, a fluttering in the air and a clattering of branches overheard and then, as the branches swayed, a splashing bright sunlight down over the cowhides and the clay mound, and the hot dust spirited up from the ground, whirling between the trees. A dust devil. As it whipped up into their faces, the lady who had spoken to Karl and who had just brought the water—the mother of the boy, likely—knelt beside him, with her dress spread over the boy' face. Soon the sudden wind spent its force in the tower of leaves above them.

Outside the grove, the flames on the flame trees reappeared and then the crown of the other solitary mango, and then, out of the red mist far below, the dark shape of Karl. He was still running, coming back. When he saw that they could see him, he slowed.

"Now, we must set him up—help hold him, Rob."

They held him up and tried to make him drink. He drank some and spluttered some, and coughed, and seemed to swallow the three yellow pills that Karl gave him, but all the time he was far, far away somewhere and showed no sign that he would wake.

Karl stayed with the boy to watch over him, and Robert set up the hammocks to camp in the trees not far away. It was well after dark when he returned, soundless. He sat down on the edge of the hammock, very still for a long time, his breathing laboured. Robert rolled over and caught the reflection of his eyes, glassy in the moonlight. "How is the boy?"

"Dead," Karl replied, sucking in one long breath. He let it out and looked up in silence at the blanket of stars overhead. He did not say more.

THE BATHING PLACE

5

Picheery Dam

Even before they'd left, the sun had risen over the eastern crags of the valley and thrown flakes of shining bronze onto the sad leaves. It blazed gold into Valery's hair where she stood watching the final packing of the jeep. Fast and gaily the sun went up into the blue sky. It shouted a promise and command: *I am here and you are young, all will be different this day from any ever before...*

Thus, the shadow of death did not remain for long. The little boy—Edie and Valery's cousin—was not the first to die, and by now, it was as if the girls had almost become used to it and had resolved not to dwell upon such things. While they were together—for Robert at least, the morning was a drive through paradise. Karl, however, was in a gloomy mood. "If only I'd gotten there sooner."

Valery put a hand on his shoulder. "You couldn't have known."

"That bloody doctor," he whispered, but even then, his spirits seemed to be returning.

All morning, on a narrow-angled road, they followed the vale down. There was no further ascent to the level of the moors and the volcanoes remained hidden except once when a turn in the road showed them both at the far end, spanning a dazzling vista of the valley. Now they were no longer hanging in thin air as they had done yesterday, but poised on a dark and uneven lawn

137

made from the succession of far tree-velvet ridges of the plateau stretching up to the mountains' feet.

It was a land of streams, now no longer dry. Springs burst from the roadside banks. Twice they drank from fonts splashing out of hollow bamboo stems that had been thrust into the pebbly soil. Robert let the girls drink first so that he could watch them, and each time he thought how perfect Valery was, from wetted hair to the fingers she used to break the falling crystal stream. Then she would turn and smile, and the drops would shine on all the leaves behind her, and, later when he drank it himself, the water seemed the best that he had ever tasted. Edie drank differently, using her hand as a shallow cup which she carried lightly to her mouth many times, sipping her fingertips.

Lines of palms followed the streams across the meadows. The palms met other trees and together they thickened into the bands of forest that accompanied the larger streams and the main river at the bottom of the valley. On the far side were similar tree lines and, above them, palms dotting the grassy slopes that inclined up to the crags and the dark green fringe of the moors. The meadows beside the road were full of lilies. The streaky heads of these nodded in the tall grass and brushed with some old familiars, the white and yellow oxeyes, the moon pennies of England. But such lilies! In his father's conservatory, or on the tiny rockeries of the small front gardens of West Wickham, these great, streaky blooms would have pride of place, whereas here they were nothing, for the trampling of cattle. They needed no gardens here. He gazed at the passing farms and the flame trees over them, and at the ponds cut for the cattle in the hillsides, at the rice fields in the valley bottoms that were of such brilliant green they seemed to be lit not only by the sun, but by a light rising from deep in the earth below.

Sometimes they saw people in these fields. Usually they were women, and in the flat rice, dwarfed by the palms, with their bright coloured or black clothes against the luminous green and their thin arms moving in gestures of work that he did not understand. They seemed to Robert more like landed Martians than real people, floating, not standing in the emerald mist of leaves—mythical creatures apart from the world, far, far away from what the prosaic part of him told him that they must be—simply poor farming people weeding a rice field.

The late sun made all the colours deeper, and the red soil of the roads glowed, like the rice had done, as if from within. They drove down a valley where there were two red streaks instead of one cut in the slope facing them. Together, with the straight and very steep road that they were descending, these streaks made the arms of a luminous red Y; but the right arm was thinner, and even from here they could see it was deeply rutted with channels and crossed with vines. The reds glowed against the black-green of the forest where the humpy, sparkling green crowns stood over their black shadows and looped webs of creeper. Small palms, more delicate than those at the restaurant, grew around the bridge at the bottom of the valley. Just beyond the bridge, a flat space had been bulldozed beside the road. The space looked new but must have been cleared long ago, enough for the full-size palms to have grown up on the edges of the pile. To the left of this place, the creek made a pool, with a palisade of sticks forming an enclosure in the shallow water.

Karl paused when he reached the space. There were several people on the main branch of the road. A woman was just setting off up the road with a shining petrol tin balanced on her head. She stopped and slowly turned to look at them when she heard the jeep behind her. She turned back again and went on. From behind the palisade came shouts and splashes. Presently, three men appeared, coming out with wet hair.

"I remember this place," said Karl. "But I have forgotten its name. Isn't this the settlement which was just starting when I was last here, where there are no wells, and all the water has to be got from the river? There was a dam being built with diamond money."

"It's called Picheery Dam," said Valery. "First it was called the Diamond Dam, but it was a silly name because it brought bad people. So, they changed it. The people who came thought they could find diamonds here, but there aren't any at all. But my father said that Picheery Dam was silly too, because after they had called it that, men came and cut down all the picheery trees. Now you have to go a long way to fetch fresh picheery milk."

"It was a wicked and a crazy thing," said Karl, "although people who know the forest well say that you can still get picheery easily. But wasn't the settlement started for people building the dam?"

"Yes, miners came here to work when their mines had run out. But lots of moors people live here as well—my aunt lives here—so they are not all wild!"

139

She laughed. "But no one works on the dam now, because of the disease. The supervisors have left."

"All thanks to the good doctor," said Karl to Robert, scowling.

"Yes. But lots of the men have stayed, all the same, as you will see when we reach the top."

There did not seem to be an epidemic of disease—or ague, as it was called here—in the village. The settlement on the plateau above the far slope was very new. Fresh-looking, mud-walled houses straggled on either side of the road, which here ran straight and level for about a mile from the edge. Some huts had walls made only of palm leaves.

They all four drove down to the bridge again. It was sunset. The sun was gone from the valley but still, behind them, it was lighting orange banks of the cuttings up by the village. Karl chose a place across the road from the palisaded bathing place for the camp. Some palms on the bank overlooked a rippling stretch of the river. The palm trunks served for the hammocks and the jeep could be close by. It was more public than was ideal, but it was not bad and there was no time to search elsewhere. The girls looked on as they laid out a few things, staking their territory for the camp; intrigued by the idea that he and Karl were going to sleep in hammocks at that very spot.

Robert said he would like to take a walk up the other eroded track that went to the dam to try to see it before it was dark. Valery said she would like to see it too. But she seemed unsure.

"Edie, will you go?" she asked.

Edie looked up the track and then glanced at Robert and didn't reply. Karl said he would not come; he had to string the two hammocks and then sort out the pills for anyone who might need them.

"You should go, Edie," he said, "but be quick, whoever is going. Night's almost here." He swung open the back door of the jeep and pulled down the hammocks.

They went. The red soil of the track was deeply crosscut by rain. At one place rainwater flowing off the hillside had made a miniature canyon deeper than a standing man. Robert stood to help the girls, but they went into the pit and out of it more easily than he did, running lightly on earth slopes and pillars of soil that his own weight brought tumbling down. Beyond this, there were barriers of creepers across the road. The track was cut in some general clearing:

trees had been felled recently, shortly after the road was made probably, and Robert could see where old logs and stumps were buried under the creepers. Some of the stumps had been the boles of truly enormous trees—bigger, he thought, than any trunk sections he had ever seen. He said this to the others.

Edie looked at the ground and kicked the clay where she was standing. "It's the red clay," she said as though she was answering Robert's remark.

"What does that mean?"

"Wait, then I'll show you. She darted to the side of the road, took a leaf from a sapling rising from a root of one of the great felled trees, crushed it, smelled it, and passed it to Robert.

"Well? I still don't see," Robert said.

"Why, it's carrotwood," Edie said, surprised and smiling.

"Well?"

"That is why the trees are so big. Where carrotwood grows the earth is always the best. And it is the red clay also. So," she added thoughtfully, "what I do not understand is why no one has planted."

"Not everyone wants to be a farmer, Edie," Valery said drily. Then, more animated, she said, "Look! A sky rose is coming!"

The sun had gone, and it was quite dark. Now suddenly a pale pink arch spread back up the sky. Flowers they had not noticed before seemed to spring into bloom on the creepers and bushes all around them. The place, the light, the flowers glistening on the waves of creeper like foam, the glowing faces of the girls, all made up magic that struck deep into Robert's heart. He felt great strength and his heartbeat raced. He pointed out a huge tree at the very edge of the clearing. He said he wanted to go up to it to see if the trunk was really as big around as the stumps by the road were.

Soon they had scrambled up through the tangled vines and felled trunks to the towering column that Robert had pointed out. It turned out that the tree grew on a small, level space on the hillside with a steep ravine at one side. Robert had intended to show off by climbing the vertical lines that he had seen from the road. He thought first he would go right to the crown of the tree, but then as he came nearer, he thought that he would go up only to the lower branches, that would be enough. When they reached it, all the lines were cut at the bottom and were swinging free. Now he guessed that they might be rotten up above and that it could be very dangerous to climb—and, although he hardly liked to admit it, the height of the tree as he stood under it, and even the mere eighty feet or so to where the line hung clear from the west branch, also appalled him. Beyond that branch would be only the half-rotten strands of the line, and the thought of using those to go higher, or even just holding them to steady himself at that height, made him feel dizzy. His eye traced the smooth black curves of the branches out to the leaves. They were black bomb bursts, hand grenades of exploded darkness, scattered across a pale sky. This was no English tree; it was a monster.

He pulled on the wooden rope and shook it. A shower of dead twigs and leaves came rattling down from far above.

He looked down. Valery was standing near him. She smiled at him and the smile seemed to flow over him the way a wave falls and flows on the beach. He threw his weight onto the line. It dropped a little but then held firmly. Another dark stem came swinging towards him, disturbed by its ties to the first. He threw his weight on that in turn and this too was firm, and it was good and rough to his hands. More leaves and twigs pattered down from high above. He pulled back the second line, letting the first go. He walked back across the level until he held the stem high over his head and then ran forward and launched himself, hanging by his hands on it, over the ravine.

All at once, he seemed very high above the logs and the tangled greenery of the clearing. He could see the rose grey trunks on the far side of the ravine rushing towards him. His forward rush through the air seemed to go on for a long time. He let out a call of glee that echoed through the forests as the black crown of the great tree turned slowly above him. Coming back, two pink figures appeared, gliding out of the back of the forest towards him, as if on skis. Really it was only he who was moving. At the very end, over the level again, close to the girls, he dropped off.

After he released it, Valery ran to the lip of the level and waited for the hanging stem to come back. "I must go too! Catch it for me, Robert! I won't reach it! I must go!" she called, jumping impatiently.

Robert caught it but held it out beyond her reach.

"It's dangerous. It might break the top."

"It didn't for you."

"I know, but I may have weakened it."

"I am lighter."

"I don't think it will break. It is only before last rains they were cutting here," Edie said calmly.

Robert put the stem into Valery's hand. She walked back as far as she could. Then she said, "I'm not as far back as you were. You must lift me."

Robert hesitated. His heart fell in a momentary dread—it was almost as if she had challenged him that he must climb.

"Aren't you strong enough to lift me then?" she said, peering towards him with a smile.

"Of course," Robert muttered. He went to her and lifted her onto his arm. He thought, *I must think of her some other way while I do this, like she was a sister—if I had one.*

He turned her in both arms so that her back was to him and his head against her side, in the narrow of her small waist. He went back until he felt the line pull, turned, and then with a heave put her right up onto his shoulder.

"My! You are strong," she said with a gasp.

"Do you still want to go?"

"Yes," she said faintly.

"Hold really hard." He let her go.

The rose flush in the sky was fading now. At the far end of her swing, Valery was a tiny pink ghost moving against the black of the opposing trees. Then she was coming back, she was a girl again, and she was like all the beauty in the world rushing towards him. He thought even that she might be the beauty he had so long sought and to which he meant to dedicate his life. He raised his arms, wanting to catch her.

"No!" she shouted. "Stand back!"

A moment later she alighted beside him.

"That was great! Great! Edie, you must do it." Her words jarred on Robert a little: they were girlish, unfitted to that acute hope which had passed through him a moment before.

He caught the line again and turned to Edie, but Edie hung back. She looked angry, absorbed, and scraped her sandals on the ground. Robert was about to let the line go when she said suddenly, "Send it by itself."

"Don't you want to go then?"

"I want to see how it swings first."

He swung the line out over the ravine. He turned and saw Edie going swiftly back from him under the tree. He was puzzled and wondered if she was cross with him about something. Then she turned and crouched, and he saw her angry look fix on the vine that he had sent far out and guessed what she was about to do.

"Edie, you mustn't!" he shouted. "It's too dark. Too high. You'll hurt yourself!"

"It'll be your fault if you get in the way…" she said in a low voice, not looking at him and watching the creeper.

Robert stepped back and the rod of the line passed him, going high over Edie's head. Then it passed him again, going back to the ravine on its second swing.

Edie began to run. She leapt and caught it just at the edge and flew off into the darkness. She seemed gone a long time and was a white spot way out at the far side when they heard something crack in the tree overhead. With horror, they thought to see her fall and indeed the spot did drop, but then suddenly it was caught in another arc, as if taken by some other force of the mysterious night, and it went swinging down very far and fast to the right. Doubtless some second thing on the line, one holding it to another branch farther out, had held when the first had broken. They saw Edie come out suddenly against the sky under the canopy of the tree in the grove opposite, at the end of a steep swing. She was not white now but like a dark monkey clinging to the rope of the line. She crashed into a cluster of other hanging hand-cut lines of the trees she had reached. They saw her arm go out for one as she went among them. She had it and let go her own and then she was swinging there back and forth far away in the other grove. She caught yet another stem, one that seemed alive, for it had leaves, clung to that, and began climbing down.

They heard a crackling of twigs far down the ravine and then her voice. "Did you see me?"

"Edie, Edie!" they shouted. "Are you all right?"

"Of course!" They heard more crackling and again her voice up: "It's quite hard to get back, and there might be snakes. I'm going straight down to the track. It's easier."

Robert and Valery started down the way they had come. Valery paused a moment at the place where Edie had started her run and looked back over the ravine. "She is very, very brave," she said.

"She shouldn't do it, in this light. She would have broken something falling among those logs," Robert said. "But, wow!"

"So, they might have dropped for us too. But my sister is like a boy in courage. She is like you or Karl." Now they were picking their way among matted creepers and over the logs and the stumps, trying to see in the half-light the track they had made in climbing up. "For me, I am not brave. Not at all like a boy."

"Why, you went too. And you wanted me to lift you for the start." Suddenly Robert surprised himself, saying, "By God, you looked lovely swinging, Valery! I wish you had let me catch you coming back."

"You are trying to say that I am like a boy too?"

"No, you're not like one."

"Sometimes I think I would like to look more like a boy. I would have my hair short. I have seen that in magazines. Would you like that?" She gave a quiet laugh, and she suddenly stopped and faced Robert. They were between two big fallen logs of the destroyed forest.

"No," said Robert stopping also.

"Why?"

"You are better like you are. Like a girl. You're..."

"Well?"

"You're very beautiful." This came out in that strange deep voice that surprised him before. It surprised him what he had said. Why had she stopped? Was the impossible to happen here (and Edie perhaps already on the road just below them). What was she expecting of him?

Valery scrambled up onto the log on her side. She sat on its downward slope and sat clasping her knees in the arms and looking out over the valley.

"I love the evening like this," she said. "I love just this moment when you can start looking for the first stars."

"In England, when the stars are coming out, it's usually too cold to just sit around," Robert said. He at once thought that this was an incredibly dull thing to have said and not even true. Sam and Linda never liked being outside, but the night was his parents' favourite time. They often all sat in the yard, staring up at the quiet sky.

But Valery seemed not to have heard. She lay back on the log and smoothed down her dress and laid her arms along her sides. "Look, the stars are coming through already. The rose sky is gone."

"There are stars there already. They were there when we were swinging," Robert said.

"I know. But my favourite isn't out yet."

"Which one is that?"

"It will be near that bright one by the tree. It's red."

"Where? By what tree?" He dragged his eyes away from the faint mound in the dress over Valery's chest and tilted them rather hopelessly around the sky.

"Come here and see where I'm pointing. Yes, it is there already. There! No, you must put your head down close by mine and look where my finger is. It flashes red and sometimes green. There!"

"We must go down to Edie," Robert said, standing up from where he stopped beside her.

"Why?" Valery said sharply.

"Oh! Valery, because I can't be so close to you and just look at stars."

Valery gave a sound that was like both a laugh and a gasp and she seemed to relax again. "Why is that?"

"Because you're lovely."

He saw her nod very slightly. She had turned her face towards him, and her eyes were very big and dark but still sparkling with the length of the pale sky that was behind him. He was standing very close to her and looking down at her on the log. He tried to read something in the tense and beautiful and slightly mocking face that was watching him. He could not read it, but the effort to do so seemed to draw him down towards her. He put his hands on her shoulders as if he would steady dizziness that had come over him. But still he bowed closer and closer above. He kissed her cheek clumsily. The touch of her cheek and of a trail of hair that was across it—hair so much coarser and less silky than he had expected—were strange to him and made him draw back almost in disappointment, but then, as he looked at her again, it was as if a steel band at the back pressed his head down towards hers once more. He kissed her lips. Valery was not smiling at all now; she looked tense and frightened.

He wondered if he was doing it the right way. God, for himself, there was no doubt it was right, the touch of her lips was a joy past speaking. There was that softness too of her shoulder that he held in his palms. It was—

"You mustn't," her voice cut the silence.

His eyes went wide. "What?"

"Edie. She's very keen on you, or haven't you noticed? Are you that blind? She asked me to get you alone so I could ask what you thought?"

"About what?"

"Don't be daft!"

Suddenly her shoulders had gone from his hands. She was standing up on the far side of the log.

"But—" He struggled to stand. "I don't feel that way—"

Valery stopped. "You should. She's much better than me in every way. And she must be there now," she said, speaking in her old voice as if nothing had happened. "We must go down. She must be waiting."

When they ran down the last clayey slope to the track, Edie was there on the track coming down from the ravine. Robert could not think of anything to say. Edie looked strangely at Valery and then for even longer she looked at Robert.

Of course, she fancies me, Robert thought. *It's written all over her face. Why hadn't I seen it before?*

"We were watching stars come out," said Valery. "That's why we were slow. But, oh Edie! You did the best. It was like the trapeze in the circus! Did you get scratched?"

"Only going down to the road. This clearing is very bad. No one has planted... Did you see how I went?"

"We did see. It was amazing, as if you were flying," said Robert, trying to force his mind back into the shade of the big tree and what had happened before. He couldn't help being sour at Edie for making Valery stop. "But you shouldn't have done it."

"Well, nor should you either."

Going down the track, Robert wanted to keep close to Valery and to help guide her through the now dark drifts. She might have been wary, but she seemed to see the ruts of the track better than he did and always moved away from him, ahead or behind, whenever he tried to come near.

6

Souls

Valery insisted on travelling in the back when they left Picheery Dam, as if she didn't want to be near Robert ever again. When they arrived at the aunt's house, Karl, as usual, bounced out on the road almost before he had pulled to a stop. He went inside to give the pills to the aunt that she was to pass on to a sick family.

Robert also got out, and slammed the door behind him, almost in Valery's face where she stood in the road waiting to mount to her place. When he did not reopen it and when, worst of all, he stared at her as if not seeing her, she grew impatient; she opened the door decisively, folded the seat forward, and climbed quickly into the back.

Robert too late exclaimed, "Oh, I'm sorry," and reaching to catch the door she had left swinging, collided with Edie, who had also been waiting. She giggled and ducked under his arm. She folded the seat back up to its place and climbed up to sit in the middle at the front.

That Robert had something on his mind was likely very obvious to all. He frowned, scarcely glanced at the scenery or anyone; and often, when he thought no one was watching him, his eyes would close and his features contort as if he had bitten a lemon. Valery from behind watched him rather scornfully now; nor was she much placated when he said, "It's nothing. I had a bad night, is all."

Edie, oblivious, kept chattering on to him, saying things that made him feel even stupider about not knowing her affections for him. She asked about his bicycle, and where he would have camped if he had gone to "Devon and Cornwall" with his mates. And what the roads were like there. Trying to answer some of these questions, Robert gleaned that she had never even seen a tarmac road before.

When he asked her that, she blushed deeply and lapsed into silence. Valery talked to Karl. Robert was again glad to be left alone.

He laid his head into the fluttering wind and thought about the diamonds. It had been a long time since he'd seen Annetta last, and he wondered how she was getting on with Dr Paul, and if she was indeed in league with him to find the diamonds. Did Karl really have the crucial clue in the drawing he had bought? If so, they just might do it, once the delivery of pills was over.

Souls was the biggest town in the moors' area. This meant a fair criss-crossing of streets, more than the usual one or two. Several of its buildings were brick, and among these was its church—a rather beautiful, steepled one, stuccoed and painted in two shades of blue. Tiled roofs were more common than palm thatch, especially in the ancient-seeming centre. A brick aqueduct arched over certain streets, bringing water to the whole town from a stream of a nearby hillside. Although vastly remote from the sea, coconut palms seemed to grow well here, their graceful stems supporting heads like green hair combs in clustered handfuls above the brown tiles.

There were signs of a coming modernity too. They passed a new blue and silver bus bearing a destination sign AIRPORT/HOSPITAL bumping along the mud road. Valery pointed to a part of the roof of the hospital just visible over a shoulder of a bushy hill which was scarred with red tracks that probably meant that it, too, was soon to be built on. Valery said proudly that the hospital had three stories and was the best in the whole province. A new settlement, as large as Picheery Dam, had grown up around its site in merely the past three years. The airstrip was somewhere out in that direction too, about two miles from the town. The helicopter brought malaria or accident cases to the hospital.

Valery was proud of the town's shops and she pointed out the more important ones to the boys as they passed. As a particular sign of "progress," she noted a photographer's shop. It had come recently, and the photographer took very good pictures. She and her parents had all theirs taken.

"And I suppose you looked smashing," Karl said.

"I didn't. It wasn't the way I liked."

"She did," said Edie.

Karl asked if she had a spare print of herself—one or another that she could give them.

"I might have. Why do you want it?"

"Just for me and Robert to fight over," he teased.

Then he told Robert that he wanted to be out of the town quickly, to be seen by as few people as possible. He said he would stop only briefly to drop the girls at their aunt's house and would leave there also the half carton of pills for them to deliver to the hospital. The boys would not lunch in the town and would not take on fuel.

As it turned out, they left the pills but not the girls at the home. A maid standing in the high doorway of the big, one-storied building told them that both their aunt and uncle were away in Cintra, another town, for the next several days. The tall doorway with the dark hall behind, the chipping stucco on the walls, and the brown packed mud of the street where they stood—and indeed all that was around them—brought to Robert an image of a medieval town.

Now both of the girls wanted to go on. They said there was no way they could miss finding the lorry at Cintra, or else meeting it on the road, which was the only one. It was due back to Souls that evening. Karl was reluctant but at last, he let them, and so the four set out from Souls together.

Because he had needed persuasion, Valery teased Karl that he preferred her photograph to herself.

"We've tough times ahead," Karl said.

"Well, why don't you want us to come and help?"

"If this was a picnic, it would be just super. But it's not. Willy-nilly, you two drop in Cintra. And in Cintra, you'll have to go to another of all your many aunts if we can't find the lorry."

"Oh, there is one, of course, that is who our aunt went to see. You needn't worry, Karl," she said mockingly.

"I knew it. Every town on the moors has an aunt of yours, evidently. Or two."

"Karl, what is the danger you are going to?" asked Edie.

"It's hardly worth explaining. Let's just say some people don't like us for bringing those pills."

"I know that. Mummy told me something about it. She says you're very brave. But she says you ought to be looking for bad men at the road camp, and not out here."

"I know she thinks that… Anyway, I'm not looking for them just here."

"Karl, Valery and I want to help. Isn't there something we can do—something that's not too dangerous?"

"Well, you could. Valery can make sure that the box I left goes to the doctor whose name is on it. There is nothing you can do for us in Cintra, I'm afraid."

"Is it true you're driving to the road camp?"

"Yes."

"If you think the road camp engineers are all right, why don't you leave the pills for them with the doctor at the hospital? He could give them to the engineers when they come in the helicopters."

"You're sharp as a tack, Edie. I've thought about doing that many times. It would save us a big risk. If I could trust everybody, I would. But I want to get them right into the hands of the people I know myself—or else straight to the sick families. The last people I want to pass them through are administrators, whether they're at road camps, hospitals, or anywhere else."

"I think it's wonderful if your pills really cure people of ague."

"Well, wait and see, Edie. If they do work, especially in the hospital and in the road crews, I hope there'll be some tests and then a big clean-up of what's going on, and that a lot of administrators and the so-called doctors will be sent to jail."

They were climbing into a westering sun. Grassy hills rose to the left and south, while on the right the country dropped off towards a distant and steepening valley in which they could see lines of crags suggesting the lip of a canyon. Their road passed little woods in damp ravines and there were tree ferns again. The roadside meadows and slopes of the hills were dotted with cattle and here and there a farm was marked by the usual dark grove of mangoes and the blue-green of banana plants. Apart from the cart tracks to the farms, there were no side roads at all. It was perfectly true that there was almost no way to miss a lorry unless it was stopped back of a farm.

After a long silence, Karl said suddenly, out of the blue, "Robert is gloomy, today. What is it, Rob?"

Robert started and looked guiltily around. "There is something. But I can't tell you about it now, Karl."

He knew from being asked that Karl had already decided that the trouble was Valery. Valery probably guessed it, too. At that moment, he *wished* it were something else. Anything else, but her. He added, "Concern about the deliveries. That's all."

They came over a crest and beheld Cintra, a tiny, tight cluster of houses in a flattish crook of the hills. It looked like a child's toy village built on the bulging and sagging seat of an old green armchair—a chair they were seeing as tiny dolls themselves perched on one of the arms. The houses made the three sides of a square, or rather they made the sides of a J, because a few straggled out from the rest along the tiny road leaving on the far side. That road descended into a series of bare spurs toward the craggy, broken country Robert had noted to the northwest. Here they were high: there were almost no trees, only bushes and guavas, and banana palms with brown and tattered leaves behind the houses. Everywhere was grassy and open. The ravines on the slopes were like the creases of the old soft leather of the chair, and there were little knolls and bare places of sand as if a dog had bitten and scratched there.

In the middle of a smooth greensward that Robert supposed was the village green, there stood the same lorry, with the same bright tailboard, that the boys had first seen at the White River crossing.

"They're here," said Valery cheerfully, vindicated, and she clapped her hands. Karl, too, looked relieved.

Taking the zig-zags down, as they drew near to the big slope at the back of the village and the moorland went out of sight above them, Karl said, "The next drop would be the head streams of Diamond Creek. Beyond that, the land rises all the way to Elmin. It's very deserted country."

"Does anyone live up there?" Robert asked.

"Not a soul from this village to way on the other side of Elmin. Same towards Pandora too. There's not a soul from here to—well, really, to the other side of the Vascoma Valley, six hundred miles, come to that—save an odd lorry that might be on HPD, boats on the river, indigene or two in the forest."

"There used to be shepherds on the moors," said Valery.

"Not now," said Karl grimly. "Disease."

"I know."

"So far, as it happens, other villages like this have suffered, but not Cintra. So far, it's been spared. But it's only a matter of time, I suppose."

Beside him, Robert felt Valery shudder.

DR PAUL EXAMINING EDIE'S EYES

7

Cintra

It was a brilliant late afternoon. The girls had been delivered to their aunt's home. Karl had gone off on foot to a farm a mile away to see a sick child and give her parents his medicine. Robert had stayed behind. They were also awaiting the return of a man who, they had been told, would sell them dried meat for their journey. Karl, who had been in high spirits ever since they had come into view of Cintra and the lorry, had promised Robert that they would be camping that night in a fairly extraordinary place—a belt of wild rocky limestone country that formed a natural bridge over the gorge. "The river goes right through the limestone in a tunnel about a mile long and as big as a cathedral," Karl had said. "It's a thousand feet down under terrific crags."

But if Karl's enthusiasm for these natural wonders was high, Robert's was low. He didn't know why. He wandered a little down the road and tried to take an interest in a very large millipede that was creeping across it. He considered whether he might collect it for Karl, but he didn't. His eyes instead strayed to the lorry and the house behind it. He realised that his melancholy was at least partly to do with the fact that, whatever wonderland they might be camping in, Valery and Edie would not be there.

To take his mind off it, he made himself busy, exploring the area. He climbed a hill with a deceptively sharp incline. There was a mortar slab there on the summit and the rotted stump of a post that probably had once been part of a crucifix. As he reached it, he heard the sound of voices. He went cautiously to the front edge of the flat place in order to look down. He wasn't thinking anymore about whether Valery and Edie would see him on the rock; now he just wanted to see where the voices came from and why some among them might be familiar.

But Valery and Edie *were* actually there, below him.

He suddenly felt cold and knelt on the rock. He was high above, looking steeply down onto a group of about twenty people, all looking at the same thing. No one was moving; their shadows lay long on the grass. He saw Edie. She was a little apart from the line, standing very upright. In front of her here was something quite horrible that seemed to have power over her, which was making her stand close to it and preventing her from running away. It was like a polar bear, or some other tall upright animal, but not like a bear, it had a long black beak like a crow, aimed straight down into Edie's face.

Edie's upturned face was half towards him, her lips thin and white and her mouth half-open. Her arms were straight down by her sides at first, but soon she raised one hand to the level of her breast as if to have it ready to shield her eyes; only to have the thing with the beak take her hand in his—it was a man's hand—and place it back down by her side.

He looked closer. The black beak was some kind of a loupe attached to a man's head, with a black strap at the back, crossing his rather thin and pale hair. Yet somehow, seeing that it was an optical instrument and that the "animal" was merely a man who was evidently examining Edie's eyes, didn't at all take the horror away. For one thing, Edie must've known what was being done to her, and yet she was clearly terrified.

As Robert was wondering what to do, the man suddenly stood up and lifted the beak thing onto his forehead.

Dr Paul.

He took Edie's hand and led her to a big rock that lay in the grass. Edie sat down in the grass at its side. She made nervous and confused movements. Dr Paul seemed to be telling her something that she did not understand. Then she laid her head back upon the rock. Dr Paul stepped astride of her; he clapped the beak back over his face and bent down. He made signs over her, moving his fingers in what looked like a sign of the cross. He held a finger first to one side then the other, then over her forehead, moving it around. Robert couldn't see Edie's face anymore because the man's big body was in the way; he could only see her skirt and feet were visible.

Sickness swam in his stomach. He backed to the edge and started to climb down. His limbs were watery but, as he slid down to his first foothold out on the bulge, he suddenly felt coming back both strength and anger. He climbed down and ran out onto the grassy slope.

When he came round to the side of the pinnacle where the group had been, everyone had crowded at the door to a shop. The crowd blocked his way, but he was taller than most and could see inside. Dr Paul was behind the counter and Edie was still with him. There were papers on the counter. Edie had a pencil in her hand and was staring at the papers. Still blind and stricken, she moved as if about to write, but hesitated.

"Write, child write," he heard Paul say. "Write in that place where X is. Write 'Edie' or 'Edith,' whichever you like. The paper won't bite you. Once you have signed, everything is taken care of. They will bring you to the hospital; treatment is free. Come, sign. Here, just by my finger. Think what I told you, child. Blindness can only be prevented if the disease is in the early stages. Your infection is not early. It has been neglected. But we may still have a chance."

Edie suddenly straightened up and looked over the faces in the room. She could not see Robert against the light. She was a hunted animal at the end—a deer checked in brambles and letting hounds come to it. She looked at Dr Paul, who smiled gently and tapped the paper again with his finger. Edie suddenly bent over the paper. She put her face very close to her pencil and started to write.

Dr Paul did not watch. His smiling gaze wandered. When it came to the doorway it stopped, and for a moment he stopped smiling; he had seen Robert pushing forward through the crowd.

Robert broke through the crowd and came up to the counter.

"Edie!" he said, rather breathless. "What's going on?"

"Just my name."

"Ah, I know you now! It is my friend from the Bar Palace!" said Dr Paul suddenly, beaming at Robert. "How well I remember our interesting discussion about rivers! But—you are out of breath! Have you been running?"

"Sir, out of curiosity, what was my friend writing? Was she signing something?"

Paul responded slowly, holding his head high so that he could look down. "Yes, as it happens. For the benefit of her health. A matter on examination and treatment at the hospital. Yes. Now—"

"What's the matter with her then?"

"Really, it is no concern of yours."

"I don't think she will mind if I know."

"No, I don't mind," Edie said.

"It is an infection."

"Of her eyes?"

"Yes. The trachoma," Dr Paul snapped. There was no smile now and with the pushed-back instrument still capping his fair and serious face, he looked very much like a doctor. He stared at Robert. His eyes were pale and black pupils small. He had on clean pale trousers and a pale shirt. Sunglasses and the top of a silver pen showed in the shirt pocket. A narrow black belt dented his soft but still muscular waist. He held the paper which Edie had written on, lightly folded. The black side was outward, but it seemed to be a form of some kind.

"Are you sure it's that—trachoma?" Robert asked.

"It will be confirmed at the hospital. If I am wrong, excellent. But I fear not."

"I've never noticed anything wrong with her eyes."

"Of course not. You are not a doctor." He looked down at Robert and raised pale eyebrows still higher.

"What is the treatment?"

"That is a matter for discussion only among the colleagues—and with the patient, if she has to make a decision. If she wishes, she may tell you later what we advise. Now leave us, please."

"Is the treatment some kind of—fish pills?"

A moment of anger creased the broad, well-shaven face; then the smile was there again and in his next words there was even a trace of the friendly tipsiness of their last meeting.

"Ah, so you remember! Surely you will not have forgotten the rest of our conversation then—even our little difference about the rivers! We may hope, perhaps, for an opportunity to resume that fascinating discussion. Yes, I use homeopathy a little. It is very effective for some—ah—types of illness. But not for trachoma."

"Is—Miss Oliveira old enough to sign consent for treatment? Why does she have to sign now? Why not at the hospital, where her mother—"

"Young man, you know nothing about the laws and the medical services of this country. If this form is not signed, she cannot go to the hospital."

"I'd like to see what the form is like. May I have it for a moment, please?"

"No."

"Then just turn it so that I can read it from here. I want to know exactly what she has signed."

"You are not her guardian or even a relative."

"It doesn't matter. Tell me why you don't want to show it to me."

"You certainly may not see it. It is no concern of yours."

"Look, I'll fight you to see it, if I have to," Robert said fiercely. He leaned over the shop counter and made a snatch at the paper, but Dr Paul quickly drew it out of reach.

"What is the boy doing? Stop him!" said a woman's voice from behind Robert.

"Young man, you are being ridiculous," said Dr Paul.

"Robert, it is only a form that they use at the hospital at Souls," Edie said in a low voice. "It's about how you agree to make medicines and things."

"I want to see what this form says." But Robert's voice wavered.

A man tapped his arm sharply from behind. He was shorter than Robert but very broad.

"You are troubling the doctor. The doctor is a friend of the town. If the talk is of fighting someone, let's you and I step outside."

Robert scanned the crowd and saw many hostile faces, heads shaken in affirmation.

"I see you're all his supporters," he said angrily.

"Oh, come, young man," said Dr Paul in a changed voice behind him. "I understand how you feel; you wish to protect your girlfriend, who has had a shock because I have been obliged to tell her about her eye condition. She should not be nervous—I have told her that the prognosis is very good if treatment is begun in time. However, she is naturally still upset, and you are on the edge and therefore you turn on me. Do you think that I like to frighten her or that I am pleased with the result of my examination? Convince yourself then, if you must—take the form out into the light and read it."

He thrust the paper towards Robert.

The tension had gone from the crowd now and some people were drifting away. Robert took the form outside.

It was a hospital treatment consent form. Across the top was printed, "Federal Government of Santania" and underneath, in typescript, "St. Aulun's Hospital, Souls." A scrawly but readable hand, doubtlessly Dr Paul's, had written, "Edith Olivera," and "Suspected trachoma. Re-ex and treat if n." At the bottom, the name "Edith," was pencilled in large and uneven script.

Back in the shop, he found Dr Paul alone with Edie.

"Here is your friend again," said Dr Paul, not looking very pleased to see him return. "Well, are you satisfied that she hasn't signed her death warrant?"

"Yes," said Robert reluctantly, giving him back the form.

"Well, you may both leave me now. You may go and discuss this ogre who uses a loupe to sharpen his Hippocratic eye and see what you make of him. He likes to nip blindness in the bud when he can. In any case, leave me. I have some things to tidy up here among my medicines."

"You keep medicines here?"

"I do," said Dr Paul very curtly.

"You are not the owner of this shop, are you?"

"No. But I—the owner permits me to keep medicine chests here for my visits."

"Do you treat people for free?"

"So far as in my power, my services to the people are always free. Antibiotics and treatment from the hospital, of course, may sometimes be another matter."

"So, my friend will not have to pay?"

"Of course not."

"How do you make your living, if people don't pay you?"

"Young man, you will have to learn in life to ask fewer questions and to be able to see when a person has other affairs to attend to. But I'll give you this last answer: sometimes rich plantation owners seek my advice, and those I—" He paused, hearing a footstep. "Wait, who is this coming?"

Robert looked outside. "It's the shopman," he said, stepping back as the man came in.

Despite their friendly greetings, Dr Paul did not seem particularly pleased to see this man, either. He fussed out from behind the counter. "I will come back later when you are less busy, to tidy my things," Dr Paul said, and he went out. Robert and Edie followed.

The sun was about to set; in minutes it would touch on the black, ragged line of the horizon, far off across Furnace Valley. A great shadow was flowing up from the gorge, drowning its green slopes and rising towards their feet.

"Ah, wonderful land!" said Dr Paul, breathing deeply.

"I must go to see if my aunt and uncle are ready to leave yet," said Edie.

"But you won't go without coming to say goodbye, will you?" said Robert in a low voice.

"No. Of course not." She gave Robert a questioning look.

"I can't come with you," Robert whispered, remembering how Karl had wanted him to stay near the jeep.

"I know," she said. "You had better stay and talk to him."

She left, leaving Robert facing the man's big back, heaving as it drew in breaths of the pure cooling air of the plateau. And with each breath, he seemed to dilate, as if he would grow to giant size like the rock pinnacle nearby. Now he turned to Robert.

"You left too early last time. As to our mutual interest in rivers…" he began.

Suddenly there was the sound of the door of the jeep opening. Both he and Dr Paul looked around, and there was Karl putting something that looked like a black cricket bat into the back. It was the dried meat he'd gone to fetch.

He slammed the door, turned, and saw them.

At long last, Karl and Dr Paul were face to face.

8

Reunion

"**K**arl! Greetings! I was waiting for you here," said Dr Paul, turning to Robert. "You two are friends, eh? I thought so."

Robert fought the urge to shrink back like a cornered animal. Karl stared at him, unwavering. If this meeting was a surprise, his face did not show it.

"So you came back to my country," Dr Paul said.

"Yes, I came back. What have you two been talking about? Robert, I saw a crowd here earlier, from up on the hill."

"They were watching him—Dr Paul—and Edie. Dr Paul examined her. He says Edie has trachoma."

"Did he give her medicine?" Karl asked sharply.

"No. But he's arranging for her to be treated at the hospital. He's sending in a form." Robert spoke sullenly, still puzzled.

"A form? Did she sign the form?"

"Yes."

"Where is it? Did you see it?" Karl said quickly. His shoulders tilted in the way that Robert now well knew. Even in the half-light, his lips were white. Dr Paul coughed.

"He has it. But it is just the usual sort of form about consent for treatment, Karl. I did look at it."

"One piece of paper?"

"Yes."

"Where were they when she signed it? What was the paper resting on?"

Dr Paul, who had been listening in silence, shrugged at the point, turned on his heel, and walked away towards the shop.

"They were in that shop at the counter. But, Karl, now I remember something I didn't before: when I picked it up and held it—"

But Karl had already left him, sprinting to the shop. Dr Paul glanced around and saw him coming and broke into a run. Karl, at full speed, went by him and shot in through the door of the shop. The man followed a moment later, swinging himself towards the counter by the doorpost and making the whole building creak. Robert, now running just behind, saw that Karl had reached the counter first and was down behind it, pulling out drawer after drawer under the top board. Now Dr Paul was there too, trying to reach something, and Karl was bracing his shoulder against the bigger man, pushing him away whilst still rabbiting in the drawers. Dr Paul was kicking and pulling at Karl and was calling urgently, although not shouting: "Simon! Simon Oakley! Come quickly! There's a thief!"

Karl made a sharp gesture with his left arm that shook off the man's grip from his shirt, and then suddenly shot up from behind the counter as if impelled by a springboard. With one hand, he vaulted over it in a single bound. His other hand held a clipboard with papers waving from it.

The boys ran onto the lower slopes of the pinnacle. They stood where they could watch the door of the shop, but the doctor did not appear. The top paper on the clipboard was a hospital form just like the one Robert had seen, perhaps the actual one. Karl flicked the form back, and then another, and at last, a piece of blue paper fluttered out.

"Ah, what I thought," Karl hissed between his teeth. "The swine."

"Why? What's it about?"

"See, here." Karl held the third paper on the board between them so that they both could read it, turning it to the fading light to the west.

Written in black ink and a gracious, steady, cursive hand, Robert read:

"I record that of my own free will I promise body and soul to serve Dr Paul and his high purposes. I promise to do as he directs and to be his third arm until he no longer needs me or until one of us dies."

Then came the signature just as Robert had remembered in pencil on the form, except that here it was in blue ink, as if with a pointed pen: Edie.

"You'd think it was real ink, wouldn't you?" Karl muttered, holding it close. "At least, you would in this light. By day, I guess it wouldn't fool any but backwoodsy people such as these, who've hardly seen copy paper before. But of course, those are the ones he wants." He gritted his teeth.

A flood of light burst over Robert and a return of rage.

"Karl! I must talk to you." Dr Paul's voice boomed from very close to them and startled them. He was just below them on the slope. Robert suddenly wondered how they could have been so foolish as to be still standing there, and why they hadn't gone further away.

"Right," Karl answered after a moment's silence, with weight in the last word. "And I to you."

He waved his hand as if to mark exactly the spot where Robert should wait; then he nodded at Karl and they walked off together. They used the parallel tracks that the cows had made along the hillside. Karl was two paces apart down the hill and he looked very small.

He waited in the dark. Soon even Dr Paul's pale form was out of sight. So was the pinnacle, but he could see the serpent of orange lights that was the village above him. Kerosene lamps were being lit in all the huts. Above them was the black outline of the hill and a dark blue sky was filling with a fine dust of stars.

They did not come back. He peered for a while longer into the darkness, and then thought he heard raised voices, not along the slope, but some way down to the hill. He started towards the sound. The cow tracks were like steps, but in the darkness, he had to go carefully. He went a long way and so far from levelling, the slope became steeper and steeper and soon he realised that no one could stroll and discuss in this place, one would have to scramble. He started up the hill again and he found he could not be in the same line as he had been when he came down because he was hitting prickly bushes and some patches of steep, loose, sliding soil. Then he heard a sound just to his left, a cry of pain.

He ran towards the sound. He came to a cuplike grassy hollow in the hillside—perhaps it had been a very small sand or lime pit long ago. In the bottom of the cup on the grass two dark things, the size of the sheep, were moving. It was Dr Paul and Karl fighting. Both were down on the grass in the bottom and were struggling there. Dr Paul had gotten on top of Karl and was gripping him by the shoulders, pounding him against the ground.

"Karl! I'm coming!" Robert shouted, trying in vain to find his way down in the dark.

Dr Paul, with an unexpected lightness for such a big man, sprang off Karl and crouched in an odd position, facing Robert with one fist on the turf. Robert had thought to hit him with his thrown body—as he would sometimes hit the man who had taken the ball after a kick-off.

But as he came, Dr Paul lunged forward and a little sideways and caught Robert's body against his shoulders and flung him, sprawling, off the ridge of the hollow and down the slope. He did a roll and came to his feet again and at once turned to scramble back up. He was surprised and winded, but thought, *it's no matter, Karl will be up and will have him from behind now.* But when he came up, Dr Paul was standing with his hands on his hips and looking down at him calmly, and Karl was sitting on a grass step behind. He was holding his shoulder and rocking to and fro. He moved on the slope warily, watching to see what the man would do.

Dr Paul was laughing.

"Karl, are you all right?" asked Robert, coming around to Karl, keeping just out of range of the man's arms.

Karl said nothing.

Dr Paul shrugged and stepped off a few paces. "Well, talk to him if you wish," he said. "I have finished this discussion."

Robert crouched by Karl. "Did you get it back? Hey, Karl! Are you hurt?" he whispered.

Dr Paul laughed again, turned his back on them, and started to climb the way Robert had come down.

"Rob," Karl said in a voice of pain. "Wait for me by the jeep. I'll explain later."

Robert peered into his face. The look of pain was going and in its place was one of fear and misery. He stood up and would say no more to Robert. He went up the hill after Dr Paul.

Robert called after him, "But we should—"

"No. Leave him. It's no good."

"Karl, what's the matter?"

"I'm done."

He bowed his head onto his knees. Robert crouched beside him. "Karl! He's hurt you somehow! What did he do?"

Silence.

"What, Karl?"

"Stung me."

"How?"

No answer.

"The paper, did he get it back?"

"I gave it to him."

"Why? Karl, what is wrong with you? Anyway, you said it didn't matter much. We know his game. We'll get him some way or other, won't we?"

Robert stared at the dark oval of his friend's hunched body, hardly able to believe what he heard. Coldly indifferent stars glittered over their heads. "I'm done," Karl said softly.

Out of the darkness, two forms emerged. Robert stiffened, expecting it was Dr Paul, come back to rob what was left of Karl's spirit, but it was Edie and Valery. They'd heard the commotion and followed them into the clearing.

"Karl, look. Edie's here. She's come to say goodbye to us."

At last, something seemed to stir him. He clasped his fingers in his hair. "Oh, Rob, why did we—her mother! Edie—where is she?"

"I'm here, Karl." And she was indeed right before him, a slim darkness in the starlight.

"Edie! Now listen. This is one thing I must do. I must tell you. Listen carefully. You must go home. Don't let anyone take you to the hospital. Don't believe in the trachoma. If you're worried, and think there might really be something wrong, make sure you see Dr Clemson—only him." He was speaking clearly now. He had things he had to say clear in his mind. "Back at the farm, you must stay close to the house and your mother for a long time. Don't go to the washing place—not even with someone with you. Never go to the moors. Do you understand all that?"

"Yes. But why, Karl?" Her voice quavered.

"Will you do it?"

"Some, maybe. But say why."

"There's a danger."

"From Dr Paul?"

"Yes."

"Oh!"

"You mustn't be frightened. But you are, aren't you? ... Has he done something to make you frightened before? Before today?"

"No, never," Edie said quickly, "but I don't like him. I don't think he's good like he pretends to be. When he looks at you—but I don't know how I know. Even when he seemed to be so kind, asking me if I would like him to examine my eyes along with others, I knew there was something awful going to happen. Oh, Karl, I think I'm not very brave if it's him."

Out of the darkness, Valery said, "I don't like him either... Am I in danger too?"

"You? No, I don't think so."

She exhaled. "Oh, good. I'm not nearly as brave as Edie."

Karl went on, "So you must both go back home now. Forget about everything as much as you can, except that Edie must do what I said." He spoke in a decisive, authoritative tone that Robert had never heard him use before, but which seemed to come out of him with an effort, as though he was very tired.

"But, Karl, we can't just let them go like this, without explaining anything," Robert whispered. "You'd be frightened to think what might happen to you; anyone would. At least tell them we're going to fight him till we can be sure the danger's gone."

"Just leave it!" said Karl angrily. "Valery! Edie! Go away!"

The two girls stood silent just down the slope from him.

Though he was still sitting on the ground, Karl stamped his foot at them.

"Go away! Robert and I need to talk! GO AWAY!"

"Yes, and then thank you for bringing us," said Valery coldly. "Come on, Edie."

The girls went.

"Why don't we just go and kill him?" Robert said fiercely, after they had left. "We know what colours he fights under now. Karl, I believe everything you've ever said about him. He's a monster. It's like you said: it's war."

"I'm a yellow shit. I'm not brave enough for anything."

"What?—I don't know why you're saying that. You're the bravest person I know!"

His shoulders slumped. "I'm not and I never was, and now he's made me a real coward. I'm not even brave enough to die."

"Why? We might not die... If we could get the paper again and show what he was doing to the police, and if we could find his hideout and just end him—I don't believe a judge would treat it as murder."

"I didn't mean that. I can't. It's not possible. If I kill him, it'll kill me."

"What on earth are you talking about?"

"I need a long time to explain. It's as if he has made me into his Siamese twin. Just can't cut us two apart."

"Well let's go somewhere to give you some time. We can hide away till you've got your strength back, and then—"

"That's just it. I can't. Hiding and waiting would do just the opposite."

"I don't understand."

"He's instructed me to go to Chalcie Wells. It's the next town across the gorge. Then I'm to wait there until I get orders or until he comes. He says you are not involved and can go home, but he wants to see you once again before you do, I don't know why. But you must do it, Rob, because otherwise, all that will happen is that you will end up like me."

After a pause, Robert said, "I want to go on. I'll try to do the rest of it myself if you can't. At Chalcie Wells, let me take the jeep. You stay there, if it's true your life so depends on it."

"You'll be picked up within hours now that he knows where we are. That's in the worst area. If you defy him by trying to continue this trip, then you'll either end up dead or you'll be like I am now. Don't imagine that you being a British subject, or having an old school tie, is going to hold anyone back."

"I am a coward and a shit. Why aren't I brave enough? If only it would help..."

"I am as much of a shit as you. So, we both are shits. Just let me think. It would help you to get off the moor at least." He was tugging at his hair again with both his hands.

Then his hands left his hair, and he was fierce in thought; without being able to see anything because of the dark, Robert could feel like electricity in the air the tension of Karl's old self returning.

"Look, there's yet one other way out of Chalcie which hardly anyone knows because it's so bad. It goes back to the HPD, almost to Pike. They wouldn't expect me to flee through Chalcie now, because that's where I'm supposed to go, and if when I get there I do go on through, the last place they'll expect me to be heading for is Pike…" He went on. He was speaking more and more excitedly, almost incoherently, talking about a road or "non-road" as he called it. Then: "I'd have a few days before I'd die. If we could reach the Vascoma River, we could hide the jeep down the bottom. Or you could take it while I go… Decide later. Phew! We might get him yet! But there's one snag. I've never driven that track and don't know the turnoff from the other road to Impeya—and it's the kind you need to know it. That's why it's so good: no one else knows it either."

"There must be wheel marks, mustn't there?"

"There may be, but those go all ways. You'll see. We could ask in Chalcie—but that would give us away."

"I know where the turn is," said a girl's voice out of the darkness nearby. It was Edie. She was standing a few yards away along the slope. "I'll go with you and show you, if you like."

"Edie!" Karl shouted at her. "Get out of there! Spy! Get back to your mother! I told you."

"I don't believe Mother would mind my going if she knew it was with you. If I could help you, I would make her not mind when I got back."

"Get out! Shameless!"

"I'm not a spy."

Edie ran off into the dark.

Robert was breathing hard. "She mustn't come. It's too dangerous. How do we find this track, then?"

"So, you still want to try it, eh?" His voice was still harsh and mocking. "I told you I was a shit, and I'm going to get worse, I warn you. But you still want to go—even with a raving sodding turd like me? Well then, Mr Stupid, let's go. Let's set off right this minute."

9

Stowaway

Karl drove all night almost without stop. By midnight they were across the Furnace Gorge. They saw nothing of its splendours except sometimes a black space below them to left or to right, or in the form of the yellow circle the beam of their headlights made on some distant cliff face or pinnacle over a dark void. Mostly for Robert the great natural bridge that both Karl and Paul had told of, was just a hillocky and a very, very stony and rocky road. After the gorge, of course, they were climbing again, or least, were going more up than down.

Karl drove with a manic energy Robert had never seen before. He seemed to be trying to keep himself in a state of frenzy and anger. As a result, the promised revelations about Dewey's picture were at best disjointed, even though Karl was obviously endeavouring to load Robert with every detail that might help him—for he seemed to have little hope of being active himself in this or any other search for much longer.

He told Robert where the picture was hidden in the jeep. He told him that it was a rather poor pen sketch of a native's head. He said he could only think that it was of an indigene who knew the whereabouts of the treasure, or of some clue which, combined with another, might reveal the place. The native had unusual tattoo marks on the upper lip that might help to identify him if he could be encountered—he described the marks to Robert as well as he could

173

remember. When he had an opportunity, Karl had meant to consult those he trusted along the way, to see if anyone had ever met such a man.

Karl wrestled the wheel as it if were a live animal, continually cursing and muttering at the rocks and the steering mechanism. "I can't take much more of this landscape, but it should end soon," he muttered.

An unexpected voice answered from behind them.

"No, it won't."

It was Edie's voice.

"What!" Karl shouted, and the jeep jerked to a standstill.

She popped her head up from beneath the hammock in the back of the jeep. "I'm still going to show you where if you're not too mad at me. Don't send me back. I shall cry again if you do."

Without waiting to see if he was mad, she began to.

Karl turned abruptly and began to speak, but it couldn't be heard over the sound of Edie's crying.

"Edie! Stop already," Karl groused.

She sniffled. "You won't leave me in Chalcie?"

"In Chalcie—while I run for it? Where we know he's coming to pick me up! He owns you. You really will make me mad again if you even suggest I could do that, Edie…. I didn't mean it about you being a spy and all. I am sick. That's what makes me talk like that. Come, don't cry anymore!"

"I know you're sick," she said through her sobs. "It's why I came."

Five minutes later, the jeep was whining and rumbling onwards, in low gear, up the now smoothing slopes.

"Does Valery know where you are?"

"Yes. She was there, she's going to tell Mother. It's all right."

"Look, Edie. This is serious. I'm not sure if you realize what you're doing. Someone may be killed in this—"

"I don't care."

"I might get so sick that I too have to stay behind somewhere. Then you must go on with Robert to show him the way. You mustn't stay with me because I'm sick. Do you understand that?"

"Yes, Karl. If you say that's best, then I'll do it."

He looked at Robert. "And you must deliver Edie safely home. No matter what. Do you understand that? Her mother would never forgive me for that."

Robert nodded.

Karl let out a relieved breath. "Now that that is settled, how do you know about this track beyond Chalcie, Edie?"

My father used to use it. He made it the first time. He was the first ever to find a way down off the moors to the new road—except for the old way back by our farm in the dry hills. Afterwards he took me."

"What is it like?"

"Lorries and jeeps can do it—going down. And only jeeps, but then hardly ever lorries at all, can come up."

Chalcie Wells was on an open, grassy savannah. It was a straggle of moors fronting a waterless marsh that was waiting for rain. Azure morning sky arched up from a horizon level on all sides except in the southwest where the white cones of the two volcanoes floated on a band of darker blue.

They merely passed through, in case Dr Paul was already there, waiting for him. Beyond that, the turn off for the road to Pike would indeed have been hard to find without Edie. It was in the bottom of a shallow and rock-sided gully. Tyre marks hardly showed on the stony ground and from where they were the upper end of the gully appeared blind. Sometimes the ground was hard, and they bowled along merrily as if driving on an old airfield, and other times it was soft and their wheels churned and they crept slowly, using much fuel.

With or without any of Karl's growing strangeness, it was a crazy drive across that level moor. They had to wander to left or right from the road always to find better driving: this was because where there were dried marshes that had mud and not sand, which was often, the wheel ruts of previous lorries were gouged deep and square and had set hard as rock. These ruts were all across the marshes, and because the wheels of the lorries had been bigger than those of the jeep, they could not follow them, and so must keep out well to one side from the whole tangled and braided mess.

Yet the mess was the road, and to be prudent, the road should've been kept within sight. There was no need to wander from it.

But wander, Karl did. It seemed as if at the first of those steep ascents, the thread of his mad endeavour to escape Dr Paul snapped. He babbled on incessantly, making no sense. He had not slept but did not seem sleepy. Robert soon came to realize, after many useless hour-long diversions and tedious reversals out of the maze of ruts, that not only Karl's will but his actual sense of direction had gone. They began trying to point him the way more often.

It was soon clear that Edie had by far the best direction sense of all three. So, she came to sit between them. It didn't seem to worry her; even with no sun, she was still able to point confidently to landmarks on the horizon ahead. Sometimes Karl would disbelieve her and would insist on following his method, which was usually to veer more and more to the left or the right. Sometimes this veering did bring them back to the road, but sometimes Edie would at last shout, "But now you're heading backward!"

Karl would stop and give her some foolery and argument, and then would finally take the way she had said, or roughly so. Eventually, after many minutes of wandering and bumbling, he would re-find the tracks.

The wandering was wasting petrol. More low sandy rises, more dried marsh, more herds of antelope seen far off on the plain (even these seeming the same herd over again), more of the road's entanglements and its vanishing altogether. They were lost again and again.

They saw no one. All through the day, belying the brilliant start, grey clouds had crept over the blue sky out of the west. The high sun was shaded, and once gone, the grassland was a prey moor. The volcanoes had vanished also without a trace. Robert's idea of direction came from the remaining band of blue sky which he believed to be in the east, but Edie's directions often ignored this—and if she was indeed keeping in a straight line, the blue band must be oddly flitting around them. Sometimes, Robert sensed from her hesitation that she was lost too, and then they would begin mutual recriminations about their mistakes, all against all. Yet always, at last, the road came back to them, and Edie would bounce a little on the bench seat and unclasp and reclasp her hands, and say, "You see?" And all the time, except when she was pointing, she kept her arms together on her lap and did not touch the boys except when forced into it by the swaying of the jeep.

"What does it matter? It's flat enough: why can't I have fun, drive where I like? All you need, all I ever need, is one idea: drive to the west," Karl grumbled.

"It's because there's only one place you can get down the rocks," said Edie.

"And it's because nothing could matter more than keeping enough petrol to get where we want," said Robert.

"It's all downhill from here," he argued. "We're fine."

"So, you think we're going to be fine, freewheeling off this mountain cliff Edie says is coming?" said Robert angrily. "Why don't you wake up and look where Edie's pointing!"

"Okay, I see her, Great Bear, I see her." He turned left and the linkages of the jeep clanked. "Well, Edie, you didn't answer. Could it mean a moorswind?"

Edie cast a glance around the sky. "I don't think so. The wind is east."

She did not sound very enthusiastic.

Though he tried to joke, there was a huge pit in Robert's stomach. He was brittle, easily angered, and eager to blame Karl if anything seemed to be wrong. It was clear now: Karl was going dotty; he was abandoning their agreement and ceasing to lead.

Under the grey sky, the tor half behind them on their right, a dark blue expanse like the sea came into sight ahead beyond the pale grass and the yellowish rock towers of their low horizon. Sweeping ever farther to left and to right, like a flood tide coming in over sand, this sea was their first sign from above of the forest of the Vascoma plain.

Bushes, growing each mile more substantial, were reappearing on the grassy upland and making it harder to get away from the tracks. At last, Karl landed heavily into ruts so deep that the back wheels spun free and he had to use the four-wheel drive to pull the jeep out. All the time as he drove, or stopped to change ratio or drive, or reversed to avoid the traps among the deep ruts, he talked incessantly about his theory of dreams.

"So, in my belief, people can make the dream world more real by planning to dream the same thing. Once into it, it could be as real as the other world..."

"Karl! Watch!"

"I'm watching it okay—but can't you think of anything else?—Why don't you drive, since you're so critical."

Robert shrugged and they changed. He'd gotten much better at driving, by this time.

Now the crags and tors which marked the edge of the drop were close on their left. Sometimes they could see the blue waves of foothills far below. Beyond these, far out, to the very limited of vision, stretched the forest out as if it were reaching for the edge of the world.

But they were not turning down the slope towards the crags and the foothills yet. Edie said they had to wait for the opening in the cliffs, the place that her father had found. And for Robert, this was just as well, since he needed some flat places and gentle slopes to practice his steering on. The machine was far worse than he remembered when he had driven last. It was a constant effort to keep to any course. Besides the clanking and loose rods, the accelerator pedal was crazy also, wanting either to roar or to run so slow that it would stall. The clutch was spongy. The whole machine was a living protest: it had been driven too far and too fast and now it wanted rest—or else, perhaps, sensed cliffs and danger at its side and in front a general gathering of its doom.

Still, they waited for the turn towards the edge. There still were several shallow valleys to cross, with tiny marshy rivulets, dry for the time, running to the crags and many small bushes and trees. Shallow and flat as these valleys were, they were hard going because they were so marshy and clayey. The scrub forced the jeep to follow the deep wheel lines of past lorries, and with the terrible steering, Robert realized now how tiring the driving must have been for Karl.

Just when Robert thought he was through the worst, a small tree forced him back to its very deep edge. The steering bucked on him and his back wheel hit a root of the tree. Both wheels of that side went into the rut together. With a terrific crash, the jeep fell almost on its side.

Edie and Karl came down on top of Robert. The baggage behind hit the roof and a lot of it fell forward on top of them. A stench of petrol filled his nostrils, and he could hear it gurgling out of the half-filled can. Robert struggled to reach it but by the time he got there, it was upside down and empty—the whole two and a half gallons had gone into their clothes and their bags—into everything.

Afterward, Karl did little except to pick up the step of the jeep which had broken off and fallen into the rut. He wandered with it in his hand and then sat in the grass in front of the jeep and laughed—or rather giggled—and would burst out, again and again, every time he looked at their vehicle's front wheels. He scoffed at Robert, but more in true amusement than in anger, "You were so much better at it, huh? Well, now we can travel lighter. The step's gone, half our juice is gone, and now we can try driving with front wheels like Donald Duck's feet."

"It wasn't my fault."

"Well, whoever's, what of it—out with the spade. Let's get some traction under it. Edie can try to repack while we dig. You may have to do most, Robert." He waved his hands about in front of him, vaguely, but with a familiar motion. After a pause, he said, "Well, anything is better than back there."

For a moment, his smile disappeared. He faced the empty air over the toppled jeep with a look of fear and horror.

Robert and Edie regarded him, then looked at each other. The worry was clear on Edie's face.

"I can dig quite well," Edie said.

Karl, without getting up, took the step of the jeep that he had laid beside him and hurled it away into the bushes. The effort of throwing it seemed to have hurt something because he gripped his shoulders and rocked to and fro, and he flexed and unflexed his muscles.

"You dig then, farm girl—dig, Edith of Oliveira," he gasped. "Only let me talk. I can't think like I used to think; I can't think things through anymore without talking them out loud."

As Karl rocked, the odd smile, which was rather like the drunken one Robert had so hated on Dr Paul, came back, and a flush appeared on his cheeks. It made Robert feel utterly ill.

THE OLD CITY

10

Old City

It was hard to believe there was any road at all where they, at last, went down the cliff. It was merely the ledges and grassy slopes of the mountain. The jeep swayed and balanced on slanting twisted rocks, jolting down stone stairways. There were strange shapes—like towers or ruined walls—among the trees on either side.

"It flattens out soon and there's a stream. You'll have to stop there unless you use the engine," Edie said.

"Then that's where we camp," Karl said suddenly.

The strange rocks were still around them as they bumped and bumped down.

"These are like walls and ruins." Robert tried to sound relaxed. Really, he'd been worried by Karl's silence, and besides, he did not like to be rolling down a bad steep road without any power, and nor did he like knowing that they were down to their last can of fuel and were wasting their battery.

Edie said the place was called the Old City. Her father had been the first to find it and he had given it that name. Now, some called it the Old City, but some called it "The Rocks of Leopards" because a party who had once camped there had said they'd been attacked by two leopards. Her father hadn't believed them; nor had he believed another story by travellers claiming to have been dwarfish ghosts of the people who built the city. Although he himself had called it the Old City, it wasn't a city, just strange rocks.

When the road levelled out Robert turned off to one side on a flat pebbly place where there were rushes. He stopped. He and Edie jumped out. A three-quarter moon had come up over distant ragged rocks that were the lip of the plateau. The moonlight shone in black wetness on the slabs of the road, and on Edie stooping there. Robert went over to her and saw a faint sparkle of moonlight in a film of water. He said, "A pity the water's so little. We can't use it for our camp."

"It isn't too little."

"Why, even if it's running, we can't get it into our billy."

"Into the lid, we can. See, it's dripping quite fast here. And there will be more when the rocks are cool. This is a good place to camp."

She guided his hand, and he felt the warm trickle coming over an edge from one slab to another. When he took his hand away the wetness at once became cold. And it seemed to him there was a warmer coldness too, on the back, where Edie's fingers had been.

He watched her going away to fetch the billy lid. She was going to prove herself right. She was practical, and yet at the same time, in that moonlight, she was the least worldly thing of it all, a spirit, strangeness itself. She had known this place beforehand, knew these rocks as if they were old friends; and, as she walked from him into the darkness, she seemed like a part of this place herself. As if, having her with them, letting her guide them, she was leading them into a strange new world of her own.

Around where she stood, and around the silent, unlighted jeep, grew top-heavy columns, rounded towers, and broken, curving walls. Between the rocks were stunted trees. Edie stood close to him and told him again how she had camped here before with her father and had got water in just this way. Her voice was low and vibrant. She seemed pleased with their camping place. She said again how most people were afraid of it, either because of the leopards, which might be real but were harmless, or of the ghosts of an ancient people who had built the city, which was only a story.

"So, it doesn't scare you to sleep in a place like this, Edie?"

"No. It doesn't at all. It makes me feel safe."

"Safe? Why?"

Edie seemed to hesitate.

"Well? Go on. Why?"

At last, she said, "The helicopters. They couldn't possibly land here."

"Helicopters?"

"Yes. That's how Dr Paul's men get around, most of the time."

"Well, we're out of the worst of that. We're down off the tops."

Edie was silent.

"You don't think we are—out of it—then?"

"I hope so."

"Look, Edie, things are okay, aren't they? You said there are only three leagues more to the road: that's nine miles. We have plenty of fuel for that. We hide the jeep. Then you go to Pike and your aunt's until she can arrange a lift to take you home. Karl will get out of here, away from Dr Paul. Our plan's working out fine. I don't believe Karl's affliction, whatever it is, is so bad that he can't be cured. He was cured all the time he and I were coming down here from London. In London, they have marvellous medicine, too, real medicine… It's very modern."

Edie was silent, fingering plant leaves on the rock.

"Don't you think the plan's working fine then?"

"Maybe. But there so many things that could happen still. And—really I would like to be staying with you until Karl is better."

Silence. Robert thought of his friends, so much bolder with girls than he was. What would they do? "You're tremendously brave, Edie."

"Why?"

"The way you plunge into all this along with us."

"Oh, stop." She moved away. "Don't smoosh on me."

"Smoosh?"

"It's something my mother says. Besides, no one ever says that about boys. They're expected to. Why should I be any different? Just because I'm a girl?"

She turned and left him, and he followed close behind, back through the trees to the fire, feeling awkward and a little hurt that his attempt at a compliment had not been appreciated. He lumbered near to her, now at her side, now pausing ahead to hold twigs so that they did not swipe her.

Almost at the camp, they both stopped, suddenly, listening.

The sound of a helicopter seemed to spring out of the night sky. It was coming over from the moors, was somewhere up near the ragged skyline of the edge, near to the moon. It was coming fast towards them.

The fire! How could they hide it? His mind raced for something dark that they could spread over it. He thought of a leafy branch, but it would be too thin. He thought of water, but they had not enough. All the things in the back of the jeep were soaked with fuel. There was only one thing he could think of.

"Quick, Edie! A hammock! Over the fire!" He ran towards the camp. He grabbed the machete and with two slashes cut the ropes at each end of his hammock. He flung an end to Edie and they raced to the fire. They held it over the flames, placing it to face where the noise was coming down over the hills.

Karl was there too, near to the fire, standing and looking towards the sound. His face was red, stupid, and smiling. He smiled and muttered and swayed a little, still looking up.

The helicopter was not right over them. It passed along the line of crags. They waited, still, in dread for any falter in the machine's fluffing beats, but the sound kept steady. It was passing.

"Always you wake. Always. Always. I was wrong, stupid … It does not matter … Power. Always. Over us … This marsh of crime…" Karl's muttering came to Robert as the last sounds died away. He sounded insane.

In case the helicopter might return, they ate their meals in darkness. Only some dull red embers that would be easy to stamp out glowed at their feet. They hardly spoke. Robert said that they might as well try to sleep after the meal; they ought to be up and moving again well before dawn. A chilly wind was now blowing off the plateau. He tried to persuade Edie to use his hammock and she refused.

"What will you sleep in then?"

"As I am."

"But it's going to be quite cold."

"Then—those." She nodded rather disdainfully towards the scatter of sweaters, anoraks, and groundsheets that Robert had pulled from the jeep, hoping to dry them a bit from the petrol.

They re-tied the cut ropes and reslung his hammock. When it was done, Edie went away into the dark. Robert, tugging on the last knot, watched the pale arc of cloth that they had strung sway in the moonlight. "All right then," he told her. "Goodbye."

184

She watched him curiously as he took his sleeping bag under his arm and went off with a bounding stride, searching in the faint moonlight for a place where he could stretch out between the rocks. "Where are you going?"

"I'm not letting you sleep on the ground when I'm up in a hammock," he said. "It wouldn't be right."

11

Karl's Capture

Robert only went over the next hill to sleep, but it didn't matter. A few moments later, they were all up. A flashing halo over a tree-fringed hilltop changed to two brilliant beads of light and the distant whine of a motor came to them again.

"Now they can see!" shouted Robert.

"They can't, stupid, we're much too far away," said Karl. "But what would it matter if they could? They're nothing to us, or we to them."

"Well, they are not going away like you said," Robert said angrily. "They are not on some other road: there isn't another road. We must be off this road; we must hide! Come on, Karl, there's still time."

He knew that he shouldn't be saying this as if he were begging; he ought to be ordering—or he should be just starting up the jeep himself so that Karl had to follow.

He was standing close in front of Karl and could just see, faint in the moonlight, that his face had a stupid grin.

"I say we should just ride it out," Karl said dully. "Chances are they'll pass us by on some other track."

"Look, they've just gone into the next gully. It's coming nearer all the time. There is no other track, Karl. Edie, tell him, for God's sake tell him—there's no other track!"

"There is no other track, Karl." Edie's voice came out of the dark. She sounded very scared. "Karl, Robert's right! We should have gone."

"There are lots of tracks," Karl persisted. "You can hide if you like; go off by yourselves. Go now. Try what you like, but if you do, whatever you do"— and here for a moment Robert heard a sharpness, a bit of his old self—"Don't think of me. I'll be fine."

"Listen—I think it's climbing a hill again. The light's flashing up in the trees. I'm going to take the jeep on, Karl, whether you come or not…"

"When I want you to lead, I'll ask you," snapped Karl.

"Edie! Get the can and put petrol in! A half can," Robert shouted. "I'm going to cut the hammocks down."

Edie ran to the jeep. Just then the lights broke out again on the near shoulder of a hill much brighter than before. The twin beams swung across them but then turned back up towards cliffs. The noise of the engine was very loud now, it seemed a roar among the rocks coming from all sides. It was some fairly big vehicle, bigger than a jeep.

Robert couldn't find the machete to cut the hammocks down. Where had he thrown it when he cut the ropes last time? Then he remembered they had used it for the dried beef at the fire. As he ran back, he saw that Karl was with Edie at the side of the jeep and heard him saying, "I'll do that. There's a knack to it. Come on, Edie, you'll spill it, you don't know how."

So, Karl started to pour in the can. Edie ran to the fire. She threw away the sticks and swept the ashes onto a groundsheet with her hands. The fire had been on the flat slabs where the road bottomed near the trickle of water. There was a burning plastic smell from the sheet.

"Don't bother with that," Robert said. He picked it up as best he could, with some of the embers and ashes falling out through the burned holes, and he tossed it behind a bush.

He stopped when he smelled something else besides the burning plastic smell from the groundsheet. Petrol.

"Karl! You must be spilling it all!" he said in agony.

"No, it's almost all gone in," said Karl cheerfully, peering down at what he was doing. He tilted the can up more to show that it was almost empty. Robert felt around the funnel. Well, he was surprised, it did seem to be going in. He bent down. It was splashing on his hands, his ankles. They were standing in a puddle of petrol that was spreading over the rocks.

"Stop!" he shouted. He stood up and shook Karl by the arm. "Stop, idiot!"

Karl put the can down and it rang hollow on the ground, nearly empty.

Reaching his arm in beside the back wheel he found that the rubber hose from the filler was detached from the neck of the tank—it must have happened when he tipped the jeep over. All of their petrol had gone onto the ground.

The roar of the coming vehicle was louder still, the light flashing on the treetops around them.

Robert shook the can. There was still a little there. He wrenched at the rusty body beside the back wheel and managed to bend it outwards. He went on his knees and forced himself between the wheel and the body.

Mud and rust showered on him and stuck to the sweat on his face and coldness spread up his thighs, soaking his trousers from the puddle of fuel where he was kneeling.

He wrenched at the rubber pipe and tried to get it onto the neck, but he could only just reach the pipe with one hand. He couldn't get it over. Then at last he thought he had it half over in a way that would let the petrol trickle in—though he could only guess at that from the feel—he was so twisted he could hardly tell which way was up.

"Pour it now—slowly, Karl," he shouted.

Then he knew that it still was not right: the petrol was splashing on the ground again and running down over his wrist.

"Stop!" he shouted.

"It's going in okay."

"STOP!"

Karl stopped. In almost his old voice, he said, "Well, it's not working. I'm sorry, Rob. It doesn't matter. We couldn't have got out, anyway."

There was a little more splashing by his hand and then silence. Robert felt the last of it shower down. He wriggled out and snatched the can from Karl.

"You shit," he said in fury. He shook the can and then threw it over the bushes, and then realized he shouldn't have because that was exactly where he had thrown the embers.

He waited a heartbeat, two. But nothing happened.

He ran to the driving seat and tried the starter. The engine started. He let in the clutch and the jeep jerked forward. At that moment there came a blinding light in his side mirror and light came out all over the rocks and trees ahead.

He stopped. It was hopeless.

The truck now had them in full view, its headlights blinding. He passed his hands over his face and hair to brush off some of the dust and mud and rust, and then he got out and went to stand with the other two at the back of the jeep, facing the lights of a lorry coming down the track.

Some twenty yards away, the lorry stopped. Behind the still blazing lights, the doors on both sides sprang open. Men came out from the doors and they were also jumping down from behind. Then six were coming forward in a row into the light. Robert could recognize two, one short and one tall. One was a mechanic who had looked over their jeep at Chalcie Wells, and the other was the tallest man in the group, the greyhound man from Bar Palace, Scoreman.

Robert, Karl, and Edie put up their hands.

A small man in the centre seemed to be in authority. He was one of three that held guns. A fourth man carried something that looked like a bunch of iron rings. Scoreman also had a gun.

The leader went on, "You three are coming with us. You'll come under guard in the back of the lorry. From there, Karl goes on—to the place he already knows. For you other two—where you go will be settled later. You will wait for orders."

"How did you think you could escape us, Karl?" This was Scoreman.

Karl still did not reply. Robert looked sideways at him. His face was red and he had a stupid, vacant grin. His hands had sunk from their position over his head, and he was holding them rather like a bishop who was about to bless.

"I'll remember this, Karl. That you would not answer."

Next the man in authority said, "Okay, hold it right there. Karl, first you must do this. In your jeep, you have a drawing which you bought in London. Go to the jeep and bring that paper out. Scoreman will be behind you. If you try anything at all, there'll be two dead kids here as well as you. Understand?"

Robert looked sideways at Karl as he nodded, his smile a bit faded now.

"Colonel Scoreman is not a patient man, Karl. If the thing is deep in your stuff, you'd best be very busy once you're there. And no tricks."

"I know what it is and where it is," said Karl dully.

"You might tell us for a start then. What's the picture?"

"Why it's a picture, a drawing. That's all."

The speaker didn't reply. He looked at Scoreman and after a moment's pause, Scoreman said sharply, "You know it is more than that." He took a step forward. "Now find it."

"No problem," said Karl. "I know where it is. But after I've fetched it, what?"

The short man said, "You hand it over to Colonel S here, and then we travel on the way I said."

Karl laughed suddenly. "What if I don't fetch it? What if I haven't got it… I hid it, I lost it—a ways back?"

"You have got it. But if you had done that you'd soon tell us—and tell us where, make no mistake."

Karl turned and walked towards the jeep. Scoreman stepped sharply forward then to one side and raised his hand. Meanwhile, Robert watched, hands still raised. Should he run if there was a shot? Was Karl going to run? What would Edie do?

There was no shot. He heard the front door of the jeep open, and the rustling of items in the back.

"Your friends die if you make any wrong move, brother. Fetch it out here quick, and no fooling."

"All right, I have it now, it's in this box," Karl said.

"Okay, out from behind the door then—" said a new voice. "Keep in front. Take it straight to Scoreman. And no tricks."

Karl appeared from behind Robert, holding in front of him the big matchbox that they had on the front shelf of the jeep. Then the small man with the big head also passed him, walking a yard behind Karl with his gun held level just behind his back. In the space between Edie and Robert and the other men, Karl hesitated.

"Now that I can see it in the light, I'm not sure I got the right box," he muttered.

"It had better be right," cracked the small man. "See to it, now—"

"This one seems to be full." Karl rattled it.

He opened the box and pulled at something in it.

"What is he doing there?" said Scoreman, suddenly loud. The small man moved to Karl's side so that he could see, because Karl was holding the box close to his chest. He stepped sideways, keeping his gun on him all the time as if held to him by a thread.

"It's okay. It's there," said Karl. He pushed the tray back.

"Throw the whole box here on the ground in front of me. Now!" said Scoreman, still loud and angry.

"Here's the whole jolly junket of a sketchbook—all that matters. Here it comes."

He said it sullenly and faintly mocking, and Robert's heart leapt. Something was going to happen. Karl's shoulder drooped, his arm swinging back for an underarm throw. Robert noticed then that he had two matches held under his thumb against the side of the box. A spark of light and then the box went flying—with it, under it, there flew two drooping arcs of light and in a moment, a huge tulip of flame sprang from the ground, engulfing everything within sight.

12

Edie

Karl and the man beside him were lost inside the wall of flames. The rest of the men vanished behind it. Robert staggered and leapt back as the buffet of exploding fuel hit him.

A man ran out of the fire to the side and rolled on the ground, in flames. It wasn't Karl. The great petals of the fire swayed towards Robert. He could hardly bear to face the heat but still peered into flames trying to see what had happened to Karl—had he gone from the other side?

Then he saw him, his head, wearing a ruff of flames and strange, looking like a skull, because all his hair was gone—crumpled into black dirt. The strange, blackened skull that was like Karl was shouting at him: "Run!"

Then, there was a boom like the beat of a huge drum, a glitter, and a splash of flying glass, a sideways rush of the flame that carried the face out of sight: the back of the jeep had blown up. With a sound like a sneeze followed by a roar, huge jets of flame flowed from its exploded windows and arched upwards. Within a black V, behind rocking yellow spires, Robert had a glimpse of the greyhound's profile, racing beyond the fire.

Again, Karl's voice came yellowing over the roar, "Run, can't you!"

Robert peered once more into the flames for Karl, shielding his face with his elbow, and could not see him. He looked around for Edie. She was gone.

He turned and ran for the wood.

Moments later, dazed and lost and trying to comprehend the last few moments, he was walking between high, rocky banks in the valley quite like the one they had camped in, except that it was dry of water.

He was utterly alone, in a strange land. And that, he felt, was the least of his problems.

Karl. I must go back and help him. Find him.

But he didn't know where "back" was. Everything was lost in darkness. He knew he'd run downward, and that he needed to go back up, but that was all. He put fingers of both hands over the ledge and hauled himself up. As his head came above the shelf, he saw a smooth brown thing close to his face, and then swiftly it came to him that the thing was a sole of a human foot. Almost at that exact instant, the foot hit him between the eyes, knocking him backward.

Ten seconds later he found himself lying on the rocky ground, with Edie's anxious face bending above.

"I didn't know it was you," she said. "Did I hurt you?"

"The fall, worse," Robert grunted, sitting up and holding his head. "I'm okay, just wait a minute."

He blinked and sat up, trying to regain his focus.

"I am afraid I kicked hard, as hard as I could. I thought you were one of them."

"Well, I wasn't," he said, still stupid from the blow. "You don't need to tell me you kicked hard." He was trying to twist out a smile for her, but the pain made that difficult.

"Oh, I am pleased to see you!"

He cracked a smile back at her, and just then, voices echoed nearby. The men were still there. "I think we need to get away from here. As fast as possible."

Her eyes went wide. "Oh, poor Karl. If we do that, how will we ever find Karl?" She looked around at him swiftly and then back down the valley.

Robert, at once, felt guilty. He knew that Karl was hurt, burned. But Karl had been so insistent that if something happened to him, Robert must go on alone...and deliver Edie home, almost as if he'd expected it all along.

"Edie, Karl won't even be trying to join us. You heard him talking about going with them. He needs to, because of his illness. He told me he's attached to Dr Paul, now, and can't live without him. I don't fully understand. And to me, he said as clearly as he could that we were to escape. I was to—"

Edie suddenly faced round on him. "No. That's horrible!"

Even to him, it sounded false. "But it's what he wanted. He said it many times. Almost the only sensible things he has said since his illness came on, have been about that. He pulled himself together, even when he was most sick, especially to make sure we understood that."

But now Robert too was imagining Karl lying somewhere, badly burnt, and perhaps dying. And he couldn't erase the image from his head.

"I don't know what we can do," said Robert urgently. "That's just the way they'll catch us, if we hang around here hoping to rescue him."

"Karl's badly hurt and you want to leave him? You'd really do that?"

He nodded. "I need to. To get you home. Really, Edie, Karl would be very angry if I did anything else. He's very worried about his promise to your mother. It's just how we're to do it, now that we're on the opposite side of the moors, that's the problem."

"I can get home whenever I want to."

"How? Where would you dare to try for a lift?"

"I'll walk."

"In bare feet?"

She nodded.

"Through all that rocky and thorny country? With bare feet? You can't, Edie."

"Of course, I could. I'd go around on the moors from here, not through the rocks. It's easier." She lifted her chin in defiance. "But I'm *not* going. Not until I've seen what's happened to Karl, and if there is anything I can do to help him."

She walked away, although not very fast. Robert hurried after her.

"Edie—you absolutely mustn't follow Karl. It's suicide." He put his hands on both of her shoulders. "You don't know what Dr Paul was trying to do when he made you sign that bit of paper. He was intending you to become his slave, just like he did to Karl. You'll end up like him."

She balled her fists tight at her sides. She bit her lip and looked at him as if at a mysterious animal. Then she turned impetuously away to stare again down the valley the way they had come up. Suddenly she stood rigid and listened. A loud whirring came to them, funnelled by the rocky walls. It was a lorry moving in low gear. It seemed close.

"They've started!" Edie said. "They're going on down! Quick, we must follow."

Before Robert could tell her it was madness, she turned down the hillside to the left. She dashed between the rocks and bushes as if they were completely familiar to her, although so far from the camp, it must be that she had never been here before either. In less than a minute they were among some big rocks that fell sharply away and looking out over the lower foothills. The drop was almost a cliff.

Edie paused there as if deciding how to descend.

"Edie! You are not to go down! You'll kill yourself!"

"You can't stop me," said Edie fiercely. "Coward!"

"I will stop you," said Robert. He grabbed her thin wrist and held it tight. She swung her arm about in his grasp though not with her full strength and he held her easily. They glared at each other. Then she tried to prise off his fingers with her other hand.

"Look, why did you run away last night, if you are going to give yourself up now?" Robert asked desperately.

"I thought Karl was running too. Instead, he's there, I know it, and he's hurt, he's hurt—" She was still struggling to open his hand. Then she stopped suddenly and looked out where he was looking, at the track.

The lorry was swaying across the open shoulder. It was out of the woods and going away from them. They were looking down into the back. Two men were standing behind the cab and holding on to the boards, their legs wide to keep their balance. Behind them was a folded green tarpaulin and on it lay a black, shapeless thing that looked like the charred trunk of a savannah tree, a bit crooked like trunks always were.

"Oh, it can't be Karl! It can't be!" Edie bounced up and down on the rock. Robert let go of her wrist and they both stared at the object in the back with mounting horror.

"Oh, Edie!" said Robert. "Why didn't he run? Why didn't he? I didn't think he'd be like this. I hoped he would have run out and rolled in the wet rushes—"

"It *is* Karl! He moved—he's alive!" She cupped her hands around her mouth to shout to him, but Robert grabbed her wrist.

"Edie, don't," he began.

Something was happening in the back of the lorry. The black log had rolled to the edge of the tarpaulin. It hunched itself into a knot. It was crawling forward, unfolding into a human shape. It was standing up. The blackened thing, Karl, stood there between the other two, his legs astride on the lorry's deck like theirs, swaying with them as the lorry itself swayed to the rough track. He was not even trying to get away.

Meanwhile, Edie was rigid, her eyes wet with tears. She stared out over the broken hilly forest where the lorry travelled, frozen long after it disappeared from sight.

13

Profession

Amazingly, Edie *did* know where to go, or seemed to, even though, as she said, she had never been in this part of the highland before or had taken any walk such as this one. From the first hilltop, she pointed to some high crests on the blue horizon, which was toothed with rock tors. She said that they should get at least as far as those before they slept.

"You mean, that's about a third of the way?"

"Yes."

"How do you know those are the right hills?"

"By the rocks."

"But we passed others like those in the jeep. How do you know those particular ones if you've never been there?"

"I know that's the direction we must go in and I know there are hills with rocks on the top on the way: I've seen them from the other side."

"Do all the girls of the region know these moorlands like you do, Edie?"

"No, I know them the best. I can find my way in this country better than anyone that I know."

The way-finding far-from-home look faded from her face as she said this, and she gave Robert a very broad grin.

"So, you're the best in the land and you know it, huh?"

"Yes, and I know why I am the best too. I learned from my father. He knew better than any. And he taught me."

"Your father sounds an unusual man, taking his daughter everywhere, especially in such wild places." He smiled. "My parents were the same."

"Tell me about them."

She leaned forward eagerly and listened intently as he told her of his parents, adventurers who had taken him everywhere, and died, seven years before, in that accident at the seashore. When he was done, she had tears in her eyes. Robert realized he'd never told a soul about that, and when he finished, he felt relieved, more than ashamed, and ever more drawn by the strange girl's face that had at first repelled him. "You miss them."

He nodded. "Sam and Linda, they—"

"Who are they?"

"My foster parents. I've lived with them all these years. They—" He shrugged. "Well, they don't make me too eager to go home. That's all."

After a while, she said, "I miss my father, too. When he got sick, things were never the same. It's been four years since I went off with him, and yet I remember every step of this place. Isn't that queer?"

He didn't find it that queer, as he knew exactly what she meant. Though he barely recalled what he'd done the morning Sam and Linda left for Spain, he remembered so clearly the adventures his parents had taken him on, so many years before.

By nightfall, they were in the higher hills that had the rocky tors but had not yet crossed the ridge. They made a fire at the foot of a small cliff above a stream and roasted wild sweet potatoes they had grubbed from the bottoms of stony screes beneath cliffs, under Edie's direction, along their route. Edie said that you must look for birds' nests on the cliffs first, then turn over the rocks and dig for them with a stick in the loose blackish soil underneath, pulling them from around the tangled roots of the plant, which at this season was very hard to see from above because it was all dried up. They carried the potatoes with them in a basket which Edie had woven on the spot from a leaf of one of the ground palms that grew amid the mountain grass.

"How do you know all this?" Robert asked after the meal.

"All of what?"

Robert waved his hand, taking in virtually everything from the red western sky where the sun had just disappeared, to the moorland hill spread out before them, and to the basket which still held the breakfast reserve of the potatoes. "Finding your way; knowing where potatoes are and what other wild fruits and seeds we can eat; making baskets in a moment just when we need them. Don't tell me your father taught you all this. I wish I could do such amazing and brilliant things for you as you're doing for me."

Her face pinked. "Don't be silly. You mustn't—"

"I'm not smooshing you, or whatever that was, if that's what you're going to say. You are amazing. Karl wanted me to look after you, but really, it's you, caring for me. If I were alone, I'd be half-starving by now, as well as lost."

Edie's eyes sparkled. She seemed to like being praised. But the reserved, sceptical look was still there.

"Well," she said thoughtfully, "you know quite well why all this is so easy for me. I live here. I have to know how to live on a farm. You, of course, from London, would be cleverer still."

"I don't believe I would. I may have had more school…"

"Of course, you'd be," said Edie, quick and bitter. "You know you are much cleverer really, don't you? You are just smooshing me."

"I don't know it at all."

"What about marktak? There, I see by your face—I have it wrong already! What roads were made, in the towns? Oh, *tarmac*." She was blushing. "You said all towns have it. Well, here, in our region, even St. Flor doesn't have any—and that is the biggest town I've ever been to, far away from us as it is."

"Tarmac's nothing. Forget it."

"It's nothing to you because you know all about it," she said fiercely, at once blushing redder. "It's the sort of thing I want to know. I cannot imagine it—you say a carpet of tar. How can you drive on that? You are from a different world from mine."

"The hell what anyone can see! School learning isn't brilliance. You seem to me almost uncanny at times, the things you see and know, and what you can do."

"Why, Robert, you are still being silly. I just have to know these things by being up here every summer, getting cloudberries for Mother to make jam to sell… Let's talk about something else. Truly, I do like it when someone says I am clever, but it makes me dizzy. I'm afraid that I like it too much. And how do I know why you say it?"

Robert tried to think of something else to talk about, but he couldn't seem to shape his idea anymore. It seemed as if something like this was happening to Edie too, as if the dizziness she spoke of affected them both. There was a long silence. Night fell over the moor. The embers of their fire were spread behind them and had mostly gone out—partly because they had had to scatter the fire in their search for the little blackened potatoes laid among the ashes. Robert felt more and more charged to say something, but this was very difficult. Yet, was it wrong to say something which was undoubtedly true, or for that matter, right that they should proceed together without his saying it?

Edie said suddenly, "I'm going down to the stream to wash. Will you wait here till I have finished, Robert? Then I'm going to sleep." She stood up.

"Yes. But Edie, wait a moment."

"Yes?"

"There is still something I wanted to say."

"Yes?" She looked at him strangely; he thought he could see a frown.

"Edie…I think I'm falling in love with you," Robert said quickly, trying to say it before she could either speak herself or start down the slope. He waited for whatever might follow his speech, which he had thought he would never have dared to say to anyone—at one time he thought he would die a monk or an unmarried scientist like Newton or Mendel. His heart beat so loudly that she would surely hear it.

She stared at him, really frowning, and then said, "Oh, this is hopeless! Not here!"

She took two steps down the slope and then stopped and looked at him again.

"I knew something like this would happen." Again, she paused, and then said rather fiercely, "And what about Valery? What has happened to her?"

"What do you—"

"I know that you two…you know." She sighed. "Boys *always* do, with her."

"I *don't* know," said Robert, not sure whether she had hit back at him more or less angrily than he had expected. "I don't know. I can't explain. There never was anything really… She was just—very pretty. It's true, I was attracted to her.

I know now that you are much, much—more right for me to love than Valery ever was. And so, what's happened now—is much stronger—by proportion."

"By what?"

"What?"

"What you said just then."

"Proportion? Oh, I don't know. I can't say that right. I mean, I think that what's happened—what *is* happening—is something..." He winced. He knew he was fouling it up, but he couldn't find the right words to convey this explosion of feelings inside him. "Uh, love."

"Oh, stop it, Robert! You only think you love me because without me, you'd be dead in a ditch right now." She stamped her bare foot on the grass. "And so, what do we do now?"

Without waiting for an answer, she went quickly down the slope.

He peered after her until he saw her, bent over the stream, splashing in the water. Then, she went off down the far bank and disappear around the first bend of the valley. He thought he would soon see her appear at the same spot coming back; but presently, to his surprise, she went away from him, up the moorland hillside beyond—an upright shadow moving fast on the slope. Her silhouette shone against the pale grass, running. She went over the crest and disappeared.

He sat down on the grass and waited for her. Misery and darkness made him recreate the horrors of the night past, the mistakes of the day, Karl burned and gone. How could he have said such things on such a day? She was right. Now he had made a worse mess.

He stumbled along the hill. He called "Edie!" as he went, but no one answered. Soon he realized that in the now almost complete darkness he was not even going to recognize the crest where she had disappeared. He scrambled up to the highest point of the hill he was on and, climbing up on some loose rocks, called out the loudest that he could.

Still there was no answer.

Then he went down to the stream and followed it back to the cliff. He sat down where they had been before and wondered when and in what mood she would come back the next day if she came at all. But she must come, eventually. It was true what he had said, that she was his protector rather than he hers. Even if she didn't care for him, she wouldn't desert him, after that, would she?

He felt the grass she had crushed. If she ever did return, now she would probably never sit so close to him again.

A moment later, he moved to the grass at the very foot of the rock face, where Edie had said it was going to be warmest through the night, and he stretched out there. Miraculously, it was warm, even while bitterly alone. Eventually, he fell asleep.

14

Love

Awaking again in a grey light of early dawn, Robert thought he heard an exclamation of pain. Craning his head back to look along the cliff, he saw Edie standing up and leaning against the rock. But when he rolled over—slowly because he was not sure what he ought to do—and sat up, she was lying down again, her grey dress heaped around her knees, one foot moving gently over the other.

He raked together the dead embers of their fire and found a live spark, which he blew upon until it rekindled the rest. He went to the dead tree they had raided before and brought more wood. Soon the fire blazed in the chilly wind. Sunlight was just beginning to illumine the moorland tops into the same thin bright colours as the flames.

He put more of their supply of potatoes into the embers. He was puzzled. He had made plenty of noise breaking off the branches of the tree. Go or come, angry or friendly, he wished she would give him some sign. She was still moving her feet so he did not believe she could be asleep. It wasn't like her to be resting while he was busy and it made him think there must be something other than just the anger of the night—was she sick, perhaps?

At last, trying his utmost to keep his voice steady and cool, and as if the scenes of the previous night had never occurred, he called, "Edie! The potatoes are ready. Won't you come?"

She sat up and faced him.

"Aren't you hungry?" he called again.

"Yes, I am," she called back. There was a strange flatness in her voice.

"Then why don't you come? Edie, you shouldn't be so mean to me... I am sorry... It was true, but I shouldn't have said it."

"I'm not being mean. Robert, you must bring me the potatoes."

"That *is* being mean. You're going to not eat with me."

"I'm not. I will. Oh, Robert, don't just stay there. Can't you come and help?"

He sprang to his feet and stared at her. It was hard to see, but she seemed to be smiling at him. No, in fact, she was wincing.

"If you want me to come to you, you must help me," she called again. "I think I've broken my ankle."

Robert ran to her along the slope. He could see immediately that one ankle was very swollen. He should have noticed it before.

"Edie! What did you do?" He knelt by her.

"A rock turned and my foot went into a crack."

"Where were you? Didn't you hear me calling?"

"Yes, I did."

"Was that before you hurt it?"

"After. You called from the rocks where I fell, and I was lying just nearby. I wouldn't answer you then because I was afraid. And I was thinking about what you said. That word."

She looked at him and looked away and he thought that she blushed. "What word?"

"What do you mean?" he asked.

"That word. You know."

"Love?"

"Yes. Here, everyone says—to girls—to be careful when you hear that."

"Why?"

"Because men who say it will hurt you."

"Oh, Edie! How could you be with me all these days and still think that?"

"It's not very long," she said sharply. "That's the whole trouble with you. You think it's an age. But I am sorry about it all the same. I was wrong to shout at you so last night."

"It seems like an age to me. And I've loved you much longer than I loved Valery—since we were at Picheery Dam at least."

"Oh, don't start. You're so silly."

She was shivering. The first thing was to get her to the fire. She leaned on Robert's shoulder and hopped along the slope. When she was sitting down again, Robert felt the ankle and said he thought it was only badly twisted. "A swelling like a plum comes up over where a bone breaks. I've had it at football."

"It does really hurt… Couldn't we just stay here all day, Robert? To see if it gets better? You could find more potatoes. And other things that I can tell you about."

"Of course, we could."

"Plovers are nesting. I saw where they are flying. I can tell you where to look for eggs. And, Robert,"—headlong, she went into another topic—"I really did know that you were kind and not dangerous, even when you were calling me in the night. I don't know why I was so afraid."

"Oh, it doesn't matter."

They stayed two whole days by the cliff. By the evening of the second day, Edie could hobble quite fast with the aid of a crutch, and they were sure there was no break in the ankle. That evening, their third under the cliff, there was a very beautiful sunset, and after that, the weather changed—here, it seemed, a red sky at night was more of a shepherd's fright than the English interpretation. Next day, a cloud was up over the whole sky, and Edie said that a storm or a mist was coming. Although that particular night had been warmer than any other, she shivered. She said her foot was good enough to walk on and that they ought to pass beyond the main ridge that day before the cloud reached them. On the "inland" side, it would be brighter and drier and also easier to find their way.

They were happy enough as they set off. They had gone about two miles up the valley, when Robert said, "I came to like that place. I even liked just lying there after we had eaten and looking at the cliff and the little plants that were on it. And that stream which kept on running even in the heat—and the tree giving us wood."

"I love the place too. And the things on the cliff. I always like plants in rocky places." Then she added, more to herself, smiling awkwardly, "You said that word, Edie."

"What word?"

"Love."

"I didn't. I said 'like'."

"*You* didn't, but I did. And in a way, by the place, my love reaches you."

Now even his arms swung stiffly, like the thing he had said, and the grassy slope was uncertain under his foot.

Edie crutched a few steps beside him and then laughed.

"Crutching is wretched. I think I'll just try to walk."

She tried it, but only for a few steps, and then stopped. "Yes, it was a lovely place, I did love it," she said. "Kiss me for that place then, Robert, if you want to? Just once."

Robert stared at her. The moor behind her had suddenly gone far off and had changed. He could only see her face, her smile, which now seemed a mixture of appeal and laughter. Somehow, he had moved on the unsteady slope of grass and was standing close to her.

"Just once," she said faintly, as if breathless. "And only here." She touched her cheek.

Her hands were held up like a boxer's. Robert kissed her awkwardly on the cheek, and as he did so his arms moved as if with a will of their own and closed around her shoulders.

"Once," she said again, and then in a moment, somehow, she had ducked and twisted out of his arms and was hobbling away from him across the short grass. "You mustn't think things are different because of that."

"I don't."

"Good." He was glad to see that she was still smiling. "It was for the place only. Everything is the same."

"I understand."

"Then let's go on."

But everything was not the same. Nothing would ever be the same. Robert carried the crutch and they had not gone far before Edie said, "Walking is wretched too. Perhaps I could try leaning on you."

"Edie!"

"Just leaning."

Robert knew, though. *Nothing* would be the same. Leaning together, twining arms like lovers, they fled from the grey-black sky that followed, looming over the cliffs they had left.

15

Storm

The storm caught them and drove them to the dripping heights where the tors were. They sheltered under one of the great slabs, although Edie would not let him kiss her again, or speak of love, or touch her except when they were walking. Robert felt happiness such as he had never known before. Instead of the aerial predators of the mist that they feared, rain and mist this time brought them only joy. The air was sharp and tense with joy. It spread out like ozone from the lightning that crackled on the rocks above and fell softly with the rain. The rivulets on the rocks were joy itself; joy trickled from over their heads, spilt among tiny plants at their feet.

Robert said, "If this is the highest place and the mist keeps down, how will we know where to go?"

"By the way the wind blows. And if it stops, by the side of the rocks that moss is growing on."

"Edie, you're shivering."

"So are you."

"Edie, couldn't we hold and warm one another?"

"No. I know very well what would happen." She paused and then went on suddenly, "It's not just you I don't trust, Robert. It's me. And look now. The wind's blowing the mist away! The sun will warm us."

Then they were out in the high moorland meadows alight with the most wonderful and strange flowers Robert had ever seen. Edie, bending beside him, told him name by name; she had names for every sparkling, dripping, swaying bloom.

"Who give them these names, even ones that have no use?"

"I never thought of why they should have names. Some sound like the tongue of the old people, like the names of our villages. And I expect some are made up by people like Mother and me, from the farms, when we come here to pick berries; or given names by the shepherds…"

"I don't mean just the big bright ones. What seems so strange to me is that these tiny ones all have names, ones that I would hardly notice if you didn't show them to me."

She gave a short laugh of puzzlement. "I don't know. But I think it must be people like my uncle Ramon who must give names to such dull ones. He says everything should be named, and he also says that every plant will also have a use, when we know what it is."

"Everything should be named? So even the stars, though there are billions and billions of them?"

"Yes. I suppose. Even the ones in the dark parts of the sky, the ones we cannot see. I'm sure all of them have use to someone or something, even if we don't know it, yet. We are all very small, aren't we, after all?"

That night sleeping six feet apart in the long grass, they talked not of names but of that forbidden word. Somehow it was allowed. Robert said he had never known what love was.

"And do you still not know?"

"I may. I'm not sure."

"Why are you not sure?"

At first, he would not say, but she pressed him and at last, he said it was because he had not felt what people seemed to in books. She was silent for a while and then said, "Then what is different from what they say in books?"

Again, he didn't want to tell her, but when he sensed that she was cross and saw that she had turned away, he said, "Well, in books, people seem to be better versions of themselves, when they are in love. And yet what I feel, makes me think I'm fouling everything up."

To this Edie said only that they must sleep, and now she really turned away and would talk no more. He had a feeling he had said the wrong thing again.

16

Stinging Grass

The next day they were in a lower, drier country although still quite high on the plateau and near to its rim. They came over a ridge to a shallow, straight valley, which descended slowly to their right. It had narrow woodland down and centre and open, scrub-free meadows on both sides. The head of the band of woods was about a mile away to their left. Edie said that it would be easier to walk around than go through the woods. Robert could not see why. He said he thought they should stick to Edie's original line and go straight ahead across the valley. But Edie was the guide and they walked around, even though this meant going not only of their line of march, but even a little backward. An hour later, exactly the same situation faced them again: another valley, another strip of woodland, gentler meadows both before and beyond it, and again Edie insisting on going away off to their left to get around. When it happened yet a third time, Robert said to hell with detours and why should they not go straight through?

"There's a plant there," Edie said.

"What? Is it poisonous?"

"No, but—"

"Then let's go. I'll hack you a way through with a machete so that you won't need to touch a single leaf or thorn anywhere. Okay?"

"Very well. Go straight through." She smiled at him sarcastically and sat down.

Robert descended to the meadow. Almost at once, he found that it was of a grass that was much deeper and coarser than he had expected: it was not exactly a gentle meadow. Soon, he was shoulder deep; the grass was very tough and would not cut easily. Under his gym shoes, the ground was soft and yet not wet. It was more marsh than meadow but was also dusty with some sort of dust that came from the grass itself. It was extremely hot, and the dust rose and settled in his sweat. He forced his way through the marsh until the woodland wall stood over him. This wood, too, was much higher than he had expected. And even at this point the unpleasant grass of marsh didn't end, it continued scrambling up into the creepers and the trees in an absurd kind of aerial meadow, parts of it hanging in festoons from the branches high above his head. He began slashing an opening through this wall of grass and bushes that blocked his way, heading for the dark shade behind. One of the grasses leaves cut his hand as he slashed. It was only a touch and yet the cut was quite deep, and it bled. He cut off the leaf that had injured him but as he stepped back, another grass blade caught on his elbow. He felt the pull of its sharp, hooked teeth and even though he tried to turn carefully to release it, it cut his elbow as it came away. Now he saw that this climbing grass was actually something very different from the grass of the marsh and was extremely sharp.

He gave a hard slash at the wall of grass stems in front of him, hoping to cut as many as possible. He did cut them—and the weight of the strands he had cut pulled on the grass meadow above him so that a great necklace of the climbing grass fell from a branch. Its coils and long, green, razor-like leaves wrapped him round as if a big and loose-woven basket had been dropped over his head.

Standing still, he heard Edie shout, "Robert! What are you doing?"

He didn't answer. Very slowly and carefully, with little slashes of the knife done mainly from the wrist, he began cutting off all the leaves that were touching him, one by one. As he cut, more of the grass settled down from above.

He was winning somewhat and was about halfway free, having suffered only a few small cuts, when he heard Edie shout again from behind, "Robert, what are you doing? Are you all right?"

Crouching, he turned around in the chamber he had made under the fallen coils of grass, and shouted back fiercely, "Yes, I'm all right."

And then he took a swiping slash at the stems that blocked his way out. These stems were cut—but by his movement, a grass left settling from above touched his ear and another his forehead. He was almost out: but then he felt something wet in his eyebrow. Cuckoo-spit from the grass, probably. He raised his hand to wipe it off and found it red with blood. In fact, the marsh ahead was showing pink through the blood that had flowed into his eyes.

As he shut his eyes, a sharp pain sliced across his eyelid. In a surge of panic, he crouched and then dived with his whole body for the open marsh beyond the remaining stems. He felt the leaf on his forehead pull hard back against his scalp.

When he stood up, he was out of the climbing grass and blood was pouring down over his right eye, wetting his hands and shirt. He felt his forehead and found a big flap of flesh hanging there. He pushed it back up with his finger, and with his bloody eye closed and the other open, he stumbled forward, spying Edie's horrified face coming towards him. Everything else in front of him was reddish and blurred with the blood in his eyes.

"Robert! Robert! What have you done? Didn't you see it was that grass?"

"What bloody grass?"

"Razor grass! I thought for sure you'd take one step and turn back!"

"You didn't tell me. What do I know about razor grass? Edie, look, quick, at my eyeball and tell me if it's cut."

"Oh! Oh! Robert!" She held her hand to divert the blood and then with her other fingers opened the eye. "No, I don't think so. There's a speck in it. Oh, I thought everyone knew about razor grass: I thought you would see it when you came close and would come back. Oh, Robert, I am sorry, sorry."

"I can't see anything, stupid. Can you help guide me out?"

She did, and outside on the slope she sat him down in the shade of a bush. She placed his finger against the flap of skin on his forehead again and told him to hold it there. Then to his surprise, she went back down the path into the marsh. He stood up and watched, incredulous, as her black head moved further out and at last vanished away among the brown heads of the grass. He shouted to her but got no answer. Then he noticed a branch of a tree moving right under the curtain of the climbing grass. She had not even taken the machete.

Presently she was back with a small old gourd shell and a leaf held to it with her thumb. She looked pleased.

"I found good ones," she said as she came up.

"Good what?" Robert eyed the gourd.

"Ant stitches."

"Ant what?"

"Shh. Hold still." She showed him how they were to work with the cut on his hand first so that he would not wonder what she was doing when she was sewing the cut on his forehead.

She slid the leaf on the gourd to one side. At first, there was only a black hole, for the gourd was dead and hollow. Suddenly, a rather large and hideous ant ran out of a hole, onto the back of Edie's hand. She caught it with her fingers and then slid the leaf back over the hole and gave the gourd to Robert to hold. She held out the ant to Robert so that he could see, projecting between the nails of her finger and thumb, and the ant's red head with fearsome gin-trap jaws gaped very wide. The ant's legs were struggling between her fingertips. She brought her finger-hold of the ant down to his hand.

"This cut doesn't need stitches really, but it will show you how they work."

Robert felt a sharp prick and Edie pinched her fingernails together and then threw something on the ground. He saw the ant's detached head stuck to his hand. Its jaws were closed through his skin, neatly holding the two edges of the cut together. Its antennae were moving but, without any body, the head was still in no mood to let go.

"Most people here know how to use these," said Edie, answering the amazement in his face. "Everyone here knows razor grass. But I was very stupid to let you go in there. I'm so sorry."

She began work on his head, making him let the ants out of the gourd one by one. Some of them escaped, but she had brought plenty.

Robert thought that he would have fought through many another wall of razor grass to have her stand so close before him and to feel her cool hands moving over his head: she could prick him all day long with the little biting buggers' heads if she would say "sorry" to him again in that tone that seemed to care. While she worked, she told him about the ants, how they marched in long columns, and how these big ones she had collected from the woodland strip were the guardians of the columns and stood at the sides. She could find the armies by listening to the calls of certain birds that followed them through the undergrowth, eating the insects that the ants disturbed.

While she talked and worked, her breath fanned warm on his forehead and her hair tickled his ear. Dust from the grass seemed to have worked into his skin even where the leaves hadn't cut it and it was hot and itchy. The touch of her fingers felt wonderful.

"I'd think you were cracked or were pulling my leg if it wasn't that you're actually fixing me with those crazy things."

"Let me see." Her hands pushed his head away and then pulled it close. He felt a soft pressure on his forehead and opened his eyes and saw Edie's chin just above. She was bending very close to him. She quickly drew back and stood up and said, "They're done now."

Robert put his hand up, not to the stitches but to where the soft pressure on his forehead had been. Then he felt along to where the strange knobs were holding his skin and then back to the other place. "Edie…" he said, but he was really speechless to say more.

"Now we must find water so that you can wash off the blood," she said, filling in his stunned silence.

17

Swim

They did not find water until late that afternoon after a very hot and thirsty march. Robert was so thirsty that he could not eat. It was because of the amount he had sweated in fighting the marsh and the razor grass. At last, from a hilltop, they saw keeper valleys folding to their left. Edie was puzzled about what valleys these could be, but said they were bound to save water. They followed a furrow of the grassland in their direction, moving even further to the north and west of their original line than the woods and the razor grass had forced them already.

Their high valley flattened and suddenly, at a bend by a small drop, they found indeed the stream that Edie had predicted, with marsh-loving maraati palms dotted in the gently sloping open grassland around it. Right below them was a spring that started the stream, gushing up, and yes, actually making a bubbling mound of water in its pool like a broken water main does in a street. The tiny pool of the spring poured over palm roots into another pool which, itself dammed by boles of other palms, poured into a yet bigger one bordered by slabs of sloping rock; after that, the stream set off down through the meadows of the valley, going towards what looked like some edge, or at least a steepening, where their valley plunged over into another and bigger one.

Robert and Edie threw themselves down beside the spring and drank from its pool. The water was wonderful, fresh, and cool. When he had drunk,

Robert braced on the edge of the big pool. Remembering Karl and the pool way to the north where the spider had been—he swung his arms, gave a long whistle, and dived from the upper dam of palm roots straight into the pool's depth. Actually, it wasn't deep, but was quite enough to swim in. He swam to the order end and stood up, waist-deep in the water.

"It's absolutely lovely!" he said.

"Why, you went with all your clothes on!" Edie was surprised.

"Of course. I need to wash out the blood—and wetness in your clothes makes you cool for a long time when you get out. Karl and I always did it. Why don't you swim in your clothes, Edie? Come on, it's deep. You can even dive."

He dived to show her several times and once held himself down to some palm roots on the bottom to surprise her by staying under the water for a long time.

Edie didn't come in right away although she looked longingly at the water. At last, she said, "Do men and girls bathe together in England?"

"Of course."

"But they wear special clothes, don't they?"

"Ye—es. But much smaller things than you're wearing now."

Edie seemed hesitant and sheepish. Robert had his shirt off and was flapping it about in the water to wash out the blood when at last he heard Edie dive. She came up some five yards away, standing shoulder deep.

"It's lovely," she said, throwing her hair back. She sank again and swam breaststroke towards him; her body and even her dark hair were lost in the black water, and only her brown face showed.

"Robert," she said, "let me look at your stitches now. Perhaps it was bad for you to dive."

She swam toward him. It was shallow near him and she had to stand up and walk for the last few yards. As she did, a startling shape came from the water. Her thin cotton dress clung so closely that for a moment he thought that it had slipped off and she was naked. Robert had seen ever since they first had met on her mother's farm, that, unlike Valery, Edie wore no bra, and now the outlines of her small high breasts showed under the dress almost as if nothing covered them at all. Her body was thin, reed-like, and very beautiful. Robert could not turn his head from her or hide his astonishment.

Edie detected his imprisoned look because when already near and leaning forward a little to peer at his forehead, she suddenly looked down at herself and then without a word, turned and swam back into the deeper part of the pool. Afterwards, she bathed there silently, not looking at him and not showing more than the upper part of her shoulders.

As soon as he saw that she was upset, Robert felt dreary and ashamed. He flapped his shirt in the water to clean it with much splashing to act as if nothing had happened. At last, he said, "Well, the stitches do seem all right, don't they?"

"Yes," said Edie, still not looking at him.

Shortly afterward, she got out at the far end of the pool and went away into a clump of bushes. Robert stood for a long time in the water to his knees, trying to flip minnows onto the shore that came to nibble his fingers. He caught some but they were very small.

Later, when they moved on, he saw that Edie had wrung out her dress to dry it as much as she could. It was clinging much less closely and was very wrinkled. She tried to walk at a distance from Robert and seemed cross. To his surprise, she was not leading them back to the dry ridges, but further down towards the big valley, following their stream.

When Robert asked why they seemed to be going still farther out of their way, she said, "I know where we are now. I am a very bad guide. If we cross this valley here, we will get to high moors again on the other side and after that, we are quite near to my home."

Robert tried to sound cheerful. "Edie, there seem to have been cows here. Look." He pointed to pats in the grass.

Edie said nothing. They went down. A herd of cattle came into sight, grazing on the slopes.

"There's a boy," Robert said.

"Where?"

"On the ridge, just above the cows. I think he's seen us. He's looking at us, not the cows."

"He'll be up there to drive the cows down. They may be milking cows: there's good grass here, and water."

They kept watching him, and Robert said, "He seems to have left the cows. He's coming down the ridge on our side."

They were on a dirt road across red fields. There was an orchard of orange trees on one side and a maize field on the other. They were walking fast because Robert was carrying a bunch of the maize cobs he had picked from the field and they didn't want to be seen by the farmer. Their road crossed the flat valley and branched at the far side. One branch led up the valley to the farm. They could see buildings in a grove of high trees. There was a big log there that had been cut with a chain saw into the shape of a seat. It looked inviting—civilized—in all this wild, and he wanted to rest on it.

"Couldn't we camp somewhere here?" said Robert.

"We ought to go higher, and be on the moors again," said Edie.

"Why, that's where the danger is, isn't it? And here we could get some more food in the morning to carry with us—we could even go to the farm for it."

"I think we should stay away from these farms. I do not know these people."

"Edie, please." *I'm leader*, he thought, *I should be telling her, not pleading.* But still, he went on, "Maybe it's the blood I lost or something. I feel whacked, Edie."

They climbed the bank. The grass was like a shaggy rug thrown over the knoll. Its velvet leaves were sticky to the touch and dotted with red road dust. The whole mat was soft and springy. There was a palm on the hillock that had a bitten-looking trunk, so bitten it was a wonder it could stand. Behind the palm, the ground dropped a little, so they were out of sight of the road. An old rusty barbed wire fence—a single strand—passed the palm and crossed the dip and ascended the hill behind.

"Edie, it's really soft here," said Robert, stopping again. "And we're well hidden."

"We can't make a fire."

"We can eat maize raw. The sprats too. We've only to last one more day, Edie. And when we're in the hills tomorrow, we can make a fire and roast more maize that we'll take up with us."

Edie stopped too, her back to Robert, and looked away to the west. It was very quiet and nothing had passed them on the road. The sun had already gone behind the hills.

They sat and ate some maize. The first half of the first cob tasted good to Robert but soon he thought he didn't care for it much. Still, he forced himself to eat two whole raw cobs. A little better were the fish, which they ate raw and whole, along with mouthfuls of maize.

"Why are you cross?" Robert said, biting at his second cob, holding it with both hands.

"We should be farther on."

"It's not just that. You were cross before I even thought of stopping here."

Edie didn't answer for some time. At last, she said, "It was a mean thing to tell me to come in and bathe while you were there. You knew what would happen."

"What *did* happen?" Robert asked, but at once saw such anger gathering in her face that he went on quickly, "Well, I guess I know—but really, Edie, I didn't know, or I wasn't thinking. Anyway, I hardly saw you."

Edie hissed, "How can you lie like that?"

"Like what?"

"Saying you hardly saw. Do you think that I did not see you?"

"Of course, you saw me. Why—?"

"I mean, that I didn't see how you looked at me?"

"Oh, Edie, what does it matter?" There was a pause and he said, "Edie! You are lovely! How can I help looking at you? And it wasn't a trick. We neither expected it. You have to believe that."

"Perhaps I do believe that. But you are not sorry."

After another silence, Robert said, "Really, I don't understand all the hiding and the shame we have about our bodies. I understand those feelings," he added to this hastily, "because I have some of them too. But I can't see why people can stare at, say, a sunset and say, 'How lovely!' and yet aren't allowed to stare at each other and say the same?"

Edie smiled but still eyed him drily and sceptically.

"You know very well why looking at sunsets is different from looking at—what you said you wanted to look at last night," she said coolly. "Looking at sunsets doesn't go on to anything that matters."

"Then what does looking at people go on to?"

After a moment's pause, she said quietly, "You know that very well too. Babies."

Robert hadn't expected this and couldn't think what to say. After a moment, he burst out laughing. "Babies? You know that is not what I want."

She laughed rather harshly. "I'd be surprised if it was." She sighed. "The thing of it is that you are taking your time. We should've been to my home by now. And yet you are straggling...and I don't know why. Don't you want to see what can be done about Karl?"

He did. He *had*. He'd thought about that often. But he'd also settled in his mind that he was on this mission to deliver Edie home *for* Karl. And once she was safe at home, he'd be alone in a strange land, and that was when the real uncertainty would begin. He wasn't sure what he'd do then...in fact, he'd been putting off thinking about it for that very reason.

Before he could respond, she looked away up the hill that they ought to have climbed. Robert thought with delight that she might have turned away because she was smiling. But then her eyes fixed on something.

"What do you see up there?" he asked.

"There is that boy again."

"What do you mean—again? The boy we saw was on the other side?"

"It looks like the same one. See! You can see his head over the grass. He's looking at us. Now he's gone. I think he saw that I'd seen him."

"How could it be the same one? We would have spotted him following on the road."

"He could have come across in the orchard."

"Damn him! I wish he wouldn't follow us about. I suppose he's just being nosey."

"I hope so. He hasn't had time to go to the farm and tell anyone yet..."

"I suppose we *are* a bit rare. Just think, two people, looking dirty like we do, come out of the hills on one side of your farm, go straight through your dad's fields, and start up the hills on the other side. It's not surprising he's curious."

"We haven't gone up. We should have."

He stood up. "I'm going to talk to him and find out what he's up to." He set off fast up the hill.

"Be friendly to him," Edie called after him. "Don't hurt him."

"Yes. Of course."

In a quarter-hour he was back. Edie was sitting on the grass.

"I saw him, but he ran off. He went towards the farm. I don't think he will come back." Robert let out a deep breath. He had been thinking the whole time since he left her, practicing his speech. "Now Edie, you must listen for a minute. I'm not trying to change you or anything…" Again, he petered out.

"Robert, please don't," said Edie faintly. "But you and I can never be."

"Why never?"

"Never, never, never. You don't see how different we are."

"You mean, I've had more education? That's nothing. You have things I can never have." He waved his arm at the hills and the sunset. "I don't understand all that you do out here anymore than you understand London."

"You never lived on a farm like ours," Edie went on in a softer voice than Robert had heard before. She plucked at her skirt. "I'm sure in London, girls' hands should be soft. The town magazines say this too, that hands are important—I saw one that Valery had, and it had a picture about cream for a woman's hands. Look at mine."

She held out her hand. He seized one. "It's lovely, like the rest of you, like the way you talk, all of you…" He was feeling the palms and fingers. He bent his head down and pressed her fingers to his cheek, first the palm side and then the back.

"Let it go!"

"It's soft as can be. All that is nothing, nothing, Edie. My mother's hands were like yours—much more so…because of her gardening and her work at the hospital. I loved her because they were like that."

"Your mother!" Edie's voice was still faint and now indignant. She stood up, and Robert stood too. "Let it go!"

He let it go, but suddenly, in some way he did not understand, her shoulders were inside his arms and his cheek was brushing her hair. Her hands were there in that boxer's position pressed against his chest. She was rigid and her fists pushed him back.

"Edie! That is all nothing. You must believe me."

Suddenly her body changed, was soft in his arms and he was holding her up. Her whole body pressed against him. He held her right and saw with amazement the top of her head leaning slowly back just below his eyes, until, in the faint light of dusk, her face came into view framed by her dark hair.

He whispered, "Edie! Edie!"

"And we in such danger!" he heard her say. Her lips were parted, her eyes were huge and black, as she pulled away from him and rushed off.

"Edie!" he called, but she did not turn.

18

A Visit

Robert wakened to the noise of a vehicle's engine running, not far away. There was a light on the trunk of the palm above him, bright against the black and still starry sky. Raising himself a little, he saw rivers and islands and haloes of silver on the grass. He sat up quickly and found headlights blazing at him through the tops of the undulating carpet.

A child's voice said, "One is there. The other is yonder."

He didn't hear the response, but he knew the voice. It was, unmistakably brusque and low, Dr Paul's.

His eyes went wide, searching the area around him. Where was the machete? He cursed silently that he had not laid it beside him.

The top half of Dr Paul came into view, a stooping black silhouette edged with light. He was looking down at Edie. Then he came towards Robert. Robert lay and feigned sleep, watching through half-closed eyes.

He paused and kicked in the grass and stooped and felt around in it with his hands. He set off up the hill, and Robert saw him jerk something up from the ground. All around, even under Robert, the grass mat shook: Dr Paul had pulled upright one of the fallen fence posts. He came down the hill again, going hand over hand on what must be the fence wire, although Robert couldn't see it. He was pulling it up from where it was buried in the grass; at every step, he gave it a rough jerk so that the grass shook under Robert again and again. He stepped over the fence wire once again and turned to go back to Edie.

Robert sat up and groped in the grass beside him. He said as steadily and clearly as he could, "If you make one move to touch her, I will shoot you."

Dr Paul swung about to face him. "Oh! You are awake," he said. "I was dismayed that you did not come with your friend Karl."

"Drop the machete you are holding," Robert said through his teeth. "Drop it now."

"You don't have a gun," said Dr Paul coolly, peering at him through the half-darkness.

"I have a gun. Karl's. Drop the machete."

"Karl had no gun."

"You are wrong, he had—and I have it here." Robert's voice threatened to waver, though he hoped that the darkness of his hollow was enough. "I tell you for the last time: drop the machete."

After a moment's pause, Dr Paul said, "Then I this, if you that. We should talk, not play at guns and swords. I am not your enemy—not yet."

Robert lowered the right hand that he had held up. He saw a faint flint of metal in the starlight as Dr Paul tossed the machete into the grass.

"That's better. Now we can talk," he said. He stood with his feet apart and his back to the light, looking down at Robert. "Young man, you are not of these parts. You are not even a Santanian. Certainly, you are no enemy of mine. You may go back to your country in peace. But I also warn you: whether you go or stay, do not try to interfere any more with me or my people."

"Suppose I refuse not to interfere."

"Foolish boy. Don't try to play a part with me. You do not know me yet. I am power. Robert, I esteem your boyish spirit, your willingness to challenge facts and the opinions and courses of your elders. I have no wish either to break or to extinguish you. So here again is my main advice to you: go home. I say it yet again. *Go home.*"

"Not after what you did to Karl."

"Do not worry about Karl. Luckily, I am fond of him and he came to me in time, and I assure you he is happy. I am caring for him, and you need not fear about his burns." The outline of his face softened, and Robert guessed he was smiling. "I came to my farm here today especially to await you. You brought this girl, Edith, with you, who, as I believe you know, has already agreed to be mine. You brought her to my farm. You have eaten my crops... Do you know that in the USA, farmers may legally shoot trespassers that they find on their land?"

Robert wondered if, in a dash for the machete, he could reach it first, but he remembered the agility the big man had shown at Cintra. He said, "I told you that if you touch her now—or any time—I will shoot."

Paul only chuckled. "'Or any time,' you say. I guess you are feeling your own weakness when you say that; in fact, I can hear it in your voice. For me, to-morrow, another week, another month... I tell you I will take her when I wish, and you cannot stop me... Like Karl." A pause. "Go ahead, shoot me now."

His face was black; the light was behind him, but Robert could imagine the smile there: he was not so cool now; he was even a little drunk with his belief in himself, like he'd been at the Bar Palace. Robert answered him, "I never killed anyone. I hesitated because of that."

"And I'll add one other reason—quite apart from your not having the gun that you boast—killing me would not protect her. I think you guess this already, but we may as well have it clear. You would exchange only a benevolent king for the pitiless wolves of the king's guard. Oh, they are waiting, I can assure you. Your little Edith will fare far worse in their hands than in mine. And you also."

"You mean your private army and air force? Where are they?"

"Not far. And let me tell you this, Robert," he went on in an unexpectedly familiar tone, "there are many of them. They will take it out on dear Edith first; then the mother, Liberty Oliveira; then, I guess, that other child, the pretty sister whose name I have forgotten..."

Was there a hesitation, some slight flaw in his confidence? A hint even of disgust at his own threats, threats which, perhaps, he was contriving on the spot?

Robert bristled. "Those names are nothing to me. I hardly know who you are talking about."

"Do not be absurd. What is it—nine days with Edith? And how many of those did you spend with her sister?"

How did he know this too?

"Edith would go with me. We'd go far beyond the reach of your thugs. I'd take her to London."

The man laughed. "You think that London is beyond me? Have you forgotten our conversation at the Bar Palace? Did I not tell you about my flat in Westbourne Terrace? Little you know me yet… In any case, Robert, the long and short is this: You dare not kill me."

"To rid the world—" Robert started again between his teeth.

"Come, this is enough. I have limited patience at midnight. You and I should both be asleep. I came to tell you, out of an unnecessary kindness, what I felt you should know. Power does not need to make explanation, nor apology. Guard the good fortune that has saved you, Robert. You hardly know what you have escaped. And look, I make you still one more concession; tomorrow, if you wish, go to Pike and find a carrier to take the girl to her mother: that way you may discharge your obligation to her in good conscience. I am not sending for her yet, and—who knows?—my need for her help may never come. But at Pike, you must take the road for London. Do not come to my country again and do not lay foot on my land, here or elsewhere."

He turned and walked off toward the lights of his vehicle.

Robert went to Edie in the grass. Dr Paul stood still and watched him. She was like a black smudged question mark on the ground, upside down. He stepped beside her, looking where he could sit down without disturbing her. He sat down, still and upright, and watched to see what Dr Paul would do. Then, he lay down carefully alongside Edie. He was between her and the doctor and just behind her back.

The man shrugged, turned, and walked away. After a moment, there was the noise of the jeep engine. Robert watched the beams of the lights go off the silvery grass and swivel like searchlights over the orange orchard, lighting the massed and golden fruit. Then the jeep was gone.

Robert lay for a long time on his back, tense with anger, listening and thinking. At last, he turned towards Edie and nestled himself deeper into the grass. Edie turned over and came into his arms. She was asleep but restless. He tried to move away gently, but she seemed to struggle with him, and yet all of the time lay heavily on his right arm. As they moved, he found he had come to lie on her hair. She was close, her breathing warm on his skin, and there was a strange smell to her that made him wild and drunk; his temples throbbed and his brain hummed as if he were breathing ether. He ached to close his arms about her; not only to repeat that evening's earlier feverish drawing in and holding, but so that, in torrents of a new caress, he could drown for a moment thoughts of his own vileness and treachery, and his weakness and fear in the face of crime.

He cursed silently and tried to herd together thoughts that had gone wild-scattered like sheep, and to draw his focus away from that strange scent and the curves that he could dimly see. Thinking fiercely about plans, he succeeded at last in finding sleep.

EDIE IS CAPTURED BY THE HELICOPTER

19

Capture

At the first light of dawn, she awoke and found him there and was very angry, and Robert, only half-awake, stumbled after her as she walked away. He tried to tell her what had happened in the night but as he followed, he noticed the boundary fence wire was still deeply buried in the sticky grass and the broken posts were lying on the ground with the veined, delicate, red earth runways of the termites upon them, undisturbed. Had it just been a dream?

Next, they quarrelled over which way they should go.

Even if he had dreamed it, Robert said they should go over the moor as fast as they could, straight for Edie's home—hadn't she said that it was not far away now? Edie said that the sunset had foretold a change of weather, a mist, and, because of that, they should go down the valley to the HPD, take lifts to the Bar Palace Hotel, and then walk to the farm. When he explained his reasoning, she said she did not believe in any new threat from Dr Paul—all that was just a stupid dream and an excuse.

"Then all the more, why not over the moors? You admit it's a far shorter way and yours will take two days at least."

"Because of the mist."

"Look at the sky. It's going to be a clear day like all the others."

"It means mist or rain, Robert, I know it."

"But there are no clouds now. You see how high the cattle are here, and herdsmen. They don't fear the hills."

"I thought your dream told you why herd boys in his valley might not happen to be safe," she said bitterly.

"So, you do believe my dream after all? Do you think now, perhaps, that we may be standing in Dr Paul's own farm?"

"Oh, I do not know. I do not know any people in this vale. I'm afraid of Dr Paul, but I am still more afraid of the helicopters. I don't want to be up on those heights between here and home in any mist."

They went up the hillside near where they had slept. As they climbed, Edie said, "Now, I am glad we are going this way, after all. I will be able to see Mother and Annie and my birds this very night." She climbed strongly like she had done when they had gone onto the plateau the first time.

A soft rain was beginning to fall and distant parts of the plain were blotted in grey. Edie said they could follow a gully down to the right: it was likely that the trees and bushes would thicken up there and give them cover. They did this, but the going was slow due to the deep bracken and thistles and a bayonetty stuff that Edie could not run over with her bare feet. They trotted a long way. It was fairly slow. Edie was limping more and more.

Robert caught Edie's elbow and they stopped. He pointed left.

"What is it?" said Edie in a low voice, catching his fear.

"I saw someone there in the mist. He moved. I can't see him now."

They both peered into the mist where Robert had seen the faint grey upright shadow but could see nothing. "Is it that boy again?"

They trotted the opposite way, going as quietly as they could. Edie took Robert's hand but held it only for a little way because it made it harder to run.

"Look! There again! It's brown! Edie, what is it?" Robert was whispering now. "It seems like a dwarf."

Again, Edie had missed it.

"He was so close, he must have seen us. But he moved off. It wasn't the boy." It really was a mist now, less than before, cloaking around them so that they could hardly see.

Edie was looking at the ground. She snapped her fingers.

"What?"

"Wait! We are coming to a channel. Then we will see. They will be there."

"Why, we should go the other way!"

"No, wait. It is just here."

They came to the edge of a gully and with their first steps down the slope, there came a thudding of hooves and surge of brown and white shapes like deer passing below them and clattering up the far slope out of sight.

"Antelope!" Edie said. "That is what your others were too. I should have guessed before. It is all right."

It was not all right for long.

This was the last gully that they saw. After it, they were on open moor—bare grassland without even the fern. There was heavy mist again and light rain. At last, stooping over a stone, she raised her head and after a moment said, "Robert, I hear something."

They both listened. Soon it was clear. It was the fluttering engine of a distant helicopter. Robert looked at Edie and saw that she was white—white as he had not seen since Dr Paul had bent that black beak of his loupe over her at Cintra.

Shivering, her voice faltered. "We must run back. This is a very, very bad place to be. We must get back to those gullies and try to find trees and ferns to hide in. The wind is slowing, and that's bad too."

"But which way is back? Where is the sound coming from?"

"I'm not sure."

She stooped over her stone, straightened, faced one way and then another, lifting her white cheeks to catch the wind. The noise of the helicopter was coming rapidly nearer. The mist was clearing just a little.

Edie started running. "This way!"

"It's going by behind us! It can't see us!"

"There's another! There's two! Not so fast, Robert—I can't—because of my ankle!"

"Run in front. I'll follow. We must keep together now, Edie—all the time."

She nodded, breathless.

The mist cleared suddenly, and a helicopter appeared, high up in the blue sky between scarves of the low cloud or mist that was sweeping across the moor. There was a gully with bushes and a set of tree ferns looking like bright green fishermen's umbrellas along the stream a quarter-mile down a slope to their left. The helicopter banked and swooped lower, turning towards them, its tail held high. Another scarf of mist blew over them. They couldn't be seen now but neither could they see. Edie ran with an uneven, galloping movement and Robert ran quite slowly to stay with her. They crossed a gully, but it wasn't the one they had last seen; it had no trees of ferns. Robert could hear Edie's gasping breath. She ran straight up out of the far side of the gully ahead of him.

The helicopter was very loud and low now, just to their left. Its beat had changed, perhaps it was hovering. Then the mist lifted again, speeding away in the wind to the front, and there again was a blue sky. The tops of the tree ferns bowed and there too was the helicopter, banking and turning to follow them. Edie lost her limp and ran flat out for the trees. Robert tried to look back to see where the chopper was coming and caught his foot in a rain channel. He felt something tear in his shoe and stumbled, sprawling on the ground. He jumped up at once, but his shoe sole was off and flopping. As he tried to run again, he tripped on it once more and fell.

There was a cage hanging from the helicopter. He flattened himself on the ground when he saw it. As the machine passed close over him, the wind of its blades buffeted his cheeks.

As he scrambled to his feet, somewhere, Edie screamed. He spotted her, somehow down to the right of him now—she must have swerved. She was racing for the gully again, the chopper swaying after her like a hawking dragonfly, skimming ferns. It was small and agile, and the light cage swung below, like the grabs used for lifting rubbish to the jib of a crane.

As he ran, he pulled his broken shoe from his foot and threw it off. He ran again, but now had to run limping like Edie, so he had to stop once more to throw off the other shoe. He raced barefoot, faster than he ever had before, following Edie and the machine.

Edie tried to swerve again but stumbled and fell. In a moment, the helicopter had checked above her and come down. She screamed again and again, flat on her face and clawing at the grass, as the dangling cage was dropping over her. The cage broadened as it touched the ground, and even over the beat of the rotor and the engine he could hear the rattle of its metal links. The helicopter was bouncing in the air a little over the cage.

"Hold, Edie!" he tried to yell.

He ran, clawing the air to reach it.

He couldn't, though. As if bouncing upon the cage, the helicopter sprang skywards and in a moment was above him. All hope of touching it, of grasping its bars, was gone. Edie was above, lying in the cage except for one of her arms, which reached out between the blunt metal spikes that had closed under her. Her fists held bunches of grass that she had pulled up and her white face was frozen in a soundless scream.

"I'll find you, Edie!" Robert bawled at the top of his voice, as he watched her lift higher into the sky.

He stood still and fell into a panting that seemed to split him apart. *Oh, why could I never run?* he thought, over and over; *Had I been Vic—any of the others—I'd have made it, I'd be there: I'd be on the bars, riding on the top, and I'd go wherever she goes.*

Another cold scarf of mist came over. Edie, the cage, and the machine vanished into the grey, leaving Robert alone in absolute, deafening silence.

PART 4

Volcano

1

The Farm

When Robert saw the horseman coming, he slowed to a walk and moved aside, head down, to let him pass. Of course, the man would surely pass him. He knew he looked a fright, dishevelled and dirty, carrying his big knife, his eyes wild and queer.

Sheep bleated on the slopes as the man's horse neighed and tossed its head at him. When Robert thought the horseman was far enough behind him, he broke into a run again. But something must've aroused the horseman's suspicions, because he'd run only fifty yards when he heard the beat of hooves on the road behind him.

"Boy, are you out here all alone? What happened to you?" the man said, not unkindly, when he pulled on the reins and slowed the horse beside him. "You look like a wolf's son."

Even so, Robert could not trust him nor tell him of the day's terrible happening. He forced his frenzy to die a little and felt in its place a heavy weight that seemed to press somewhere beneath his shoulders and deep in his chest. He stood still and silent, facing the man. Despair drained like a cold liquid down from his head and hardened in his limbs. *Edie.*

The man lifted him onto the horse and brought him to a small farmhouse. He entered a bright farm kitchen where a woman stared at him.

"What is this?" she asked, first the man, and then him directly.

He sat very upright on a seat beside the table. No one spoke for a long time. The farmer tapped his fingers on the table, waiting. When Robert tried to leave, the man turned him back from the door almost by force and made him sit again at the table where the woman had placed food. He ate, watched by three silent, wide-eyed children. He choked back nausea and ate because he knew that he would soon need it, and after a little, he ate with real hunger.

The woman beckoned to one of the children and explained something in a low voice. The child was reluctant but she insistent until at last the boy ran from the room. Soon, he was back carrying a broad leather belt. The boy put the belt on the table beside Robert and ran out as before. Another child was called away and then a worn-out pair of boots were placed on the floor beside Robert's feet. Lastly, with the last child, came a leather scabbard for his machete, dusty as the belt.

After he had finished eating, he unthreaded the long woody root that held his trousers and put on the belt. As he did, in the side of his vision, he noticed the woman making gestures, as if in some kind of sign language, towards the man. The man raised his eyebrows in a question, and the woman made another sign with her hands, and the three children filed out of the room.

"So, it was a friend that you lost," the woman said, coming up to him. "A helicopter came and took her away?"

Robert faced her as he had before and did not answer. His throat felt tight and sore. He thought of his promise to Mrs Oliveira and Karl and wanted to weep, but he didn't have the energy to do anything more than stare.

"Was she young? Your age? Or older?"

Robert shook his head.

"A girl then of these parts? Of the Vales?"

Robert nodded slightly. The woman relaxed a little, but her next words sounded sharper still.

"Was there anyone else with you?"

"No. Only we two."

"Why were you there?"

"I was taking her home."

"Why? Where was her home? From where did you come?"

"I don't know. We had travelled far together and became lost."

"How was it you escaped when she was taken?"

Robert did not answer. The man said, "You should reply to that. How came you to escape without your friend?"

Robert looked at him and then burst out, shaking his head as he spoke, "I did not want to escape. They did not want me. I ran and fell. My shoes broke..."

Now he hung his head and tears pricked his eyes, thinking of running to help Edie, and his failure, and the cage, pulling her farther and farther away from him. But he couldn't cry, though a great sob still gathered in his throat and nearly choked him.

Then the woman asked him many other questions, most of which he answered, until at last she said, "Do not think that we disbelieve you. Though your ways and your manner of living may not be ours, we see that you speak the truth and have a feeling of great sorrow. Everyone knows that a great evil had come into these parts. It began with the new road that they are building. Here you are far from the hills where your companion was taken—yet that place you describe, the moor with the flat channels, is the nearest to this farm it has ever happened. Your story makes us afraid."

She said more, but Robert did not hear her. He was still thinking of Edie's face, the way she looked, face pale, eyes wide, gripping the metal bars as she disappeared into the clouds.

After his meal, Robert lay on a bed in an empty back room of the farmhouse, staring up at the ceiling. It was now long after nightfall. He spread his limbs to make the heat more bearable, but it never happened.

A moment later, he could stand it no more. He got up and quietly moved to the window. He lifted the latch that was on the inside and found that the shutter was swinging free. Good. Slowly he swung it wide open. Then he took up his boots from beside the bed and, as quietly as he had opened the window, he climbed onto the sill and jumped for the soft ground below. The herbs were cool under his bare feet. He groped his way back from the house until he touched the trunk of a big mango tree and looked right and left. No one. He slipped on his boots. He passed the backs of several houses, stumbling among bushes and spiky pineapples, dreading the bark of a dog. Then he stepped out into the dusty wheel tracks, still moving as quietly as he could until he was beyond the last house of the town. At last, he broke into a run, under the stars towards where great Orion dived for the pale triangle of the road and the dark trees.

WAS IT A SAINT'S DAY?

2

Vascoma

He managed to hitch a ride in a lorry in the morning. Not long after, they passed Taxim's Bar Palace against its forest wall of tree trunks, under the sea of leaves, and he thought about Annetta. Then his mind went to Karl, and then to Edie, where it stayed.

He'd lost all of them, one by one, and now here he was, adrift.

The driver must have noticed Robert's hands gripping his knees with whitened knuckles because he said, "Relax, son. Relax. We'll be there in time enough, you'll see."

But he could not. Oh, the others were hardened; they could fend for themselves. But not Edie.

The driver spoke non-stop, warning him of a coming desolate stretch of the road. There would be thirty leagues empty of habitation: first, great forests over low hills until he reached the rocky gorge mouth of the Furnace River and the ghost village of Gullet and then the ox-bows of the Vascoma itself. Beyond this began the foothills of Elmin. The road climbed to a great height on the shoulder of the volcano. From the account, it sounded as if it went to the very snows. On that shoulder, too, must be those loose slopes where, it was said, the bulldozed cuts could slide away for a half-mile under the wheels of a lorry. From there the road passed over and down into a drier country but still ran for a long stretch without farms. Then came a town called Cashie Flats. At Cashie, good land would begin again; there were bamboo savannah and rich sugar farms. Before that, he would see a fruit canning business—nothing near it, but desert itself, and after the town an alcohol refinery, with nothing likewise.

"And how far from Cashie Flats to St. Flortwy?" Robert asked when they finally had to part ways at Chalcie Wells.

"Forty. And four days."

"Forty what? Miles?"

"Why, leagues, boy. What are miles?"

"Miles, why everyone—"

"I know miles. We have no use for them. Keep miles for London."

There was a pause and then Robert asked, "Isn't there another place beyond Gullet—another mining village—called Diamond Creek? I heard there was, and that it is abandoned, too."

The old man raised his head and his eyes showed not whites really but yellow; and they were streaked with the red of meandering veins.

"Diamond Creek," the man said slowly at last. "And what business have you at Diamond Creek?"

"I haven't any. It's just a place that I got to hear of."

"To hear of. Boy, what heard you of Diamond Creek?"

"Well, for instance, that once a man found a huge lot of diamonds there. And that he buried them."

"And that he buried them." The tone in which he said this seemed to bury them again, and, with them, to bury a conversation that had gone on too long. He scraped his unshaven upper lip with his long yellow lower teeth and gazed over Robert's shoulder. Suddenly, his blank stare was gone and he looked eagerly downward, as though seeking the disturbed soil where buried diamonds might lie. Then he rolled the yellows of his eyes up to Robert again and said slowly, "Boy, if you were told by strangers about Diamond Creek, I'd pass it by."

"I was planning to. But no one does live there now, do they? Isn't it a ghost camp, as they say, like the one at Gullet?"

"As they say… I know nothing o' that. Gullet's no camp. It's a town—it was, and I wish you may have a good journey."

No sooner had Robert shut the door of the lorry, the man took off, leaving him in a cloud of dust.

So, Robert travelled on until he reached the last town that was not a ghost town. As he walked along its only street, he thought that none of them, living or dead, were towns anyway— just rows of hovels. He went to the petrol post to wait for a lift.

There, Robert sat under a tree to wait. It was a fair way to St. Flortwy, yet. Across the road was an empty football pitch. It had coarse, patchy grass over orange soil. At the side of it, not far down the road, was a church built of red brick. It was shaped more like a mosque than a church because of the cross on the top of its dome. Over its door, a graceful palm tree, and ladies in dresses bright as jewels in the sunlight were passing under the palm and going inside. Was this Sunday? If so, he hadn't known it. Or was it some special service, a saint's day perhaps? Or a wedding? The darkness of the door swallowed up the bright-clothed people. He fell to wondering if Edie possessed dresses as bright as those to wear on Sundays. He could not imagine it. He thought of the limp, clinging cotton dress he knew so well. Then he thought of what might be happening to her now and could not bear it, so he stood up and walked to and fro in front of the pump and the shack and a corrugated iron roof under which the mechanic was working on a tyre.

Dark visions painted the beaten ground under his eyes. The brilliant light that had fired the luminous dresses had become blackest night. Sweat ran on his face and seared his eyes and dripped from his chin and his eyebrows. He saw Edie's face as he had last seen it, distorted into a scream. It was silent, as it had been then.

Shaking the horrible thought away, he became aware of real silence around him: the clang of the mechanic's levers and the thump of his mallet on the tyre had ceased. He looked up and realized the mechanic was looking at him queerly. There was the sound of a distant heavy lorry and a dust cloud could be seen rising among the alms at the far end of the village.

The driver was all too happy to give Robert a lift, and they passed the afternoon in silence, headed south. More blue hills came up in the south like ships on a sea horizon. First, they were unreal mesas, sliced by clouds and vistaed in the long converging tree walls of the road; then they were nearer and rising over the forest, even over the greatest trees, all across their front. It was a mass without limits, with a grey drape over it and huge clouds piled above. Silver of sunlight dulled on the cloud tops as the travellers went in underneath.

Now more and darker shapes showed, blurred under the cloud, a hunched mass of hills. Hills were behind hills, and hills riding on hills' shoulders. A clearance showed chevroned valleys going up and up, a velvety forest that was blue and silver in a flash of resumed sunlight. Grey mists drifted off, like steam from a doused campfire. Now the clearance was widening, silver, tinted pink with the later sun; a firework of sunlight exploded up over towers of clouds to their white tops, blossoming in a sudden pale blue sky. And there in the gap, far beyond, above everything, whiter than the white cloud on which it rested, an icy cone…

It was Elmin. Robert gasped to see it so high; and he could not understand how the cone was rounded as he saw it here; where was the flat edge, marking the crater, that he had seen from afar? Then he thought, *I am looking up at it now, the crater is farther still, up beyond those curved icefields, still far out of sight.*

A witch's sleeve of lower cloud closed the gap and the vision vanished. As if conjured by the same sweeping, violent arm, the ramparts of the plateau swung with the swaying movements of the lorry frontwards and crawled to the feet of the mountain. Only in Chinese paintings had Robert ever seen, ever imagined rocks such as what was now raised before him. Pinnacles leaned darkly together, capped with trees. They were monkish conspirators, hidden in cellars of the closing cloud.

He watched the clouds, thinking of Edie, disappearing into them, and twisted in his seat. "Edie," he muttered, his lips trembling.

"Say again, mate?" said the lorry driver, slackening speed.

"Oh, I'm just off to myself. What's that gap between those two—those two big hunks of rock? Where does the gap go to?"

"They call that Furnace Canyon. The river comes out there. Comes down out of the Vale country, off of all the moors," he shouted over the noise of the engine.

"Okay, but if that's the Furnace River, where's Diamond Creek? Isn't that around here, too?"

He felt the man's glance on him and an answer withheld. They drove in silence for a while. *People here sure are sensitive about Diamond Creek*, Robert thought.

But at last, the man said, "See that other white cliff up there, more in front, against those hills behind?"

"Yes. Pink, isn't it, really not white?"

"Sure, mate, you can call it pink. It's getting sunset. So what? Anyways, that cliff isn't as close to the mountains as it looks; it's way out this side. It's over Diamond Creek." He looked around at Robert as though sizing him in some way.

Again, they drove on in silence a few minutes. Robert was thinking that that was the cliff in Dewey's sketch, the same crag. It was beautiful. Somewhere below it must be the hanging green valley where the hut had stood; where he and Annetta had lived, and possibly, where a trove of diamonds was buried.

He heard the man say, "And there's the mighty Vascoma."

THE COLOSSAL HORSESHOE

They were breasting an edge. A flat forest lay between them and the hills. Across the flat lay the river. It was bending to the foot of the crags and the mountain, washing at the black limestone, the ash, and the diamond clays. It was a colossal horseshoe thrown into the forest, steel grey in the fading light, a lake in size, but with the stiff sweep of a river. Farther ahead it appeared again, but only as grey flecks in the black forest—ox bows perhaps, or braided channels around a maze of islands. To the right of these flecks was another block of the high country, a real mesa this time, not very high, but cliff-sided at the top above forest slopes. The river divided the mesa from the mountain. Perhaps it was ash of the volcano choking the path that was breaking it into those channels, like a delta. Out to the right of the mesa and beyond it there lay the endless sea of forest that he had seen before from the plateau edge. But then it had been under a dull and serene sky. Now, the smoke-like black clouds rushed in towards the foothills of the volcano, scarf behind ragged scarf, fighting over the land.

"Wow. It's some river. It's even more beautiful than I imagined. Everything is here. Everything wants to be here. Even the clouds."

"Not people, not most of 'em. There's two things you haven't seen yet."

"What?"

"One's the dead camps. Only it'll be dark by then."

"And what's the other thing?"

"The long legs. Skeets. Biters. Every kind."

"They won't change what I think," he said, as they drove into the gathering dark through a forest of furious and tumbling luxuriance.

3

Mosquitoes

The brakes of the lorry creaked and hissed and creaked again. He slumped forward, braced himself, and looked up. The engine idled and a door slammed. He must have been asleep. They were on a downhill and had stopped.

Lit by the beam of their headlights, there was a long wooden bridge ahead and he could see the driver walking out on it. He was walking on one of the two separate plank causeways that were made to take the wheels of traffic. There was nothing between these planks and nothing outside them, only the trestles of the bridge and blackness from which came the sound of fast running water. The driver kicked at the boards. Some were loose and when he dislodged any, he kicked them back into the line again. He reached the far end and came back along the other causeway, testing it as before. Beyond the bridge, at the farthest reach of the headlight beam, were some rickety wooden huts up against the forest wall. They looked dead, windows covered with creepers that seemed to want to swallow them whole.

Over the noise of the water, he became aware of another sound, a rather vibrant whine. At first, he thought it was inside his head, some part of the headache that he had. It became louder, but he ignored it, wishing he could go to sleep again, but his companion's inspection above the river made him worry that the lorry was about to undertake a perilous path he should stay awake for.

As he yawned and stretched, it felt like soft feathers were brushing his face. He put up a hand to see what they were and at once there was redoubled whine all about him with a pinging note added to it that he hadn't heard before. Mosquitoes! He slapped his cheeks and passed his fingers over his shirt. There were clouds of them, in his mouth, all around. They were there like a feather duster that someone was teasing him with, touching him and whisking it away. The feathers touching his face suddenly seemed prickly and his cheeks began to feel hot and heavy with bites. He wound up the windows of the cab and slapped his face again and all over his shoulders and arms and pressed himself against the seat so that they couldn't bite him behind. He held up his hands to the reflected light and saw that they were smeared dark with squashed bodies and his own blood. With the windows closed and the warmth of the engine under him, the sweat sprang from him in streams. It didn't stop the mosquitoes. They went on, stinging his legs like they did his face and his arms, biting through his trousers. He slapped his calves, his thighs, his knees, everywhere.

The door opened and the driver dropped into his seat behind the wheel.

"I always check a wood-trestler before I go out on it. Just one wheel down through a board can finish you out here."

He revved the engine.

"You weren't kidding about the mosquitoes," he said miserably. "Where is this place?"

"Why," the driver eased the motor and looked round at Robert. "This is your Diamond Creek."

"It is?"

"Want to stop, hey? Look for diamonds, like I said? Go up the creek to-morrow? Have a nice peaceful sleep first, hey? Plenty of huts here to choose from!" He waved a hand frontwards and chuckled.

"NO! I have other business here."

"Business of what kind?"

He frowned. "I'm searching for someone."

"Who?"

"My business is my own. And look, how do we get these damned mosquitoes out of the cab?"

"I told you," the man said laconically.

"God, what do we do when they're like this?"

"Just move. Once we're across and moving, they'll soon be out."

"So, we've passed Gullet already?"

"Five mile back. Houses all empty like here. Same problem. I didn't wake you, though I thought the bridge over the Vascoma would. That one's a real banger. Steel." He revved again and they jerked to motion.

With the timbers creaking and cracking below it, the lorry went slowly onto the bridge. The spans dipped under their weight and the trestles swayed— the whole thing was a zig-zag. Robert gripped the handle of his door, goading his limbs to be ready for a jump.

No jump was necessary, fortunately. After the bridge, there were some steep little hills and then flat again. They must be back on the flood plain of the big river because here were the flood-dumped logs once more and the diversions. Later, through layers of sleep, he was aware of a long, long ascent, the engine roaring it seemed for hour upon hour. He was cold but managed to awaken enough to close his window, and then he was hot again but still sleepy. Opening his eyes briefly, he realized the lorry was going over the flank of the volcano.

There below him, a hundred yards away, was a big double-storied farm-house with barns behind it.

"That's where I leave you," the man said, seeming all too glad of the fact.

Robert climbed out of the lorry and thanked the driver at the road, then walked the rest of the drive to the farmhouse. It was a square building that once had been plastered and painted white. Now the plaster that was left was yellow and brown and much of it had gone, showing crude brickwork underneath. The roof had the same curly tiles that Robert had seen at Souls. The farm was very old. It was similar to others which Karl had pointed out to him north of the plateau. They had been built for plantation owners in the days of slavery. And in fact here, behind the barns, he could see the roofs of a low line of huts that would have been for the field slaves to live in. Beyond the farm was a vivid green marsh, strange to see on the sloping foot of a volcano.

To the left of the farmhouse was a well-beaten drive which must lead to the main road, perhaps a mile or so back from where he had stopped. He hadn't seen the turning, but that wasn't surprising; there were many turn-offs into small beaten tracks, some of which led to farms while others just evaporated into the savannah. On the side of the building which faced the fence, he could see the corner of a lean-to-patio with a carved wooden railing. There was another shed on that side, separate from the barns and newer looking, although built in the same style. To one side of this building, was a neat vegetable garden with thriving eggplants, okra, and tomatoes, as well as some less happy-looking cabbages. The garden caused Robert to warm to the farm. It made him think of Mrs Oliveira's homestead and Edie. And yet, although so friendly and beckoning, the garden and the whole of this unexpected level land had an almost surreal look: it was so green in contrast to the savannah behind him, and so surprising the way it backed off into a level blue haze where he expected to see the rising slopes of a mountain. The silent red house was as in a dream and seemed to be pulling him to go to it.

An orange tree was laden and bowed with fruit, and the ground under it littered with still more. The tree glowed with its abundance. But as Robert looked, it seemed to him that all the finest oranges were higher up, just out of reach: no doubt the farm people had picked the best from lower down.

He looked down again at the farm. The house was silent, as though deserted, but he could hear sounds of cattle somewhere beyond, perhaps at the barns. Silent as it might be, he felt sure the building was lived in; water had been splashed on the ground near the well, making a dark patch, and there was similar darkness along the rows in the garden where the plants had been tended to. The garden didn't look so much like Mrs Oliveira's after all; it was too neat and square and too clean of weeds. It was an oddly laid out garden to find at an old farm. Indeed, he didn't like the place so much now. It looked lived in and neat, but in some way, eerie.

Was someone watching him? The small windows of the house were all dark. They had no curtains, he couldn't see any more there, but he knew how a person could easily stand at the back of a dim room and look out without being visible. But then, why should they? Really there was no one, and anyway, why should anyone mind him taking a few oranges off this loaded tree?

With both hands, he grasped a smooth-barked branch and shook it. The branch seemed to shake back at him as if it were alive; it released a load of fruit, far more than he had expected. Oranges came tumbling down around him, thudding onto the ground. They seemed to go on falling long after he had stopped shaking, as if he had triggered some mechanism hidden in the trunk. The thudding of the falling fruit was quite loud, and sure enough, a dog barked somewhere beyond the farmhouse. He realized there was a man on the corner of the patio, half-leaning, half-sitting, on the rail of the balustrade and facing inward towards the part of the patio that Robert couldn't see. He wasn't looking at him now, but Robert had a strong feeling that he had looked and had seen him. He certainly hadn't been there before; he had probably come out at the sound of the fruit falling. Robert watched, standing very still, but the man did not look round again. *Probably he has seen me and he doesn't mind me taking them,* Robert thought; *but probably, too, I'd better go down and say something. I can ask for a drink of water at the same time.*

When he reached the level, he clapped his hands. The man looked up and the noise of barking behind the house redoubled. It sounded like a lot of dogs, but they must've been penned, somewhere.

"What do you want?" the man asked. He had a countryman's clothes; Robert thought that he might be the farmer or the farm manager.

"Would you mind if I took a few of the oranges from your tree up there?"

"What brought you here?"

"I was down on the road waiting for a ride. Then I saw your tree and I thought it was wild. So, I came hoping to pick some. I'm very thirsty."

"Where are you going by bus?"

"Oh—to Criteery."

The man said something to someone who was out of sight on the patio. Then he turned to Robert again and said, "Take all you want. Shake the tree and take what you want, and go."

"May I have a drink of water from your well too?"

Again, the man spoke to the person whom Robert could not see. "Not from the well," he said to Robert. "That water is not good. Take it from the filter,"—he pointed onto the patio—"but be quick. Men are in conference here."

Robert went around and up the steps onto the wooden decking. There were two people there besides the man he had been speaking to. At the far end, a man in sunglasses and a light clean jacket was sitting in a wicker chair. On the flat rail of the balustrade just by him, there was a glass and a bottle. Between him and Robert, a hammock was strung across the patio and another man was sitting in it, facing away. Robert could only see a few wisps of sandy or grey hair over the top and two big feet in black sandals underneath.

Robert went to the filter which was on a shelf against the wall. The man in sunglasses watched him rather coldly as he filled his glass and drank. All three men seemed to be waiting, as if by silent agreement they had suspended their talk until he should have gone.

Robert filled his glass and drank a second time. "Thanks, that's lovely. It's wonderful how cool it keeps. I'll rinse the glass." As he filled the glass again half full, the man in the hammock stirred. Robert ran his finger around the rim, swirling the water in the glass, then went to the rail of the patio and threw the water out onto the red beaten earth of the yard. He turned to take the glass back to the shelf when he noticed the big man had stood up and was looking at him with a surprised smile.

Dr Paul.

Robert did not smile. He tried to keep his face calm and flat and to let his limbs complete the action which they had started. He went towards the shelf and placed the glass down.

"So, you came to see me," Dr Paul said. He looked hard at Robert, his eyes narrowing, although his smile did not change. His stare, his look, somehow brought Robert to a standstill in the middle of the patio and made him turn to face him again. "Perhaps you were seeking me?"

Robert was too stunned to speak.

"Welcome," the man went on again, after a pause, "I am glad that you drink my water and that you come in peace." He looked at the glass in Robert's hand. "You should not trouble with that washing; leave it, the servants will do it. But do not leave us yet. Sit down and talk."

He waved to a chair with a cowhide seat. Then he swung the hammock up and over himself and put it behind with an easy gesture, hardly stooping as he passed under. He seemed suddenly much closer to Robert although he had moved only one stride. Dr Paul sat down in the hammock again, now on Robert's side, spreading his feet wide on the floor. He was wearing a light pink shirt and a narrow black belt that held up cream-coloured trousers. His bare feet were in big, loose leather sandals. He leaned back in the hammock and beamed at Robert who, for his part, did not smile or sit down.

To the man in sunglasses, jerking the words over his shoulder and not taking his eyes off Robert, Dr Paul said, "You see that we are acquainted, this young Englishman and I. I would introduce you, Spence, except that he has never told me his name. Why he has not told me it, even after all the meetings and the conversations we have had, I do not know. But sometimes I feel that my liking for him is not quite reciprocated. I think that he distrusts me a little." He laughed.

He spoke clearly, but his speech had a soft edge, a drunkenness, likely. *And I am not the only one who is distrusting; see how he watches me.* Just as Robert thought this, the man's smile vanished. He looked towards the man whom Robert had seen first and who was now standing behind him. He seemed as if he was going to speak but said nothing, only frowned a little and pursed his lips. In a moment he had turned back to his companion in the wicker chair; the stiff look was gone and the smile back again.

"Name or none, Spence, you should know this young man. He's sharp as a tack and one to go far. Pour him a drink. You, lad, sit down and join us. Relax; join our discussion."

Robert didn't move.

"Pour for him, Spence, pour. And we have ice. You had not expected ice on this farm, I think?" He was addressing Robert again and he paused, pouring him a drink, which he pushed over to him. "When you came, young man, we were talking—"

"Where is Edie?" he growled.

The smile faded. The man gave Robert a cold look and went to replace the glass he had brought beside his own. He brought his chair under the ropes and placed it by the steps of the patio and sat down there.

"Now, that's unkind. I thought you had more manners than—"

"I know you and your men took her," he sneered. "Caged her like a wild animal. Enslaved her as your own. Does your friend know that?"

There was a beat of absolute silence, and then the smile returned to Dr Paul's face. He did nothing but shift his eyes slightly to the left, at something behind Robert.

It was a signal. Suddenly, there was the sound of footsteps, drawing closer, guns being cocked, and dogs, panting with a blood hunger.

Without a moment's thought, Robert broke into a run, leaping over the balustrade. It was a long drop and he fell on the hard ground but was up again in a moment. Before he could dash for the orange tree, a dog came around the house's corner on his side and then another, closing in fast. He swerved from the dogs and ran past the patio again heading for the barns. Dr Paul stood at the balustrade, pointing and shouting with a red face and slicing a finger through the air towards him.

When he reached the open barn door the first of the dogs had already closed its teeth in his trouser. The brute's weight made him stumble but he crashed against the door and did not fall. The dog was still with him when he gained the inside and slammed the door against the bared teeth of two more rushing at him, to a furious barking and scratching outside. He kicked the dog that had got him, hard several times with his free foot and it ran whimpering into the darkness. The barn was high and dim and almost empty, except for the far end where there was some hay—and over there by the hay was a streak of sunlight around another half-open door.

He ran to this door and swung it open and found himself looking out onto a moving pavement of grey bodies. There were fifty or so cattle pressed into the V between the two barn buildings. They were pulling down hay from a rack just below the level of his feet.

There was a raised path between the wall of the barn and the drop to the rack and the ground where the cattle were, and on this edge stood a man with a pitchfork. He was a dirty, small man and he looked at Robert with surprise and dislike. They stared in silence for a moment and then the man came forward, levelling his fork and dropping the hay that was on it and waving the points as if Robert was an animal that must be herded back into the barn.

Out beyond the massed backs of the cattle, Robert could see the big fence and beyond that the sunlit savannah and the mountain rising into cloud. He stepped down onto the top wooden rail of the rack and set off running across the backs of the cattle. They were sharp and unstable; it was like running on floating logs or worse because the cows he had just stepped on were heaving wildly behind him and the shock of their movement went through the herd faster than he could stride.

He missed his footing and fell between them, thudding against the hard ground, hooves kicking and churning close to his face. As he scrambled to his feet, he was caught between two brown barrel-like sides and carried along with them as they surged for the open, pressing together in the mass. All at once, the brown sides parted and his feet hit the ground.

Finally free, he took off for a small metal gate in the fence. The gate was padlocked, something he saw from a distance away—still, he reasoned it would be easier to climb there.

As he reached it, the barking of the dogs came loud and furious. They were coming round the barn. The cows ahead of him checked and came rushing back. Now, barking came from the other side too. The cows checked yet again and then for a moment it was as if the herd of fifty had exploded to a thousand: cows were on all sides of him, rearing, and running, bellowing, and trying to flee from the dogs which were dodging the hooves and trying only to get to Robert.

Three were at him again when he reached the fence and when he started to climb, one bit at the cuff of his pants. Again, halfway up the wire and clinging outstretched as one crucified, he kicked at it savagely with his free leg and it dropped away. Others jumped at him and he kicked as they came.

A twang in the wire near his hands sent a violent sting through him. He let out a cry as the sound of a shot rang out from behind him.

Ducking instinctively, he saw the man with sunglasses was not wearing them now. Instead, he was kneeling by the balustrade, shooting a pistol. *I'm hung like a target for him,* Robert thought frantically. He gave a last kick to the dogs and turned and climbed. Another shot and again the wire shook and a dog fell, howling. He swung a leg up and then lay along the fence top under the barbed wire and rolled over; his shirt and trousers tore but he dropped.

A furious firing from the farm, many guns now, broke out as he ran clear of the mess of dogs and cows that were milling beyond the fence. He sprinted for the nearest belt of trees.

He plunged into the wood and scrambled down through the trees and creepers to the little stream that he knew would be there. He ran up the stream keeping to the water but with the bottom rocky and slippery and the turns that the stream took. He swung up a sapling onto a tree trunk that was fallen above the stream and balanced along it to the far slope. He ran at that and up and out of the wall of the wood into grassy savannah beyond. The narrow woodland was a screen against the farm. He ran uphill towards a crest.

He hit something very hard with his knee as he landed on the branches and he fell forward and rolled on the pile. It had not been springy as he had expected. But he had been lucky, he was all right; it was only a bruise on his knee. He shut his eyes. It had been quite a drop and he could easily have fallen badly on the stump or whatever it was under the branches and might have broken an ankle or a leg.

When the pain would let him, he stopped holding his knee and turned over, but as he straightened, it hit him again so that he doubled up once more, now on his back. He had rolled down between the tailboard and the pile of branches. He now saw that he was lying on a green tarpaulin which was covering something hard and knobbly, under the branches.

His feet touched ground and he swung forward and dropped. He could not take the speed and went down forward on the hard rock. Not too bad. Then he was up again and was running and skipping and limping for the trees at the left. He climbed among broken rocks and tangled vines. Once under the trees, it was very dark because of the great crag overhead. The grey bulk was shelving out over him; it was overhanging here, and indeed, under the trees, seemed almost like a cave. Shortly, it was a cave; he could see it now; he would be able to rest here and to nurse his knee, and there might be trickles of water on the rock that could quench the thirst that had been plaguing him since his run from the dogs. He stumbled forward into the dim opening, slipping on old rotted leaves that lay thinly over the smooth rock. There was a breath of moisture and coolness in the air. Then, as his eyes became more used to the dark, he spied what he thought to be the rock wall of the cave on his right was a wall of dark and rotten-looking wooden boards. He touched the boards, and they were indeed wood, and his fingers came away black with a damp slime of the algae on them.

"People may have once lived here." He breathed the words aloud.

"People may have lived here," a sharp voice said beside him, "still do. Put up your hands. Stand where you are and don't move. I am right behind you. Don't move, don't look round or I'll shoot."

A man had come out of the darkness and he was holding a small black gun. Robert stood still with his hands up and the man went behind and prodded him in the back. "Keep your hands up and don't move," he said. Keeping the cold hard thing that must be the muzzle of his gun pressed into Robert's back, he ran a hand down the outside of each of Robert's thighs, pausing over his pockets. He lifted Robert's machete out of its sheath and let it clatter to the ground. Robert heard someone else coming in through the trees the way that he had come.

"Move," his captor said. "Move straight ahead and when I tell you, start turning to the right. Don't try anything; this little thing just wants to get you and it'll shoot out your spine." He poked Robert in the back again and Robert started to walk.

"So, we have him," another voice said behind. "After all that fuss."

He knew that voice. It was Dr Paul.

HUTS AT
DIAMOND CREEK

4

Prisoner

It was daylight when he awoke and even from where he lay, he could see treetops out of the windows, waving in a breeze and lit by sunlight.

He guessed that he would be on the first floor of the big farmhouse. His room had one armchair and one narrow bed where he lay. It was like a barrack room. But here, instead of the lapboards and wallpaper, there was cracking white plaster and paint. It was clean like the barrack rooms had been too, but unlike them, it was light and airy. There was one picture on the wall. It was a painting showing an out-of-date small propeller aircraft in the background of clouds and sky. It would've been a pleasant room to awaken in, if not for the chains on his ankles, tethering him to the frame of the bed.

His wrists were free, at least. He moved his arms widely to feel their freedom and then used his elbows to help him to sit up. He strained to look out of the window. He could see, far off, between the nearby mango trees covering a level landscape until, right at the skyline, a blue hazy line of mountains were sloping upward.

He looked at the fetters on his ankles and stretched down and handled them. After some time, he concluded that there were just three things he could think of that would easily get them off: the right key, a hacksaw, or a sharp file. He looked around the room. Of course, there were none of these things here, nor anything like them. So, the fetters would stay on. Next, he looked more carefully at the metal frame of the bed. It was clear there was no way that it could slide off.

He lay down and tried to think. Sitting up for even a few minutes had given him a headache, and already he didn't feel as well as he had when he had first woken up. The second his head hit the pillow, one thought hit him, square between the eyes.

Edie. Edie was here. She had to be.

Stupid, he said to himself. *Of course, you'd run into Dr Paul and be unable to keep your cool and blow it. Now how are you going to save her, like this? You're likely in just as bad shape as she is.*

He sat up once more. *Was he?*

He thought of the construction of his old iron bed frame at home. Before long, lying on his back on the floor beside the bed, almost under it, pushing up on the main frame, he wriggled the legs of the bed back and forth. Eventually, he began to feel a looseness as the old paint broke and a conical metal dove-tailed joint came loose in its socket. At last, with a crash and a clatter, the joint at that end came free.

Holding the loose chains so that they wouldn't drag on the floor, he shuffled to the door. Of course, it was locked.

He shuffled across to the window and now, standing, found himself looking down past the branches of a mango tree into the beaten earth of the yard. To the right, he saw the two joined barns he had run to when the dogs were after him. Looking to his left, mostly hidden behind the tree, there were some other low buildings. He paused to listen but heard no sound except but a bird's call, coming faintly through the glass. It was a bit like when he had first seen the farmhouse—oddly silent and eerie.

The window was not locked or barred and opened easily. Now the call of bird—a jay, he thought—came clearly. Another was flashing blue and green among the leaves of the fruit trees farther out.

He leaned awkwardly from the window. It was quite a drop, likely more than one floor. Too far for a jump.

He wondered if he might climb to the tiled roof whose eaves were just above his window and would be within reach if he stood on the sill. But he remembered how simple and square the house had been as he had seen it from the orange tree: there would be no lower roof to jump down onto.

Then, still looking at the tiles, he noticed that just under the eaves there was a projecting board that ran right along the wall. It had one inch or so projecting above the drop. A very strong person might just get along it going hand-over-hand. Of course, there was the window he had to pass, but that might even be a help. If anyone was in there, he had had it anyway; if there was no one, he could take a rest.

He thought of the apple tree in the garden at his home in London, and of how, to get away from his foster parents, he'd spent quite a bit of time doing pull-ups there. He did fifteen in a row, most days, quite easily.

You'll gain nothing by waiting, he said to himself, rubbing his hands together.

He climbed out of the window and reached up to it. It had a firm square edge. There was dirt and grit on it but nothing his fingers couldn't grip.

He looked around. No one. With his cheek almost against the wall, he swung off and began to move along it, moving his hands very quickly to be most of the time with his weight upon both arms. Hard cakes of pigeon dung gave him trouble, but he found places between them or knocked them free. Soon, he was stooping on the windowsill and looking into a rather well-furnished and empty bedroom. The bed had been used and there was a feminine perfume in the air.

But no Edie. No Karl.

He made to go on, but then drew back. There was a long stretch ahead and perhaps more pigeon trouble. Now he clung to the upright of the window frame, thinking of Edie. Could it ever be her room—another "prison cell" next door to his own? He smelt the perfume again.

No, it couldn't, she couldn't possibly use that. And yet, there was some-thing about the smell that was familiar.

He stopped at once when he saw a hanger with a silken blouse upon it, as if put out to wear, attached to the closet doorknob.

Then he realized at once that someone did occupy the bed, but the form was so small and frail and covered in blankets that he hadn't seen. The figure let out a feminine moan, as Robert moved closer.

It was Annetta.

5

Annetta

nnetta was lying on the bed. She was pale and she was changed terribly. Her face was aged and sick. But there was something else that was not just change brought by suffering. She had ever been pretty, but now it was as if, under creased and fever and the faded suntan and the red spots of her cheeks, and in her wide, staring eyes, Robert saw innocence, and the beauty of a child. She had on one of her satiny blouses that had once been white, but which was now soiled and damp, and a short, blue pleated skirt like a schoolgirl's, clearly not her own. She wore stockings, and beside her feet on the rumpled bed there lay a pair of high-heeled shoes. She lay on her side with both of her hands behind her and there was something else on the bed coming from under—a length of chain that went to a manacle clipped to the steel bed frame on the near side. Although she lay without turning, she was moving all the time, changing which foot rested on the other, laying now the side of her head and now the back of it on the dirty pillow. Strands of damp, uncombed hair clung to her forehead.

Two pillows that looked better than the one she had were thrown together on the floor in a corner of the room: and there was another on the armchair.

She did not seem to notice Robert there, but after he had watched her a minute, unable to realise what he was seeing, she said suddenly, "Well, if I look a fright and you want my hair combed, you must do it yourself. You can see why I can't so don't blame me."

She looked at him for a moment after she said this. Robert still stood by the door. Suddenly, she stiffened and lay still, and then raised her head and really stared at him. She began to struggle to sit up, but fell back, and her chest heaved. Now she curved her body so that she could lay her head on the side of the bed and look at him, although still without turning over.

She said, "My!"

To his disbelief, she was suddenly smiling. It was the same lovely smile that he had last seen in the dim light outside the hotel where they parted, with the flint of her gold stars.

"Robert!" She gasped and then began a fit of coughing in which she doubled as if in pain, but before the coughing was finished, she gasped out again, "Robert! Robert!" and was again smiling and even laughing while she coughed.

"You came, love! You won!" She cried. "And where is Karl?"

Robert looked at the door behind him… They must not hear this. He could not answer her.

"And you did win, love?… You did! It's Karl's triumph! I didn't hear any firing, though that's no surprise: I've been sort of dozing and not caring. There could have been an earthquake since I've been in here and I'd not know. Oh, you've won, even in time for Annetta to see—that's sweet and it's all I need! And Karl is coming, isn't he, dear?"

Her voice was husky and breathless but clear enough. She spoke fast, even faster than he remembered.

Robert whispered, "Karl isn't dead. At least, I don't think he is. Annetta, you're sick!"

"I know, love. I'm more than sick. Dying is more like it."

"Dying! What is it? The cough?"

"Yes, love. And more."

"Annetta! Oh, Annetta! Does it hurt?"

"Yes, it does, love, but not so much now you've come."

"Oh!—"

"What can you do, you're thinking? Nothing. Just stay by me—if you can. And keep the others away. Bring Karl…I really badly want to see him, Rob… But he's a prisoner too, isn't he?—and you? But if you can get a chance, bring

Karl to me! I know he and I have had our differences, but I should like to see him, just once, before..."

Her husky voice trailed off. She looked at him and smiled tiredly. He tried to smile back at her and couldn't and they were silent for a few moments.

"Annetta—" he said, and stopped.

"Yes, love?"

"Annetta, you're right, I'm not free and neither is Karl. I am going to try to escape. But I don't know if I can."

"I guessed that, love. But can you find Karl for me?"

"I'll try to. I'm not sure if I can."

They were silent. After a moment, she said, "What if none of us do get out of here? Will it all be for nothing?"

Robert thought for some time, about what Edie had said about the flowers, being named, even if they went unnoticed. Then he whispered, "I do think something will last, Annetta, even if we both die. Something drifts out: it's like a faith that I have. I don't believe in it completely, but I do a bit. Maybe there is ether after all, and that it might carry this for us."

"Carry what?"

"Oh, it's probably all nonsense. The dark of the stars. Carry the record of our not giving in. Carry love."

"That's too much for me, dear. I'm also getting tired. I'm going to close my eyes for a bit. I'm so hungry."

"When did you start starving?"

"As soon as he took me—Dr Paul—after I left you."

"How soon after was it, Annetta, that you were taken here?"

"The day after," Annetta said. "I told you I had a mission. I told you I needed to complete it. I tried. I had some of Michael's poison, and I tried to use it on Dr Paul. He was too smart for me. I failed."

Robert's heart soared and fell back. "That was very brave of you."

"I don't think so. It was just necessary. Something I should have done long ago...before..."

Her head drooped, and she seemed to turn inward in her thoughts. "You said he killed your son. Is that true?"

She smiled. "Did Karl say it was not?"

Robert nodded.

"Then I will let him tell it to you, perhaps. One day. But I would like to see him again. Do you have a mother, love?"

He nodded. "I did. She died."

"Oh, I should have known that about you. Come here. Let me hold you."

He had been sitting on the side of the bed. Now he fetched the pillows that were in the corner of the room and sat on the floor beside her so that his head could be very close to Annetta's. But before he would let her go on, he muttered, "These pillows are much softer than yours. Do you want me to swap one?"

"It's no odds to me, love. You take it."

He smiled. It did remind him of his mother, who would always give him the best of everything, taking the least for herself.

"Tell me more about your story," he said as she wrapped an arm around him. "You were a singer, too?"

"Yes, before Michael. I didn't sing much when I was with Michael. I did actually sing, but I hated the other miners so much that I didn't want them to hear me, so I used to go quite far out and sing to myself. Actually, it needn't be very far, because of the noise of the falls on the creek and the miners being almost always near it. But my favourite place was a bit further, a white cliff that I'd climb up to. It was lovely on the grassy slope at the bottom—you came out of the forest—and sometimes I'd see antelopes and their babies and they'd made me think of mine to come. The trees shut you in so much down below, and here you could see over them, you could even see old Vascoma way down the valley. But I wished I had had someone to listen: I always sing better when someone is listening and I can see they like it. It shows what I thought of the miners...I was sad that Michael didn't care for music; he'd listen to me, and he liked me to do it, but he'd hardly notice if it was good or bad and you could see he was thinking of other things—bugs most likely. He was a funny man, most would say, but very, very kind and gentle, and far different from another I'd ever been with. He loved me, though, and our son...now, he loved my singing..."

"I'd like your singing, too, I think, if I ever heard it," he whispered.

"Well, then I will sing to you. But there's one more thing I can tell you, love," she said huskily, "about the diamonds—if ever you should get free and want to look for them. But to me, Michael seemed to talk in riddles when he said it, and I don't suppose it will help."

The diamonds seemed a thousand miles away. "I don't care about that much now."

"Ah, but you should care, love. Karl was right, they should be used; I was wrong for not trying like Michael wanted me to. I took the easy way out and took up with the doctor, and look where I am now. Perhaps it's a kind of punishment for that, that I am here."

"Oh, well, tell me, then. But talk low, Annetta."

"Michael said something about how he was going to put them into safe-keeping with some great chief of the Criteery tribe. Part of the trouble is that he kind of smiled when he said it, so I didn't quite know if he was joking, and the other part is that the Criteery tribe is tiny, and doesn't have any chief at all, leave alone a great one. I asked him about it once, but he just smiled and said: 'You must wait. You'll find out, Stella (that was my name then), if you do what I say.' He said he'd tell one thing more: the chief had a rough and a fierce look, 'But he'd keep the stones safe for you, and give them when you need.' I said: 'Mightn't he die?' and he said, still with that funny smile: 'He won't; he knows all secrets of his people and one more: how to stay alive.' After that, he wouldn't say more. He may have meant the man knows their medical things, herbs for illness, and such; but then I never did see a Criteery looking very old. They certainly die plenty of ways, like being shot, and herbs wouldn't stop that."

"I hope to God no one is listening now," Robert muttered. "Can anyone hear this?"

"I don't know, love. Does it matter?"

"Yes. A bit. I don't want Paul to get the stones even if we can't."

They were silent. Robert was thinking of the sketch. It must be of the chief who she was to find and to recognize by his tattoos. Where could he be? Clearly, there must have been other clues that had been lost. But how had Dewey been so confident that the native would be still alive when Annetta needed him? Then he thought, oh, of course, Dewey must have been thinking in terms of only a year or two, not the years which had passed until now.

Even so, was it what had happened? It was just possible that the man might have survived.

"Did any of the Criteeries you spoke to have tattoos on his lip? Or have you ever seen any that did?"

"No love, but I know what you're thinking of—the sketch of Michael's. Yes, Dr Paul wanted that picture too and fetched me to get it, but I don't know anything else about it. But it all goes round in my head, dear. No, I never did see a tattoo on a Criteery—any kind."

A moment of eagerness died. He didn't have the sketch anymore, anyway, to revive the details. It was hopeless.

"Let's talk of something else now," said Annetta, seeming to realize the same thing. "Tell me about Karl. Even though I know it is something bad, because you haven't talked about him already."

He opened his mouth to tell her about the horrible fate that had befallen Karl, when she stiffened and sat up on her elbows. "Someone is coming!"

Listening, he, too, heard footsteps outside. And Robert watched the door and felt his strength and his resolve going. "I will come back for you."

She laughed, which dissolved into a wracking cough. "No, you won't."

He headed for the window, wanting to help Annetta, but knowing deep in his heart that he would never see her again.

"Don't look at me anymore, love," Annetta murmured. "Don't say good-bye. Go—but break if you can, before too long. And promise me you'll try to send Karl to me. Go, now. All my love goes with you."

6

Dr Paul

L ater, when Robert was back in his place, Dr Paul came. He was smiling, more his old overbearing and contemptuous self. He looked less pale and tired, even was flushed: Robert guessed that the day's irrigation had begun. He thought that he was like he had first seen him in that pub, just south of London—no, no, that was another man, though similar—no, rather, like he had been at the Bar Palace Hotel. Dr Paul put down a black bag on the armchair and tutted when he saw the state of the bed frame. "You're unhappy with your accommodations?"

Thinking of poor Annetta, he scowled but said nothing.

Dr Paul laughed. "Oh, come now. You can't expect me to let you traipse around my lands, knowing what I know about you. And make no mistake, they are my lands. As well as everything that is in them."

His eyes turned cold for a brief moment, and Robert understood his meaning at once. "I don't care about the diamonds. I just want Edie back."

He snorted with disbelief.

"It is all well explained," he said cheerfully. "She is in the hospital. She will be sent down when she is well enough to travel. She is unharmed and will remain so. You may rest assured of it."

Now it was Robert's turn to look with amazement. Dr Paul had begun to unpack something from his bag. He was relaxed, urbane. A faint smell in the room, familiar to Robert from one that sometimes came home in his father's breath, told him that his guess had been right. Dr Paul had been drinking.

"I have learned from the hospital that you were right. She has been ill, but not seriously so. I have already given instructions on what antibiotics she is to receive. She will be here in a few days."

Now it was Robert's turn not to believe him. He wanted to, but he knew better.

"I will not say that she may not have been punished for something or other. In any military unit that may happen, as it happened to you. All who visit there must accept rules… And, I may say, no one goes out: that is one rule that affected you. And now," he sighed, "I have to do the same for you. In short, even earlier I could see from the way you were holding your hand that your fingers are developing a septic inflammation."

Robert, who had been lying on his back, suddenly rolled onto his side and began watching intently what Dr Paul was doing.

"With her, it will be per orem; with you, intro-muscular. The effect is so much faster that way. I do not trust them to handle syringes, or I would order the same for Miss Fairby."

"Miss Fairby?" he asked innocently.

"Oh, yes. I'm sad to say, she is ill. Near death, it seems. Come, come, I know you know that. You've been to see her, yes?" His eyes went to the chains that Robert had done his best to replace.

Robert didn't answer. Dr Paul continued to rummage through his medical bag, making Robert even more nervous. "I don't want to be injected with anything. I don't believe I am sick."

"Then I am sorry, but I insist. I am a doctor and you must defer to my opinion of what is best for you."

"I will fight it."

"Don't be silly. I can easily hold you down."

"I see you are sad and troubled," Dr Paul said, watching him. "Is it for me and my problems? No, it is not that yet. But understand that I do have problems. Karl understands it well."

Robert snorted.

"He does. The moors people do not like the government. The people want development, but they want it at their own pace, on their own terms. It is this movement that I have planned to aid, and that I can lead. In twenty years there will be a new principality of the highlands here. It is an area, which, including that to the east, is half the size of Europe. The whole range will be ours, even to the sea. This is not an unplanned dream: I already have my air photographs of the site of the harbour and my sketches for it all."

Robert listened with amazement. His mother had nursed madmen; she told him how they can draw a listener in. He said, "You want the diamonds."

Dr Paul looked at him, startled and puzzled, and then muttered, "You don't understand, you don't understand. I want more than the diamonds. I want all of it."

There was a knock on the door. Dr Paul went to it and opened it a little and looked out. Robert heard a low voice outside. He raised his head to listen.

"In a minute, in a minute," Dr Paul said through the door.

"Who was that?" Robert asked.

Dr Paul ignored his question. "No, what happened, happened. I did not ask for this responsibility. But it is happening, and these people need a wise ruler…"

"Where is Edith?" Robert asked, his voice shaking.

"She is not far off; like Karl, she is alive and well. I told you."

"Can I see her?"

"No."

"I am not going to join you," Robert said.

"Then I shall have no use for you… Shall I send you elsewhere, see if they have a use for you instead?" Now he was clearly angry.

Robert did not answer.

He shoved the syringe back into his bag. "Then I will. I was trying to be benevolent, but I am done. It is your funeral, boy. At best, they will find a use for you in chains heavier than these; at worst, the body of a silly boy who did not know his good fortune will be tumbled down among the rocks—and there a ghoul of the mountain will come and will strip the flesh off it and eat it." He was now cold and fierce in a way that Robert had not seen before.

Robert slumped forward over his knees stretched on the bed and felt ready to cry in his fear. He thought of his parents and missed them so desperately at that moment that he wished he'd died that day, instead. Once, his mother had told him that one could make courage and defiance out of fear by catching them suddenly, before one knew what one was doing, short of the point which forced one to screams. He'd always wondered, if one could make courage out of something so opposite, couldn't one make other emotions, too, like love? He thought of Annetta, too. These things, the love, the courage, he imagined would be a soft, flowing ether, buoying him onwards, out into the dark of the stars.

Almost while he was thinking this, he heard himself beginning to say in a quick, sputtering voice, "You're not benevolent. Any chance of my thinking that went away early on, when I saw that trick you'd done with Edie's signature. Your 'cause' couldn't ever be mine. I won't—"

"Oh, that? That was nothing."

Robert looked at him, startled. The voice was booming, but it was gentle again, half-amused.

"I would never have used that in her case. Sometimes it is a help, that is all. It becomes a joke between us—between me and the person who has signed. I only use it when the person is better able to understand that she is…"

"Can I see Karl before you send me to wherever I'm to go?"

He expected a quick refusal as for Edie, but the man looked at him as if confused and did not reply. Instead, he pulled himself to his feet and picked up his bag. He turned from Robert, shrugging his shoulders and shaking his big head. For one moment Robert should see that his eyes were tight shut. Then he walked to the door. He took hold of the handle and then, turning to Robert, said, "Here is your breakfast coming."

He went out, leaving the door open.

7

The Servant

A servant came into the room carrying a tray with food. He was small and quite young, had very short hair, and a bit of a limp. Robert looked at the tray and realised suddenly that he was ravenously hungry. It was a whole meal that they had sent for him, not just breakfast: a mound of rice with reddish-brown beans and yellow sweet corn piled beside, and a slab of freshly fried steak with a thick brown gravy. He could not think how long it was since he had eaten that, since his foster parents had been vegetarians. The tray also had a knife and fork, a large glass of some cloudy fruit water, and, on a separate plate, a large tomato and a sunset-coloured mango.

Is this supposed to be my Last Supper? He wondered grimly.

The man came toward the bed hesitantly, as if expecting to be told where to lay the tray. Really, as any fool could see, there was only one place to put it—the bed. Anyway, who was he, as a prisoner, to say where?

But he patted the bed beside him and smiled and nodded at the man the way one might at the waiter in a foreign café, not knowing his language. Something in the hesitancy of the man's movements touched Robert painfully, even while his main attention was on the food. Mainly, though, he was just in joyful anticipation of a good meal for the first time in days and days.

The man laid the tray on the bed. Robert said, "Thanks very much," as he stared at the food, wondering which of it to attack first. He picked up the knife and fork.

"Do you want me to stay and talk while you eat it, Robert?"

Taken aback by the use of his name, Robert looked up and saw Karl.

"If I don't stay with you," Karl went on in a low and spiritless voice, "you would have to eat it with your fingers because I'll have to take the knife and fork away with me."

Robert stared at him. Karl's hair had been cut very short. Some of it must have been burned like that by the fire, as on one side, there were blackened and frizzled ends. But only some; the rest had been cut. There were large scabs on his temple and his ear on the side where the hair was singed. The burns were healing but would doubtlessly scar. Karl looked well and was plumper than Robert remembered as if he had been eating more. Robert was amazed that he had not recognized him—but then, after staring at him, he was not so amazed. Something in Karl's manner had changed so utterly. Yes, his face was rounder, but the edge of the old sharp hatchet was dulled. He walked and spoke like a servant.

Robert couldn't think what to say. At last, he said, "Stay, Karl."

Karl sat down on the arm of the armchair. He interlocked the fingers of his hands and rested them on his knees.

"I suppose you're going to ask how I came to be like this," he said dully. "I can see you're disappointed in me. I expected that."

He looked at the tray that was now on Robert's lap.

"Eat, Robert," he said. "We can talk while you're eating."

Robert started to eat. It was good to have something to do—to have something, actually, that would keep him from having to talk. Soon he was putting all that he could get onto his fork at the time and biting and swallowing fiercely.

"Where is Edie?" he said at last, with his mouth still full.

"Edie is in the hospital."

"And you know about Annetta, then?"

He nodded.

"She said she wanted to see you."

He pressed his lips together but said nothing.

"So, you've gone over to this side?" he said. "You don't look as if you're acting."

"No, I'm not. It's a case of force majeure, Rob. You remember how I said I might turn out to be a shit when we started? Well, now, from your point of view, I have."

"You said you might—for a few days or a few weeks—but that you hoped you were getting to be curable."

"Well, it's worse than that," Karl said in his new weak, toneless voice, and then added with a sigh, "The trouble is, at this point, I don't want to be cured."

"So you've really come to approve of what he is doing here?"

"Sort of. He has to win in the end, doesn't he? Even if we had been able to halt it just for a little with our pills, it wouldn't have done much. I've come to believe that. And, Rob," he said a little more eagerly, "more of the things I value turn out to fit in what he's doing than I thought. You've talked to him yourself—to Dr Paul—a bit now, haven't you? I heard you. Well, don't you have to admit that there's a lot more to him than you thought? In what he's saying and doing?"

For the first time, Karl was looking at Robert, a faint challenge flashing in his grey eyes.

"Come, admit he is the most egg-headed, all-around panjandrum you ever met. He knows about everything. I beat him a bit on insects and plants—that's about bloody all."

Robert said, "Maybe. But he's also the most all-around super egotist that I ever met. He thinks he is so important it excuses anything he does. I told him I'd never join him, and I'm disappointed you didn't do the same."

The challenge faded from his eyes. "Rob. The best thing for you now is to fall in with us too. I have to tell you that, Rob—we have absolutely no other option."

Robert said nothing for a while and went on eating. Then with his mouth full, he murmured, "Even if you don't want to escape yourself, Karl, you could do me something else. Help me to."

There was another pause. Karl fidgeted and smiled slyly. "I can't. That's impossible. I'm a coward."

"You're not a coward at all, Karl, and you know it."

"I am. I lose my nerve. Like I did at the circus. Like I did when my father died, and I had a chance to change everything. My father, you know, he taught me everything there was to know about bugs and things, and what did I do?

I betrayed him. And I've lost my nerve here. I'm a shit. Even more so when I'm—like this."

"Are you drugged now?"

"Of course. I have to be. I have been all the time you've known me."

"How? I never saw you take anything."

"Oh, Rob, I thought you would have guessed all that by now! It's in that lump on my shoulder."

"What is? What do you mean?"

"It's in what they call an implant. You cut a hole and put it in there, sort of bury it in the fat layer. A plastic capsule. It leaks the stuff out and gives me a dose all the time. All the time—and I have to have it. It only needs replacing every three years. I haven't needed even the first replacement yet. So long as I keep steady in my life and don't bump that place where it is, I'm pretty much a normal person. The trouble is when I get too much or too little."

"So that was what happened when I bumped you at the pool then?" asked Robert, his mind darting around among so many of Karl's acts that had formerly puzzled him. "I squeezed it and it gave you too much?"

"Yes, and after that, there was too little. That was why I started to be so ratty the next day. A pool of the stuff builds up in the scar tissue around where he put the implant in. When it's bumped or squeezed, a lot gets into the blood at once. What it does depends on the mood you're in when it happens. Sends you high or low. Then, because the scar tissue's been emptied and more only leaks out of the capsule very slowly, you always get some withdrawal signs a day or so later. If that bump's hit or squeezed a lot, then I know that I'm going to just about die—or worse than die, for what it feels like, in the next few days."

"Ah! So that is what Dr Paul was doing when he was banging your back on the ground at Cintra?"

"Yes. He got a little behind me as we were walking along and then punched me right on the lump. Then of course I hit him. We fought and rolled into that hollow. He's much heavier and fitter."

Robert glanced hard at Karl looking for anger, but there was none.

"It is horrible. Karl, how can you work for a man who runs the company that makes this fiendish thing you've got in your shoulder? And puts it there himself, makes you his slave? And how can you approve of a company whose reports keep a whole land dying of disease?"

"I was young, when I did, at first. When my father died and I was alone in the world and had no one. I was just a boy and had no choice. I thought you, of all people, would understand that."

"But now—why—?"

"Why do I put up with it now? Sometimes I don't know, Rob," said Karl wearily. "I suppose a small part of me has always approved of Paul. You won't make me say anything else. I am sorry I got you into this. I thought it could be different. I thought I could..."

He stopped, and a silence fell.

"But you can see the point of what he's saying about the population, can't you?" Karl said sadly at last.

"I see that he's hungry for power. That's all. And I refuse to help him with that."

"Maybe. But you might have no choice. Like me?"

"No."

"So you'd go back to Sam and Linda? Is that it?"

"He's not going to let me go."

"So you'd rather die than—"

The edges of Robert's eyesight began to fade, and he shook his head. It did no good. He suddenly felt overwhelmingly tired and dizzy. "No. Even if he did, after what he did to you, to Annetta, to Edie, I'd never be able to—"

Karl chuckled sadly. "I was once like you. I thought the same." He sniffled and wiped a hand over his nose, and his eyes drifted to the food, which was almost gone. "I was wrong. Things happen."

Karl spoke more, but Robert could no longer hear it. He heard the rushing of blood in his ears. He squeezed his eyes closed and opened them, trying to get his bearings, but it suddenly occurred to him, why he was feeling so queer. He dropped the fork. "What..." he began, but he couldn't hear his own voice. All he could see was Karl, bending over him, a sad expression on his face. And then, the world faded to black.

8

Reunion

When Robert woke, he was lying on a stone floor in utter darkness and silence. He had a throbbing headache and felt sick—the sort of sickness one has when trying to stand after a blow. In contrast to sickness, he also felt a gathering strength and excitement, as if his mind would soon seize something that it had forgotten—anger, perhaps—and then he would stand and rush again at the man who had knocked him down. Fairly soon, he realized what was probably the cause of the feeling of new strength—his legs were spread wide on the floor. They were in blessed freedom. He was not bound!

Still lying where he was, he reached out in the darkness and started to feel the floor on both sides with his outstretched arms. No bed. This was not the room he'd been in before.

There were cool flagstones under him, smooth and clean. They smelled damp and rather like bleach; they might have been washed not long ago.

First crawling and then walking, and all the time carefully exploring before him with his hands, he found out the shape of his prison. It was simply a corridor about five yards long with a door at each end. The walls and the ceiling above him that he would just reach, were bare and smooth. There were two grates in the wall near the ceiling and one was emitting a faint draft.

More interesting was a deep recess that he discovered near one of the doors. It was at the level of his shoulder, and, at the end of the recess, almost at arm's length, his fingers could touch a metal plate a little roughened by rust. Even without the plate, though, the recess would be too narrow to admit his body. The door near the recess was metal plated in the same way, and it was this that made him feel sure that he was indeed in some sort of a prison and that this door was the main entrance. It had a keyhole but no handle. He listened at the hole. Utter silence.

Treading back through the dark to the door at the other end he again listened at the keyhole. Again nothing. This door had a handle, but he had not tried it yet. Listening carefully in the recess, he thought he made out a soft, colourless noise, or perhaps the mere illusion of sound, as in a seashell. Another noise that he was beginning to hear everywhere, he decided, at last, was not the noise of the fan that ran the ventilator, but rather the faint reverberation of his own blood.

When he had satisfied himself that there was nothing else to be touched in the corridor, he tried the handle of the second door. It turned and the door opened and led him through into yet more utter darkness. He went forward as quietly as he could. Walls went off to left and right and the sound of his own movements told him he had come into a larger room; the ceiling too was higher and now out of reach. He thought he heard for the first time one sound, a faint creak, coming from in front. He stood still and listened, but it did not come again. He started feeling his way along the wall to his right. It was as bare as before, but in his circuit of what proved a largish room, he found two more doors with handles. Finally, he was back at the open door where he had entered.

He skirted along the wall towards the larger of the two he had felt and then heard again the same creak as before. This time it definitely came from out in the room. His imagination now painted unpleasant pictures. Scoreman might be there waiting for him. Surprisingly, he didn't feel very scared. Perhaps it was the drug Paul had put into his food, killing his fear, making him reckless.

In order to have a landmark to start from, he went back to the door he had come in by, and then set off crawling across and room. When he reached the opposite wall without finding anything, he stood up and turned around. Steadying himself with his hands against the wall, he started slowly back. He reached out and, at about the height of the top of his head, touched a stretched rope that slanted down towards his left. He began to run his hand down it.

After about a yard, his fingers came to a big knot. He felt the knot carefully and found that it joined the rope to some bigger loop of soft cord.

Suddenly, under his fingers the knot and cord he was feeling jerked into violent motion and went completely loose in his hand. He thought he had released a trap of some sort and instinctively jerked back and held his arms by his face to shield it.

Out of the darkness behind him, a voice hissed, "Who is it? Don't touch me!"

A few moments later, the room blazed with light.

He blinked: he was in a bare yellow room with a hammock strung across it, which accounted for the rope he had been touching. Beyond it, right in the doorway that opened to the passage he had come in from, lay Edie. One of her hands was reached out to a light switch in the main room—he must have missed it, too high or too low, in feeling the walls—and her other held the handle of the door. She was poised, ready to close it.

"Don't come—" she said, and then with a gasp: "Robert!"

"Edie!"

To his dismay, her look of horror stayed fixed in her face. "Robert!" she gasped again. "What are you here for?"

"Edie! Why?—I don't know."

"Why didn't you turn on the light?"

"I didn't know there was one."

"How did you come?"

"They gave me something that put me out. They must have left me in that passage and—" His words came out in a rush, until he noticed the expression on Edie's face was not one of happiness but of worry. "Edie—why are you afraid of me?"

"I was frightened. Why did you come so quietly, Robert?" she said, looking at him again with a frown and fresh horror in her face, and still as if she might try to slam the door against him and hold it.

"I didn't know where I was, Edie. I thought there might be a chance to escape and I didn't want anyone to know I was looking for a way." Robert felt defensive, not knowing quite why.

"You're not on his side then?"

"No, of course, I'm not!"

"Karl is now," she said.

"Yes. How did you know? Have you seen him?"

"No. But Dr Paul keeps telling me and it sounds like he really is."

"He is. But he's sick too, with those drugs. You can't blame him very much, Edie. So this is where Paul has kept you, Edie."

He didn't know if it was a question or a statement he was making. He was unsure of himself because of the way she was looking at him. He felt at once overjoyed and disappointed in his finding of her.

She didn't answer. There was still something very wrong between them. He felt guilty, although, again, he wasn't sure why he should be. He said gloomily, into the gap of silence, "Then what is the matter, Edie? Aren't you pleased to see me? I am to see you."

"I suppose if this is his prison for you, too, then there can't be any way out," she said with a sigh. "I had some wild idea that you might come to save me."

"Oh," he said. Yes. He had fouled that up.

After a silence, she said, "Why didn't you run with me when the helicopter came? Why did you keep behind?"

"Oh, Edie. I was sure you would have looked back and seen! My shoe broke and I tripped and fell. I was running as hard as I could to catch up when the cage got you. The shoe broke, it came in half. I had to take it off—and the other."

She looked at him doubtfully.

"Don't you remember what my shoes were like? The toe was broken open— when I ran, it tore right along."

"You should have called me to stop, so we could have stayed together."

"I didn't have time to do anything. Edie, it's mean of you to think I was running away or something!"

She looked at him keenly and in silence.

"Oh, well," said suddenly, and with the sound of her voice, it seemed that some cloud had partly lifted. "Robert, I am glad to see you, now that I know you are not on his side. But there isn't any way out. We are in a prison here."

"But we will escape."

"You are very sure of that?"

He nodded.

She smiled. Her lips arched up and her funny nose arched down. She let go of the door handle and held out both of hers towards him.

A moment later Robert had flung the hammock behind him and was holding her tight in his arms. "Edie!" he said breathlessly. "Yes! I've found you at last! Edie! I've looked for so long and never thought I could! We are together now, Edie."

"Don't squeeze me so! And now let me go," she said, swatting him.

He let her go.

But Edie, standing there, was the best thing he had ever seen. He moved to take her in his arms again, but with the fists that had been patting on his chest, she pushed him away, saying, "Not again, Robert. Now we must talk."

They sat down and she started to tell him all that had happened since the helicopter took her.

9

Escape

Robert listened to Edie's story and hated Dr Paul more. Apparently, she had been here all along. He came to her room for these long "chats" every day. Edie thought it was every day, but she could not be sure because all was timeless here except for the meals. By the meals, she said, she judged that sometimes the doctor came in the morning, but that more often it was in the late afternoon or evening. If he came late, then he was tipsier and more egotistical, and in some ways, more pleasant to be with.

So, he makes himself her whole world so that she must end by liking having him come, just for company, Robert thought bitterly.

After Edie had told Robert how she had thought the meals told her the time of the day, she started to cry. They were sitting in the room where the hammock was, side by side, their backs against the wall. After a while, still crying, Edie let Robert put his arm around her shoulders. They sat like that for a long time, Edie rather stiffly neither encouraging nor discouraging Robert from keeping his arm there.

"What does he want? What does he want?" she asked over and over.

Robert thought that he knew, in part, what he wanted; he thought that she knew it too, but some barrier stopped him from saying it.

Gradually, she stopped crying.

"Do you ever let him put his arm around you like this?" Robert asked at last.

"No!!" said Edie.

"I think that's the sort of thing he wants. The start. He wants you to like him and to need him."

"Oh! I never will!"

He asked where they sat when Dr Paul was there. She said in the bedroom. She would be in the one armchair, he in the other. He told her "puffed-out" stories about himself and lectured her on science and things that she couldn't understand, and he told her of his plans for the future. When she pleaded to be let go, he would say, "Not yet awhile, not yet. I am waiting. First, something must happen." And later he would say, "If there is anything I can do to make you more comfortable while you are here, tell me." He would ask her about the food and how she liked it. Almost every time he came, he expected her to have changed into the new, clean clothes that he had brought last time, and he would take the last lot away. At first, she had refused to change, but later she did.

Robert punched the air with a fist. He was fairly sure now that the drug he had been given was just a knockout so that he could be brought here without seeing where he was going. Did Paul just want them to see each other and that each was unharmed—so that they would think better of him and bend more easily to his will? Or, worse, was it some cat and mouse game? Was he watching them, listening somewhere? Robert looked with distaste at the two ventilators high up in the walls of the room where they were sitting.

"He's power-hungry and mad. We have to get out of here."

She sniffed. "I miss my mother. I'm sure she's worried."

Robert found her hand on the floor beside him and now he held his hand over it. It was smooth and seemed very small. He stroked her fingers. He wished he knew how he could steer her away from the subject of her mother's grief. He asked other questions about her life, but although she answered them, he sensed that her mother was still foremost in her mind. "Yes. You will see her again. I promise."

She didn't withdraw her hand and didn't particularly give it either. She let it be where it was, on the floor, underneath his. Robert was sure that she distrusted him still. But touching her hand and listening to her voice, she seemed to him every minute a thing of more and more intricate beauty and delight and knowledge, a precious thing which he must never harm. A being who, whether she yielded or not. Whether she ever liked him or no, he wanted to be near forevermore.

It seemed like long years since their flight together on the moors and there was much to say. Even so, at last, they were talked out. Even Robert's fever of longing became worn out also. Their silences grew long. Edie said she wanted to go to sleep. Robert was anxious to let Edie decide this time how far apart they must keep, so he went out to the bathroom first and came back and lay down near to the wall. Presently, to his disappointment, he heard her feel her way past him and go to the far side of the room.

So they lay ready to sleep, almost as far apart from one another as the room would allow. Sleeping, when they were here and did not wish to be, seemed so wasteful. He wanted to get out. But he also wanted to protect Edie. She'd been through too much. So he lay there, on the ground, trying to think of a way out, and as he did, he heard her restless breathing.

He tried in his mind saying to her "Edie, good night" and "good night, Edie," but after the lapse of silence, neither seemed at all right. So, at last, he said, "Edie, why don't you use the coverlet Dr Paul put there for you?"

"I don't want it," she answered. "You use it."

"I don't, either. Good night then."

"Good night."

Once he had said it, she seemed to calm, which allowed him, finally, to think.

After about an hour, Robert asked Edie softly if she was awake, and then said, "When I was standing up before, didn't the ceiling seem a little higher over my head?"

Edie thought a moment and answered that perhaps it did. Her voice showed that she had not been asleep either.

That's where it must be. It was an entrance passage. The oily smell fitted his idea too. He jumped up and switched on the light. He had been right; it was higher. The place was poorly lit, having no light of its own. It was especially dark at the far end where the shelves were.

Robert scratched at it with his belt buckle but to his disappointment found only hard concrete again. His last hope then had to be the side wall away from the hammock room. After a few moments of scratching, he said excitedly, "It is different here; this is plaster."

She came over and looked. "I think you're right."

Together, they dug in the plaster with their fingers. At last, they were able to force the crude tools behind the plaster and to prise it away in large slabs. They saw a well-made brick wall behind.

They started on bricks at the bottom. The lowest was about at Robert's waist. There must have been wooden steps from there on down into the passage. But the cement was hard and after about an hour of work the grooves were only half an inch deep and they had not even begun on the sides. They worked furiously but the cutting went more and more slowly as the grooves deepened. They couldn't judge time easily, but it seemed that it would be well into the next day before they could move out the first brick, if that.

Robert thought that if the wall was only one brick thick he might be able to burst it. They dragged the mattress from the bed and put it across the passage under the wall for Robert to fall on if the wall gave. Braced between the walls of the passage, Robert worked his way up until his head was nearly at the ceiling and then pushed with all his strength on the bricked wall with his feet. Edie brought pillows and he worked those in behind his back to shorten the span and to give less pain to his shoulders. The wall was unyielding as solid rock.

Below him, as he gave up, he saw Edie sitting in an odd stiff position on the mattress. He thought something had happened to her. He started to work his way down. By the time he dropped to the mattress, she was up and gone. He found her in the bedroom, apparently measuring herself on the wall beside the big bed.

"Edie, what's this?" he asked puzzled. She had a serious and strained expression like she had had when she was looking for landmarks on the moor.

She answered at last, in a low and hurried voice, touching the bedposts, "I am measuring these. There is another way—these may be right for it. If we can get them. Robert, can you break the bed? If you can, I will show you a way that may work."

It was the big head posts that she wanted. She explained her plan but Robert couldn't understand it. He was holding a bottom corner of the bed frame and shaking it to see what might be loose. Then he started to rock the bottom board to and fro: this was all that would move, and he would have to start there even though it was not the piece he wanted. The rest was too strong.

"I learned the way from my father," Edie told him with pride, watching Robert work the tail boards and evidently confident that his strength would soon smash through to the pieces she wanted.

"He knew many ideas like this. He used this one for felling a tree the way he wanted if there was another trunk near, or to lift a heavy thing onto the lorry when he did not have the winch."

Robert was amazed that she was so sure that her plan was going to work. He could tell she was thinking of levers but couldn't see what she hoped to lever against: besides, the posts would easily break at the thin places between the knobs.

The bed was heavy and well made. When the bottom was off, he needed a strong lever to break the boards. He tried to break the stem of the shower above the tap, but the whole shower came away from the well and a water pipe broke somewhere up in the plaster of the ceiling. After that, water from the pipe poured steadily into the bathroom. They shut the door, and with the new levers made from the long pipes, Robert was able to work faster on the bed. But in a minute, water was flooding out from under the bathroom door. When, about an hour later, they had cleared one of the bedposts into the usable condition to be what Edie wanted as a mallet, the water was already round their feet and far out into the hammock room and near the corridor.

They had already closed the door to the corridor to muffle their noise. Edie tried to make the door into a dam against the water. She packed the coverlet of the bed under the door and then strips of the coverlet into the crack at one side. She used the hammock to block the crack up the other side. Finally, she packed the pillows against the bottom of the door. But they couldn't really tell how far her barrier was stopping the water.

Robert didn't bother to break all the boards off the second bedpost. Already, the wreckage in the room was beginning to float. Broken boards washed around his ankles. They carried the posts across the hammock room and into the cupboard and saw at once that the strut that was to break the wall was too long. Only one post needed to be the right length, the other was to be the mallet. They started to cut off the big lathe-turned ball that made the top end of the first post. For this, they used the ragged metal ends of broken shelf brackets, and they took turns to file at the wood and deepen the groove. When halfway through, Robert tried to break off the ball by taking it into the bathroom and bracing it between the pedestal of the water closet and the wall, but this only broke the earthenware pedestal, and they had to resume cutting with the shelf brackets. At last, Robert broke off the ball by propping it on other bits of wood and hitting it with the other post.

The breaking of it made a tremendous splashing. They were soaked and the water was calf-deep. Edie was not ashamed to be a mermaid as she had been those weeks ago. She brought plaster dust and sprinkled it into the water by her dam at the door, but she called to Robert that she could see that water was going out at several points: the corridor beyond must be flooding also.

Robert dropped the beam he was carrying and waded to her, having to go around the mattress and the pillows, which had now floated free and had drifted away from the door. He stood by her and looked at the eddies she was pointing to, where the water was pouring through the crack. When she stood up, he put his arms around her and pressed her to him, and he kissed her cheek.

"Edie," he muttered. "This is for luck—don't stop me, don't talk, I know, I know all that—it's so that our beam will fit now. Or it's because it's the worst time to hold you—I don't care."

"I like you holding me," she gasped, breathless from his pressure. "For the moment it doesn't matter. Will we drown here if we don't get out?"

"I don't think so. The water will run out, or they will see it, finding everything. By the way, Edie, don't ever touch the light switches now. Anyway, I believe we are going to get out. Let's try—"

He kissed her again and released her and they fetched the beam and carried it into the passage. Now it was the right length. They jammed it up between the walls on a slant and Robert started to hammer the end, which was against the inside wall, using the other bedpost as a mallet. He was trying to drive this end down the wall to the straight across position, while Edie kept the other end from slipping by holding it up with a board. That end was placed on their target of pressure, which was the centre of the bricked space of the doorway. The beams were above the level of their heads and the light very bad, and twice the strut beam fell and had to be started again. At last, Robert's end began to bite.

"One wall—or the other—must go now," Robert jerked out between his blows. The blows were making a terrific noise. The whole flat seemed to shake.

Robert paused and craned to look at the gouged trail that his end was making through the paint of the wall. "It's moving in," he said.

"And a crack is coming!" said Edie, peering at the bricks.

"Where?"

"Right down here."

"Keep back now, Edie. It's going to go."

The end he was hammering was moving along quite fast now leaving a grey gouge in the paint.

Then suddenly, the wall crumbled, and bricks and plaster fell with a splash into the water along with their beam. Dust and water were everywhere.

Through the gap they found themselves looking up from the bottom into the narrow and oily concrete pit. They could see a wooden roof covering the pit, with streaks of faint light between the boards. Robert climbed up into the hold. Standing on the floor of the pit, he had to stoop beneath the boards but found that they were loose, although quite heavy—they were squared-off logs. He pushed one up and turned it over to one side. He saw that he was in a big wooden shed. A tractor stood nearby, and various farm implements were stacked around it. The pit he was in had been made—or was as if made—for servicing vehicles from below, just like the one in which Karl had worked on the holed tank of their jeep. In the side of this pit, there must once have been a low door leading into the underground flat. It looked like a hatch covering drainage well below the pit. Perhaps it was meant as a fire escape from the flat.

"Edie, we're going to get out!"

The shed was deserted and seemed little used. In one corner, a black box whirred on the ground. They guessed it to be the fan for the flat, which they had heard from below. They peered from the dusty window of the shed and Robert saw a high chain-link fence not far outside and beyond that, savannah trees. He knew now where they were and where the flat had been dug out and built: they were in that new-looking shed that he had looked down on when he had first come to the farm. And the flat was below this shed and below the garden with the vegetables that he had first liked and then had not.

It was a little after sunrise. They peered through cracks on the other side of the building and could see the farmhouse and the patio. There was no one about. The building was like when Robert had first seen it: deserted and still.

When they had carefully opened the window, they could look sideways up to the steep rise where Robert had come down from the orange tree. That was one way that they could flee now, but it was both in the full sunlight and in sight of all the windows of the house on the same side. The other way would be along the fence towards the metal gate. There between the gate and the old barns was the same herd of cows whose backs Robert had tried to run on. They looked peaceful enough now. Some were standing and some were lying on the ground.

"The gateway is better—if it's unlocked like you said." Edie sounded decisive. "The cows will help us to get there without being seen. We have only a few steps in the open and then we can get behind them and crawl to the gate, and when we are through, we can run along the fence on the far side. The fence is endways to them and they cannot see us through it—see how from here it looks like a grey wall?"

"That's only from here," Robert objected. "And it will be taking us the opposite way from the road."

"Soon we will cross to the wood. Then we will go down its stream."

"That'll be the stream I ran in before," Robert said. "Edie, going up there first will be a terrible zig-zag in our way."

"It's the best way. We are concealed there."

There was a pause. Robert cleared his throat and then said, "Edie, if we do, it'll be far too hard to double back to get you home. We'll have to—"

"We're not going home."

"Of course, we're going home. You said yourself, your mother is—"

"We're going to get the diamonds."

He froze. "Don't be silly. I need to get you home and then I'll let the police deal with—"

"The police don't care. He owns them, like everything else. He plies them like he does everyone, with promises of great wealth if they help him." She crossed her arms. "I'm not being silly. He told me all about it. How much he desires those diamonds. He told me that the person who has those diamonds holds all the cards. If we take that precious stash from him, we'll have a better bargaining chip. Isn't that what we need?"

He stared at her. "We have no idea where they are. The map, or drawing, or whatever it is that was the key—it is gone forever."

"Then we start from where we left off with Karl. Where we left his jeep. And we are in luck. Because my way will take us right there. Oh, Robert!

Promise me we will. We must find them first. If he gets those diamonds, Santania is all but lost."

He paused for a long time, thinking. Here, he thought all Edie had been doing during her time in prison was missing her mother. Now, he saw that she'd been doing much, much more. Thinking foolish thoughts, or maybe brave ones, or maybe a little of both.

"Edie—"

"*Promise* me."

He could see in her eyes how much it meant. When she was like this, there was little he could deny her.

"I promise, but *we're* not doing anything. *I* will go after them alone, when you're safely home. Until then—"

"I'm going to go whichever way you go," she said fiercely. "If you won't let me come with you, I'll go down to the prison again and just wait for them to come."

"Edie don't be silly. The prison's flooding."

"Oh, I won't drown, "she said scornfully. "I'll come out and wait here when the water rises."

"You *are* silly, Edie. You know that is not what I want. Let's go your way then… But I'm not sure that the cows like me after that last time. They'll make a noise."

"They won't care. They have been fed and are happy."

"Then it's bad. The man who fed them must be somewhere."

They heard someone shouting in the house. Edie clutched Robert's hand. "Help me up to the window, Robert. We must go!"

They climbed out. They ran across the open ground until they were between the cows and the fence and then they crawled towards the gate. Edie made clucking and breathing noises to the cows as she crawled. Robert hissed that she should stop it, they were too loud, but she still made them. The cows watched the two go past but only one climbed to its feet, and then merely to turn to them and to stare.

10

Pursuit

It worked well until long after they were out of sight of the farmhouse. But after they had turned from the fence towards the belt of trees that ran parallel to it, looking back, Robert spied a man some two hundred yards off on the other side of the fence hurrying down towards the farm. He wasn't running but walked very fast, and in this country with its great heat, even in the cool of the morning, it was unusual for a man to do that.

When they reached the other side of the trees and were out of his sight, they went downhill themselves. They crossed between two hillocks to another valley and then headed downhill again towards the open savannah and the big sheds of the plant depot which they could see from time to time. They tried to keep the buildings out of full view in case a watchman should see them against the pale hillside.

After they had come out from behind another hillock which they had used to go even further to their left, Edie called to Robert to stop. They sat down to be less visible, and Edie strained her eyes over the broad bowl of threadbare grass and over the big sheds and the hummocky country beyond which slowly levelled out into the far blue haze of the plain.

Far beyond the grass and even the hummocks, sunlight was flashing from the distant windows of a building. Edie said it was the fruit cannery. If they could reach that far, perhaps they could escape.

It was freedom: already its heady scent was on all sides, over their heads in the blue sky, and under their feet in the tall, sharp grass. Freedom was in the rough bark of saplings that their hands gripped on crossing streams in a wood, in the fireflowers of the meadow, and the parakeets whirring and screaming from one tree to another. It was even in the strands of razor grass avoided at the woodland edge, and in the ache in their chests that had come from this real, real running in the open air.

At last Edie panted, "Now I know exactly where we are. You see the hill there, nearer than the factory, and to its left? Yes. We must go there. That is by the road, near where my aunt has a house. They will hide us until the search is over, and then they'll find a lorry to take us to the jeep."

"It seems as if Vascoma Province has aunts for you like England has Youth Hostels. And you always know where to go—but how are we to pass the sheds, Edie?"

"Behind these small hills." She pointed to their left where the savannah was changing into dry woods and the hillocks into real hills; above these again rose the grey and velvety slopes of the mountains, whose heights were shrouded in the rainbow clouds. "We must keep near enough to the mountain to be in the trees. We might go up into them if they come."

Robert thought of the dogs but did not say so. They were full of hope as they ran off. Refreshed by the rest, Robert could even ask as they ran, how many aunts Edie had. Edie ran some way and seemed to reckon something before she answered: "Twelve."

Keeping inside the woodland margin was difficult. There were creepers, bushes, razor grass, and cacti all tangling and about at body height. So they were tempted all the time to move down into the open savannah. They were halfway along and already beyond the sheds when they saw a mile or so to their right between two grassy hillocks, four horsemen go galloping by in the same direction. The riders were only in sight for a minute and certainly did not see them.

After that, Robert and Edie trotted and scrambled along faster and hardly spoke; for fear of being discovered.

In a tongue of deeper woodland, they came to a narrow dirt road marked with many tyres. The exit onto the slab was shielded by some large fig trees, and Robert guessed at once that this must be one of the main roads up to the base in the mountains, probably the very one on which, higher up, he had jumped onto the lorry.

The slab and the trees would prevent a route coming up from the sheds from being visible on an aerial photograph. Robert suggested that they should use the track to go a little higher into the hills themselves, to keep away from watchers who, he guessed, were being rapidly deployed in the savannah. They had just started up the track when some faint metallic sound from up ahead made them stop and race into the bushes to the right. A moment later, peering out, they saw a Land Rover coming down the track.

"Quick!" he whispered to her.

They ran and crawled further into the undergrowth of the wood. The descending vehicle clanked as it came to a stop behind them, under the fig trees. A door slammed and there were some shouts.

Edie glanced his way, looking as though she were holding her breath.

She let it out when the vehicle moved on, but a few minutes later, voices still came from behind. Reinforcements for the search were being brought down from the base, and, doubtless, more watchers had been posted. The voices did not sound urgent, so it was likely they had not yet been seen.

Quietly, Robert motioned to her. They slipped further into the wood and found a deer track which led them down into the shrubby savannah again; on their left, there now came a rocky open slope which, for the time being at least, closed any chance of their getting unseen into the higher hills.

Now that they knew that the four horsemen were in the country between them and the road, plus the other men, doubtless who had been in the Land Rover, they were more hesitant to leave the trees and to set out towards Edie's wart-topped and bitten hill, even though they were now near to it—perhaps only three miles away.

Edie said there soon would be a river coming down from the mountain, and that its valley would have trees and cliffs which would help them to cross the open land unseen.

They came to a shoulder from where they could see such a valley, although not yet the stream itself. The valley was more open than Edie had hoped: trees and palms and patches of scrub were scattered along it but there were no real woods—at least, not here. Nearer to the hill, a black line of treetops suggested that there might be some woods further down.

The valley itself was quite sharp and its small bluffs made cover. Still, the risk of going into the open was great and they discussed whether they should try to wait for nightfall, or even wait for a whole day, hiding here, crawling to some vantage point in the open, rocky slopes on their left so that they could watch what their pursuers were doing.

But quite suddenly they heard the dogs, and that thought was gone. They were near, coming round the last shoulder of the rocky slope, not a mile away. Yet it would be twice that distance to reach where Edie and Robert stood if they followed the scent, because of a deep re-entrant. The dogs were moving and yelping amid the brushwood just out of sight. What was fully visible to them was a Land Rover that had come out with the dogs into the open. Also, a little ahead of the Land Rover, there were two horsemen.

Robert and Edie ran on through the scrub until they were over the next shoulder and then out onto the grass and straight down towards the river.

"We must run in the water down there," Edie said.

"But the dogs can try for us both ways—up or down."

"There is no other way, except to climb the cliffs—or to climb trees."

"I know."

But actually, there was no river to run in. They looked out over a dry wadi: the only water was two stagnant pools.

"This cannot be the river I meant. That one never dries. But this goes the right way and we must use it. We have no time—no time." She moved to run and then stopped. "Robert," she said.

"Yes?"

"I am sorry it is not the right river."

"Oh, it doesn't matter." He looked at her puzzled. She was just a yard away, strangely looking at him as if both frightened and puzzled herself. Then he guessed why she had paused, what she wanted, some sort of a possible goodbye in case they were taken, and in a moment he had her in his arms again. He held her so tightly for a moment that her bones creaked and he feared that he had hurt her. But still, even when he let her go, she clung to him.

"Of course, it doesn't matter," he muttered. "You are wonderful—how you always find our way."

"We'll stay together whatever happens, won't we? Even when the dogs come?"

"Of course… Now, we must go."

They scrambled down steep grassy slopes and screes to the sand banks and pebbles of the wadi. On the flat, they could make good speed running and knew they could be round the first bend before their hunters were in sight on the hill. But the dogs too would come on extremely fast once they were here.

It was very hot in the wadi and they poured sweat. Edie, who had been running as strongly as Robert up to now, began to lag a little.

The stream bed brought them to a cliff that must be a waterfall when the river is active. It cut completely across the wadi, but some trees whose branches grew close to the edge enabled them to get down. Edie's grassy hill with its wart of rocks on the top was now close above them. Edie, gasping in a brief pause, pointed out that this valley must join with the bigger one with the river in it not far ahead, but that the valley of that must turn back towards the mountain a mile or two before it went out. Their shortest way now would be to climb up and out of their present valley and over the shoulder of the rocky hill, leaving it to the right.

They clambered up out of the valley, taking a steep course between bluffs. They found themselves on a bulldozed track and, when they had got their breath back from the scramble, ran along it. It went around bend after bend, and each time they could see the track farther ahead, and finally could see where it snaked out into open grassland on the hillside. Edie was excited and said that they would soon see the chain-link fence at the far end of the depot area—and the road, which was just on the other gate where this track joined it.

"We will roll under the gate: that is easy."

Edie was focusing only on the road ahead, waiting to see the gate. Robert watched the hill above them, thinking that if it was true and this was the last hill within the depot area, as Edie said, then it was the obvious place for a sentinel. And at last, with a sinking heart, he saw one.

There was a man on a horse standing near the big rocks at the top of the grassy slope. They were brown against the brown and domed rock, and both hard to see. The man had not seen them. The steep slope was out of his sight, and the road which had led to it was under some trees. He was looking back across the open country. If they could get around the hill a little more, he would be left out of sight again behind the rocky top.

She panted, "I am sure we can do it now. I still cannot hear the dogs; now they won't be able to catch us before the fence anyway."

Just as she said this, three things happened quickly. First, they did hear them. They were much closer than before and directly behind them, but a bit muffled by the trees and the bends. Second, they came within sight of the gate. The track went straight down into a level grassy savannah and, not half a mile away, they could see the chain-link fence and beyond it, a glimpse of the yellow sand of the road. In the fence was the big wire-covered gate.

The third thing was that Robert saw the second watcher up on the hill, and now his heart fell like a stone.

This was another on horseback. He had a red shirt. He was on the other side of the hill from the first and he was looking down directly over the track to the gate. Of course, he had been right, they were no fools, they would have known the importance of this natural watchtower, and that one watcher could not watch both sides at once. His worst fear was now realised: this horseman could not fail to see them as they went into the open and he had an easy slope below him and must reach the gate ahead. Even at this distance, Robert could see the gun at his belt.

There was a high bank on their right now, so for another hundred yards, they would run unseen.

They set off running soundlessly on the ridge of sand that the grader had left along the roadside. Soon they were running flat out, and it was taking less trouble to be silent. Another hundred yards ahead was a bushy promontory that they had passed as they ran. The dogs also were still not in sight. His plan was going well. Everything was in the right place: the cutting, the big rocks, the promontory.

Hooves on the road came thundering ahead of the dogs. Robert thought that he heard an engine too. And then he heard a helicopter start its motor way down on the slabs. The sightline to the overhang and the far cliff was at that moment clear: shortly, he saw the machine itself rising from the rock with the immense reddish face of the cliff behind it.

Behind it, a second machine was being dragged out. Some way out towards him was a big rock, a broken slab lying on others. A man was standing on this. Robert saw him suddenly raise both his arms above his head. He waved at them, lowered, and then raised one arm yet again. He watched it slanting and turning. Then he turned also, faced into the rock, and climbed on as fast as he could. "Come on, Edie..." He panted. "Climb!"

The thing's intent was already clear. It was coming straight up the canyon towards them.

But Robert would not let Edie be taken again. That much was sure.

He boosted Edie up to the side of the hill. She reached for him. "Come on."

But she did not have the strength to pull him up. He wouldn't attempt that. He'd pull her right down. He motioned her back, as something sounded behind him, very near. Robert found a place where could put the ring of his belt into a crack and he turned to look. It was hovering a little below and at some forty yards out. The sliding door was open, and through the door and the glass dome, Robert could see the pilot and one other man.

Scoreman.

Seated beside the pilot, he had a gun on his lap, probably a rifle.

He slipped from his seat, sat on the floor opposite to the open door, and leaning back against the seat, rested his elbows on his knees. The helicopter swung about a bit, turning slowly around sideways again until Robert could again see Scoreman sitting just inside the open door. He raised his weapon.

"Edie!" he shouted up to her. "Get back."

The rising barrel of the gun became a black spot in the lower half of Scoreman's narrow face. But not quite all of the time yet: the helicopter was swaying a little and he was waiting for it to steady. Robert turned his face to the rock and held hard to his crevices. The shot came and a spatter of broken rock stung Robert's cheek and fingers. It had struck two feet to the right of his head.

Robert wondered if it was worth making some gesture of defiance. No, the man would enjoy that, it would show that he, Robert, knew who he was and cared; instead, he would simply climb. There could be no doubt now but that he would soon be shot. Only another cloud might save him. He looked down the valley. Others were coming but far out. The valley was clearer than ever before.

Now, a second helicopter was on its way up. All for them.

He climbed again. Another shot barely missed his ear and then a third splashed a string of chips of rock and lead just beside his thigh. The leader was dropping refinements, Robert thought, he'll settle for a shot in the body after all. But then there was silence except for the engine and the loud fluffing beats of the rotor. Robert looked around and saw that the helicopter had turned and was facing the second one that was now coming in almost on a level very fast towards them. Through a corner of the glass dome, Scoreman was leaning forward speaking into a microphone. Still, the other machine came fast; it almost looked as if they would crash. Then it suddenly veered left, away from the cliff. A little way out it started on a tight turn, leaning steeply. The first, Scoreman's, also started to turn—going back to the way it had been earlier.

He climbed again. He still couldn't understand why the second had come, why the two seemed to be squaring off in the sky like bulls, ready to charge. Scoreman would have finished Robert already, if not for that.

There was one more shot, a poor miss. The other copter was still getting in the way. He could hear it coming close along the canyon wall from the direction of the waterfall. It was easy here; the cracks and pits were good and the face was at last sloping in. When he turned, he saw that the first was again facing the second, and at the same time was slowly backing away. Scoreman was on the floor and was re-winding his arm in the sling. Again, Robert could see his face; he was angry.

The other machine came slowly on. It was very close to the cliff and alarmingly close to Robert. The two machines kept face to face. Robert hung there and watched the second edging in…so close he could finally make out the people inside. Two men, the pilot and someone standing, leaning over the pilot's chair from behind.

Karl.

The second machine had moved right in and was there where the first had been before it, hanging and bouncing on updrafts just opposite to Robert. Scoreman's had backed off, although it was still very close. Scoreman was shooting again, and repeating shots faster than before, but he was now at quite an angle along the cliff and firing from twice as far off.

Now, still leaning over the pilot, Karl turned his narrow and white face up towards Robert. He smiled and jerked his head towards the top of the cliff. His other hand held a knife, its point pressed against the pilot's neck. The pilot, face pale, was leaning forward, clutching the control.

Karl loosened his hand on the shirt while still keeping the knife where it was. He pointed to Robert, made some gestures around his chest and shoulders;

then he held up his thumb and grinned. It was a moment only; then he was pointing once more to the cliff above.

Climb, his gesture said.

Robert waved and turned back to the face. He unhooked the buckle from its crack and began to climb fast. A new strength had come and his heart sang. Oh, even at the very worst, he could die better now, when he knew that Karl was with him.

Karl! It had been Karl there on the rock! He had seen Robert climbing. It had been no fist he had raised, or, if fist, had been his salute! He had come to help him—Karl, Karl—at Robert's last trial he had turned to his own dear and brave self once again.

The wind up the valley was strengthening more. Clouds came; both copters went far off from the face, although Robert could still hear them in the mist.

The cloud passed. A finger of green branches was there above—branches, blue sky, and still the silvery unlit rockweed on the red stone. Out of the blue sky, the two helicopters raced down towards him.

He climbed.

One of the machines was very close to him. He climbed until he could find a place to jam his belt and hung and turned quickly round to see which it was. It was Scoreman's. It was turning again to bring its open door opposite and Scoreman was there again sitting in the door with a different, much shorter gun of pale metal. The other chopper was close by also, nose to nose, and was trying to edge in again along the wall. Robert saw furious gestures passing between Scoreman and his pilot. Scoreman was shouting, but the pilot was ignoring him, slowly backing, and Scoreman still not in a place to fire from the open door. Scoreman's copter turned slowly outward from the face. He's defeated again, his pilot again chickening to the other, Robert thought joyfully. But it wasn't the same. Somehow both the copters were ignoring him now and were sinking below his level, each focused on the other. Robert climbed. When he looked again, it was into the dome of Karl's just below, seeing it through the black flashing of its whirling blades. There it was like watching a violent happening on a television screen after you have just come into a room and do not know the story—a dream act going on in a bubble or a crystal ball. The pilot of Karl's copter was making wild gestures, stabbing with his finger towards the other, shaking in his chair, half-turning to Karl who still stood over him leaning on the back of his seat and holding the knife on his back. Robert looked to where the pilot was so violently pointing. The other machine was turning. It turned outward from the cliff until its door faced the one below. Scoreman was kneeling in the door, his face distorted with hatred and fury. He had raised the white gun to his shoulder.

Robert heard him fire and saw the line of holes spring in the other copter's dome and flaring cracks and a sparkle of chips flying in the sunlight. He saw Karl crouched low behind the pilot's chair. Scoreman lowered his gun and turned to his own pilot. Karl's chopper rose, swung unsteadily towards the cliff. It drew level with Robert: the wind of its blades was thumping on his shoulders and for a moment he thought it was going to hit him and crash on the cliff. Then it steadied, and Robert looked again and saw it was much closer to him than either had yet been. Karl was sitting on the lap of the pilot. The pilot's head was laid sideways behind Karl's back as though he was asleep. Karl looked towards Robert and smiled at him again but with tight lips. He was holding the control bar by the ends as if he sat at the steering wheel of a car.

Now he grinned and scratched his short hair. He reached down beside him the way a man would grope for the gear lever or the handbrake in an unfamiliar car. He pointed vaguely into the mass of dials in front of him and scratched his head again and put a crooked finger against his puzzled and yet smiling lips, biting his nail. Robert smiled despite himself, and with leaping heart, thought, *He's pretending he doesn't know how to drive. But he must know a bit how to fly or the thing wouldn't hover as close and steady as it did. Or is he crackers again?*

Karl was looking at him and grinning as if nothing mattered now except for the little dumb show that he was putting on, the joke between them two, with him pretending to be a learner driver out in the road too soon; and again, Robert could only watch him amazed, could only think of the dead pilot lying soft under his arse, and wonder how—Karl would ever get down. And he smiled back.

Scoreman's helicopter had been rising and turning again the way it had been when he had last fired. Karl didn't seem to have seen it. Robert pointed to it. Even then Karl didn't stop. He gestured back with the flat of his hand. Contempt, no problem, the gesture said. And as the doorway of the other machine again swung into view, Karl leaned forward and with a sort of—hell, an imperious dignity!—waved at it, a curt sign to tell it to go down and away. The

310

other still rose. Scoreman was kneeling there, still more fury on his face. His pale short gun was already raised, but he was waiting to be level, or perhaps, fearing a crash, until he was above the other machine.

Karl hunched over his control. He pulled down on the peak of an imaginary hat, turned to Robert, and grinned, and waved. Quite suddenly, his machine tilted steeply down.

Fear dawned on Scoreman's face. He looked astonished; he lowered his gun and leaned swiftly across towards the pilot.

Karl's machine seemed to hang for a moment, and then it went sliding forward and down, and Robert knew in a flash what was to be the finale of the act that Karl had wanted him to stay and see—

But he could not look. He pulled himself close to the cliff, turned his face away, closed his eyes.

There was a tremendous bang and an explosion that rang against the rock all around him. He opened his eyes. There was only one helicopter: it was whirling towards the cliff, its rotor spinning, its entire tail was gone. There was a noise of a giant stick run on a paling fence as the rotor struck the cliff; he saw the body of the copter bounce on the rock and then vanish below into the cloud. Some long seconds later a crash came far below; then, seconds after, another, finally a softer creak and crash—that of a falling tree.

He clung to the cliff. Now he knew only that he had wanted more time— to be with Karl again, speak to him, and to say goodbye.

PART 5

The Forest

THE JEEP

1

Flood

Robert was dreaming of home. He was dreaming of Sam and Linda, telling him to be a good boy, before jetting off to Spain. *Be a good boy,* he thought bitterly. *I am not a boy. You mean to keep me here, away from the world. I have seen more than either of you. My parents...*

He woke with a sob in his throat, the image of his parents, beckoning to him that day on the shore.

Something was gently tickling and stroking his feet. At first, he remembered Edie and thought it was her, playing a trick on him. But when he sat up, he saw her, curled beside him, asleep. His heart leapt at the memory of the pleasant night they'd spent together. They'd found a town after their escape from prison, and rented a lorry, and headed out to find the jeep, just as he'd promised her. And then, darkness fell, and they'd been forced to camp out on the banks of the river.

But when he looked, he realised that the sensation was wavelets, touching his feet, from a great sheet of brown water that had already come up to the wheels of the lorry. Now, even more than what had begun in the past few days, it was as if he and the lorry were on a beach and this was the tide. He looked out at the trunks, now standing deep in the flood and then under the lorry. The white sheet of the oxbow lay out before him, the wall of the forest beyond it and the tops of bushes showing just above the water, like reeds.

315

"Edie!" He got up quickly, cursing their stupidity.

She woke and looked around, then slipped away from the encroaching water. "Oh!"

Although he considered everything was now lost, he walked around the margin of the coming flood, trying to see if there was a way he could salvage the vehicle.

"Robert! Look!"

He followed her outstretched finger beyond the lorry, which was still mostly in sight above the water, to the top of another vehicle, this one, in a terrible state, blackened and battered.

The jeep.

They'd found it, but now, it was almost gone. He could only see the top of the wrecked cab, as it was in danger of being fully submerged. Water was lapping at the level where the windows had been.

Great. We'll have lost two vehicles, here, now. And if last time was any indication, it'll only go downhill from here.

"Maybe I can salvage some of our things from the jeep?" he asked, starting to wade out there.

"Be careful!" she cried. "The current!"

Indeed, the current was stronger than it appeared. He looked along the water's edge to the lorry and saw that its wheels were already deeper in the water than they had been moments ago. The flood was coming very fast and that was current to the brown water now. Between him and the lorry, there was a small log touching the shore, a smashed branch shaped like a Y. He crawled to it and pushed it with his foot. It was some light soft wood and was floating.

Suddenly, from away up the valley behind him he heard the engine sound again. A grader or something was coming back. He could get to it this time. He crawled into the water pushing the floating branch ahead of him.

He could walk most of the way down to the jeep, but, when he got near, he found that there was quite a strong cross current and he had to work hard to move on towards it. The current was from the marsh and towards the oxbow.

When he got to the cab, he peered in the open windows. Everything was submerged, some of it floating on the surface of the brackish water. He felt carefully everywhere, probing the corners under the water with his feet. He wasn't so sure now that, if it had stayed sunk, eddies of the current might not have lifted it sufficiently for it to be carried out through a window.

At last, the only thing he pulled from the water was the soaked toilet roll that held Dewey's drawing. He recalled, fondly, something Karl had joked about, long ago. *In the art fraud business, they call this giving the work a patina of age.*

He looked in the direction of the current and saw that there was a dam of floated branches and trunks that were forced against the few still upright trees that separated the makeshift road from the open water of the oxbow. There was a lot of small twiggy stuff and some green floating plants—reeds—held up behind the jammed logs.

He let himself down into the water again and pushed gently off and floated. He knew it was crazy and dangerous even as he did it. The current carried his floating body quite swiftly down to the dam of logs. Already, he realized that the space to it was further than he had thought, and that the water was much deeper and that he had no plan about how he was going to get back.

He ended up among all that myriad, floating rubbish of the forest—seeds, old dry fruits, palm leaves, twigs alive and dead, brown scum, and floating plants. There, almost against his chest, deep in the water amongst the debris but easily seen, was the toilet roll from the jeep.

With the roll in his teeth, he climbed up a branch onto one of the big logs of the dam. The whole set up rocked a bit as he put his weight on it, but at last steadied, and he found he could sit on it right out of the water. Eagerly, he pulled the roll apart, not tearing it as he had before but carefully, taking off layers until he was nearly to the inner cardboard tube. At last, he gently detached from the roll a sodden sheet of a thicker and stronger paper and laid it on his knee. It was the picture of the indigene's head that Karl had bought from Mrs Foster, the page from Dewey's small sketchbook. Robert looked at the drawing with a growing delight and triumph. Though wet, the picture was perfect still. He looked out across the oxbow towards where the butte was. And of course, from here the face of the rocks was behind trees. Anyway, it was not needed: it was clear from memory. It was the same face—it had been just touched and rounded a little to make it seem like a sketch of a real man. He counted the holes in the upper lip: in the part that you could see of the man's half-turned face, there were exactly seven. The second one from the right in the picture was not just a hole but had been made to a cross by two diagonal cuts. Perhaps it was scarred and torn—the native had suffered a blow from a stick? A special insignia of some clan? He looked at this widened hole in the lip very carefully, and it was nothing like this and was as he had thought. It had been done later, added—added the time Annetta had told to Karl, after the diamonds had gone from the bed, after the dying man had returned to the hut that last time.

The proof was this: Despite the wetness of the paper, Robert could see that the draughtsman had been careless. The line of the crossways cut in the lip was not drawn so firmly as the rest and a trace of a pencil stroke wandered a little up on the man's cheek. Dewey had been very sick. And these strokes had been done in a different pencil, harder and not so black. He had prepared the drawing beforehand, sketching there at the old hut, when he had decided what to do. After he had done it—with what canoe trip, what climb, what effort—costing him his life!—then he had added that cross to show which cave. Now there was one last test needed to confirm Annetta's telling. Robert felt carefully on his own lip, looking at the drawing, and his heart danced in triumph. Yes, it would be so—that wider hole, crossed by the pencil, would be just above the man's left eye-tooth. Had the rocks been a man.

Robert grinned and tried to snap his fingers, but no snap would come. He scrambled slowly to his feet on the log and looked out towards the river. He wished he could see, could salute the rocky shade whom Dewey had made guardian to his diamonds, to what reliable witnesses had called the world's greatest hoard. Now Robert would face his silent and mocking gaze more surely and would reply.

Of course, even standing, he couldn't see the cliff; tree trunks and vines were in the way. And beyond the oxbow, the trees would probably still be too high and too near to allow him to see even the top of the butte. But unless he could see past the nearby trees and vines. Robert couldn't be sure of this. It was needless to do, but he wanted, if he could, to look once more at the cave where he now knew the diamonds must be. Behind him, the sound of the grader had become very close and loud. Finally the sound stopped, probably just up the hill at the point where he had left the other lorry, there where you could look down on the broken one which then had been dry and now was wheels down behind him under the flood. Robert turned to see the place but could not; it too was hidden by the trees; just as he hadn't seen the jeep and the second mired lorry from up there, so now he couldn't see the place. But he was not quite by the lorry or the jeep now and he thought that from the other end of the log the people in the grader might see him. And also, looking the other way, he might see the butte.

He was unsteady, but he held to one upright branch and then to another and moved down toward the bole. There he swayed and tried to regain his balance.

The log rolled, and with rolling, the dam burst. He found himself down in the water again clinging to a branch, and in a moment, he was being carried out in a swift current towards the main river. He called, "Edie! I think I've found it!"

2

The Map

The next morning, Robert and Edie walked up the footpath through the bush-filled channel, the remains of the once hopeful road. The forest was coming back, all eating itself in the new way that Robert had learned to see, but evidently not fast enough to cancel out its growth, for that went on, and the channel, so neatly cleared not long ago by saws and dozers, was filling fast with saplings and vines. In the greenery on all sides, Robert could hear the forest's strife. He could hear the pulling of the leafy hair, the crashing, the groan of strained branches, the skins splitting as the parasites came through their victims. He could see it too: everywhere were baby leaves bitten the moment they burst from the bud, and so many blotched by moulds, and so many others decayed and starved of light. Spiders had made their webs across the path between cassia and cassia and tall grass and horse tomato bush. There in the webs, the spiders fed on their moths and flies, and when you looked closely at the spiders themselves, as Edie showed him, nearly every one had another red or yellow blob-like creature on it, or even many, sucking the spider's own body. They were attached to the back or to a leg or any place where they could not be pulled off by their victim. Edie told him to look closer and he saw the legs of these blobs—eight. The blobs were the spiders' kin.

The day arched brilliant over this tremendous war—blue sky and fleecy clouds—and up to the left, through gaps in the trees, the volcano reared its far-off head of snows.

Robert held the map in his hands. As for those stones, was it true that they crazed everyone, as Annetta had said? If so, they certainly had crazed him oppositely. He found that he wanted none of the fame or fortune. All he wanted to do was keep them out of the hands of the vile Dr Paul.

At last, they had climbed really high. Their track, which had been uphill all the way, was flattening out. They were out of the forest, and in one more mile, had reached the road. Almost opposite their own disused track, there was another, smaller but much-used. It wound off amongst the grass and bushes of the savannah. Between the two junctions, on their side, there was a seat of the type which Robert had now seen twice before—a big log cut by a chain saw to give it a crude flat seat and a back. He looked curiously and with some fear at the track and the savannah opposite. For savannah, it was rather unusually green and well grazed and fertile, and it reminded him of a landscape that he had seen once before—green and level cattle land stretching away into a haze and, behind the haze, rising, tier upon tier, the dim velvety ridges of a mountain.

They went to the log seat and sat down.

"That is the path that goes to the cave on the map," said Edie, scooting over to allow him to have a seat as she buried her nose in the picture. "See?"

"How far, do you think?"

"Not far. Of course, there are no markings on this map but I think it shouldn't be more than a day. Otherwise, we'd cut right into the river."

For a moment, he thought he heard the sound of helicopter rotors. They still didn't feel far enough from Dr Paul's farmhouse. He stood up. "Let's go. I don't like this place."

"Nor I," said Edie quietly, and she looked sharply at Robert again. "I'm ready when you are."

They were silent for quite a long time. At last, Robert said, "Edie, it could be dangerous. Perhaps you should stay here."

"Oh, you do keep me—you keep me always," Edie said, changing her manner and flashing a big smile. "Whether we say goodbye or do not say it, I do not think we can ever part now."

"I—Why?" Robert exclaimed, stupidly. "You mean that?"

"Of course."

"Even—even when I go back to London?"

She pushed ahead. "Oh, let's not talk about that now."

Robert felt his shoulders grow heavy. Then he braced himself and sat upright, thinking that there would be little further time to talk. Edie as usual had read his thought, for she added, "I am still thinking about that."

Robert said no more, but his hopes were buoyed by the thought. Maybe she would come with him? He looked up at the mountain and saw that the high clouds were parting and showing its shining snowfields. It was so splendid to look on that he felt cheered. Yet still, he could see no foothills beyond the level savannah. The mountain was magic, floating—just now he could easily imagine that it might float farther and farther away, just as once in London the same one had seemed to come close, by some optical trick, through an immense distance. He looked at Edie again and felt troubled—there was an undercurrent of fear, excitement, flowing between them and he felt himself standing on the edge of a gulf just as when he had reached the top of the cliff.

"Tell me," she said after they went another short distance. "Do you think we will see Karl again?"

He had been thinking about that for a long time. He didn't think Karl would be able to go back to Dr Paul, not after the helicopter stand-off. But then, where would he go? Perhaps even now, he was trying to get back to his old self, to look for those diamonds. But without those drugs he needed, the ones that tied him inexorably to Dr Paul...could he? He'd likely have to go back to Paul, and accept whatever punishment was given him. "I don't know. I don't think so."

She sighed. "I think you are right." She stopped and pointed. "Look. That's the one."

He followed her outstretched fingers to the mouth of a cave, only partially visible beyond the vegetation.

His heart leapt. Only when he started to walk toward it did he indeed hear the rotors of a helicopter. This time, it was not in his head. They were approaching, incongruous to the conversation, out of the west, over the forest.

It was too late to hide. The first plane was now past them and the other coming up. The droning of the two combined was quite loud. It nearly drowned for a while the noise of a Land Rover bumping through the woods, toward them.

When he heard it, he looked round very startled and at once saw clearly through the window Dr Paul driving.

The Land Rover passed and turned into the side road. The canvas hood was off the back and two men were sitting just behind the cab holding onto the metal frame. As the Land Rover turned on to the track one of the men stood up, still holding the frame, to look at the aeroplanes over the cab. The other, however, was looking out behind and he saw Robert and Edie. Suddenly this man reached over and began to knock on the back of the cab. Some forty yards away, the Land Rover came slowly to a halt. All three men were now staring at Robert.

He thought of dodging into the cave but shrank back. He realized that he was not going to run, he could not. One of the men moved swiftly to the tailboard and bent over something there—it would be the toolbox, Robert guessed at once—and that was where weapons would be.

"Edie—" he said urgently.

"Oh, no!" he heard Edie say quietly beside him. "What will we do?"

Somewhere way ahead, there came a shot and then another and then after a pause, a burst of automatic fire. Then there was the loud distant noise of a car engine drawing rapidly nearer. Then an intense, staccato burst of firing came from several points among the trees ahead. After this second firing, the sound of the car engine stopped.

Dr Paul stepped out of the car and went to them, smiling benevolently. "I see we are all here for the same purpose, then. Shall we go in together and see what we can see?"

3

Diamonds

Robert and Edie were brought to the central hall of the cavern. There, two men now bound them tight to a stepladder. They tied him at ankles, knees, waist, and shoulders, while his hands, still behind him, were left tied with the wire.

Men were busy putting trees back in place where the Land Rover had come in.

When their knotting was finished, the two men shoved the ladder to its upright position.

Now, just as before, the leader came on alone, a nightmare, within the dream of the dark cavern. He paused by Robert with a smile. "You are probably wondering how I found you."

Robert spat, "These are your lands. I thought you knew them like the back of your hand."

"I wish I did. I didn't know these lands. Not like Dewey did. If I had, I'd have taken the diamonds when he died and at the time Annetta and Karl came to live with me."

Robert stared. "Annetta and Karl?"

Dr Paul smiled. "Did Karl not tell you that Miss Fairby and the good scientist were his parents?"

Robert simply could not speak, because now, when he thought of it, it seemed that he'd known it all along. Of course, that would be why Karl was so educated in insects and plants and things. And why he and Annetta...

"However, before I knew it, Annetta went off and sold his last sketches in London. Which made things quite impossible for me, you see? Had it not been for all that, I wouldn't have needed you or him. Or Edie." His eyes shifted to her. "Karl told you about his implant, didn't he? Did Edie tell you about hers?"

Robert's stomach dropped.

"Doctor!" a voice called from deep within the cave.

Dr Paul looked as though he was about to say something, but held up a finger. "I'll let her tell you. I've been waiting too long for this. It's time to see what's at rainbow's end."

He quickly turned and hurried off. When his footsteps faded, all Robert could hear was Edie's heavy breathing. "Edie," he whispered. "Are you drugged?"

"No," she said in a small voice. "But he did implant something inside me. Under my arm. It hurts. I think—they said it was a tracker."

Robert's head fell back. So, Dr Paul had let them escape. No wonder they'd gotten off so easily. He'd taken Edie because he knew Robert would come back for her, and that together, they'd find the diamonds. He'd told Dr Paul he'd never help him, but he had. He'd unwittingly led him right to Dewey's diamonds.

"I'm sorry, Robert," she whispered and started to sob quietly. "I should've told you."

"No. Edie. It's not your fault."

"They're going to kill us," she whispered. "Now that they have what they need."

When Dr Paul returned, he held something up to the firelight, for them to see. It looked like a cloudy pebble, but Robert knew what it really was—an enormous and very valuable uncut diamond.

The men that were with him hooted and hollered. "Thousands of them!" someone shouted. Robert swallowed the lump in his throat. Wrists still bound, he reached over to find Edie. He wanted to hold her hand, but only managed to stroke it with his fingertips. It was as cold as ice.

"It's all right," he said to her. "It'll be all right."

Robert didn't want to view Dr Paul's ultimate triumph. It meant that they had failed, that all of Santania would fall under his hold and Dewey's cure would never get to all the people who needed it. Robert looked instead at the man coming behind and after a moment's disbelief, realized that he had seen him before. He was the man who had passed him and Karl on horseback at that stream crossing way to the north—where they had washed and had that mock battle, where the spider had been, and the crickets had run on the sand. He was the man who had given them milk and the cocoa fruit. It seemed a million years ago.

The man was looking closely at him. Then, the man did something Robert did not expect. He winked at him.

At that moment, Robert remembered what Karl had said. He was a police officer from St. Flortwy.

Edie shuddered, and Robert heard, almost in a whisper at his elbow, "Oh, this is terrible."

But that little movement, small as it was, had given Robert something that had all but left him—hope.

"What are you—" He stopped when the man put a finger to his lips and quickly advanced into the darkness, where Dr Paul and his other men were pulling the diamonds from the trove.

Edie tensed. "What is happening?"

"I don't kn—"

While he was saying this, Dr Paul had broken into a run towards Robert and Edie. As Paul came near, Robert saw pink bubbles bursting from his lips. His shirt and hands were dappled red. Paul pitched forward as he ran and crashed in the road at their feet, a knife buried between his shoulder blades.

The cave went absolutely silent. Dr Paul lay in the sand. A crowd of soldiers from the trucks had gathered: all looked down silently at the dusty, blood-spattered man who, with the knife removed, had been gently rolled onto his back. Then there was a scream and a woman burst through the crowd from behind and flung herself on the dead man, kissing him, and feeling with her cheek for any breath coming from between the bloody and disdainfully smiling lips, wiping blood from his face with her blue-dyed hair and her hands.

Robert and Edie could not watch and turned away. Others among the soldiers turned away also. The man from horseback carefully untied them and whispered, "For Karl. Now run."

They took off, running.

They never saw the diamonds, or Dr Paul, ever again, but as they reached the mouth of the cave, they came upon dozens of police officers, rushing their way, and as they climbed down the hill toward the road, there was the unmistakable sound of gunfire.

Edie said, "But Robert! The diamonds."

Robert did not slow, not even a bit. He'd promised only two things during this journey; that he would keep the diamonds out of Dr Paul's hands, and that he'd deliver Edie safely home. Now that he'd done one, he was ready to finish the other.

4

Homecoming

hree days later, Robert and Edie travelled down the long slope of the world towards her home. In the reality of the plateau, of course, it wasn't all down. In fact, more of it was up, because of the long valley he had to go up that carried the road towards the dry hills and the moorland rim. But the hills were green and the farms happy-looking, and even the floods in the fields and the streams onto the road that he must wade through, flowed for him cheerfully and warm, under a blue sky.

A lorry brought them to the town nearest to the flooded Furnace River. Then the long, long walk with nothing coming by and taking him most of the afternoon. As they descended to the moors, the sheer beauty of the place struck him. He hadn't noticed how lovely this valley was before because, when they had arrived, it was misty, and when they had left, his thoughts had been too much drawn to the girls they were carrying. Back then, he had thought Valery was the beautiful one and so she was, but she was a lone spark in that landscape, bright and different; she did not unite with his love for this whole natural world like Edie did.

A turn in the road brought him to the banana grove. And a person was sitting on the roadside in the shadow of the arching leaves. It was Edie's sister, the little girl who had met them at the same spot the last time they had come.

"Annie!" Edie cried.

She, looking very much like a miniature Edie, suddenly uncoiled from the roadside and stood there, slim and dark in the shadow of the tattered, arching leaves, shading her eyes to look towards them, and broke into a run towards her. Edie, too, started to run, and the two met each other in the middle of the bridge, Edie gathering the small girl into her arms. "Edie!" she shouted with glee.

"Yes, it's me," she said, smoothing the girl's hair.

It seemed only a few seconds, noticing nothing of what he passed, before they were at the door of the farmhouse. It wasn't open. The farmyard was very silent: he couldn't even hear or see chickens. A slab of the blue-painted plaster, perhaps loosed in the recent heavy rain, had fallen into the yard from the wall and lay there in fragments purple and brown. The vine was low over the door; its sombre, heart-shaped leaves had no flowers to welcome him this time.

The door swung open, and an older woman stood there. At first, Robert did not know her, but then pieces of her—her eyes, her hair, became familiar. It was Mrs Oliveira. Surprise, and then joy, lit her eyes.

"Ah—you!" She said, stopping short in the half-darkness back from the doorway.

"Mother!"

In seconds, Edie and her mother were locked in each other's arms, both weeping.

"Mother! Mother! It is you! I am home! Oh!—home!"

When Mrs Oliveira pulled away, her eyes were red with crying and her cheeks wet, but she looked immensely happy. She was younger again. She breathed the air and looked out over the farm as though she had returned from a long journey.

Annie took Edie by the hand. "Oh! Come inside. I have so much to show you!"

Robert went in and saw Edie standing at the table and staring at the window with a rapt smile. Annie was in front of her and holding her two hands and pulling at them, but Edie wasn't looking at her, or with no more than one downward glance, and was instead gazing out of the window and was saying: "Yes, Annie, in a minute, in a minute. We will see my birds. Annie! I am home!"

Mrs Oliveira seemed to change course from whatever had taken her to the door. Now, she talked of making a great feast for their return. "And of course, I will want to hear the story. I'm sure you have a lot to tell us. As we have a lot to tell you."

Edie nodded and held out her hand to her mother. She placed something in her palm. "The first is that Dr Paul will plague us no more. He's dead," Edie said solemnly.

Her eyes lightened. "It's true?"

Robert nodded.

Edie smiled. "I'd say that is cause for a celebration. Yes, Mother?"

The darkness returned to her face. "Before that, there is something I should show you."

5

A Tragedy

Mrs Oliveira silently led them through the house, to the bedroom at the back of a long hallway. When she stopped at the door, she glanced back for a moment, then quietly opened it. The lamp showed a pallet in a far corner of the room with a mosquito net over it. Through the mosquito net, he could see the thin shape of a man lying asleep. He could hear his raspy breathing.

He went over to the net and lifted it and saw that the man was lying on his back on a pile of sheepskins. Evidently, he had been very badly hurt. Both of his legs and one of his arms were tied between sticks of wood with bandages of bast. From the splinted limbs and the thin waist, Robert's eyes travelled to the man's pale, skull-like head—

Then he saw that the face was Karl's. After that, all was easy: of course, it was Karl. He was thin indeed, but—then, of course, this had to be. Skull-like, his head was still its old shape: it was narrow, a hatchet, like it had always been. And everywhere you could still see the fine outline of his muscles; you could see that this boy, this skeleton, had once been strong. His hair was short, and some of the black-burned ends from the fire were still there. The red scars were also still on his face.

And among the red scars and the pale skin, on his forehead, there was the new mark which Robert was to see in his dreams ever after as the final badge of his friend's courage. In the lamplight the mark was black. It was the shape and size of an old wet beech leaf fallen on him. Robert at first thought it was the swelling of a bruise, but when he held the lamp close, he saw that it was a shallow pit punched into the bone of his forehead. Karl's mouth had a strange, tight expression which Robert had never seen there before; it was because of this expression helping the face to look skull-like, that he had not recognized him immediately.

Though his eyes were closed, Karl was clearly alive, breathing regularly. His throat was moving.

"How did he come to be here?" Robert said with amazement, rushing to his side.

"I don't know. He was brought in here by some passing travellers. He was found like this."

Karl gave a croak and his eyes opened: Robert saw with horror that the pupils were pointing in quite different directions and one almost out of sight; he was seeing nothing. Now his face began to contort slowly into a meaningless grimace, his lips drew back to bare his teeth, and there began the long groan that changed slowly into a scream, while at the same time, his whole body convulsed and writhed, his splinted limbs straining against their wrappings.

When the scream came, Robert seized his friend's one free hand—it was a clenched fist already, but he held it against all its strainings between his own palms, and he knelt beside the bed and leaned over and said, "Karl! It's me! It's Robert! It's all right, Karl! I have come!"

The scream went on completely unheeding his words. Robert flung his arm across Karl's thin shoulders and pulled them towards him saying, "Karl! Karl!" Still, the scream took no notice; only in its own time did it begin to die away. Karl lay limp again.

Robert released his shoulders and held his hand. He began to sob.

"You must not think that the crying hurts him," he heard Mrs Oliveira's voice behind him, "or that he does that because of pain."

Robert looked around and saw that they were both there, standing behind him.

"We understand how you feel. We have felt it too… But think, Robert, a screech owl screams like that and that is not for pain. Nor is he in pain. It seems to me that it is to be thought of like this… Karl is gone to some other world, some other life, when he does that. There are many levels in our mind—often it seems to me, by his movements, that he is now a fish, out in the Great River, and, who knows, perhaps out there, swimming, he is even happy!"

The leg moved stiffly inside the bandages. Karl lay as if asleep and gave no sign that he noticed he was being touched. She pointed to the beech-leaf mark on Karl's head. "I do not know what happened to him."

Robert guessed. Dr Paul had come to him and this had been his punishment for helping Robert escape. The thought tore at him, making his insides tight, his eyes welling with tears.

Robert held Karl's hand and watched him sleep as Mrs Oliveira said, "He is unhappy because he is lonely. I think he has been waiting for you. I think he wants to talk with you."

"Then does he wake up sometimes?" Robert said with a faint note of hope.

"No, he has been always like that since he came here."

"Then how can he talk with me?"

"That, I do not know."

"Karl!" he said, bending close to him. "Karl, now that I understand, we can talk. And I've wanted so much, so long to tell you something! We've done it, Karl! We won! I finished the climb! I got out! You did save me! And better than that, Dr Paul is dead. You're free. Do you understand?"

There was no response.

"Karl, not only that; I found the diamonds! I found the key in that sketch. I nearly lost it by drowning but didn't. The sketch was in the jeep—charred but I could read it. Now it's gone… Karl, Annetta died—but you knew, didn't you? She was ill, and—"

"His mother," Mrs Oliveira said.

Robert looked up. "So, it is true?"

Mrs Oliveira smiled sadly. "Annetta was his mother. He didn't tell you? I suppose that is right…there was some great falling out. He was upset because Annetta chose to go with Dr Paul, so soon after his father's death, and of course he was young and had to go, too. Dr Paul treated him abominably. But really, she had no choice. I've heard—"

Robert found himself squeezing Karl's hand. "His father…you mean Dewey?"

She nodded.

"So that means, the diamonds belong to him?"

Mrs Oliveira shrugged. "I suppose. But it was never them he cared for. He wanted to carry out his father's wishes and cure all the people of the disease. That was what Dewey had been doing there, trying to find a cure. He found one, which was the one he was trying to get out to the people, but unfortunately, Dr Paul found out about it, and did not like it. He did not want anyone having more power than he had."

Robert fell silent. He felt again the answering twitch in Karl's hand. In the pitch dark of the room, for a moment Robert tried to think of something to say. The only thing that came to mind was, *Thank you.*

So he told Karl, and followed it by telling the whole story of his escape, starting where he had last seen Karl in the big house.

He could feel through the hand Karl's eager listening now. It was easy. In the faint light coming through from the other rooms, he saw that the shaking was Karl's head banging to and fro in a monotonous rhythm. Worried, Robert stood up and tried to steady the head with his hands; he felt then that Karl's tight cheeks were wet with tears.

"Oh! I forgot to tell you this all along," he exclaimed. After this, only now and then his whole frame shook; Robert held his hand tight and felt the departing sobs seem to shake and hurt in his own throat, as if they were his. He steadied his voice and said, "I will make all the plans. When you are better, we will make sure the cure gets everywhere. All of this country will know your name. You, my friend, are a hero."

And the best friend I have ever known. He felt a hand patting his shoulder. He knew what it was of course. He turned and saw Mrs Oliveira with a bowl of soup. She looked radiant with delight, as if she'd seen some improvement in her patient after Robert's presence there. She nodded at Karl and then leaned forward quickly to take his hand. They both held him while he went into the prolonged convulsion and scream that must have been dammed up whilst Robert had been talking. It was so bad and went on so long that Robert was terrified by it again.

As Mrs Oliveira fed Karl, Robert told Karl the rest of the story, all those things he had felt too estranged to tell when they had met in the farmhouse: of the flight across the moors, the snatching of Edie, and on and on. He didn't tell him that he had fallen in love. Not while she was there, of course. But of course, Karl would be guessing that; Robert knew that he couldn't say her name and not let it sound that way to him. Would Karl guess that this was so much more serious than the thing with Valery? If Karl were to get better, oh, perhaps he might marry Valery himself. The two certainly seemed keen on one another. And then, would they be related? Brothers. As impossible as it sounded, the thought warmed Robert.

After the patient ate, Robert decided to carry Karl out into the open air. Outside it was a glorious day of sunshine with small white clouds. There was a promise of heat coming, but as yet it was fresh and warm, and the pall of the past few days—that white sky, seeming to melt with sweat and lassitude—was gone. Karl was easy to lift and yet hard to carry through the narrow doors of the hut because of the splints. Really, he was terribly light, a mere shadow of his former self.

Robert carried him out into the bright channel of the trees and laid him down on some soft grass and sat down beside him. Karl's head flopped to one side and he lay as if not knowing that he had been moved. Robert started to tell him in more detail than he'd done before how he and Edie had smashed up Dr Paul's basement flat and how they had, at last, managed to break even its very walls. He thought it was an amusing story and would cheer Karl, but he made no sound, no movement at all.

Big bees, like bumblebees yet much faster in their flight, were visiting purple blossoms close above. Robert thought that Karl, if he could, would give the scientific name of each one, and expound upon their many eccentricities. Though he'd always thought Karl rather pompous and long-winded about it before, now, he almost longed for the education.

Instead, Robert told Karl how he had deciphered the sketch. He told him how he was planning to go back to London after the last of the medicine was distributed, and how maybe, one day, Karl could visit him again there. "It certainly is dreadful to think of going back to Sam and Linda," he said, "after all that has happened. The world seems too different now. I don't know how I will. I'll need you, mate. And perhaps…you will need me a little, too? It certainly was an adventure. Not all good, but adventures rarely are. I still think I am better for it."

As he was speaking, he noticed a movement beside him. He prepared to take Karl's hand and to hold him in the coming struggle, but, looking, he saw that Karl had stiffened and had started slowly to shake his head. Even his eyes opened, but then contracted with pain and closed.

"Well, I won't go back to London if you don't want," Robert said quickly, breathing fast and watching.

The head shaking stopped. "Is it that you don't want me to go?" Again, the head began to shake. "Well, I will, and you'll come, too. Karl—you're moving for the first time: I think you are getting better! And I wish you could tell me what you do want!"

Karl could tell him, sort of. But it took a lot of beating about because Karl's only signals were this shaking of the head for a negative and the other, a slight pressure of the fingers, which sometimes worked and sometimes didn't.

One thing that Robert found out quickly enough from the negatives was that he didn't want a hospital or anything like it for himself.

Sometime later, there was a lot of head shaking that Robert could not understand. It was slow and faint. Karl seemed very tired, and Robert wondered if he was hearing at all.

"Well, what the hell do you want me to do, Karl? After trying to see to Dewey's wishes? What am I to do if not to go home?"

The battered and skull-like head lay to one side and Karl seemed far asleep and made to move. The beech-leaf dent, in this bright light of day, might have been beautiful if it had not been what it was: it reminded Robert of one of those photos of the sun taken at the full eclipse—where from under the moon's black disk flames of green and yellow spread over the sky.

"I can't just vanish, can I? Where should I go, Karl? Do what we once talked about? Go south from Cimoul—way down—to those new farmlands—and those mountains farther south?"

Karl's head, still turned to one side, made the faintest shaking.

"Do you want me to come back here?"

Karl made no move and Robert reached for his hand and held it, as he had done before, to see if he was saying yes. He felt the faintest twitch.

"To Edie?" he said, puzzled. "You want me to stay here?"

Karl's hand withdrew. Robert looked at him sharply knowing that he seldom moved a limb except when in a convulsion. Sure enough, his lips were moving in those tight, pulled grimaces and his mouth opening—but there was something different and no sound came. His free arm was scrabbling for something, he was trying actually to do something with that arm. At last, trying to steady and control him and meeting jerks that seemed like irritation, Robert guessed: Karl was trying to sit up!

At once, Robert had rolled onto his knees and knelt beside him, gripping both his shoulders and holding him down. "You mustn't, Karl," he said. "You're not ready for it..." He looked around. "But what is it, Karl? What is it?"

Instead of pushing Karl down as he meant, he found he was pulling him up, helping him, or perhaps it was Karl who was pushing him, now that he had his elbow firmly planted to the ground. Both the boys' heads were up among the prickly stems of the bush, breaking the spiders' webs and shaking down dead leaves into their hair. Robert couldn't take his eye from Karl's slowly moving lips. They were twisted, baring teeth to the gums—it was like in one of the pictures in his biology book—a chimpanzee which looked as if it were laughing or afraid, but the caption said anger.

"What is it, Karl? What is it?" he whispered again and again. But again, he had it wrong, the lips weren't trying to say anything, yet still, still, there was something else he was trying to do. A hand shaking like a flag's halyard in a gale came to Robert's shoulder; against his other shoulder came the wooden splints in a stiff clasp. So they held on to one another, and then the separate, wandering pupils of Karl's eyes, which Robert, during the convulsions, had so often watched with horror, came together and looked into Robert's own. Then he saw what it was that Karl was trying to tell him by all this long struggle and the stiff grimace: He was smiling, laughing!

He saw the shadow of his head on Karl's and the bright lit stubble of his hair and, for a moment, the flash of sunlight in his eyes. Then the eyes closed and the shoulders he held were limp and the shaking hand on his arm fell away. He laid him down. It was a limpness such as Robert had never felt before—always, always in this illness, even in deepest sleep, he'd been tense. Robert thought that Karl had never in his whole life relaxed, had never let the fight go, not even when under the drugs, like he was letting it go now. As his friend's head fell sideways on the grass, his eyes opened again.

And the smile was still on his face, even at the very last.

6

Goodbyes

Contrary to what he'd expected that morning, when they returned to the moors with the sun shining overhead, there was no celebration that night. Instead, Robert went off by himself, to a corner of the weed-choked garden, and sobbed.

He was not sure how long he stayed there, alone. The sun had long since disappeared, and the mosquitoes were biting.

Edie came and put a comforting arm around him. "I am so sorry," she said.

She smelled like soap and her hair was damp around her shoulders. She let him dry his tears on the sleeve of her dress, a soft, new one he didn't know she owned. Then Robert started as though suddenly awakened and tried to press her closer. She pushed at him gently.

"You shouldn't hold me like this. It is bad for me to allow it. But it is nice—so nice." Instead of drawing away, she put her forehead on his chest again. "I always knew Valery would have this, and I so long hoped it could happen to me, too…and now it has. But holding each other like this is wrong."

"Edie, why is that wrong? It is only for you to say—it's if you like it."

She sighed, hesitated, and then said, "I say it because I am not what you think."

"What do you mean?"

341

"I mean that it could never work for us. I heard what you told Karl about going back to London. So, it's impossible."

"You can come with me."

She laughed. "Oh, I couldn't! For one thing, this is my home. My mother needs me. And I told you already. I have never even seen maktak, or whatever it is called. It'd kill me."

Her shoulders, which he now held again, quivered. "No. You mustn't keep saying it! Whatever you are, Edie—Edie, I have tried to stop and I can't. I can't stop loving you. I love you, love you—every minute of every day. I can't stop thinking of you."

Her white-dark face turned up to him again.

"Robert—You must not, even now…"

He drew her to him again and this time she did not resist. He kissed her cheek and then her lips, her hooky nose was turned and pressed upwards against his. He whole lithe body pressed on him, sung in his arms.

When their lips parted, he whispered desperately, "Edie, then—now—can it be the same as before?"

"No, I think," she said faintly. "It is—just so impossible, like this—you and I."

"What does it matter?" He said fiercely.

"You have to think, Robert. You need someone more like yourself. Someone from your world."

He stamped his foot. "Edie—"

"Oh, it is one thing," she went on, "when we are in hills far away in danger, or prison. It is another when we are in London, in a place that is all yours and none of mine. I would not understand a thing! I'm sure everything would have to be written, and I cannot even read or write! Now that I have thought about it, even *you* would seem different—how could you not? Oh, Robert. Do not be angry."

"What is my world like then?"

"Great. Terrible."

"Edie, you make me crazy. This isn't my world! It's not England! And yet we still fell in love. At least, I fell in love with you. Anyway, don't you remember about us? How I had to learn everything from you. And I am more of your kind now than ever I was; I have learned so much—so many things from you. *You* are my world. Edie, you must—"

Somehow, they swung together again and he didn't finish. This time it was she who spoke first when they broke apart. She gasped a little for a breath and then smiled cheerfully and pushed him a half arm's length distant. "I love you, of course. I will always. And maybe you will come back here. But I cannot leave."

He held her tight. "Then I won't leave."

She shook her head. "You have to. You promised Karl you'd finish his dream, and the country needs you. There are still more doses of Dewey's medicine to get, to spread throughout the world."

Robert shrugged. "All right. Then I will come back. As soon as I can."

She smiled faintly and stood up. "Then I will be waiting."

"Now, in the light, I can see your dress. Edie—it is lovely."

She laughed. "Oh, Robert, don't smoosh me! Still, I like it if you like it. It seemed lovely to me when I saw it in the shop in St. Flortwy. But now, here I see that it is nothing of a dress. I wish I had had Valery to help me choose because others were brighter, but I was afraid I'd look silly." She laughed nervously and added as if as an afterthought, "Valery sees magazines. You know how she is."

"It's absolutely perfect for you, Edie. It's others who make themselves foolish with their clothes and their make-up, not you."

"Then you don't like bright dresses?" she asked suspiciously.

"Oh, I do—some. But dull ones are often more beautiful."

"Dull, yes it is—there, I knew you were smooshing me again."

"You are beautiful to me, no matter what," he said, and kissed her again. "And I will always think of you. Even if you don't or can't wait, I promise. I will come back for you."

NEWSPAPERS

7

Toward London

Robert thought of Edie's trouble with the word when he first hit tarmac again on the trip north. Fifty miles on, cities loomed in the distance. He'd been here before, but how strange everything looked! It seemed strange to see the skyscrapers of civilization when for so long, it was only palm trees, rustic huts, and mountains that shaped his world.

He'd contracted with a lorry driver named Kenneth Tosti to go the whole way back to London. At first, seeing his clothes, the driver wanted to take him for nothing, but after learning that he had money, he accepted a reasonable fare. On the first day of their ride, he stopped in a town for lunch, paid for Robert as well, and then made sure that Robert had time to buy a new shirt, trousers, socks, and pants before they moved on. He was a hearty, joking man, careful in his work and yet one on whom all care seemed to sit lightly. Above all, he had the gift of seeing another's trouble, and by the second day Robert could feel silences that began to answer to his own heartache, silences the more obvious because they would cut off the man's usual, cheerful flow of speech. For a long time, the driver said nothing to him directly about this, but at last, while his ten tyres were drumming the tarmac of a straight, black, and empty road, he burst out, "I can see you have woman problems, brother. Don't tell me. I know the signs."

"Yes. I guess so."

"Someone has died?"

"Yes."

"The woman? No, I think not her."

"No."

"The pal, then?"

"Yes."

"Malaria?"

"No. Some disease similar to it, yes."

"Ah, I know the one. But this girl…she's the worst for you now, isn't she? Look, brother," he said, "take it from me, there's plenty more out where she comes from… But maybe you don't want to tell me."

But Robert did—very much. He told a rather brief tale about how he'd been thrown together with Edie—how he found her lost (what an insult to her!), and how they had made a long journey together over the moors towards her home. They had encountered bandits, had fled different ways for greater mutual safety, and had both escaped. Then, when he had reached her home—he gave an almost truthful account of the discussion that had led them to separate.

The man listened intently, and then asked suddenly, "And the pal: where was he in all this? Where did he die?"

Robert had nothing ready. He hesitated, then rambled on about their entire adventure, and what had led him to breathe his last.

When he had finished, Tosti said, "Then where was this place that he died?"

"Oh—in the moors."

"Ah, I know that place, brother." A silence followed. "And this guy, your friend, was he older than you?"

"Yes. A bit."

They were silent for quite a while.

"You been mixed up in some strange going-ons, specially these bandits and all."

"Yes."

"Pretty bad luck."

"I suppose so. A bit."

"Those moors are lawful places, as a rule."

"Well, there have been a lot of kidnappings and things going on there. You may have heard about that."

"Sure, I've heard," the other said, alertly. "Everyone's heard… Were your bandits the same lot as that?"

"I don't know. They didn't catch us."

"You don't know, huh? And you don't think you were unlucky to be mixed with bandits—or only a bit unlucky?"

"Only about the girl."

"What's luck with a girl? Well, it is luck I suppose."

"I had to leave her behind. That's all."

Again, silence, and then he burst out with, "Look, Robert, with the girls, it's like this. You've got to learn to take them and then let them go. Let them decide it, see? The less you bother, the more they like you. And when they don't like you, then, of course, the less it hurts. Be good to them when you're with them, treat them kindly and…that's all. The rest is up to them. But you're on to London, eh? You'll soon forget her."

He doubted that very much.

They stopped in a small town for lunch at a crowded restaurant that was the ground floor of a double-story building. Robert sat down at a counter and opened a menu while Ken was outside, parking the lorry. He was watching a man in a white cap splash cups of water on a marble slab while fielding orders.

When Ken returned, he slapped down several newspapers on the table and sat down in the seat beside Robert. Then he seemed to wait. Robert hardly looked up, as he was deciding whether to have a Scotch egg or soup. He hadn't seen a paper in a long time, and truthfully, didn't care about news of the outside world much. On the top paper, he saw a big red headline "TRIUMPH AND TRAGEDY" and a photograph filling most of the front page. The bulky tabloid didn't say what the triumph was, but the photograph said it clearly enough: evidently some mountain peak had been scaled. And the tragedy was probably that someone had fallen off; but what of it?

Then curiosity got the better of him. Did Santania have peaks that were all that worth it to fall from?

"Are you ready to order?" he asked.

Ken didn't answer, and Robert glanced at him. He realized that Ken was looking, not at the paper, but Robert himself with a peculiar, half-suppressed smile, and then that he glanced from Robert to the paper and back.

"Have you read the story the papers are carrying?" Ken asked at last.

"I don't much care," he said sullenly, but even so, pulled the top paper towards him and turned it around. It certainly looked as if the climb had been quite a feat; the view and the expression on the climber's face were enough to show that. Where could they have possibly had the camera? Hanging in the thin air, it seemed. "So, what? The guy fell?" Robert pushed the paper back. "Where was all this then?"

"Can't you guess? Can't you read?"

Robert glanced at the photography again, looking for some clue. There was no gear: it had been a free climb, evidently, and that must rule out the Himalayas. He looked next at the rocks. Horizontal, sedimentary. The ledge itself was white: the photo showed the white continuing into the cliff, looking like a layer of cream in dark cake…

Suddenly he pulled the paper sharply back to him and opened it out that he could see the whole photo. He frowned and his stool seemed to sway under him. He stared at the ledge and then again at the climber's contorted face.

The photo and the headline were so huge that there was little space on the paper's front page for anything else, but now that it was flat, below the photo he read: HOW CHAMARD'S UNIT FELL.

Beneath was a small section of text:

"Escape from the valley of the shadow: The unknown Englishman, Robert, climbs amid rifle fire, carrying the secrets of Chamard's terrorist unit… Alas, not for long. Has DEATH demanded a return match? We do not know. Reports yesterday suggest that the hero may have been drowned in the flood crest of the recent rains while he was weakened by his ordeal on the mountains. More pictures and the full story on page two."

Robert now bent in astonishment close over the photographs.

The climber was himself.

Impossible. Impossible. Absurd.

There had been no one there—only empty air was at the angle where the photograph must have been taken. His mind reeled and he pulled the next paper from the pile towards him. It had a different headline: DUEL IN THE

AIR: MYSTERY OF A HERO'S MIRACLE ESCAPE—AND WHERE IS
HE NOW? And then there was a photograph of two helicopters facing each
other off the rock face; in a blur, out of focus, he could just see himself fastened
as a lump on the cliff just above. He turned over more of the papers. All had
parts of the same story, but the photos were often different.

"How?" he muttered aloud, glancing up at Tosti.

Ken Tosti was leaning across the table, watching Robert as he read.

"You were up there recently," he said, grinning. "You said that you had
been to Impeya and Diamond Creek. Maybe you have some clues that might
help the colonel find this Englishman that they talk of!"

Robert stared at him stupidly.

"Come, Robert," the man said, reaching across the table and grasping his
hand. "Don't try to fool me anymore. Look at me. You are him. You are the
'Robert,' aren't you?"

Robert saw that several people were standing behind Tosti. He looked
around and found there were more still there, a dozen or so close by watching
him—in fact, everyone who was in the café had gathered near their table.
One man was holding a paper and looking from Robert to the paper and back
again and grimacing and shrugging and shaking his head. Another face in the
crowd caught Robert's eyes at once; it was the man who had shouted at him in
the other restaurant. He had his hat on now and from under its broad brim,
his deep, red-rimmed eyes stared fixedly. He stared at Robert, his former hate,
but his expression was quite different from what it had been before. He had a
half-smile, like a man who waits to be surprised by a new conjuring trick. His
face was also much rosier than it had been.

"Come, Robert. It's you. Admit it."

Robert glanced at the first photo he had looked at and thought how incredibly the terror of the moment had disguised him, even from himself. Need
he admit it? Should he?

"Come, admit it... It was hooey, what you told me, most of it. Admit
it—from now on, you're safe." He laughed and tugged at Robert's hand again.
"I was suspicious of some of your story. I guess I'm a sucker. I believed you in
the end. That is you in the photo, isn't it?" He put his finger on it yet again.

There was a tense pause and then Robert said, "Yes, it was me."

A gasp went up from the crowd.

"But someone did die," Robert added.

"In that crash of the choppers? Of course, how wouldn't they die?"

"No, he survived that... I mean, he died after the flood. I can't explain. And I don't understand these." Now he was muttering. "The photos are plain impossible... These must be fakes...and yet...it did all happen."

"And now we hear it from him!" Ken gave a big burst of laughter and banged the table.

But why? Why had it all happened as it had? Why had the man followed him and Karl to the moors—or why gone ahead? Why had he been in the shop, and why, later, had his hide and his vultures been just where the canyon plunged and the rockweed path led up? Why? Why is life as it is?

What is it?" said Tosti. "What have you thought of?"

"Oh—I am just thinking I know how he took pictures now. He had a very big lens—a telephoto. And he had a hide—I think I saw it."

"So, you admit to everything now?"

"Yes."

"And to the diamond story too?"

"Yes. To that too."

Robert felt somehow breathless.

There was another gasp from the crowd that pressed closer to their table. It seemed to have grown. Voices were saying, "It is him—yes, it is him, is he—he is the same as in the picture—I see it easily."

The driver seized Robert's hand again and pulled him to his feet. "Come, folks," he shouted. "Give this sick boy a cheer. This is your 'Robert'—and we've found him—here! This is the guy who smashed Chamard's army for you, the guy who found Dewey's diamonds! Now he's telling us all of it was easy, nothing... Come, give him a cheer."

There was shouting and cheering. A forest of hands reached towards Robert; they grasped his hands, his arms, his shoulders. Others beat almost painfully on his back.

"It wasn't me," Robert muttered. "It was... We were..." he tried to count, confused by tumult, and then muttered at last, "We were four."

He thought that no one had heard him say this, but later as the noise died down a voice shouted to him, "So the four? Then where are the others?" And there was a hush.

"Two of us have died."

"Two died!" Now there was complete silence.

Silence.

"You said one didn't die. Where is he?" the voice repeated.

"Oh. It's not… Oh, I can't tell you who they are and where they went."

"Come, Robert, who are these others? Name them. The world should know; we should cheer for them too."

"Don't press him, friends. I guess it will all be out in the papers in good time." Now, it was Ken's voice again.

"Then it was two down and two to go: less bad than might be. We're sorry, Robert, about those two, but we're glad we have you."

"Yes, yes—this nation thanks you, Robert!"

There was cheering again; the hands were reaching for him; there were the smiling, and even loving faces on all sides. Among them, Robert saw, blurred and bobbing, that broad-brimmed hat like Annetta's and under it, a woman's red-rimmed eyes, complete with shining stars. Beside her, his face clean of scars, his hair dark and tumbling down his face, was Karl. They were together. Robert saw their warm smiles and hands reaching out between the tight bodies of the others who pushed him back. Robert found himself on his feet, leaning through the crowd. He touched their fingers, but instead, found an old man's. They were knotted and rough like stems of old manioc, the plant that he now knew well.

He shook the bony fingers, found that he could not face the wild, joyful stares of the others, so he held his head down—and knew that, yet once again, he was crying.

PART 6

London, Again

As the cheers rose all around him, he kept his head down, and in a dizzy swell, he closed his eyes to block them out, to keep the tears at bay. He tried but did not succeed, for they burst free and floated out into the room like snowflakes.

It was over.

Robert fell on the bed. He was confused but the great weight was gone, and the rest lay there with him on the bed on the floor: they were scattered, tiny and melting away.

He looked up to see how they had come.

A last square of sunlight was on its slow path across the wall to the window where, outside, a clear day of the late spring was drawing to its close. He had seen this often before: the patch was not square, of course, but slanted, and it was growing narrower and a deeper red. The cracks it was crossing were an old, familiar map. At this moment one junction within the lighted square held his eyes—it was where the Bell joined its String. He knew at once that it was there, in the darkest of that joining, they had come through. And he knew too, for just that moment, why as seen from the looping plane, when it had all stood vertical before him just as it was now, it had seemed so alike and yet different. Of course! The answer was easy: it had been mirror reflected—seen from the wrong side!

Suddenly, this thought was gone and he could no longer remember it. He stood up. He rolled his sleeping bag one way across the bed and then drew it back, and stared at it, puzzled, trying to recall why he was there and what he had been doing.

Then he ran down the stairs.

Outside, his bicycle leaned in the hedge. He peered at it. The pedals! They were mended. The hammer and two pins, one sawn neatly in two, lay below. The milkman! And he, rudely, after answering the telephone, had gone upstairs in anger, and must have fallen asleep.

Yet he knew somehow that this man, whom he could not remember, would not be offended.

Tomorrow, he would catch up with the others. They were his friends still: and who could blame them if they did not come to see him at a home like his? Nevertheless, there was a pain still burning there, and he was not sure. Maybe he would not go, maybe he would go to Devon alone instead.

Or perhaps he would travel up toward West Wickham, and head somewhere else entirely.

Something odd, a new strength and a sense of terrible loss coming from somewhere inside he did not know, stayed with him, weighing on his heart. These things weren't from that phone call, which he remembered, but from something that had come after, something that had happened in his room, some thought or dream that he had had while he had been asleep. He felt as once in childhood when he'd woken to find his hands holding only air instead of the parents he'd dreamed of.

But this had been something far, far worse than that, and also better; something tremendously important had happened to him and he did not know what. He stared at the hedge—at his bicycle leaning there, the car in the next drive, the tree at the gate, houses, seeking within and without. Something, things, people, traces of a huge past, had been with him for a moment on the bed, and all of it was now gone...

A person.

The milkman!

The van!

With a suddenly pounding heart, he ran to the gate and looked both ways along the road. Mr Lampson had come home and was doing something with his red car (making it redder probably; he usually was). Mrs Lampson, too, was on her doorstep, watching him. It was a strange and fine late spring evening. The last of the sun was going and flowers of laburnum, blazing in the last light, brushed his cheek.

He didn't care.

He flung himself on his knees on the pavement under the tree and peered intently into the gutter of the road. Could there be wheel marks left, and if so, what could they tell him? Nothing. Still he peered, and at last, he reached down with his fingertip, one foot out from the kerb, and picked up a tiny flake. Another lay beside it. He rubbed the first one in his fingers and it crumbled to powder.

Pink. Brick dust.

What other trace of that purring and lurching van had he expected? Stains and oil of the road, dirt, a bottle top pressed in the tarmac, flowers fallen, milk brought to his home in the late afternoon... It made no sense. Yet the man had been here—the milk was at the door; it had come late and had not been taken in, and his bicycle was mended. Who had done that? He could not remember and yet somehow, he knew.

He had been hit, had been lying on his bed—it had been all a dream.

"Have you lost something, Robert?" he heard Mrs Lampson ask. She was at the next gate. He didn't answer, and from the side of his eye saw her turn to her husband, who was also watching curiously from over his car.

Let them think as they would. He didn't answer. He felt an endless uncaring for what they did or saw. Not with the wide world beyond this street. He was changed in that; in some way he was stronger, it was one difference. He simply did not care. Out in the road, the other fleck of the red dust that had fallen from the float glowed towards him in unearthly colour, brilliant as a flower. Around it, he saw on the black asphalt more, dusted like red stars, glowing and dimming, like lights on a chandelier in a grand hall. There was some memory of what it all had been, but he could not catch it. Things were falling, they were showering away all around, melting like snow. There were flowers, and faces—faces angry, vicious, endearing. Rocks, rocks of a desert, rocks reared impossible above him, raising a face of doom, yet these also opening a strange, silver road, shining mother-of-pearl—and dark, castellate rocks that were ruins beneath orchard trees. There was a flower of flame roaring, ants marching, human arms reaching and arms pressing away—and there was a snake, a blazing sun, a parrot on a branch, tears staining a painting of a white dead tree, a man fallen with a raw wound, and the wounded fallen heart of his own...

"Have you lost something, love?" Mrs Lampson asked him a second time, now standing close by him.

He let his breath go out slowly.

"Yes, I have," he answered. "But I intend to find it."

THE END

END PIECE

Lightning Source UK Ltd.
Milton Keynes UK
UKHW021855130322
399994UK00006B/11